Mortal Sins

K.L. Hiers

Published by Stormy Night Publications and Design, LLC.
www.StormyNightPublications.com

Cover design by Korey Mae Johnson
www.koreymaejohnson.com

Images by iStock/Lorado and Shutterstock/Vittorio Iocolano

1st Print Edition. January 2020

ISBN-13: 9798601129053

FOR AUDIENCES 18+ ONLY

This book is intended for adults only. Spanking and other sexual activities represented in this book are fantasies only, intended for adults.

CHAPTER ONE

After an intense chase, Snod had finally managed to corner the vampire down in the dark tunnels beneath an abandoned factory. He was fast, even for a vampire, but Snod was tenacious. He had never failed a mission before and he had no intention of starting now. Vampires were soulless monsters that were a plague upon the earth and it was his sacred duty to destroy them all, including this one.

The vampire's eyes were flashing brightly as he backed up against the tunnel wall, a spectacular sight that Snod had seen before when the fiends were about to die. It didn't move him in the slightest. He felt absolutely no regret killing a vampire. They were all abominations, savage and cold monsters that preyed on innocent humans and had no right to exist. He couldn't feel bad about killing something so monstrous.

"I don't want to hurt you," the vampire warned, his bright eyes narrowing fiercely. "All you have to do is walk away."

Snod was surprised to hear the vampire speak, but he didn't believe the vampire for a second. He knew it was a trick and he prepared to lunge, drawing a stake from his vest. He heard a strange sound, something creaking overhead, but he ignored it in favor of staying focused on his target.

"Look out!" the vampire suddenly shouted.

The ceiling began to give way with a deafening groan, Snod stuck staring stupidly at the unavoidable death crashing right on top of him. He closed his eyes and began chanting a prayer, waiting for the end.

It never came.

The vampire had grabbed him, pulling him out of the way and dragging him to safety. Snod was stunned, the vibrations of the crash still rumbling beneath his feet as he gawked at the vampire. This unholy abomination had just saved his life and he was completely speechless.

"You can try to kill me if you want," the vampire said quietly, "or we can find a way out of here. Your choice."

Snod said nothing to that, but he put his stake away.

They found that the various twisting tunnels only led to more collapsed areas that the vampire was not able to clear with his mighty strength. Even with Snod helping him, it wasn't enough. Snod had explosives, but those were in the trunk of his car and not very helpful. After hours of silent searching, they both came to the same dismal conclusion.

There was no way out.

Snod slumped against the closest wall, sliding down to the floor. He was furious. He pounded his fist beneath him, snarling loudly.

"You don't have a phone?" the vampire asked.

"Dead," he replied shortly. "You?"

"Dropped it," the vampire sighed, sitting down on the floor opposite him. "Was sort of trying to get away from this crazy guy trying to kill me."

Snod glared.

"Eeesssh, tough crowd." The vampire winced.

"I'm not stupid," Snod snapped.

"I never said you were?" The vampire blinked owlishly.

"You're waiting for me to fall asleep, to pass out," Snod accused venomously, "and then you'll feed on me."

The vampire held up his hands with a frustrated sigh. "If I wanted to kill you, why did I save you?"

"Maybe *you're* stupid," Snod challenged. It sounded foolish as soon as he said it, but he didn't know what else to say. He stared defiantly at the vampire, refusing to back down.

"Mmm, I'm loving that razor-sharp wit," the vampire said with a long roll of his eyes. "It's just great."

Snod glared again, and the vampire fell silent for a while. He never took his eyes off of him, ever vigilant, refusing to let his guard down.

It was easy to spot a vampire once one knew what to look for. Trained since he was a child, Snod could pick one out of a crowded room in seconds. They were too graceful when they moved, too still when they didn't. And they were always very beautiful.

Snod didn't know if that was the result of the curse or if vampires were particularly shallow when they chose their potential progeny.

This vampire was no exception. He was tall and muscular with bright green eyes and sinfully long legs. Snod tried not to let his gaze linger, staring up at the ceiling and drawing shapes in his mind by connecting lines between the rivets. He had never taken the time to really *look* at a vampire before, and there was something about this one that made his heart beat a little faster.

Snod didn't know if it was the strong line of his jaw that he found so appealing or the broad shape of his body, but he felt a stab of guilt immediately when he recognized the feeling as physical desire. It was wrong. Not just because the vampire was an unholy abomination, but he was a man.

The temptation of the same sex was not unknown to Snod and it was one he had fought against all of his life. He couldn't help but steal another peek at the vampire, glancing over his full lips longingly. The vampire caught him staring and Snod quickly averted his gaze upward once more, counting as many of the rivets as he could see. When he ran out of ones to count, he started over again.

"Been with the Order long?" the vampire asked after a while, fidgeting with his glasses. They had been broken, perhaps during the chase.

"My family is one of the original seven that founded the Order," Snod replied with a faint hint of pride.

"That makes you… a Rosario? Or a Snod?"

"You know us?"

"Yeah, I always make it a habit to learn about the crazy people that might show up trying to kill me someday," the vampire dryly replied.

"My name is Obadiah Penuel Snod, and I am not crazy. I am here to absolve you of your unholy curse," Snod recited dutifully. "It's my mission from God to cleanse the earth of your sin, to free your soul of its impure taint."

"So you're a virgin?" the vampire pressed with a sly smile.

Snod felt his cheeks burning, refusing to answer such a ridiculous question. He couldn't explain why his pulse was continuing to race and his thoughts were suddenly swarmed with all sorts of lewd thoughts.

"It's nothing to be ashamed of," the vampire soothed.

"Fuck off."

"Sorry, I couldn't help but notice you're not wearing a ring," the vampire explained. "The Order requires pretty strict celibacy, right? Until marriage?"

"To hunt the impure, we remain pure," Snod grumbled. "The Order teaches us that sins of the flesh cloud our minds. Hunters can only marry after they retire."

"You know, you're not really selling me on the whole Order thing. Doesn't sound like a very fun club to be in," the vampire laughed. "Like, at all. I mean, some cults at least have orgies."

"It's not a cult," Snod defended. "It's a sacred order that was founded hundreds of years ago, charged with a—"

"Holy mission from God to kill vampires, blah, blah, blah. Got it," the vampire scoffed. "Wow. They've really got you brainwashed bad, huh?"

"Fuck you."

"No, seriously. You can't get laid and you spend all of your time trying to kill vampires. What the crap do you do for fun? Punch old ladies? Kick puppies?"

"Is this your plan? To keep talking incessantly until I beg you to drain me dry?" Snod groaned lightly.

"Just trying to be friendly," the vampire protested, "since we'll probably be down here for a while."

"Can't you… call someone?"

"Already told you, I lost my phone."

"Not on your phone," Snod snorted. "You don't have anyone you can summon?"

"No," the vampire said, finally understanding what Snod meant. "I don't have any children to summon. And my Maker will not come even if I tried. Trust me, you wouldn't want him to anyway."

"You've never turned anyone?" Snod was genuinely surprised. "Thought you things couldn't help yourselves."

"No," the vampire replied quietly, fiddling with the broken glasses. "Most of us 'things' take turning someone very seriously."

"So. You have no progeny, and you're refusing to summon your Maker."

"If he actually came, he'd kill you on sight," the vampire said simply. "He doesn't like humans very much. You're just food to him."

"Aren't we?"

"I don't think so," the vampire replied earnestly. "We're not all monsters, Obadiah."

"Don't call me that," Snod growled.

"Fine, shit… forget it."

"What?"

The vampire didn't respond, his eyes cast down at the bent frame in his hands.

Long moments of silence passed before Snod spoke again. "Why do you wear glasses?"

"I used to," the vampire said, looking up at Snod with a little smile. "When I was human, I mean. Obviously don't need them now. Sort of a habit, I suppose."

Leaning his head back against the wall, Snod exhaled slowly. He was exhausted, hungry, and his body ached. He had never spent this much time with a vampire and he was desperately trying to squash the sinful thoughts threatening to invade his mind. He watched one of the bulbs flicker and go out, scowling at the added darkness.

"You need to eat," the vampire remarked. "You're getting weaker."

"I'm fine."

"I am not going to sit here and do nothing," the vampire declared. "There has to be a way out. One we haven't found yet."

"We already looked," Snod drawled in annoyance.

The vampire set the glasses down, frowning. "We'll keep looking."

"To what end?" Snod snapped.

The vampire looked positively sullen, crossing his arms over his chest. "I didn't save your life just to watch you starve to death."

"Why did you? Wanted a little snack for later?"

"Because despite what you think, I'm not a monster," the vampire insisted.

Snod ignored him and kept running through scenarios in his mind, trying to figure out a plan. Something. Anything.

Wait…

"Heart blood," he said at last, staring wide-eyed at the vampire. "What about heart blood?"

The vampire blinked in surprise. He scoffed quietly, demanding, "And what exactly do you think you know about heart blood?"

"It's the most powerful source of vampire blood," Snod said, his fingers inching toward his stakes. "Blood straight from your heart, right?"

"Uh, yeah. But you don't have to get it from my heart. You can draw it anywhere while my heart is beating because it'll pump everywhere," the vampire explained quickly. "You can't get it out of me if I'm dead, so don't get any cute ideas."

Vampire blood was a powerful substance. When ingested by humans, it temporarily granted them all sorts of intense abilities. It was also rumored to be an amazing aphrodisiac, but it was the increased strength that Snod was interested in.

The power from heart blood was said to be the most potent of all. Their combined efforts hadn't been enough to clear the debris trapping them down here, but with heart blood? It could give Snod the extra boost that they needed to escape.

But what the vampire was saying didn't make any sense.

"Vampires' hearts don't beat," Snod argued, his eyes narrowed suspiciously.

The vampire shook his head sadly. "You really don't know anything about us, do you? Except how to kill us."

"Tell me."

"God," the vampire groaned, appearing distressed by Snod's ignorance. "It beats when we're first born, when we lose or make a progeny, or… uhm…"

"Or what?"

"When we fuck," the vampire finished bluntly.

"You're not turning me!"

"I didn't say I was going to!"

"That's it? Those are the only ways?"

"Yes!" the vampire insisted stubbornly. "I have nothing to gain by lying to you."

"Or I can just stake you and find out for myself if you're telling me the truth," Snod reasoned, pursing his lips.

"I already told you that won't work," the vampire growled in frustration. "If you try to harm me, I will defend myself. We both know that will not end well for you."

Snod thought back to the incredible chase that had led

them here. Having learned the vampire's nightly routine in the weeks preparing for his attack, Snod had been waiting for him to leave the karaoke club he visited every Thursday to make his move. Unexpectedly, the vampire had left much earlier than Snod had anticipated and prompted the demanding pursuit.

It was like chasing a ghost. Snod had never met a vampire that could move like this one, simply disappearing and reappearing in a blink. As much as he prided himself on his skills as a hunter, he knew there was no way he could kill this vampire without taking him by surprise.

Even in that scenario and under the most optimal conditions, there was doubt whispering in the back of Snod's mind. If he couldn't kill him to get the necessary blood, that left only one option. It was one that made Snod's loins tighten up and he could barely believe what he was about to say.

"So, sex," Snod said quietly. "We should have sex."

"Wait, are you serious?"

"Yes," Snod replied, aiming for casual even as his pulse began to thump heavily with excitement. "We'll do it really fast, get the blood, and get out of here."

"My panties are already dropping," the vampire drawled, unimpressed. "Take me now."

"We have no other choice," Snod snapped. "We can try to keep waiting, in which case I'm going to die in two more days without water. You may take longer to starve, but you will die eventually, too."

Snod knew what he was proposing was rife with sin. Sex outside of marriage, sex with another man, and sex with a vampire were all damnable offenses to God. He didn't know which was worse, but he was not going to die down here.

The vampire was very beautiful. The Order wouldn't have to know about it. He could continue serving them loyally just as he always had. But to serve, he had to be alive.

"Who says I even want to have sex with you?" the vampire huffed in disgust. "Maybe you're not my type."

Snod scowled.

"You did try to kill me," the vampire pointed out. "Not exactly putting me in the right kinda mood."

"If we survive, I'll tell the Order you're already dead," Snod bargained. "No other hunter will come here."

The vampire didn't look convinced.

"If it doesn't work, and we don't survive… at least I wouldn't have died without knowing what it's like," Snod said quietly, allowing a rare moment of vulnerability to shine through. Knowing that what he desired was a terrible sin, he had resigned himself to being a bachelor. But maybe, just this once, he would finally be able to know the true intimacy of that most passionate embrace.

The vampire's face was perfectly blank, but his eyes flickered softly in the darkness. "There's some things you should know if we're going to do this. And I haven't agreed yet, but I want to be honest."

"What?"

"You know about the blood bond?"

Snod's confused expression indicated that he didn't.

"If we share blood, which we are going to, we'll be connected," the vampire continued patiently. "You'll be able to sense me, just like I'll be able to sense you. It'll be strong at first, but eventually it will fade. It won't go away completely, but you should be able to ignore it after a while."

"Sense what exactly?"

"Feelings, sensations. The more blood that's exchanged, the stronger the connection."

Snod hated that he was so fascinated. It also startled him that the Order apparently knew so little about the creatures they had been hunting for so long.

"Fine, I don't care," Snod said quickly, shaking his head. "Let's get this over with."

"Wait! I still haven't said that I'm going to do this," the vampire argued. "A pity screw is one thing, but you're a friggin' vampire hunter. Maybe I should just let you starve, huh?"

"You said you weren't a monster," Snod reminded him.

"How many vampires have you killed?"

"How many humans have you killed?" Snod snapped back.

"Asked you first."

"Thirty-six," Snod said smugly. "You?"

"Seven," the vampire replied, his expression deeply wounded.

Snod was dumbfounded. How could the foul fiend have survived without killing humans every night?

"Now who's the monster," the vampire snorted, shaking his head dismissively.

Snod didn't say anything, shifting against the wall.

A long drag of silence passed with the vampire seemingly lost in thought. He was perfectly still, so motionless that he easily could have been mistaken for a statue.

Snod tapped his foot impatiently, his stomach gnawing at itself with hunger and anxiety.

"I'll do it," the vampire said at last, "but I have conditions."

"And those are?"

"First, lose the stakes," the vampire replied. "In fact, lose all of your weapons and any anti-vampire voodoo you might be carrying around. I still don't trust that you won't try something."

Snod leaned forward, taking off his tactical vest that held all of his stakes and throwing it down the tunnel. He removed a large knife from his ankle, two more from his belt, and a bottle of atomized silver spray. From around his neck, he pulled off his scapular, a religious charm designed to ward off vampiric mind control.

Cleared of all dangerous objects, he held out his hands expectantly. "What else?"

"Second, you have to let me feed from you," the vampire said. "I won't drink enough to hurt you, I promise, but we have to bond. It'll make it easier… especially since it's your first time."

Snod made a face. "Fine. Anything else?"

"I guess that's it. I just..." The vampire cleared his throat. "Are you ready?"

"Yes." Snod nodded, licking his lips. "How do we..."

"Look. Just relax. I'll take care of you," the vampire promised. He smiled, slinking over on his hands and knees toward Snod. He crawled into Snod's lap, his toned body much heavier than it appeared.

The weight felt good, Snod's interest becoming apparent very quickly.

The vampire made no comment, guiding Snod's hands to his hips.

Snod had wanted to rush this and get it over with, but now that the moment was here and his cock was twitching, he wanted to savor every second. He'd thought about having sex for years, especially as a teenager when he first noticed that he enjoyed looking at the bodies of his male companions instead of the females.

He took his vows seriously, ignoring the urges as best as he could. What he wanted was unholy. When he couldn't stand it any longer, he would find relief in a shower stall thinking about broad shoulders and strong jaws, letting the water wash all the mess away.

As the years went by, he knew that he would never be happy in marriage to a woman. He prayed for guidance, received none, and opted to continue hunting. He rarely even thought about sex anymore.

But now with a beautiful vampire straddling his thighs, every single one of his debauched adolescent fantasies was taking over his brain. His skin already felt numb, tingling with nerves and anticipation, unsure of what exactly to do except he wanted to touch and feel.

Snod started to slide his hands up to explore, cringing when he realized he was shaking.

"Take your time," the vampire said, taking a deep breath he didn't need. "It's all right."

Snod moved over the vampire's chest with more confidence, frowning at how cold he felt. He pressed his palm over his heart, startled that there was truly no heartbeat. He knew there wouldn't be, but it was still quite off-putting.

He let the vampire undress him, expecting that there would be a rush of clothing flying off. The vampire surprised him by taking his time, divesting him with an unexpected care and tenderness.

The vampire frowned at all the scars he found beneath Snod's shirt, tracing over them with delicate fingers.

"The Order," Snod explained as if it was obvious. "Lessons."

The vampire said nothing, but there was a splash of anguish in his smile. Perhaps it was even pity. He let Snod take off his shirt, sighing as Snod's trembling fingers traced over his bare skin.

The vampire's body was a smooth sea of white, its perfection occasionally interrupted by little freckles and moles. His body was sculpted perfection, tangling himself around Snod and letting their bodies press together.

"And what about…" Snod didn't even finish the sentence before the vampire had a few condoms and a small packet of lube in his hand.

"I was headed out on a date with a really nice guy," the vampire explained with a faint smile. "I was expecting it to go well."

"That's why you left the bar early."

"Yes, stalky stalk, that's why I left early," the vampire groaned. "Wow, you're so romantic."

"Shut up."

The vampire rolled his eyes, appearing surprisingly human.

"Well, let's get going," Snod said stubbornly. His nerves were getting to him, and he didn't know how much longer he could last with the vampire's firm ass pressing down on his dick.

"Slow your roll, Casanova," the vampire griped. "You can't just flick a switch, okay?"

"Tell me what to do," Snod said, a frustrated growl tainting his tone.

"Have you ever even kissed someone?"

Snod didn't answer.

"We're going to take this one step at a time." The vampire cradled Snod's face, his cool touch soothing to his overheated flesh. He pressed close, his nose lightly bumping Snod's cheek. The vampire's eyes were so bright as they gazed into his. "Do everything I tell you, listen to my voice… and I will make this so good for you. Do you understand?"

"Y-yes." Snod's palms were sweating, the anticipation making his pulse race and skip over beats.

"Good boy." The vampire smiled, crossing the last few increments of space between them and sealing their lips together in a sweet kiss.

Snod stiffened immediately. The vampire was too cold, too male, too wrong. He wanted to push him away, knowing he should feel revolted. Everything he had been told all of his life said this was a terrible sin.

But… it felt good.

There was a strange heat prickling his flesh and a pressure building in his loins he had never known. The closest comparison he had were the private moments he had dared to take in the shower in his youth, but this was infinitely more intense. It made his cock throb and took his breath away as he shyly pressed his lips back against the vampire's.

The vampire was endlessly patient, letting Snod get used to the feeling of their mouths chastely touching before slowly deepening the kiss.

Snod groaned without meaning to, embarrassed by the needy sound and ready to end this right now.

The vampire persisted, allowing himself a small purr of pleasure, encouraging Snod to be as expressive as he wanted to be. His fingers moved over Snod's short hair, petting over the base of his neck as he slipped him the barest hint of tongue.

The taste was electric, Snod gasping at the new sensation. His hands reached out, finding the vampire's sides and waist, feeling every inch of cool flesh that he could reach. He kissed the vampire earnestly, experimenting with the angle, finally brave enough to let his tongue dart forward.

Moaning softly, the vampire let Snod explore, kissing him with increasing passion.

Snod had to come up for air, panting and staring awkwardly at the vampire. His lips were pink from kissing, and his eyes were so green they were practically glowing. He had seen vampires' eyes light up before in battle, usually right before the moment of death.

But nothing like this.

Snod had never seen anything so beautiful before, and he wished he had the courage to say so.

"Now," the vampire said, nuzzling their noses together. "Who is gonna be wearing this?" He held up the condom expectantly. He looked over Snod's flushed face, smiling as he teased, "Mm. Thinking it's gonna be you, big boy."

His cheeks continuing to roast, Snod cleared his throat. "That's fine."

The vampire shifted, suddenly completely naked in Snod's lap. The rest of his clothes were folded in a neat pile behind him.

Fuck, he was fast.

"How do you move like that?" Snod couldn't help but ask, stunned. He'd barely gotten his own shirt off and the vampire didn't even have his socks on anymore.

"That's really what you're thinking about right now?" the vampire hissed, reaching down and starting to unbutton Snod's pants.

Snod scowled.

The vampire sighed, "Shut up and kiss me."

Snod obliged, leaning forward to capture the vampire's lips in another passionate kiss. His breath stuttered when he felt cool fingers pulling his cock out of his pants. No one else had ever touched him there before.

It was too good, too much, and he panted against the vampire's lips as he struggled to control himself. The condom was rolling down his shaft. He wiggled a little at the unfamiliar sensation and the weird smell of latex.

The vampire had lifted his hips, kissing Snod eagerly, asking, "Are you ready?"

"Yes," Snod replied, determined and excited.

There was no Order here; there were no punishments, no sermons. It was only him and a beautiful vampire, whose lips made his heart race and whose touch made his very soul tremble. He was finally going to find out what sex was like. He would know what it was like to be inside someone and fall into that most intimate embrace.

Snod gritted his teeth when the vampire began to lower himself down, the tightness of his body squeezing around his cock and making him moan. It was so snug and slick, and he tried to catch his breath as quickly as it was being stolen away.

"Nice and slow," the vampire said, rocking his hips patiently, wrapping his arms around Snod's neck and kissing him tenderly.

Snod couldn't hold the kiss for long, his head dropping back against the wall with a light bang, cursing, "Fuck…" The vampire's body felt cool, but not uncomfortably so, and he marveled at how easily the creature took every inch of his cock.

"Good?" the vampire asked, kissing along Snod's neck.

"Yes," he panted, his hands racing over pale flesh, seizing the vampire's narrow hips. His cock was buried so deep. He felt overwhelmed by the beautiful friction when the vampire moved. He'd never felt so connected to another person, desperate to touch and kiss, moaning quietly.

The vampire mouthed along Snod's throat. "I'm going

to feed from you now… relax."

Snod nodded, gritting his teeth when he felt the faint prick of fangs. Oh, this was stupid. He had given a vampire permission to feed on him. This was even more despicable than laying with another man, offering himself as a meal for a monster. He braced himself for the pain of his throat being torn apart, but it never came.

He only felt light pressure and a gentle sucking, the vampire groaning beautifully as he drank. The sensation was tender and sweet, leaving Snod writhing as the vampire rode him hungrily.

As he drank, Snod was startled to feel that the vampire was getting warmer. His whole body was flooding with warmth, Snod's cock suddenly swallowed up in the new and intense heat of his tight ass.

"God… please forgive me, fuck," Snod moaned, letting the vampire take all that he wanted. "It's so fucking good."

The vampire pulled off with a loud moan and not a drop of blood spilled, gasping as he slammed his ass down harder. He began to lean back, his hands now pressed against Snod's thighs as he greedily fucked himself down on his cock. "Mmmm, you're doing so well for me, Obadiah… so fucking good…"

Everything the vampire did was perfect and graceful, Snod awestruck by the way he moved. The curl of his back, the way his hips bounced up and down so effortlessly; it was absolutely divine.

Snod was starting to lose himself, cursing and crying brokenly. It was all so incredible. He wasn't going to last much longer. The pressure building inside of him was threatening to burst at any second, and he hissed a warning, "Close."

The vampire growled, straightening himself back up and grabbing Snod's hand. Snod nodded, pressing it over the vampire's heart. "Almost," the vampire cried, never losing rhythm, still relentlessly riding Snod's cock. "Almost there."

Snod gasped when he first felt it. There it was, only a

tiny thump at first, but a definite pulse was steadily starting to grow in strength beneath his palm.

The vampire's heart was fluttering to life, soon beating as fast and hard as his own. It was beyond fantastic, and he growled as the vampire rode him even harder, intent on taking them both over the edge and into absolute madness.

The vampire tilted his head, clawing at his neck until a bright red stream of blood began to trickle down his collarbone. "Drink," he commanded urgently. "Hurry!"

The blood was so bright that it glittered, Snod feeling his guts roll at the thought that he was about to drink it. But that blood meant freedom; he had to do this.

He grabbed the vampire by his hair, ravenously locking his mouth against his bleeding neck and sucking hard. His mouth flooded with blood, the vampire crying out pleasurably.

Snod swallowed it down, his body rocked with a plethora of new feelings. He could feel enormous strength, an ancient consciousness that seemed to stretch on forever. He could sense pleasure and breath and his eyes were starting to tear up from the flood of emotions saturating his thoughts.

"Coming," the vampire snarled, his hand grabbing his own cock and bringing himself to the peak of ecstasy. "I'm coming, fuck!"

Snod had to sever the connection, choking on the last swallow of blood when he felt the vampire's body clamping down on him. He couldn't stop himself, climaxing so hard it made his head hurt, his vision blinding white as his cock pulsed over and over again.

He clung to the vampire, his body slamming upward as he tried to chase that perfect feeling. It was fleeting and gone too soon, its loss leaving him trembling and sweating.

"Good?" the vampire panted, smiling brightly.

Snod nodded feebly, replying, "Yes… it was…" *Amazing, glorious, magnificent.* "It was good."

"Come on," the vampire huffed, his smile fading and

rolling his eyes at Snod's meager review of their coupling. "Let's get going."

Snod wanted to hold him a bit longer, his arms tightening around his waist. He wasn't ready to lose this yet. He wanted to throw the vampire down on the floor and do it again, he wanted to do *that* over and over for hours and hours on end.

He could still feel the vampire's heart pounding in his chest, the beat slowly starting to fade as reality crept back in. He knew they had to move. He released him finally, knowing the vampire could have broken away whenever he wanted.

Smiling sympathetically, the vampire rose to his feet and offered his hand down to Snod.

Snod stood up, a deep satisfaction resonating all the way down in his bones. The touch of the vampire's hand made his stomach flutter pleasantly, and he cleared his throat as he tried to ignore it. He peeled off the condom, tossing it away and tucking himself back in his pants.

The vampire blinked back into his clothing by the time Snod had finished zipping, saying, "We need to go. Now or never."

"Got it." Snod was all business once more as he followed the vampire back down the tunnel. He retrieved his gear as they went, his muscles itching from all the unfamiliar energy coursing through him.

When they reached the rubble, together they grabbed the chunk of twisted metal that was blocking their path. It groaned and squealed, finally giving way from their combined might and revealing an opening big enough for them to crawl through.

The vampire zipped through first, shouting behind him, "All clear, come on!"

Safely back on the factory floor, Snod began to approach the vampire again.

The vampire watched him warily, saying, "Remember our bargain. We're done, right? You'll leave the city?"

Snod couldn't stop thinking about what it had felt like to be inside him, the lovely sounds he made, or the way his eyes fluttered as he came. He knew it couldn't happen again, and no one could ever find out. His memories would have to be enough to last a lifetime.

"Yes," Snod said abruptly. "I'm going to go."

"Wait," the vampire said, almost frantic, speeding over to Snod's side.

Snod blinked, licking his lips slowly. "What?"

The vampire bit the end of his finger, gently rubbing blood over the puncture marks he had left on Snod's neck. "Yeah, probably wanna get rid of those first," he said with a smirk, stepping away.

Snod touched his neck, surprised to feel the wounds had vanished. He knew vampire blood was powerful, but healing like that was astounding. There was so much they didn't know about these creatures.

"I never asked," Snod said quietly. "What's your name?"

"Are you serious?" The vampire laughed. "Wow. You really wanna know that now?"

"Yes," Snod replied simply.

The vampire stared Snod down with those impossibly green eyes, debating for a long moment. Finally, he said, "Francis Barnaby Temple. But you can call me Frankie."

Snod nodded, a flicker of a smile curling his lips. "Frankie."

The vampire stuck out his hand, saying, "Nice to meet you, Obadiah."

Snod shivered when their hands met, resisting the desire to pull him back into his arms. "Nice to meet you, too, Frankie."

"Don't take this the wrong way or anything," the vampire said with a nervous chuckle, "but I really hope I never see you again."

Snod smirked. "Don't worry. You won't."

"We're not all monsters," the vampire said with a wistful smile. "I hope, if nothing else, you remember that…"

Snod didn't know what to say to that.

The vampire was gone in a blink without another word, leaving Snod alone in the factory. He could still feel the vampire's lips ghosting over his, wishing like hell he had been brave enough to steal one more taste.

Snod took a deep breath, forcing himself to turn and walk away.

CHAPTER TWO

Even though he had showered last night, Snod thought he could still smell the vampire's scent on him when he woke up the next morning in his hotel room. He was uncomfortably hard, trying to will all the blood in his cock to travel anywhere else in his body.

With the memories of his coupling with the vampire guiding his hand, he had touched himself in the shower. He refused to give in to such temptation again. He glanced at the time, sighing haggardly.

It was four o'clock.

Right on time.

Snod's internal clock was meticulous, rarely ever needing an alarm to wake up after so many years of rising early. It was part of why he had done so well in his youth while training with the Order. A strict schedule appealed to his compulsive nature, and the structure of the rigid rules governing everyday life had always been comforting.

Until now.

Snod couldn't begin to count how many rules he had broken. Carnal sins aside, he had let the vampire feed from him. He had even dared to taint himself with the most foul and sinful substance on earth, the vampire's own blood.

He had been seduced by lust, and allowed his body to be violated by a fiend. Worst of all, he had let the vampire live. He felt dirty down to his bones, the guilt of what he had done oozing out of his every pore.

Disgust cramped up his guts to the point of vomiting, and he ran to the bathroom. When he was finished being sick, he rested his head against the cool porcelain of the commode. He needed to repent. He had no idea how many lashes the bishops would order him to take for all of this, but he knew in his soul these sins couldn't be beaten away.

He had liked it.

He had *wanted* it.

Regret was taking over his thoughts now and he was ashamed. It would have been better to have died down there instead of feeling like this. He hated himself for giving in and loving how wonderful the forbidden desires had felt. He especially loathed the tiny piece inside of him hoping that it would somehow happen again.

Leaving the bathroom, he got cleaned up and started packing. He had to make contact with the Order soon, but he was dreading it. He'd never had to report a failure before.

Snod didn't know how he could even begin to explain all of his sins. Would the Order even allow him to stay a member? Would he be excommunicated or something worse?

He swallowed hard, having heard many stories of members who had been executed for severe acts of treason. He couldn't imagine anything more traitorous than sleeping with their sworn enemy.

Kneeling beside the bed, he bowed his head in prayer. He knew he should be asking for forgiveness for his sins, but there was only one plea bubbling up to his lips in this vulnerable moment.

"Help me, Lord," Snod begged softly, the anguish inside of him threatening to swallow him up. "Grant me the strength to move on. Help me stop wanting him so much… help me forget him."

Forget how good he had tasted, how sweet the touch of his hands was, the wondrous sensation of his body wrapped around…

Fuck.

Snod gathered his things and hastily left the hotel. He had to get outside the city and call the Order immediately. He plugged in his phone, berating himself for not charging it earlier. He knew subconsciously he hadn't bothered because he was trying to prolong the inevitable. Cranking the car, he took a deep breath and drove out of the parking lot.

He pulled into the street, finding himself instantly blinded by the headlights of a truck driving in the wrong lane.

Well, wasn't that just peachy.

Snod tried to jerk the wheel, but it was too late. The truck was traveling fast, too fast, and he got a face full of airbag when they collided. His whole body rocked against the seatbelt as the windshield and passenger side window shattered, raining glass all around him.

His car was pushed back several feet, tires squealing from his foot being wedged against the brake. The force of the crash smashed it up onto the sidewalk and into a telephone pole.

The horn was going off, Snod groaning loudly as the deafening sound added to the awful throbbing in his head. He reached up to touch his forehead, finding his fingers red.

Blood was beginning to run down into his eyes, and he couldn't hear anything except the blaring of the horn. He could see sparks from the damaged wires overhead and smell gasoline. There was also a very large amount of explosives in his trunk.

Very illegal explosives.

He didn't want to be blown up, and he couldn't afford to be arrested when the police arrived.

He had to get out of the damn car.

Snod was able to unbuckle his seatbelt, grabbing his still dead phone and trying to pull himself free. The center console had been crushed inward by the force of the crash and his hips were pinned in between that and the driver's side door. He tried to keep a cool head, but deep inside he was beginning to panic.

He smelled smoke, and while he couldn't see any flames yet, he knew it was only a matter of time.

Slamming his elbow in the console and punching at the shattered windshield did nothing. He couldn't get enough leverage, starting to pant heavily from the smoke invading the car. He had to focus, his heart thudding with dread when he saw bright flames crawling up the hood of his car.

He might die here.

Snod's mind flooded with concern for his beloved brother, Athaliah. Though they had different mothers, blood was blood, and his younger sibling was the only family that he had left in the entire world. He had always taken care of him; who would be left to do that if Snod was gone?

He didn't know why, but he suddenly thought of Frankie the vampire.

Gorgeous and incredible Frankie who had shown him a taste of pleasure he couldn't ever dare to dream of having again. How could such a vile creature be so sweet and kind, invading his thoughts even now in what might be his final moments?

Snod took a deep breath, closing his eyes, certain he could smell him even now. At least if he did die here, he had finally found out what it was like sharing his most intimate parts with another person.

It was beautiful.

Suddenly, the windshield was ripped off like a Band-Aid, metal whining and crunching as it went flying off into the street. Snod stared in shock at the awesome display of strength, gawking at his rescuer.

It was the beautiful vampire perched on top of the flaming hood, the very one who had been in his thoughts mere moments ago.

"Frankie?"

Frankie's eyes were wide with worry behind a new pair of glasses, as he quickly reached for Snod to help him out of the wreck. "Are you all right?"

"I'm great," Snod groaned, hating how easily the vampire was able to pull him out of the car and onto his feet. He detested feeling so weak, coughing stubbornly and pushing Frankie away the moment he felt steady enough to stand on his own.

That was a mistake.

His head spun, and he immediately teetered over, finding himself once again in the vampire's strong embrace.

"You need a hospital," Frankie insisted.

"No," Snod coughed defiantly. "I need to get out of here before the police get here."

"Why?"

"Because I have several outstanding warrants for my arrest," Snod hissed angrily. He saw something leaking out of the truck and running underneath his car. He definitely smelled more gasoline. "Also, a very large quantity of explosives in the trunk of my car. We need to move. Now."

The vampire tracked the scene and quickly saw the danger they were in. He zipped away, carrying Snod to a safe distance and gently setting him down. "I'll be right back!"

"Where the fuck are you going?" Snod demanded.

"The truck driver! He's still in there!"

Snod stared dumbly as the vampire raced over to the truck to get the driver out. He had honestly forgotten about the other person, and was surprised by the vampire's unexpected mercy.

The vampire brought the truck driver over to the sidewalk, gently laying him down beside Snod. He patted the man's shoulder, relieved as he said, "He's unconscious, but alive."

Snod's head jerked toward the accident, the fire beginning to lick around the back tires of his car. Even over the blaring horn, he could hear the wail of sirens approaching.

"We need to go. Now!"

"If you won't let me take you to a hospital, where am I supposed to take you?" the vampire snapped.

"Anywhere but here!"

The explosion was deafening, the ground shaking beneath their feet. They were far enough away to avoid the worst of the blast, only a few pieces of debris landing close by. Snod quickly stomped one out that was still on fire, his ears ringing miserably as he tried to shout, "Now!"

Grabbing Snod, the vampire took off. Snod cringed as the world went flying by them, his stomach dropping uncomfortably. Moving at such high speed was extremely unnerving.

Ugh, and nauseating.

He closed his eyes, covering his mouth so he wouldn't puke, gasping as he felt himself dropped down on something soft.

A couch.

Snod looked around, startled to find himself in a very nice loft. The furniture was all antique, the colors warm and comfortable, and there were hundreds of old books crowding every inch of space on the walls except one spot where a large portrait of Benjamin Franklin was hung.

Other than the small television set, Snod didn't immediately see anything that seemed to be from this century.

The vampire was sitting next to him, a first aid kit between them, his bright eyes watching him intently.

"Where are we?" Snod demanded, certain he was probably talking too loud because he couldn't hear himself.

"My home," the vampire replied.

"This… this is where you live?"

"What did you expect? Spider webs and black velvet?" the vampire scoffed. He made a face, adding grumpily, "I didn't know where else to bring you."

Snod didn't reply, collapsing back on the sofa with a

groan.

"If you want," the vampire offered hesitantly, "you can drink from me. It would heal you."

"No," Snod growled. "I'm not doing that again."

The vampire's lip curled up.

"It was a mistake."

"Maybe rescuing your ungrateful ass was a mistake," the vampire snapped.

"How did you know?" Snod lifted up his head. "How did you know where to find me?"

"Because of the blood that you're so eager to turn your nose up at," the vampire replied. "We're bonded, remember? You summoned me. I felt your fear and your pain, and then… well, I came for you."

Snod was startled, all too aware of his thoughts shortly before the vampire's miraculous arrival. "I summoned you?"

"You were thinking about me, very strongly. That's all it takes sometimes." The vampire was positively smug. "Don't even try to deny it."

Snod glared.

"Fine," the vampire said with a smirk, reaching for the first aid kit. "You don't want my blood, that's your loss. I can at least patch you up—"

"Don't touch me," Snod said sharply, sitting up and trying to scoot away from him.

The vampire flashed his fangs as he drawled, "Really? After everything we've been through? I save your life twice, but now all of a sudden, I'm an unholy monster again?"

Snod's insides churned. He remembered all too well what they had shared together. He also recalled how vile it had left him feeling once the glow had faded. He again said nothing, his silence speaking volumes.

"Everything you need to clean up is in the kit," the vampire said flatly, face blank. "There's food and drink in the kitchen if you want it." He blinked away, reappearing with a pair of pajamas and dropping them on the table.

"Clean clothes if you want to change."

Snod watched the vampire suspiciously, trying to remind himself that even being near this creature and allowing it to live was forbidden.

But he was being so nice…

And he was still so very beautiful.

A surge of lust ignited deep inside of Snod that he tried to ignore. He was surprised when he saw the vampire's eyes suddenly flutter and his lips part as if responding to what he was feeling.

"You have food?" Snod quickly asked. "For what, all of your victims?"

"For my friends," the vampire replied dryly, now acting as if nothing had happened. He did crack a tiny smile, unable to resist teasing, "You know what those are, right? Friends?"

"Yes," Snod growled ferociously.

"You're so easy to piss off," the vampire snorted, standing up and clapping his hands together. "And as much as I would love to keep watching you make grumpy faces, I have to get ready for work. Stay here, rest up. I'll be back later."

"Work? But the sun will be up soon."

"Yes, I know, but…" The vampire trailed off, peering at Snod curiously. "You do know that some vampires can day walk?"

"No, the sunlight burns the impurity out of your tainted flesh and—"

"Oh, my God," the vampire cackled. "You have no idea. You really have no clue at all!"

Snod's cheeks flushed. He was angry, in pain, and the vampire was laughing in his face. His temper was beginning to simmer, his fingers digging into the couch cushions.

"You know, all of my immortal life I was warned about the Order," the vampire said with a grin. "The feared and dreaded vampire hunters. I was always looking over my shoulder, always making sure to change my identity every twenty years so no one would ever catch on that I wasn't aging. I did so much to keep myself safe from you! And after all of this time, wow, you're all so stupid!"

Snod rose up immediately, snarling angrily, "We are a sacred Order charged with—"

"Blah, blah, killing vampires," he snapped back. "Yeah, I got it. But you know what I'm starting to think? All the vampires you've killed that you're so disgustingly proud of? They probably weren't even a hundred years old. Maybe fifty at most? Ha! You've been killing vampire children and keeping their little baby fangs as trophies and thinking you're a big, mighty hunter."

Temper now boiling, Snod clenched his hands into fists. "I'm warning you. I appreciate your hospitality, but I'm—"

"What?" the vampire taunted cruelly. "Getting mad? Oh, yeah. I can feel it, remember? God, you really are all fools. I still can't believe it. The Order is nothing but a bunch of ignorant, brainwashed virgins who—"

"Shut the fuck up!" Snod shouted, all of the pressure building up inside of him exploding violently. He wasn't thinking clearly, blindly lunging at the vampire.

The vampire grabbed him effortlessly, pinning him down against the couch. His fingers curled around his throat, baring his fangs as he hissed, "Where was I? Oh, right. Nothing but a bunch of ignorant, brainwashed virgins who have no idea what they're being sent out to destroy."

Struggling furiously, Snod realized that trying to move a brick wall would have been easier. He had fought many of the undead over the course of his lifetime, but none like this.

He had grossly underestimated the vampire's strength, fighting hard no matter how futile it was, panting now as he gazed stupidly up at those pretty green eyes. The press of the vampire's hips against his was too familiar, and he urgently prayed for all of these treacherous feelings to go away.

They only got worse, a new wave of desire washing over him that made him groan out loud. He didn't even know where it came from, but now all he could think about was how good it had felt to kiss this lovely creature. He stared dumbly at the vampire's lips, desperate for one more taste.

The vampire's face shifted, softer and warm, his hand moving to cradle the side of Snod's cheek. Whatever spell was being cast at that moment, it seemed to affect him as well.

Snod's heart was aching, a million voices in his head screaming at him to stop, but the only one he could hear was the one whispering for him to give in to what he wanted. He grabbed the back of the vampire's head and pulled him into a heated kiss.

CHAPTER THREE

Snod couldn't explain his sudden lust. Perhaps he had hit his head too hard or maybe he had finally lost his mind. With the vampire returning his affections so hungrily, he didn't care right now. All of the disgust and self-loathing he had experienced before melted away.

How could something that was supposed to be wrong feel this good?

The energy between them was crackling and the slide of the vampire's lips was absolutely intoxicating, Snod's heart thrumming faster and faster. He was more sure of himself than he had been down in the tunnels, deepening the kiss and raking his fingers through the vampire's hair.

The vampire was touching him all over, cool palms sliding under his shirt and squeezing his hips as they grinded together. Snod had to pull away to gasp, trying to catch his breath as the vampire flung his glasses away. Snod was getting dizzy fast, but he didn't want to stop.

The vampire's tongue was so cold, like ice as it dipped across Snod's face to lick at some of the dried blood. It was soothing against his hot skin, his hands racing down to grab the vampire's ass.

When the vampire groaned softly, Snod stole away the

sound with his mouth. He wanted to be inside of him, he wanted to feel that intimate embrace once more.

There was a knock at the door, and they both froze.

The haze that had captured them seemed to fade even as Snod's cock continued to throb. He glared up at the vampire, hissing softly, "Expecting someone?"

"Fuck," the vampire cursed. "Damn carpool!"

"Car… what?" Snod didn't think he had heard him correctly.

The knocking continued more insistently.

The vampire blinked away, suddenly dressed in scrubs and a white lab coat, fumbling with a fresh pair of thick-rimmed glasses. "My job! Me and some of my co-workers take turns carpooling."

Snod sat up, grunting as he struggled to adjust himself.

The vampire carpooled.

How quaint.

"Look, let me do the talking," the vampire said quickly. "Don't move and don't touch anything. Oh, God. Especially the books, please don't touch the books."

Snod's head was reeling as he watched the vampire flit around at lightning speed.

"Okay, one minute!" the vampire called out to the door as he stumbled around. He finally answered it with a breathy, "Hey! Sorry about that!"

A young man with long braids and dressed in similar scrubs came barging right in, complaining, "Dude, you took forever, and I've got to piss! We're gonna be…" he stared at Snod, "…late."

The vampire grimaced.

The young man smiled, asking slyly, "Frankie. Who's this?"

The vampire grinned sheepishly, saying, "Uh, Lorenzo, this… this is my new friend, Obadiah."

Snod scowled.

Lorenzo was smiling even wider, teasing coyly, "Friend, huh?"

Snod wanted to stand but was afraid that it would be much too obvious what he and the vampire had been up to. Shame began to creep over him at having been interrupted during such a sinful act, and he glared heatedly at the stranger.

"Rough night, huh?" Lorenzo continued to joke, elbowing the vampire knowingly.

"Something like that."

"I mean, he's bloody… you're… well, you know." Lorenzo gestured with his hands, making little fangs with his index fingers up by his mouth. "On the bitey side?"

"He knows?" Snod growled, jumping to his feet, his hesitation forgotten in his rage. "Is he one of your foul concubines?"

"My *what*?" the vampire spat, shaking his head. "No! He's my friend!"

"Then how does he know what you are?" Snod demanded.

"Stand down, lover boy," Lorenzo soothed, eyeing Snod's bulging crotch with a loud snort. "Look, I figured it out. We share a lab together. It's not hard to notice when someone with fangs never eats or drinks or ever goes to the damn bathroom. Which speaking of, I still need to—"

"He's not going to say anything," the vampire insisted, looking to Snod. "I've been friends with Lorenzo for years. He's very trustworthy."

"Oh! Yeah! Never!" Lorenzo confirmed, shaking his head. "Frankie is my best friend. I would never tell anyone!"

Snod stared Lorenzo down, his fingers instinctively twitching. He might not be able to fight this vampire, but a scrawny mortal would be no challenge.

I will not allow you to hurt him.

Snod flinched. It was the vampire's voice whispering right in his ear, but his lips hadn't moved nor had he budged from his firm stance next to Lorenzo.

The world at large still believed vampires to be a myth. It was vital to their very survival, but it was also imperative to the survival of the Order.

No one could know that vampires or the sacred organization were real. Working in the shadows was how they had been able to operate for so long. Anyone who found out the truth and could potentially put them at risk had to be disposed of.

Without question.

Snod glared, wishing he knew how to communicate back, suspecting it had something to do with their blood bond. He concentrated, thinking a few short words as hard as he could while staring the vampire down.

You gonna stop me?

The vampire showed his teeth in a silent snarl. He definitely heard it. He looked at Lorenzo, saying quietly, "No carpool today. Go without me. I'll take the bus to keep my carbon footprint down, I promise."

Lorenzo frowned, glancing between them. He was obviously no fool, able to clearly see something was wrong here. He rested a hand on Frankie's shoulder, asking seriously, "You okay? For real?"

"For real," the vampire confirmed.

"All right," Lorenzo said, still not sounding convinced. He stuck out his jaw, saying sternly, "If you're just playing hooky to get some nookie, I'm not covering for you."

"There is no getting of the nookie, I swear," the vampire replied, patting Lorenzo's arm. "Go get Amy, I'm sure she's freaking out that we're late. Just tell them I have a stomach bug or something, I'll be in soon."

"Fine," Lorenzo conceded, heading toward the bathroom, adding defiantly, "But I'm peeing first."

Snod waited for the bathroom door to shut, stalking toward the vampire as he hissed furiously, "What the hell was that? How did you do that? Talk in my head?"

"The same way you did it to me," the vampire whispered heatedly, right in Snod's face. "The bond of blood is powerful! Very powerful! I've only experienced it with another vampire before, okay? I didn't exactly know that was going to work!"

"Bullshit!" Snod growled, feeling the anger beginning to intensify, his blood starting to heat up once again. "You threatened me!"

"No! I simply stated a fact! I will not allow you to hurt my friend!"

"The threat is implied!" Snod barked back, hating how beautiful and bright the vampire's eyes were when he was angry. He caught himself looking at his lips again, swallowing back a groan.

The vampire shuddered, stepping away from Snod as if the physical distance would decrease the lustful sensations.

It did not.

Before either one of them could act upon them, Lorenzo came out of the bathroom, waving his farewell as he said cheerfully, "Better be there before the boss gets in at lunch, that's all I'm saying."

"I'll be there," the vampire promised with a strained smile, sighing as his friend left and the door shut behind him. He narrowed his eyes at Snod, grumbling, "I'm going to be so damn late."

"You should kill him," Snod said immediately.

"What?" the vampire gasped. "Are you nuts? He's my friend! I trust him!"

"You're a fool," Snod warned. "You can't trust anyone but yourself."

"Says the guy who blindly follows a crazy cult's every command," came the dry retort.

Snod wanted to grab him, maybe choke him, but very definitely wanted to kiss him again. He shivered, wishing the feeling would go away. It was strong and seductive, and it was difficult to resist. He felt sick to his stomach, trying to pray for strength.

"What's wrong?" the vampire asked, sounding concerned. "Is it your head? From the accident?"

"Why does that keep happening?" Snod asked, a hint of fear in his voice. He had never felt so out of control before.

"That feeling between us."

"It's the blood," the vampire said calmly as if trying to soothe a frightened animal.

"You keep saying that!" Snod snapped in frustration. "Everything is because of the damn blood!"

"Because it is!"

Stalking back to the couch, Snod flopped down defeatedly. He was sore all over, frustrated beyond belief, groaning, "I should have never done it. I'll never be clean of this filth."

"Well, I can't really help you with that. I have to get to work," the vampire said with an all too human sounding sigh. "Do you even have someone you can call? Money for a cab? I still expect you to honor our deal."

"Phone's dead," Snod replied shortly. "No money. Everything I had was in the car."

"Well, what kind of phone do you have?"

Snod showed him, and the vampire flickered away. He came back, suddenly standing in front of Snod holding a charger. "Here. I used to have one like that. Take it, call whoever you're going to call, and leave the city."

Snod accepted it, staring at it with a frown. He was out of excuses now. He had to call in.

"What's wrong?" the vampire teased. "Afraid they're gonna kick you out of your little crazy person club?"

"When I tell the Order what I've done, I'm afraid they'll execute me," Snod replied softly, tangling the charger cord around his fingers. His brother, Athaliah, would be left all alone.

"Come on," the vampire scoffed, his face falling when he realized Snod was completely serious. He walked slowly and deliberately up beside him, gently touching his arm.

Snod flinched slightly, but caught himself leaning into the vampire's hand.

"There is nothing wrong with what we did," the vampire assured him. "There is nothing wrong with wanting what makes you happy. Gay, straight, vampire, human. The

Order is wrong, Obadiah. About so many things, but they're especially wrong about who you can love."

Snod bowed his head, continuing to twist the cord to occupy his hands.

"I'm sorry about what I said," the vampire went on. "About you all being a bunch of dumb virgins or whatever. There's nothing wrong with that, not at all! But it's different when it's your choice, when it's because you want to live that way; not because someone else is telling you to and threatening to kill you over it."

Snod still said nothing, tightening the cord until his fingers were beginning to turn colors. He deserved the pain, he deserved a punishment. He wanted to believe the vampire, desperately, but he couldn't shake how wrong what they had shared together was.

No matter how much he wanted it.

"You deserve to live your own life," the vampire insisted, prying the cord loose from Snod's grip. "The way that you want to, to be happy."

Snod caught his fingers, longing for his cool touch. It was comfort he sought now more than anything, holding the vampire's hand as he struggled to find the right words. He sighed, saying quietly, "I wouldn't know how."

"How about this. If you're gone when I get back, great! Enjoy going back to hunting vampires and your potential execution!" the vampire exclaimed. "But if you're still here… maybe I can help you."

"Help me?"

"Well, if the Order kicks you out, you could start over. I'd let you stay here with me until you got on your feet again."

Snod was stunned. "Why would you do that for me? I tried to kill you."

"Everyone deserves a chance to be happy," was his simple reply.

"Just like that?"

"Just like that," the vampire promised. "I know a thing

or two about wanting a fresh start. Plus creating fake identities. I could give you a completely clean slate. You could go to school, get a job."

It sounded too good to be true.

"What would I even do?" Snod demanded sharply. Despite his harsh tone, he wasn't angry. He was afraid. He had never imagined living without the Order telling him what to do and guiding his every move.

"Whatever you want," the vampire replied. "Just think about it. I mean, for all the Order knows, you were in that car when it blew up. You don't even have to call them."

Snod frowned, the temptation making his soul ache. It was terrifying, feeling lost already, though a tiny flicker of hope began to burn deep inside of him.

He would be free.

The vampire gave his hand a brief squeeze before letting go, saying quietly, "I really do hope I'll see you when I come home, Obadiah. If not, I understand."

"Obe," he corrected with a hesitant smile. "You can call me Obe."

"All right, Obe. Please. Really think it over, okay?"

"I will," Snod answered, nodding faintly.

The vampire smiled warmly with something like longing in his eyes, and then in a blink he was gone.

Freedom; the very idea was so huge and magnificent it made Snod's head pound to even consider it.

Snod found an outlet to plug in his phone and headed right back to the couch. He tended to the worst of his wounds and collapsed against the cushions, absolutely exhausted. He was so drained that he didn't even dream, only waking a few hours later when he heard his phone coming back to life and ringing incessantly.

It was a simple ringtone, a flutter of chimes, but now that chiming sound filled his gut with dread.

It was the Order.

Specifically, Archbishop Sanguis.

Snod hurled himself off the couch to grab his phone,

having just missed the call. He stared down at the screen, seeing dozens upon dozens of calls, voicemails, and texts that had gone unanswered.

Most were from the Order, including an oddly frantic text message from Sanguis all in capital letters demanding to know if this was the fiend he had battled against. Attached was a photograph of an oil painting of two gentlemen, perhaps late eighteenth or early nineteenth century.

The man in the foreground was blond, strong chin, and utterly smug. The tall young man at his side was doe-eyed, beautiful, and Snod recognized him immediately.

It was Frankie.

Snod didn't understand the urgency of identifying the vampire he had fought, continuing to scroll through the rest of his messages. A few were from his younger brother, and he felt a pang of guilt for having been gone so long and not letting him know he was all right. He kept reading, realizing very quickly the Order really did think he was dead.

It would be so easy to walk away like the vampire had suggested. New identity, new life, do whatever he wanted, love whoever he pleased.

Guilt dropped on him like a wet towel, heavy and uncomfortable, forcing him back to the couch because he didn't feel well enough to stand any longer. He couldn't do it. No matter what sweet things the vampire had told him, he couldn't turn his back on the sacred Order he had served all of his life.

His little brother was still there, Athaliah, the only family he had left in the whole world. He couldn't abandon a lifetime of training and devotion either. It didn't matter what sinful things he wanted, even deep down in his soul.

The Order came first above all else.

Snod took a deep breath and dialed the archbishop back, his pulse skyrocketing higher with every ring.

"Snod?" Archbishop Sanguis' voice came onto the line, totally in awe. "Is that really you?"

"Forgive me, Father," Snod said, dropping off the couch and to his knees immediately. "I have sinned so greatly—"

"We thought the beast had slain you!" Sanguis exclaimed. "We also heard a report of an accident, one that matched your vehicle's description. We've been so concerned, my sweet child."

"It was," Snod confirmed. "My mission has been… complicated."

"Tell me. Is the beast still alive, my son?"

"Yes, I've failed you," Snod said sorrowfully. "He was too fast, I wasn't able—"

"Tell me what happened," Sanguis said, sounding gentle and kind. He didn't seem upset in the slightest.

"The beast and I became trapped underground. There was large debris blocking our way, too much for us to move. We couldn't escape… we were down there so long, and I was getting weaker. I inquired about using… the vampire's blood."

There was a small grunt on the other line.

Snod began to sweat, continuing, "Heart blood, specifically. I was desperate. He agreed to give it to me, describing a ritual to procure it without turning me or endangering himself."

"What such ritual would that be?"

"Copulation," Snod responded shamefully. "We laid together. I let him drink from me, and I from him. With our combined strength, we were able to escape."

"Heart blood from laying together? Truly?" Sanguine sounded intrigued.

Snod was struggling with the odd reaction. He had been expecting threats of eternal damnation and being ordered to lash himself. He hesitated, saying slowly, "Yes, Father. I felt the beast's heart beat myself." He gulped anxiously. "You're not angry…?"

"Tell me more, my son," Sanguis pressed. "At what point were you able to take the heart blood?"

"At… climax," Snod said awkwardly.

Sanguis was quiet for a long moment, his voice stern as he said, "You said this vampire was fast. All the unholy beasts are fast; why was this one unique?"

"He moves like a ghost. I would have never caught him on foot," Snod replied honestly. "He simply disappears and reappears like magic. I've never seen anything move the way he does."

"This is very important, my son," Sanguis said. "Did you receive the photograph I sent to you? The painting? Was the vampire you met in that painting?"

Snod frowned.

The archbishop's line of questioning seemed erratic, and Snod was now suspicious. The archbishop was much more interested in talking about the vampire than all the terrible things Snod had done. He didn't dare question such a high-ranking member of the Order, but something felt off.

"Yes," Snod replied after a brief pause. "It is definitely him. The brunette."

"What about the blond man?"

"No, Father. Never seen him before."

"Where are you now?" Sanguis demanded.

"I'm at the vampire's home," Snod replied, rubbing his hand over his face. "After the accident, the vampire saved me and brought me here."

"Are you safe?"

"Yes, he isn't here now, but he will certainly return."

"I must speak to the other councilmembers immediately," Sanguis said excitedly. He cleared his throat, adding firmly, "Stay where you are, we will make contact again shortly."

"Yes, Father," Snod said, sighing when the line disconnected. He hung his head, wishing he understood what the archbishop was up to. He was restless, moving into the kitchen and poking around the cabinets.

There was food, but not very much. Chips, pretzels, mostly snacks. The fridge was nearly empty except for a standard selection of condiments, and the only item in the freezer was a bottle of vodka.

Snod was starting to look at the first shelf of books when his phone rang again. It was Archbishop Sanguis.

"Yes, Father?"

"I need you to kneel, my child," Sanguis said sagely, sounding like himself again, firm and wise. "We're going to pray together now."

Snod knelt right where he was standing, putting the phone on speaker and clasping his hands together. "Yes, Father. I'm ready."

"Lord o'God, please forgive Your sweet child, Obadiah Penuel Snod, for all of his disgusting and heinous crimes against nature. Forgive him for how he has sinned against You and soiled his body," the archbishop began. "I know my sweet son did not mean to stray so far from Your light, and he will repent immediately."

Snod began to take off his vest and his shirt. He knew the motions well, his body reacting practically on instinct. He didn't have a flagrum with him, having lost it in the explosion, so he took off his belt. He closed his eyes, completely ashamed of himself.

Yes, what he had done was disgusting.

He was disgusting.

Feeling that way and wanting that vampire had been wrong. His soul and body needed to be purified.

"How many, Father?" Snod asked obediently.

"How many times did you lay with the fiend?"

"Once," Snod replied honestly.

"Have you had any other impure thoughts?"

"Yes, Father."

"Ten lashes for the first sin, five more for every time after you had these vile ideas."

Touching himself in the shower, when he was trapped in the car, and kissing the vampire on the couch.

"Twenty-five, Father."

"Begin," the archbishop commanded.

Snod curled the belt around his hand, whipping it over

his shoulder and cracking it over his back. Over and over, grunting from the pain, trying to suppress all of his memories of the sweet vampire.

The more he struck himself, the hotter the anguish burned inside of him. He knew it had been a sin, but he had enjoyed being with the vampire so much.

It was beyond anything he had ever felt before in his entire life. It was sweeter than the blissful call of the Order or the comfort of taking communion. There was nothing that could compare.

And the vampire was so kind, so gentle, his mercy and charity without question. He had been willing to help Snod start a new life, to forgive him.

How could this perfect creature be the same as all the vile fiends he had sworn to hunt down and cleanse from the earth?

Snod didn't feel any better when he was done. He calmly put his belt back on as he said, "Forgive me, Father. I have put my sins to my flesh, and I pray the Lord will take them from me."

"You are forgiven," the archbishop intoned.

Such words used to fill Snod with warmth. He only felt empty now.

"I have a very special mission for you now, my son."

"Anything," Snod said eagerly. He wanted to get out of there and away from all of this.

"This vampire, he has affection for you?"

"I believe so," Snod answered hesitantly, a sharp frown creasing his face. He didn't like where this was going.

"This is vital to the future of the entire Order," Sanguis told him. "I want you to stay there with that creature. I want you to befriend him. I want you to get close to him."

"But, Father," Snod protested, "I can't do that. The Order forbids—"

"As of this moment, you are no longer a member of the Order," Sanguis said briskly.

Snod's heart stopped.

No, no, no.

This couldn't be happening.

"You are being excommunicated for your foul sins of the flesh. The council wanted your life, but I begged them to be merciful. They are allowing you to live, but you are now an exile. You may never return to us—"

"My brother," Snod pleaded. "What about my brother?"

"Your sins do not reflect on him, I promise you," Sanguis said gently, "but you will never see him again."

"Father, please," Snod begged, wringing his hands together desperately.

"Listen to me, my son," Sanguis soothed. "Now that you're no longer a member of the Order, you will have no trouble fulfilling your special mission. This will be a way for you to come back to us."

"What?" Snod was horribly confused.

"There is something we need from that vampire, and you're going to get it for us. You can only do that if you're a free man. Do you understand?"

"No, Father, I don't!" Snod was unhinged, shouting, "Please! Tell me! Tell me what you want me to do!"

"The Order will accept you back with open arms if you give us his Maker's name. Earn the vampire's trust, seduce him, bewitch him. Do whatever you have to do, but we must know the name of his Maker and if he's still alive." There was a pause. "Can you do that, my son?"

Snod took a deep breath, closing his eyes as he breathed, "Yes, Father. Yes, I can."

CHAPTER FOUR

Snod hung up with the archbishop, putting his clothes back on and returning to the couch. The cloth of his shirt was irritating his raw back, but he ignored it. He had a new mission, one that reeked of deceit, but he had no other choice.

If he didn't complete this mission, he would forever forfeit his place in the Order.

Sanguis told him that his phone would be deactivated because he had to be cut off from all the Order's resources, but he would turn it back on in one month. At that time, Snod needed to give him a name.

He remembered the vampire mentioning his Maker when they were trapped down in the tunnels, warning of his intense hatred toward humans. Snod wondered why Sanguis wanted to know so desperately or what possible benefit a name would be, but it was not his place to question a member of the council.

His place was to obey.

As for his current state of mind, he was at once elated and miserable. Being free of the Order technically allowed him to do as he pleased, but there was still an uncomfortable sense of guilt embedded in his bones that made him ache with indecision.

There was a little voice telling him that everything he had done or wanted to do now was wrong, and then there was an even tinier voice saying that it wasn't.

The lashing hadn't made him feel any better. He had simply gone through the motions, and the ritual provided no comfort. He was lost and confused, his heart and head at war with one another and unsure of how to proceed.

He had little time to process any of it. The front door opened and Snod leapt to his feet to see the tall figure of the vampire walking in.

The vampire's face lit up, laughing happily. "You're still here!"

"Yes," Snod said, his stomach rolling uncomfortably at how that gorgeous smile made his heart skip a few beats.

The vampire frowned, locking the door behind him and zipping to Snod's side. "You're hurt."

"I'm fine."

"No, you're hurt, I can smell blood," the vampire insisted, checking Snod over to look for new injuries. "What happened?"

"I was cleansing myself," Snod said stubbornly. "It's nothing for you—" He grunted when the vampire turned him around, pushing his shirt up and revealing all the angry welts.

"Obe," the vampire sighed in sympathy, "why did you do this?"

"Because I had to cleanse myself," Snod replied as if it were obvious. "The mortification of the flesh purifies my body of its sin."

"The Order made you do this?" he accused.

"I did this willingly!" Snod argued, trying to pull away, but the vampire held him in place. "What is it? The smell of blood tempting you to tear me apart?"

"Tempting me to commit you," the vampire grumbled. "What happened? Did they kick you out?"

"Yes," Snod replied, unable to keep the sadness out of

his voice. "I've been… kicked out, as you so eloquently put it."

"How else should I say it?"

"That my life is over! Everything I know, everyone I care about, my entire world! It's all gone!" Snod roared, whirling around to shove the vampire away.

The vampire didn't budge, his hands pressing against Snod's chest. "Oh, Obe. Don't you get it? Your life is just beginning."

Snod scoffed, shaking his head in protest. "I no longer have a purpose."

"Your purpose is whatever you want it to be. You're free," the vampire insisted. "Think of all the incredible things you can do now."

"Like what?" Snod asked softly, laying his hands over top of the vampire's and scanning over his lips. He told himself this was for his new mission to get close to the vampire, ignoring how it made him ache inside to touch him again.

"Like… getting drunk!" the vampire laughed, pulling away with a grin. "I'll even drink with you! We're celebrating, right?"

"Vampires can't get drunk."

"Where there's a will and a highly sophisticated laboratory, there's a way," the vampire chuckled. "Let's get you cleaned up first."

Snod allowed himself to be herded into a spacious bathroom, sitting down on the edge of the tub as the vampire tenderly peeled his shirt and scapular away.

"What did you use?" the vampire asked softly, his fingers lightly touching one of the wounds.

"My belt," Snod replied, frowning.

The vampire pricked his finger on one of his fangs, slowly dabbing his own blood over each raised welt. "These are part of your lessons?"

"Yes," Snod sighed softly as the pain began to fade.

"You've done this… a lot."

"Slow learner," Snod replied with a faint smirk. The vampire looked confused, and he added, "That's supposed to be a joke."

"Sorry if I don't find it very funny," the vampire said dryly, picking up a washcloth and dampening it under the faucet of the sink. He began to softly wash Snod's back, his movements tender and caring.

Snod was absolutely melting, closing his eyes and concentrating on the cold fingers moving over each tear in his flesh. He felt echoes of those same fingers touching him all over as his cock thrusted deep inside the vampire's tight body…

The mission.

Snod cleared his throat, glancing back at the vampire behind him, asking quietly, "The scrubs… Are you a doctor?"

"Yes, I'm a hematologist," he replied. "I work for Hazel Medical Research Facility."

"Hmm. Plenty of access to blood then?"

"Yes, to help me find cures."

"For…?"

"For diseases," the vampire said with a smirk. "I like helping people."

"Were you a doctor before you were turned?"

"God, no," the vampire laughed. "I was a printer's apprentice."

"The books," Snod realized. "They're yours? Did you print those?"

"A few of them, yes. I worked for Hall and Sellers for several years, a printing company in Philadelphia."

"How old are you?"

"Old enough," the vampire replied coyly.

"Did you have a family?" Snod paused, noticing the vampire's frown and quickly amending, "I'm sorry. You don't have to…"

"It's fine," the vampire replied softly. "They've been gone a long time. My mother died from a fever when I was a child. My father was never quite the same after losing her. He always said she was the light of his life. He lost his way without her."

"What happened to him?"

"Well, I went overseas to France for business, and by the time I returned, he had already died. Consumption, they told me. Tuberculosis."

"France?" Snod inquired, trying to keep the conversation light. "I've never left the country."

"See? Something else we can add to your list!"

"List?"

"Your freedom list!"

Snod snorted, asking, "What kind of printing business took you to France?"

"I was a secretary then," the vampire said with a grin as he finished up cleaning Obe's wounds, "to a very influential American ambassador."

"Oh?" Snod flexed his shoulders, surprised that he couldn't feel any of the markings he had inflicted on himself. He turned to face the vampire, putting it all together as he said, "Printer. Philadelphia. An ambassador to France. The portrait in your living room. You worked for Benjamin Franklin?"

"Oh! You know your history! So they do allow reading in the Order?" the vampire teased, blinking away and returning with a clean shirt.

"Yes," Snod bit back, grabbing the shirt defiantly and pulling it on. He didn't feel right wearing the scapular now, shoving it into his pocket as he argued, "We are taught very well."

"Yes, I can tell." The vampire smirked, throwing Snod's soiled clothing in a hamper. "Early American history, self-flagellation techniques, how to kill vampires… very sane and effective schooling."

"You didn't answer the question," Snod persisted, following the vampire back into the kitchen. He noticed the mess he had made of the first aid kit had all vanished.

"No, I did not," the vampire said plainly, taking out the bottle of vodka from the freezer and pouring a shot in a glass.

Snod made a face at the seemingly harmless substance. He didn't trust it.

"One second," the vampire said, disappearing in a blur and reappearing in pajama pants and a comfortable looking t-shirt. In his hand was a large amber glass bottle. He poured a shot for himself, something thick and almost black.

"What is that?" Snod asked, making another face.

"In essence, very iron-rich blood," the vampire said, picking up his glass and encouraging Snod to pick up his own. "It is possible for vampires to gorge themselves on large quantities of blood and experience sensations very similar to being drunk. So I found a way to replicate it with extremely concentrated blood. Specifically from a pig's liver."

"Pig?" Snod blinked. "Vampires can drink animal blood?"

"Of course we can," the vampire chuckled. "Now, come on. A toast." He lightly clinked their glasses together. "To freedom, new friends, and a new life."

Snod grimaced, studying the liquor skeptically. It couldn't be that bad. It looked like water. He shrugged and drank it back, gagging immediately at the sudden burn. "Poison!" he hissed accusingly. "You poisoned me!"

The vampire snorted in laughter, nearly spilling his blood, rubbing Snod's arm. "No! It's vodka! There's gonna be a little bit of a kick." He poured them both another round, a can of soda pop magically appearing next to Snod's glass. "What you need is a chaser."

"I am never drinking that foul shit again!" Snod snapped angrily. Nothing had prepared him for such a strong taste. He was surprised when the burn began to ease off and left him with a pleasant warmth in his chest.

Maybe one more.

Snod took the next shot, wincing and quickly chugging

back some of the soda to soften the burn. That actually wasn't so bad.

"How are you enjoying defiling yourself?" the vampire chuckled, the glasses filling again in a blink.

"I don't understand the appeal," Snod replied with a frown. "It burns. And it tastes like shit."

"Keep drinking," the vampire urged. "You'll understand soon enough." He seemed relaxed, his pale cheeks slightly flushed. "Mmm, what other sorts of things were you not allowed to do in the Order?"

"Imbibe any stimulants, anything that could be considered addictive or that would pollute our bodies. Alcohol, nicotine. Mmm. Caffeine," Snod said, nudging the soda with a laugh. "That seemed to be the one rule everyone broke. Even one of the archbishops took a public lashing after being caught with a cup from Starbucks."

The vampire furrowed his brows. "These lashings… they would be in front of everyone?"

"Not always," Snod said, surprised how easy it was to open up to the vampire. "Usually they'd be done during prayer or confession. Just you and one of the priests."

The vampire looked a bit alarmed.

Snod set his glass down a little harder than he had meant to, feeling a little fuzzy, asking firmly, "So. Tell me. How old are you?"

"Why are you so interested?" the vampire asked innocently, obviously grateful for the change in subject.

"Is that why you're so fast? Because of how old you are?"

"No. I inherited the gift from my Maker. Some vampires have unique abilities, you see. Some are very fast, some can turn into mist, some can bewitch you with just a look. It takes centuries to learn, but they can be passed down from Maker to child."

"You don't like your Maker?" Snod could very clearly pick up on the hostility in the vampire's voice when he spoke of him.

"No, I do not," the vampire said sharply, finishing off his drink and pouring another.

"Why? Tell me about him," Snod said as casually as he could, trying to keep his interest discreet.

"No," the vampire said flatly, his expression as blank as a marble slate. "There is nothing to tell. He turned me, and I left him as soon as I could."

Snod was overwhelmed by a sudden surge of sadness, an ache that took his breath away. He had never felt such sorrow. He had to gasp out loud, reaching forward to grab the vampire's hand. It was the vampire's emotions he was feeling, he realized, and the anguish was suffocating.

The feeling faded almost as quickly as it came, and he stared in confusion at the vampire. "What… what did he do to you?"

"Not everyone wants to be immortal, Obe," the vampire said, letting their fingers weave together. "I'm sorry. I'm not used to having a blood bond. I forgot to keep it down, I guess. Didn't mean to let my feelings come through like that."

"Can you feel mine?" Snod asked pointedly, wondering if his ulterior motives could be sensed. He caught himself looking at the vampire's lips, remembering what the archbishop said about seducing him. "What am I thinking about right now?"

"Well, you're nervous," the vampire answered immediately, "but also excited." He tilted his head, smiling wide, his fangs glittering. "Mmm. Yup. Very excited."

Snod smiled, taking another shot. He didn't even need the chaser now, warm and fuzzy all over. He didn't quite mind the taste of the booze any longer. He felt good. He felt really good. He toyed with the vampire's long fingers, laughing, "I'm starting to finally understand the appeal of drinking."

"Good, right?" the vampire laughed, looking so flushed and beautifully human. He tipped back his glass, licking his lips as he sighed, "I only drink on very special occasions, you know."

"Mmm, I'm so glad my life ending is special to you," Snod drawled sarcastically.

"No! I didn't mean it like that!" the vampire groaned. "Don't you get it? Obe! There's a whole world out there just waiting for you!"

"Waiting for me to do what?"

"To live! Look, I'm going to help you. Putting together a new identity will take some time, and I meant what I said about you staying here with me. I have a guest room. Lorenzo usually crashes there when he's had too much to drink, but you're welcome to it."

Snod felt a ripple of guilt, the happy warmth ebbing. It didn't feel right taking advantage of such kindness, especially when he had every intention of returning to the Order as soon as he could. He had to get back to Athaliah.

"What's wrong?" the vampire pressed, immediately sensing something was amiss.

"I have a brother," Snod replied quietly. It wasn't a lie. He was very concerned for what might happen in his absence. "He's still there."

"With the Order? You're worried about him?"

"Yes," he nodded. "Athaliah. He wasn't born into the Order like I was. My father had many sins of his own, and he was unfaithful to my mother. We didn't find out about Athaliah until he was already in high school."

"Is he a hunter like you?"

"No," Snod scoffed, "he's not worthy to hunt. His right eye is blemished, a deformity from his birth. He cannot receive the council's blessing to take up the sacred mission."

"Wow. Uhm. Does… does he like it there?" the vampire asked hesitantly.

"He's adjusted," Snod said shortly.

It had not been easy. His brother still struggled with the strict environment and had actively rebelled when he first arrived. There had been several failed escape attempts and many harsh lessons though Snod had always tried to protect him.

"Why don't we go kidnap him?" the vampire suggested, slamming his glass down excitedly. "If we get him out of there, then you won't feel so guilty about leaving him behind!"

"We can't just go take him!" Snod argued, laughing at the ridiculous plan. "The Order's main compound is a fortress. There's dozens of guards and multiple layers of security—"

"That you know very well, I'm sure!" the vampire cut in, squeezing Snod's hand. "I bet you could figure out a way to break in there and rescue Athelsbyah!"

"Athaliah, not Athelsbyah!"

"Whatever!"

Snod kept laughing, finding the asinine idea totally hilarious. He shook his head, chuckling heartily, "I appreciate the offer, but I think I'll pass."

"Well," the vampire huffed, "if you change your mind, let me know. Super fast day walking vampire is at your service for all potentially dangerous rescue operations."

"Why are you like this?" Snod wondered out loud, the liquor making his tongue loose. "Why are you so… nice for a vampire?"

"Have you really taken the time to get to know any of the others before me?"

"No," Snod confessed.

"Well, then you don't really have anything to compare me to," the vampire laughed.

"Seriously," Snod pushed, utterly entranced. "After everything I did, you just, what? Forget all about it?"

"People, vampire or human, are all a mix of good and bad," the vampire explained, adjusting his glasses. "I try to be one of the good ones and remember what it was like to be human. You've been raised in a horrible place, and I know the way you are isn't your fault. I think I can help you be better. I want to try, really. I can show you everything you've been missing living in that cult. Look, I haven't forgotten anything you've said or what you tried to do, but I do forgive you."

Snod's heart stopped right on the spot, staring in awe at the vampire. He had no words, lost in his bright green eyes and the gentle warmth washing over him. He wanted to kiss him, touch him, bask forever in this soft light he exuded from every pore. Dozens of clergy had forgiven Snod countless times over the course of his life, but he had never felt as comforted as he did receiving absolution from this vampire.

He was suddenly pulling the vampire closer, seeking more, wanting something tangible, desperate to touch him.

The vampire offered no resistance, allowing Snod to embrace him, giggling sweetly, "Mmm, trying to dance with me now?"

Snod snorted, saying dryly, "I don't dance."

"Wait, are you serious? Dancing is forbidden, too?"

"No," Snod clarified, feeling his face get hot. "I just… can't. So, I don't. Music has never… moved me."

"Oh, you wait right here," the vampire said, his eyes wide. "I have the perfect song! If this doesn't move you, nothing will. Hang on one second!"

Snod mourned the loss of the vampire in his arms, watching him flit over to an antique secretary desk. It opened up to reveal a modern stereo hidden within.

Music began to play, a poppy guitar riff bouncing through the speakers, and a man started to sing. It was something about being a man and waking up next to someone else. It was utter nonsense to Snod's ears.

"What is this?" Snod complained, frowning.

"The Proclaimers!" the vampire shouted, blinking back to grab Snod's hands and pull him out into the living room where they would have space to dance.

"Proclaimers of what?" Snod loudly protested, swaying slightly from the alcohol.

"Proclaimers of move your damn ass!" the vampire cackled, trying to inspire Snod to move his hips.

"This is ridiculous!" Snod let his foot tap along to the beat, but otherwise refused to cooperate.

Then the chorus hit, a triumphant declaration of walking hundreds of miles and Snod was completely captivated. Before he knew it, he was bouncing all around, his soul filled with joy, laughing as the vampire dragged him into a festive romp.

It was absolutely impossible to resist. The call of the music was more heavenly than morning communion, and Snod couldn't stop smiling.

The song played on and Snod was absolutely enchanted, though his attentions had drifted away from the music. He was certain that no creature alive could capture the beauty or grace of the vampire's body as he twirled and slid across the floor, twisting and swinging his head to the infectious beat.

Snod let himself be pulled along for the ride, moving his feet clumsily as he tried to keep up. The world was spinning around him in a bright blur, and it was utterly glorious.

Somehow his hands ended up around Frankie's waist, sliding down greedily over his back and hips.

Yes, *Frankie.*

They were spinning together, laughing happily. Snod didn't know the words, but it was easy enough to follow along into all the da da da's of the chorus.

Frankie was quite possibly the most beautiful vampire he had ever seen. He had hunted so many before him, and yet still not a one had this life about them like he did. He couldn't even think of a single human who could boast such a vibrant soul.

Snod couldn't stop himself, leaning in for a taste of it, capturing his lips in a sweet kiss.

Frankie sighed contently, his arms winding around Snod's neck and kissing him deeply. The weight of his body pressing against him was divine, Snod's head swimming in ecstasy as they moved together.

Even as the song ended and their feet stopped dancing,

they were still embracing. The tension was heating up, Snod greedily kissing down Frankie's jaw and neck.

"Oh, Obe, hmm, we probably shouldn't," Frankie moaned when Snod bit down on his throat. "God…"

"I want to be with you again," Snod pleaded, holding him tight, completely open and honest with his desire. He squeezed Frankie's ass, loving how he squirmed.

"Okay," Frankie breathed, those gorgeous green eyes gazing at him with such adoration. Instead of speeding them away, he took Snod's hands and led him into his bedroom step by step.

Snod didn't bother looking around except for a quick glance to find the bed. He tumbled down onto the plush blankets and took Frankie with him. He was frantically trying to get their clothes off, eager to begin.

"Hey, hey, hey," Frankie soothed, his hands latching on Snod's shoulders to hold him in place. "Slow down. We don't have to rush this."

Embarrassed, Snod turned his head away. Now that this train of desire had hit a stop, he had a moment to think. This was wrong.

Disgusting.

"Hey." Frankie could obviously sense his apprehension, icy fingers cradling his cheeks and craning his head back toward him. "Obe. There is nothing wrong with wanting me. With wanting this…"

Snod couldn't speak, unable to express the mix of lust and indecision clawing away at his guts. He let Frankie pull him into a tender kiss, his worries chased away by his soft lips.

"Listen to me," Frankie said firmly, his words leaving no room for argument. "Do exactly as I say and I promise it will be worth it."

"Yes," Snod breathed, his eyes fluttering as his body responded to the stern command. Their clothing peeled away at an agonizing pace, Frankie not allowing it to speed along any faster, making Snod wait.

Every time he pushed, Frankie slowed down even more, leaving him groaning and his cock painfully hard. He couldn't think about anything else now. The Order, his lashings, and even thoughts of Athaliah all disappeared as he gave himself over to this beautiful vampire.

Every new sensation was exciting and made him ache with need. He was on top of Frankie now, marveling at the cool flesh of his thighs pressing against his hips. The touch of his icy fingers raking over his scalp made him shiver and he could not get enough of his mouth.

Snod could feel Frankie's arousal, pressing insistently against his own. He groaned when Frankie rolled a condom on him and spread lube between them.

"Obe," Frankie urged, his fangs bared, greedily tugging at his cock and pulling him where he wanted him most.

"Frankie," Snod whimpered in reply, the first cool touch of the vampire's tight entrance making him gasp. He pushed forward, letting it swallow him whole, his grace lost as he floundered to be inside him as they had been before.

It was easier this time, being in complete control of the rhythm, immediately pounding into him hard. That tight body wrapped all around him was incredible, and Snod buried his nose against Frankie's throat as he slammed forward.

Frankie cried out sharply in reply, his hands digging into Snod's back.

Snod had never heard such a sound before, his head snapping up and his hips stilling. He stared down at Frankie, not sure if he should continue.

"Wait. Why did you stop?" Frankie demanded furiously.

"It, it… it sounded like I was hurting you," Snod hissed back, eyes wide with concern.

Frankie's head dropped against the pillows, groaning, "Obe, I'm a fucking vampire. You're not going to hurt me."

"Are you sure?"

"Very sure," Frankie confirmed, raising his hand and abruptly slapping Snod's ass. "Don't you dare stop again!

Come on!"

Snod grunted in surprise, his body registering the pain but something else along with it. It was new, exciting, and he didn't know what to make of it except he really wanted to feel it again. "That…"

"Shit," Frankie hissed. "Is that all right? The lashings, I should have—"

"Do it again," Snod pleaded helplessly. "Please?"

"You really want me to hit you again?" Frankie asked breathlessly, searching Snod's face for confirmation.

"Yes," Snod begged, wishing he could explain the rising well of desperation inside of him. The sharp touch of Frankie's hand made him feel alive in a way that his lashings never had, and he was certain he was going to explode if Frankie didn't spank him. "Please, Frankie!"

Frankie didn't hesitate another second, baring his teeth as he spanked Snod's ass mercilessly. The sound was like fireworks, loud cracks in rapid succession that seemed to echo inside the small room.

Snod groaned in reply, rearing his hips back and pushing his cock in deep, delighting in the loud moans that promptly erupted from Frankie's lips. Now that he knew these were cries of pleasure and not pain, he did everything he could to hear them. Every fierce roll of his hips was punctuated with the crack of Frankie's palm, sending blazing signals of pleasure up and down Snod's spine.

His cheeks were soon stinging from Frankie's hand and Snod found that he liked the burn. It was similar to the physical sensation from his lashings, but this wasn't a punishment. He had asked for it and received it at length, gasping sharply when Frankie finally stopped. There was something so deeply pleasurable in the aftermath of being struck in this manner that he immediately craved more.

Snod had certainly never been left wanting after being beaten by one of the members of the council, but he was absolutely yearning for another taste of Frankie's discipline.

Purposely, Snod began to slow down, his eyes issuing a

silent challenge as he stared down at Frankie. He couldn't bring himself to speak the words out loud, but he had a feeling that he could get Frankie's attention.

"Oh, you naughty little thing." Frankie's expression instantly darkened and there was something primal flickering over his face. His arm went up and his hand roughly cracked across Snod's ass with a loud smack. "I told you not to stop, now come the fuck on!"

"Fuck!" Snod's response was immediate, and while he was not particularly graceful with his movements, he could thrust away like a sledgehammer. He watched Frankie brace himself against the headboard to keep himself from being scooted up the bed from his powerful slams. He loved the way Frankie's lips parted as he moaned and how his eyes fluttered as he moved inside of him.

"Fuck, I want to feed on you," Frankie growled, his eyes zeroed in on Snod's throat. The hunger was undeniable. "Yes?"

"Yes," Snod whispered, tilting his head to the side.

Frankie pulled Snod down right on top of him so their bodies were pressed flush together. He petted his hair, kissing along his shoulder and his neck before finally sinking his teeth in.

Snod only felt the tiniest of pricks followed by an intense and lovely suction, moaning much louder than he had meant to. It was unbelievably intimate knowing he was feeding his lover, his breath stuttering in his throat as he felt Frankie heating up all over.

"Feels good," he grunted, his hips still thrusting away like a piston on an engine, never tiring, never stopping.

"Obe," Frankie groaned as he pulled away, licking his lips greedily. "Mmmph, here, like this." He stretched out one of his long legs, throwing it up on Snod's shoulder and pushing him back. He grabbed a firm handful of Snod's ass before spanking him hard, exclaiming, "There, now come on!"

Snod jerked from the hard smack as he got settled on his

knees, holding Frankie's thigh and experimentally thrusted forward in this new position. He cried out immediately, startled by the sudden heat and the depth that his cock could reach now.

Oh, that was good.

Snod started thrusting again, Frankie's warm hands sliding down over his shoulders and gripping his forearms as he held on for the rough ride. The slapping of their bodies colliding was positively obscene, and Snod couldn't get enough of it. He was a mess of sensations, lost to the divine feeling of Frankie's body wrapped around his cock and the heat left behind on his stinging cheeks.

Frankie was arching into every thrust, helping them maintain a fast but perfectly delicious pace. He spread his legs as far as he could, moaning and demanding more, his cock hard and leaking as it bobbed against his stomach.

Snod wished fucking him like this could last forever, but his legs were on fire and the pressure in his balls was begging for release. "I'm gonna, gonna…"

"Come on," Frankie urged, grabbing his cock and feverishly jerking himself off. "Make me come!"

Snod gave Frankie all that he had, grunting as he worked through his muscles failing and chased down his orgasm. When he came, it was sloppy but heavenly. He cursed and shook as he rocked himself through it, unloading deep inside of Frankie's tight hole.

He watched Frankie fall apart beneath him, still grinding down against his spent cock as he climaxed, pearly splashes of cum shooting across his lean body. Snod had never seen anything so absolutely erotic, leaning down to kiss all the pretty sounds from his lips.

He didn't even care about the stickiness between them. He was entirely consumed with the need to keep kissing him. His head was still light from the rush of the intense act, and he was suddenly struck by a devastatingly strong wave of nausea.

"What's wrong?" Frankie asked quickly, very concerned.

"It's not because we had sex, is it?"

"No," Snod replied earnestly, wishing he could make the queasy feeling go away. "I just feel… sick."

"Are you gonna throw up?" Frankie gazed up at him in sympathy.

"Yeah," he groaned, his stomach gurgling defiantly as the room spun. He could taste bile and vodka creeping up the back of his throat. "Definitely gonna throw up."

CHAPTER FIVE

Frankie was nothing but kind as he helped Snod to the toilet to heave up his guts, petting his back in soothing little circles. "I'm sorry. Probably should have made sure you ate something first."

Snod couldn't reply, caught between dry heaving and hacking, groaning when his stomach gave him a brief reprieve.

Oh, he was not going to drink again.

Never.

Not ever.

Maybe.

He'd actually enjoyed himself very much, and now he understood exactly why the Order forbid the consumption of alcohol. It was so easy to lose control when one's inhibitions were completely tanked.

Grumbling miserably, Snod closed his eyes. He was still drunk and his stomach was unbelievably angry with him. Frankie's hand felt cool now, and it was comforting against his flushed skin. Despite being so sick, he had enjoyed his coupling with Frankie.

Especially the kissing. God, how he adored the kissing. Sweet and tender, passionate with tongue, open-mouthed ones that were more heated pants than kisses…

There probably wasn't going to be more kissing of any kind this evening considering the state of his mouth, Snod thought glumly, slumping against the commode.

"Let's get you cleaned up," Frankie encouraged, wiping Snod's face down with a damp cloth and easily carrying him out to the sofa. He wrapped his naked body in a warm blanket, blinking around to clean up the liquor and their glasses.

Snod sank down into the cushions, staring bleary-eyed at the tall vampire as he sat down beside him. He watched as he used his nail to break the flesh of his neck, grimacing. "What are you doing?"

"Making sure you don't have a hangover," Frankie replied with a smirk, gently wrapping his hand around the back of Snod's head, bringing him toward the blood slowly leaking down his collarbone.

Snod was repulsed for a moment, but he remembered how pleasurable it had been to drink from the vampire before. He also knew how powerful that blood was, and he did feel so wretched. He let Frankie pull him close, his tongue slowly lapping at the trickle of blood.

Frankie's eyes fluttered, stroking Snod's short hair. He smiled, murmuring encouragingly, "Just like that, Obe."

Snod could sense a fresh surge of lust burning between them, sucking every last drop that had dribbled down from the small cut. It was a similar warmth to the alcohol, but this seemed to fill him up all the way down to his toes. He pressed a hand against Frankie's face, sliding his fingers up into his hair as he drank.

Frankie let Snod take all that he wanted, gasping, "God, yes… yes, Obe…"

Snod shivered to hear his name spoken like that, his nausea gone and the painful pulse in his head fading. He swallowed back one last thick mouthful, tilting his head to press his lips against Frankie's. He wasn't as clean as the vampire, spilling a few drops as they kissed so passionately.

Frankie didn't seem to mind, letting the blood smear between them as their tongues met, deepening the kiss. He was touching Snod greedily, pushing the blanket out of his way to track every inch of his muscled flesh. He nosed against Snod's jaw, his fangs lightly pressing as he asked breathlessly, "May I…?"

"Yes," Snod said, offering himself willingly, inhaling sharply when Frankie bit down. His eyes rolled back, groaning as the vampire drank. He could feel Frankie getting warmer in his arms, amazed at how quickly he heated up.

He was getting hard again as Frankie fed. It was utterly intoxicating and Snod was panting by the time he'd finished.

Frankie continued to explore Snod's body, his fingers chasing after every scar as if he was trying to catalogue them all. "God, you're beautiful."

Snod blushed, turning to press Frankie down into the couch. He knew the vampire was letting him do this, but it was still thrilling. He shook his head, glancing over the creature beneath him, sighing, "I'm nothing compared to the absolute heaven that is your body."

"Sweet talker," Frankie chuckled, though the compliment had made his cheeks rosy. He reached down to lightly tease over Snod's cock. "Mmm, seems like someone is feeling better?"

"Much," Snod said, his cock heavy and throbbing, lightly thrusting into Frankie's palm. "Can we… again?"

"You are downright insatiable," Frankie teased, pulling him in for a wet kiss.

Snod mouthed his way back down to Frankie's neck, mumbling, "Can't help it. I want you so badly, God help me. You're incredible."

"Always in such a rush," Frankie sighed adoringly as Snod was already trying to line himself back up and push inside. "Slow down."

"Don't want to," Snod argued, gasping when Frankie effortlessly pushed him off and forced him into a sitting position on the sofa. He wanted to protest, but Frankie was slinking down in front of him on his knees.

He was still amazed how beautifully the vampire moved, intently watching as he gracefully settled between his thighs, peppering his skin with warm little kisses that made him shiver.

Snod's cock twitched as he breathlessly asked, "What… what are you doing?"

"Obe," Frankie said firmly, "you need to learn about a little something called foreplay." He bowed his head, his tongue running over Snod's balls and up the shaft of his cock. "Now shut up and let me suck your cock."

Snod was not proud of the sound he made, wheezing when he realized exactly what Frankie was up to. He was going to use his mouth, he was going to use his mouth down *there.*

"God in heaven," he moaned, squirming as Frankie continued to lick and tease, not sure what to do with his hands. He scrubbed at his face, whining pitifully, watching every move Frankie made with wide, lust-blown eyes.

Frankie curled his fingers around Snod's thick girth, sucking each of his balls into his mouth and rolling his tongue over them. He was savoring the texture, the taste, applying just enough pressure to make Snod groan.

Frankie finally released his tender sack, slowly feeding every inch of his cock into his mouth. It was slick and moist, totally different from being inside of him, but definitely as pleasurable. He stared dumbly as Frankie's hand moved out of the way, the last of his cock slipping down his throat.

Snod knew there were tears falling down his face, his hands reaching back to grip the edge of the sofa. Frankie looked beautiful with his lips wrapped around him so tightly, and he was unable to stop his hips from canting forward. Frankie didn't stutter in the slightest, bobbing his head and sucking fiercely, making Snod writhe and cry out.

Frankie kept going and going, Snod unable to do anything except hold on for the ride. Right when he was certain it couldn't be any more intense, he felt a faint prick of teeth against his groin.

Frankie had taken every inch of him down his throat, and now he was drinking from him, right *there*, sucking softly and running his tongue all over his shaft. It was dirty and totally forbidden, and fuck, if it wasn't the most amazing sensation Snod had ever experienced.

Snod could feel a rush of warmth as Frankie's mouth began to heat up, shuddering all over. The pressure was too much and Snod was not able to even call out a warning. He fell right over the edge into bliss and came hard down Frankie's throat.

Frankie bobbed his head, offering a muffled moan of satisfaction as he worked him through it, lightly massaging his balls and continuing to suck at him until Snod was begging for mercy. He popped off with a cheeky grin, not a single drop of blood or cum gone to waste, humming, "Mmm, how was that?"

"Heaven," Snod gasped adoringly, surprised by how profusely he was sweating and that his cock was still half hard. "That, that was perfect. I'm sorry I was… quick."

"I take it as a compliment," Frankie said with a warm smile, crawling up into Snod's lap. He kissed him, their cocks crushed together as he began to slowly grind against him.

Snod couldn't believe how eagerly his cock stood at attention, especially after coming just moments ago. "Is this more of your blood magic?" he asked, his hands moving over Frankie's flesh, hot to the touch from having just fed from him. "This… virility?"

"Uh huh." Frankie's eyes were bright and happy, watching their cocks sliding against one another. "We can go all night if you want."

All night.

Snod seized Frankie in a passionate kiss, wrapping his arms around him. He squeezed his hips, his ass, whining as the throbbing between his legs became more demanding.

Frankie was in control now, forcing them to go slow, and it was driving him crazy.

Frankie took one of Snod's hands, trying to guide it down to their cocks, but Snod jerked away. "What's wrong?"

Shame had forced Snod's hand to move, not ready to touch something so male, so much like his own and yet so very foreign, stammering, "I-I can't…"

Frankie nodded in immediate understanding, smiling reassuringly, sliding Snod's hand toward his ass, down between his cheeks. "What about this? Is that okay?"

"Y-yes," Snod sighed anxiously, his fingers now moving to find that tight ring of muscle, nodding. "I can do this."

"I want you to touch me," Frankie said sternly. "I want you to feel good with me. It's amazing to share this with someone, to open them up. But if you're not comfortable…"

"I can do this," Snod repeated stubbornly, slowly pushing the tip of his finger inside. It was much tighter than he had expected, weirdly smooth as he slowly felt around. He pushed a little more, watching Frankie's face for approval.

Frankie was smiling, his hands gently cradling Snod's face, stroking his thumbs over his cheekbones and kissing him encouragingly. "Just like that," he urged. "Go deeper."

Snod obeyed, suddenly pressing his finger all the way in, watching as Frankie gasped, his mouth hanging open in a happy smile. Snod did it again, the tip of his finger exploring to find what Frankie liked the most.

He added a second finger, slick and pushing deep, Frankie's back arching and grinding against Snod's hand. He kept pumping his fingers, rough and clumsy, but Frankie was making the sexiest little sounds so he kept going.

"Good?" Snod asked breathlessly, kissing at Frankie's neck.

"Uh huh," Frankie sighed, pushing his body closer. "Very good, Obe…"

Snod could feel the snug muscle around his fingers starting to relax, asking quickly, "Are you ready?"

Frankie huffed softly, and Snod could sense a flash of frustration. He didn't know what he had done wrong, frowning.

Frankie nodded all the same, smiling as he replied, "Yes, Obe."

Snod pulled his hand away, hastily trying to shove himself back in Frankie's wet hole the second the condom was on.

"Easy," Frankie soothed, lifting his body and slowly taking him inside.

Snod's hands grabbed at Frankie's hips, trying to push him down, trying to buck up to bury his cock deep. But Frankie wouldn't budge, only allowing a few inches at a time, nipping playfully at his neck.

"Please," Snod pleaded eagerly.

"Patience," Frankie replied. "Let me show you how good this can feel."

Snod groaned when Frankie finally sank all the way down, his ass wonderfully tight and hot. "God… yes."

Frankie had a hand on Snod's shoulder, the other tucked behind his head as he rolled his hips. His body rose and fell in a beautiful wave, his lean stomach flexing as he moved. He was as graceful during this passionate act as he was dancing, his expression soft and gorgeous.

Snod had to touch him. He had to feel his legs, his hips, his sides, sliding his hand over his chest where he was surprised to feel a faint heartbeat. "You're close," he gasped, keeping his palm right where it was.

"Uh huh," Frankie panted.

"Don't you… don't you want to…?"

"Sometimes, it feels better if you wait," Frankie explained, smiling at Snod's hopeless expression. "Trust me…"

Snod tried to, he honestly did, but all he could focus on was wanting to come. He could feel Frankie's heart beating faster and faster, certain they were both about to tip over the precipice of pleasure.

But then Frankie slowed down to a devastating crawl, denying them both.

Snod growled in frustration, begging, "Please?"

"Not yet," Frankie commanded. "Almost." His hips finally began to pick up the pace once more, and he kissed Snod passionately.

Snod's balls were aching with the need to release, and his kisses were frantic. The passion was perfectly hot and as Frankie moved faster and faster, Snod was certain this time he wouldn't be refused his ending.

Frankie cried out excitedly, his hand feverishly jerking himself off as he rode Snod harder, panting hoarsely, "Coming… come on… I'm coming…"

Snod was utterly mesmerized, Frankie's body clenching all around him and the fire that had been building inside of him finally exploded as he came. It was intense, Snod left trembling all over as his hips jerked violently up into Frankie's.

Frankie was practically singing, his head thrown back as he moaned beautifully, rocking them through their orgasms. "Yes, Obe, yes, my good boy! Come on!"

"Fuck, fuck!" he grunted, his hips seizing as he unloaded more and more, his orgasm never seeming to end. He finally collapsed against the couch, Frankie falling against him. He was sweating, out of breath, able to feel both of their hearts pounding furiously away.

Frankie lightly petted the hairs at the base of Snod's neck, a smile on his lips as he taunted, "Mmmph… now do you see why it's good to wait?"

"Uh huh," Snod said, imitating Frankie's cheeky reply. He ran his hands over Frankie's back, loving the closeness of their embrace.

Frankie was happy, Snod could sense it washing over him through the bond. He was happy, too. There was no Order here, no shame, no punishment; just the two of them, enjoying each other.

"Mmmm... again?" Snod asked softly, nuzzling against Frankie's neck.

"Again?" Frankie echoed, laughing sweetly. "God, I've created a monster."

"Is that a yes?"

"Yes, Obe," he chuckled. "It's a yes."

Snod growled playfully, wrapping his arms around Frankie's hips and lifting him right off the sofa as he stood up. He eagerly carried him back toward the bedroom, the vampire cackling impishly as Snod playfully threw him back on the bed.

They went two more times before Snod was completely exhausted, passing out the moment his head hit the pillow. He was restless, stirring often, but always drifted back to sleep when he felt the vampire's cool body next to his own.

When he woke up, Frankie was still in bed but was already awake, watching him sleep with a little smile on his face.

Snod stretched out his legs as his eyes flitted open, grunting, "Mmmph. Morning."

"Good morning," he replied. "Sleep well?"

"Not bad. What time is it?"

"A little after eight."

"Fuck," Snod gasped, sitting up quickly. He couldn't believe he had slept in so late, his heart instantly fluttering in panic. Then again, it didn't matter, did it?

He had nowhere else to be.

"What's wrong?" Frankie asked, his brow furrowing with concern.

"I'm usually up and moving much earlier than this," Snod said, flopping back down in bed. "I think you wore me out."

"Me? Please, you're the one who couldn't get enough last night," Frankie taunted.

Snod smiled sheepishly, his eyes glancing over Frankie's muscular body. He was still naked, stretched out on top of the covers, sunlight peeking through the windows and splashing little shadows all over him. He looked absolutely gorgeous.

Snod reached out, gently touching his hip where the sun was hitting, asking, "It really doesn't hurt you?"

"No," Frankie said with a shake of his head, "not for a very long time."

"Another gift from your Maker?"

"No, this one is all my own," Frankie replied, a hint of sadness tainting his handsome expression.

"How?" Snod asked, unable to hide his curiosity.

"I walked into the sun and survived," was the sad reply, Frankie glancing away at the wall.

"You walked into…" Snod frowned. "You tried to kill yourself."

"Yes," Frankie said, sitting up suddenly.

"Why?" Snod asked dumbly, confused.

"Not everyone wants to be immortal, Obe," Frankie sighed, his eyes dark. "Especially when your Maker is a monster."

Snod's lip twitched, swallowing hard. He could tell this was a difficult subject, but he knew he needed information. He needed a name. He tried to remain calm as he could, saying casually, "You were trying to get away from him?"

"Yes," Frankie said, moving from the bed and blinking into a shirt and sweatpants. "I tried, I failed, and now I can walk in the sun. It's how I was finally able to escape him."

"He can't day walk?" Snod pressed.

"No," Frankie replied, tossing a pair of pajama pants at him. "He couldn't then, but he probably can now. Most vampires acquire the ability with age, and this century he'll be over a thousand years old."

"A thousand…" Snod couldn't hide his amazement. He sat up, pulling on the pants and ignoring the swelling of his cock due to the early morning hour. He cleared his throat, adding nonchalantly, "So, he's still alive?"

"Probably. I've done everything I can to suppress the

bond between us," Frankie said shortly, clearly getting aggravated. "I still feel him sometimes. There was one time I tried…" He shook his head, human and lost, snipping quickly, "Never mind."

"You can manipulate the bond?" Snod decided to change up the subject, not wanting to anger the vampire and lose this fountain of information. He needed to know more.

"It's possible," Frankie said, heading out into the kitchen with Snod following behind him. "I can keep my feelings from you, my thoughts as well. You can hide yours from me if you try."

Snod frowned, watching Frankie flutter around to make him breakfast, eggs and bacon quickly popping into a pan on the stove. He wondered if Frankie could sense his anxious treachery. He figured it was best to drop his questioning for now, sitting down at the table.

"Scrambled okay?" Frankie asked, smiling brightly now.

"You don't have to cook for me," Snod politely protested. "I'm more than capable."

"I don't mind," Frankie insisted. "Helps me feel human."

"Like the glasses?"

"Yup."

"Is it really so different? To be a vampire?"

"I hope you never have to find out," Frankie replied with a short laugh, "but yes, it's very different. The worst part is watching your world disappear."

"Disappear?" Snod cocked his head curiously.

"When I was human, there were no cars, no computers, no phones. Times changed, technology changed. It was amazing to watch. I still remember the first time I saw an actual working lightbulb. I thought it was a miracle. But soon, I didn't recognize anything. Street names were different, buildings I knew were demolished and replaced with new ones. Everything was changing so fast, and the world I grew up in, the world I knew… it was gone."

"I never thought about that," Snod said quietly. "Is that

why you keep all this old furniture? Something familiar?"

"Exactly," Frankie chuckled. "I tried to get my actual desk back from when I was alive, but it's in a museum in Philadelphia now."

"Would that happen to be the Benjamin Franklin Museum?"

"You are just full of questions today!" Frankie laughed, stirring at the pan with a coy smile.

Snod felt caught, blushing as he struggled to regroup. Damn, he couldn't stop himself from treating this like an interrogation. "Sorry."

"It's all right," Frankie soothed. "Why don't you tell me about you? Hmm?"

"There isn't much to tell," Snod said, glancing down at the table. "I was born in the Order, raised by them, served them until now." He felt a wave of anguish, guilt gnawing at his stomach.

It was so easy to forget what a sinner he was when he was in Frankie's sweet embrace. He had never been so happy, but he knew this was wrong. He would certainly have to repent for all of this if he returned to the Order.

No, *when* he returned.

"Well, I can start working on your new identity today," Frankie said, plating the food and offering it to him. "You'll need some clothes, I'm sure. Toiletries of your own. Oh, we need groceries. I'm afraid I never keep very much here."

The guilt was becoming almost painful, making Snod's insides clench. "You don't have to do all of that for me. I'll find a way to manage."

"Let me help you," Frankie pushed. "When you're on your own, you can pay me back if you'd like. For now, consider it a loan if you're so put off by receiving charity."

"I suppose I can find some way to make it up to you," Snod said, lightly stirring his eggs around his plate. He tilted his head, admiring the sight of Frankie bent over the sink cleaning up the pan. "Mmm, it would probably be considered prostitution if I offered my body to you as a form of payment?"

"Definitely," Frankie snorted with a sly smile. He hesitated before adding, "Which… that's something we need to talk about."

"What?" Snod asked after a small bite of egg.

"I don't think we should have any more sex," Frankie said carefully. "It's going to be hard, especially with all the blood we've shared, but I don't feel right."

At first Snod could only stare, surprised at how much it hurt. The rejection was a knife in his gut, twisting uncomfortably as he tried to understand. "Why?"

"I'm taking advantage of you," Frankie replied. "The blood, your situation… it's not fair."

"My situation?" Snod wasn't hungry anymore, dropping his fork with a clatter.

"Yes," Frankie said with a frown. "Less than two days ago, you were a virgin. You hadn't even kissed another person before. Please understand. I don't want to hurt you, Obe."

Too late, Snod thought angrily, forgetting that the vampire could probably hear him.

"I'm sorry." Frankie moved to sit beside him at the table, gently resting his hand on Snod's arm.

Snod jerked away, glaring furiously.

"It's very easy to get your emotions mixed up, especially when sex is involved," Frankie pleaded. "The last thing I want to do is to lead you on thinking this is something that it's not."

Oh, Snod hated how much this hurt, the pain opening up a fresh well of shame. How could he have been so foolish?

"I should have known you'd throw me away the second you were done with me," he snarled, too vulnerable, too raw. He moved to stand, not sure where he was going, but desperately wanting space. "This was a fucking mistake."

Frankie flickered to appear right in front of him, firmly grabbing his arms as he said, "I am not throwing you away!

Listen to me."

Snod struggled, but he was no match for the vampire's strength.

"I know how intoxicating the blood can be," Frankie explained quickly. "When we're together, I want to make sure it's because you want to be with me. Not because I took your virginity and not because of our bond. You need to know that there are other people out there! You don't have to be with the first person that comes along."

Refusing to meet his eye, Snod stubbornly looked down at the floor.

Frankie gently touched his face, saying quietly, "My Maker didn't give me a choice. I want to make sure you have one."

There was something warm in the bond, so deep and endless that it took Snod's breath away. He looked back up at Frankie and for a split second he swore he felt his heart beating. It was pounding in time with his own, their pulses synchronized beautifully, and he was not sure how or why he was experiencing this phenomenon.

It began to fade as he leaned into Frankie's touch. "I've spent my whole life not being able to make my own choices. Let me have this. Let me… let me choose you."

Frankie shivered all over, his eyes bright as they gazed longingly into Snod's. "A month. Let the blood get out of your system. Make me believe you want me of your own free will. Then we can move forward. Together."

Snod didn't want to give this up, not while he still had time to enjoy it without consequence. One month to seduce this vampire and learn the name of his Maker?

Done.

"One month," Snod agreed, hugging Frankie close. "Kiss for luck?"

"Hmmph," Frankie snorted, placing a chaste kiss upon Snod's lips. "You're gonna need it."

"I bet you won't make it a week," Snod argued defiantly, pleased when he felt Frankie's feverish lust burning between them in the bond.

"You won't make it one day," Frankie shot back, smiling slyly.

"Mmmm, guess we'll just have to see."

"Guess so."

CHAPTER SIX

"No blood?"

"No blood."

"Totally fair."

"This is the last time, Obe."

"Absolutely."

They had made it two hours before falling back into bed together again.

It had started innocently enough, Frankie suggesting that Snod take a shower before they went out to run some errands. Snod didn't have any clean clothes to change into, leaving the bathroom in nothing but a towel to look for Frankie.

The towel was wrapped loosely around his hips, his skin still damp and glistening, and Snod was surprised by the spike of hot desire that came over him when he found Frankie.

"What's wrong?"

"Do you have any idea what you look like?" Frankie sighed, his cool hands gliding down Snod's firm body. His fingertips reached the edge of the towel as he gazed adoringly down at him. "How beautiful you are?"

Snod shuddered at his touch, stunned by how emotional

he suddenly felt. No one had ever made him feel like this, vulnerable and yet so safe, his loins beginning to stir.

Frankie bit at his lower lip, hesitation slowing his exploration. "Obe, we really shouldn't."

Snod disagreed. He dropped the towel, pulling Frankie immediately into a heated kiss.

That was how they ended up back in Frankie's bed, Snod spreading the gorgeous vampire out before him on his stomach, eager for this new position. Slick and waiting, he began to press inside, any possible patience he had lost the moment he felt that tight muscle swallowing up every inch of him.

He began pounding Frankie right down into the mattress, fucking him hard and loving every scream of pleasure. The jerking of his hips was all function, completely without grace, but it felt fantastic.

Frankie took it all, moaning as his fingers clawed at the sheets, arching his ass up for Snod to hit just the right angle that made him sing so beautifully. Snod couldn't last long at this pace, but how sweet it was chasing down his climax, driving himself into Frankie over and over again until they were both shaking in bliss.

He rolled over, grinning slyly at Frankie as he panted, "Last time?"

"Definitely the last time," Frankie mumbled through a face full of pillow. He turned his head to peek at Snod. "The bond will fade faster if we don't feed from each other. It will get easier to resist."

"Mmm." Snod pouted.

"One month," Frankie reaffirmed, rolling onto his side. "Wait one month, and then we can have all the sex you want."

"Will we always have to use these?" Snod asked, wrinkling his nose a little as he peeled off the condom.

Frankie snorted. "Not always, but I think it's best to be safe for now."

"I was a virgin, and you're a vampire," Snod drawled.

"What possible diseases could there be between us?"

"None that I know of," Frankie answered honestly, "but I do know that it's possible for diseases to be passed between humans and vampires, so I'd rather take some precautions."

"Like what? What diseases?"

"Vampirism, for one."

"But vampirism is—"

"It is a disease," Frankie gently interrupted, already knowing what Snod was going to say. "It's not an unholy curse from God. It's caused by a very unique strain of bacteria."

Snod's brows furrowed up. "How do you know that?"

"Because for the last forty years, I've been studying it," Frankie replied with a shrug. "That's why I became a hematologist. Trying to figure out a way to cure it."

"A cure? For being a vampire?" Snod never thought such a thing would be possible. "You could be human again?"

"That's the hope," Frankie said wistfully. "It's part of the work I do at the lab. I help research for cures and treatments for human diseases, and in my spare time… I try to find a cure for vampirism."

"How close are you?"

"Not very," Frankie laughed, scratching the back of his neck with a sigh. "I was only able to identify the bacteria and how it's transmitted six years ago. I have to be careful so no one figures out what I'm studying, and resources at the lab are very closely monitored. Some of those machines cost millions, and they're not just going to let me experiment with them."

"I hope you figure it out," Snod said sincerely. "I can't begin to imagine a world without vampires."

"Don't worry," Frankie snorted dryly. "I'm sure the Order would find something else to hunt down and exterminate."

"The Order only began hunting vampires to save

innocent people," Snod argued.

"I know the history," Frankie replied gently, sensing Snod's brewing anger. "The Seven Families came together because they thought vampires were corrupting the church."

"They were," Snod said stubbornly. "They tried to turn the grand bishop into a vampire and take over, but he refused the poisonous vile blood so they killed him. He died with a pure soul."

"No, he definitely drank it," Frankie countered. "He got very sick, drank the blood, and died because his well-meaning physician was a fool."

Snod narrowed his eyes, demanding, "How do you know?"

"Because it was the world's first attempted blood transfusion," Frankie replied. "I'm a freakin' hematologist who works with other hematologists. We talk about blood a lot and Grand Bishop Valiant is one of those fun little anecdotes you pass around. They didn't understand that the blood had to be pumped directly into the circulatory system, like through a vein, to work. They thought they could feed it to him, and his body would absorb it in the same way nutrients get absorbed from food. They used the blood of children, as I recall, hoping that their youth would cure his fever. It didn't work of course, and he still died. A proper blood transfusion still probably wouldn't have saved him. It wasn't the fault of vampires, only ignorant men."

"No, that's not what happened," Snod said, shaking his head in agitation and sitting up. "It was definitely vampires. They wanted the power and influence of the church, so they tried to turn His Holiness into an undead fiend that they could spread their filthy blasphemy through him. They were going to start demanding human sacrifices and blood at every service. My ancestors helped stop them, and many of them died saving all those innocent people and purifying the church."

"I'm sorry, Obe," Frankie said earnestly, his cool fingers

touching Snod's back. "I'm not trying to upset you."

"You're telling me that the lives my family lost are all now part of some joke you like to tell other doctors," Snod said bitterly. "What part of that is not upsetting?"

"If that's what you believe happened, I'm not going to argue with you," Frankie said, moving to sit beside him. "I truly didn't mean to offend you."

Snod could feel Frankie's sincerity oozing through the bond, and sighed quietly, "No one believed my family or any of the others. Everyone was worried about demons corrupting innocent people into witches. Even Grand Bishop Valiant, who had endorsed hunting witches, didn't see the real threat of vampires until it was too late.

"It was why my family was shunned, why they all decided to break away from the church. Ten of thousands of innocent people were being executed as witches while vampires stalked the earth completely unchallenged. The Order tried to intervene, but then we were labeled heretics and witch sympathizers. We had to go into hiding and hunt in secret for our own safety."

"I am very sorry that happened to your family," Frankie said honestly. "I know that vampires have not always had the best relationship with humans. Many of them, like my Maker, believe that you're nothing but sustenance. But not all vampires are like that, and the Order… while they may have good intentions…"

"Think long and hard about how you intend to finish that sentence," Snod warned.

"I admire your loyalty to them, I do, but look at what they did to you," Frankie went on, unflinching. "Look at how they raised you, the things they've forced you to do to yourself. It's not right, Obe. Even with the best of intentions, they've tortured you and turned you into a killer. As soon as you broke one of their stupid rules? They abandoned you."

Snod did not point out that he had been given a way to return to the Order, hanging his head down as his stomach began to clench. Somewhere deep inside, he knew Frankie was right. He knew that there was nothing wrong with the things they did together. And yet, the guilt of his sins still weighed down heavily upon him.

Keeping the truth from Frankie was one of those sins now, perhaps the worst of all. The vampire had been nothing but kind to him, treating him with compassion and tenderness, and allowing him in his very own bed again and again.

Snod didn't know what to say. He was in too much anguish to craft a lie or any response that would mask his deceit. It was all he could do to lean forward and kiss Frankie, a kiss he knew he didn't deserve.

Frankie let him, framing his face with his hands, kissing him sweetly in return. "It's okay, Obe," he breathed softly. "I'm not going to abandon you. I won't."

Snod's heart was crushed and resurrected all at once, his eyes damp as he deepened the kiss even more. He tried to tell himself that his deception was harmless. Frankie would be angry that he had lied to him about his intentions, but all Snod needed was a name.

A name couldn't hurt Frankie, right?

The kiss became hotter and hotter, neither able to resist the call of their bodies wishing to reunite once more. Snod poured himself over Frankie, trying to take his time now, capturing each breath with a passionate kiss as he pushed his way back inside of him.

Frankie's arms and legs curled all around him, rolling their bodies together with every deep thrust. Snod was enjoying the passionate tempo, loving how he could feel Frankie's heart starting to pound beneath him.

Snod used all of the pain tearing at his soul to fuel his hips, nearly sobbing when he finally came. He kept going until Frankie was coming with him, holding him tight as his long legs continued to tremble around him.

"Last time," Frankie said with a breathless grin.

"Last time," Snod agreed.

Frankie was right. This was dangerous. Whether the blood was to blame or not, when they were together all Snod could think about was being with him like this forever.

They got cleaned up, Snod taking a set of borrowed clothing to dress in. The pants were a little too snug, but the shirt was comfortable. Frankie admired the fit of the jeans with a hungry smile, but kept his desires to himself and the bond clear for now.

Frankie drove them to the mall to pick out a few things, but it quickly turned into purchasing an entire wardrobe. Frankie had a generous nature, and he clearly enjoyed spoiling Snod. He barely glanced at a shirt or a tie that caught his eye and Frankie was already grabbing it for him.

Snod nearly passed out at the register when it was time to check out, Frankie patting his hand and telling him that it was fine. They dragged the purchases to the food court, Frankie again letting Snod get whatever he wanted.

The Order had a few restrictions regarding diet, but Snod couldn't resist the sweet aroma of the Chinese restaurant. Frankie enjoyed watching him slurp down a literal pound of lo mein and sesame chicken, chuckling at his satisfied groan when he managed to finish it all.

Watching Frankie in public was incredibly entertaining. He had to walk at a normal human pace, and Snod could see how much he wanted to run and blink around. Having to restrain all of that power had to be exhausting, trying to appear as human as possible to blend in. Even slow, he moved with an unnatural grace that made Snod question how no one else around them seemed to notice that he was supernatural.

Plenty of people did stop to check him out, men and women alike, leaving Snod with an uncomfortably angry feeling in his stomach that he couldn't quite place. His admirers certainly saw his physical beauty, but Snod knew not a single one could really see just how special he was.

Frankie's smile was so bright, always waving and grinning at children as they walked by. And babies, oh, how he adored babies, pausing often to compliment them and their parents. It was like wading through a sea of darkness with a ray of sunshine, Frankie beaming happily wherever they went.

They headed back to Frankie's home, the vampire making quick work of washing all the new laundry and putting away the clothes. He showed Snod a grocery catalogue for a company that would deliver food right to their front door. He let Snod place a generous order and even helped him put all the food up when it arrived.

Exhausted by the day's errands and humbled by how much money Frankie had spent on him, Snod collapsed on the sofa.

Frankie brought him a glass of soda and Snod cringed when he took a sip. He narrowed his eyes, accusing, "There's alcohol in this."

"Just a little," Frankie teased, sitting down beside him. "You need to relax. You're tense."

"You did too much today," Snod said, taking a big swallow and making a face. "I don't think I could ever repay you in this lifetime."

"It really wasn't that much," Frankie insisted. "Besides, I do very well for myself, thank you. You don't need to worry about what I decide to spend on you. It was just some clothing and some food, vital necessities."

"Just," Snod echoed.

"It makes me feel good," Frankie said with a shrug. "I like to help people." He picked up a remote from the coffee table and turned on the small television, flipping through a selection of cartoon films.

"Thank you," Snod said sincerely. "Your generosity is admirable."

Frankie shrugged again, smiling bashfully as he replied, "It's nothing, really." He kept scrolling through the television menu, asking brightly, "So! Favorite Disney movie?"

"Favorite what?"

"Disney?" Frankie stared at him. "Walt Disney? Come on. Please tell me you've seen at least one Disney movie."

"They're forbidden," Snod replied awkwardly, taking another big sip of his drink. "Walt Disney promotes homosexuality and paganism."

"You're serious."

"Yes," Snod said flatly.

"Well, even if they did, which they don't, you're no longer in the damn Order, and you're going to watch *Beauty and the Beast* with me," Frankie said defiantly. "In fact, I'm going to make sure we watch every single Disney animated classic there is!"

Snod felt his face heat up immediately from the scandalous notion. "I'm going to need more to drink."

The bottle of vodka magically appeared on the coffee table, Frankie winking slyly as he teased, "You just sit right there, and enjoy Walt Disney's thirtieth animated feature film."

Snod grumbled lightly as he nursed his glass, not sure how to prepare himself. Even if it did have vile subliminal content, it was a cartoon for children. He wasn't expecting much.

Before he knew it, he was completely enthralled. He was yelling at Gaston and cheering for the Beast, nearly in tears at the end when he was restored to human form and lived happily ever after with Belle.

"What'd ya think?" Frankie asked as the credits began to roll, smiling happily at Snod.

"It… it was beautiful," Snod replied, wishing he was better with words to describe everything the movie had made him feel.

"Ready for another one?" Frankie asked eagerly, already flipping back to the menu to access a new title.

"Please," Snod replied, making a fresh drink and sitting back, preparing himself for another adventure.

"This one is called *Aladdin*," Frankie said as he pressed play, snuggling up to Snod's side.

Snod was surprised, but the affection was more than welcome. Frankie had been keeping his distance since this morning, and it felt good to be close to him again. He slowly wound his arm around his shoulders, his eyes excitedly fixed on the television screen.

'A Whole New World' was in its final swing when there was a desperate knock at the door.

The sound snapped Snod out of his happy daze and into action, up on his feet and ready to strike.

"Down, boy," Frankie soothed, patting Snod's hip as he blinked by him to the door to see who it was. He glanced over his shoulder back at Snod, saying, "It's Lorenzo."

Snod made a face, plopping back down on the couch and his eyes returning to the movie. He was grumpy at the interruption, crossing his arms firmly over his chest.

"Hey, Lorenzo!" Frankie greeted amicably as he opened the door, watching his friend stalk straight into the kitchen with two big bags under his arms.

"We are getting wasted," Lorenzo said, obviously upset about something. "Well, I'm going to get wasted, and you're going to watch."

"What's wrong?" Frankie asked, his brows arching up in concern.

"Leslie," Lorenzo moaned in anguish. "He said that I'm not mature enough for him, that he needs someone like Maxwell over in diagnostics that has big plans for his life, and…" He trailed off, finally noticing Snod. "You're still here."

Snod said nothing, leaning forward to sip his drink noisily. He was buzzed enough to be pliant, staying seated when Frankie gave him a sweet smile.

"Yes, Obe is gonna be staying with me for a little longer," Frankie explained quickly.

Lorenzo forgot about his own troubles for a moment, grinning playfully as he teased, "Thought ya said it was only a one-time thing?"

"It's getting a little complicated—"

"Thought ya said you weren't gonna let things get complicated?" Lorenzo was clearly enjoying this now, pulling several bottles of alcohol out of the bags he'd brought, smirking contently.

Frankie groaned, scrubbing his hands over his face. He took off his glasses as he sighed, "I know what I said!"

"So, Obadiah, being Frankie's best friend in the whole wide world," Lorenzo announced cheerfully, "I am required to inform you that should you hurt him, I will make you disappear. I might even be able to build a robot to do it for me."

Snod scowled at the threat, standing up slowly. Frankie probably wouldn't like if he hurt his friend, but maybe just one little punch…

"But for right now, let's be cool!" Lorenzo added quickly, grinning sheepishly and mixing up something bright and colorful in a pitcher. "Tell me all about Obadiah. I'd love to know how you guys met."

"No," Snod replied shortly.

"Wow. Isn't he just a charmer," Lorenzo said dryly, pouring a glass of the colorful concoction and gulping it back. "I can really see how he just swept you right off your feet, Frankie."

"Are you staying long?" Snod demanded. "I'd like to finish the movie Frankie and I were watching."

Frankie narrowed his eyes, soothing, "Lorenzo is having some personal troubles, and he's more than welcome to stay."

Lorenzo was positively smug.

Snod glared, retreating back to the sofa to watch the movie by himself. He grabbed the remote, stubbornly rewinding the film back to the genie's first song. He liked that one.

It would be nice to have a genie, he decided. He'd use all three wishes to make Lorenzo go away.

"So!" Frankie smiled gently, looking back at his friend as he urged, "Tell me about what happened with Leslie."

As Lorenzo launched into his sorrowful narrative about his heart being cruelly smashed, Snod did his best to ignore him. He didn't trust people easily, and even though Frankie had previously vouched for this young man, Snod didn't like him.

Lorenzo was too eager, too obnoxious, too loud.

Snod turned the television up a little more, making himself another drink. A strong one.

"Well, Leslie doesn't know what he's missing," Frankie was reassuring his friend, blinking over to turn the television back down to a reasonable volume before returning to the kitchen.

Snod scowled when he saw Frankie had taken the remote with him.

"I know it's hard, but you need to find someone who likes you just the way you are, immature and all," Frankie went on without missing a beat. "Find someone with similar interests instead of just a pretty face to pine after."

"Easier said than done," Lorenzo sighed sadly. "I need a man who is seriously like, mentally, a twelve-year-old kid. That I could relate to! Because I'm mentally a twelve-year-old! I mean, it sounds screwed up when I say it like that, but someone like me who's pretty."

"Got it." Frankie nodded. "I will keep my eye out for a pretty version of Lorenzo."

"Let's go out," Lorenzo said suddenly, slamming his glass down on the counter. "Come on. Pretty please? Let's go shake our booties somewhere with other booties."

"I don't think I should leave Obe," Frankie said hesitantly, glancing over at Snod on the couch. "He's sort of in a bad place right now, and I'm supposed to be helping him."

"We both know by 'help' that you actually mean 'bang,' and you can totally bring him," Lorenzo pouted, slapping his hand down on the counter as if he was sliding something over to Frankie. "This is me, playing the best friend card."

Snod frowned, not liking where this was going at all. He

wanted a quiet evening with Frankie all to himself, not gallivanting about with the ever increasingly annoying Lorenzo. He'd been to clubs before on hunts, and he wasn't a very big fan.

Frankie groaned in frustration, looking back at Snod and giving him a pleading smile.

Please…

Snod shook his head defiantly, kicking his feet up on the coffee table and getting comfortable, making it clear he had no intentions of leaving. He lifted up his chin, thinking back as hard as he could.

There is nothing you can say or do that will move me from this couch.

Frankie smirked, quirking a sly brow.

If you come with us, I'll blow you.

"How soon do we go?" Snod asked, hopping up to his feet.

"Soon as we finish these motherfuckin' shots!" Lorenzo cheered, swigging back his drink and grabbing another glass to pour another round for them both.

Snod grimaced, but approached the counter to take the glass, knocking it back and expecting the worst. He was surprised to find it was very sweet and actually quite tasty. "Let's do some more of those."

Lorenzo cackled, eagerly pouring again while Frankie beamed sweetly at Snod. Frankie leaned close, pressing a soft kiss to his cheek that made him blush.

Snod lost track of the shots after that, and Frankie helped him quickly get changed into some of his new clothes for the evening. Lorenzo claimed the only cure for his broken heart was alcohol and dancing, eagerly diving into the crowded dance floor as soon as they arrived at the club.

Frankie left Snod at the bar with a promise to return soon, joining his friend. Snod was pleasantly drunk, glad he had eaten earlier today as he did not want a repeat of his last adventure with alcohol. He watched Lorenzo and Frankie dancing, smiling to himself.

Frankie was such an amazing dancer, and his promise of future fellatio already had Snod half hard in his jeans. He couldn't help but notice someone else was admiring Frankie, a blond man with a strong jaw and a pretty face.

Oh, he didn't like that one bit.

After a few songs, Frankie and Lorenzo came back to the bar, laughing and chatting excitedly. Lorenzo seemed like he was in a much better mood, even buying Snod a drink for coming out with them.

All the while, the blond was still watching Frankie, and Snod was starting to get angry. He didn't like how he was looking at Frankie at all, but he wasn't sure why he was so irritated.

Frankie must have sensed it, asking quietly, "What's wrong?"

Snod nodded at the man, growling, "Him."

Frankie followed his eye, squeaking and quickly turning around, his expression mortified. "Oh, no."

"Who is that?" Snod demanded.

Lorenzo looked over to see who they were talking about, laughing, "Oh, that's Mark!"

"Who the fuck is Mark?"

"Remember when we met?" Frankie asked slowly. "I had a date that I thought was going to go really well? The date was with Mark. He thinks I stood him up. He gave me another chance, and I stood him up again when you had your car trouble… look, we had gone out a few times, I really liked him, but it didn't end very well, okay?"

Snod snorted, Mark now looking his way with a sour face. Snod smiled, big and bright, very purposely winding his arm around Frankie's waist. He didn't know what was making him feel so possessive, but he wanted to make it clear that Frankie was his.

But wait, he wasn't… was he? They weren't courting. Snod actually didn't know how to define what they were to each other except he had no intentions of sharing Frankie, no matter how temporary this was.

"I should at least go say hello," Frankie said, gently pulling himself away from Snod.

Snod gritted his teeth together, watching Frankie approach Mark and awkwardly exchange a hug. He wished he could hear what they were saying, chugging back his drink with a scowl.

"Frankie had such a crush on him," Lorenzo said unhelpfully. "It really broke his heart when Mark dumped him because of your, ahem, 'car trouble.'"

"Car trouble," Snod echoed. He cut his eyes at Lorenzo as he demanded, "How much do you know?"

"Frankie likes his secrets," Lorenzo replied, "but I'm not stupid. I know something really bad happened, and he helped you out. That's what Frankie does. He always helps other people first, no matter what it costs him."

Snod scoffed disgustedly. "Was Mark really that much of a loss?"

"Frankie was like freakin' in love with him until you came along," Lorenzo said, ordering them another round. "He's a super great guy. Good job, nice car, and fuck, look at that mug. Sorry, bro, but you still might have some competition."

"Does he know? What Frankie is?"

"No," Lorenzo replied, "and I'm still waiting to hear the full story of how the fuck you do."

Watching Mark paw at Frankie's arm and leaning close to whisper in his ear, Snod could finally identify that nasty, angry feeling burning down inside of him. It was a sin he had always managed to avoid before, but now it was threatening to scorch the very lining of his stomach.

Envy.

CHAPTER SEVEN

Snod had been the victim of many sins throughout his life. He had succumbed to wrath more times than he could count, and he was getting quite familiar with lust. Pride was one he had dabbled in, having taken much pride as a victorious hunter time and time again.

But envy…

This was the first time he had felt the wicked prick of envy.

He hated how easily Mark interacted with Frankie, and he despised his confidence in how he touched him and smiled at him. He hated even more how Frankie responded, grinning brightly and resting his hand on Mark's shoulder.

Snod could feel ripples of happiness and longing in their bond, and he knew these were Frankie's feelings for Mark. They weren't as strong as the lusty desire that he knew Frankie felt for him, but that brought him no comfort. This was worse because these emotions seemed so much more genuine.

Frankie truly did care for Mark, very deeply.

Snod knew he had no right to be jealous. He had no claim on Frankie, and they hadn't agreed to any sort of exclusive relationship. Their intense sex life was the result of their blood bond, and it was simply that: sex.

Frankie's promise to explore something more once the effects of the blood had worn off held little promise when he was looking at Mark the way he was now.

Furthermore, Snod knew in one month's time he planned to return to the Order and devote himself to his old life. There was no reason to be envious because he wasn't planning on keeping Frankie. This life was not meant to be.

Even so, he found himself gritting his teeth and imagining breaking each one of Mark's fingers every time he touched Frankie.

"Calm down," Lorenzo soothed, breaking into his angry thoughts. "I can hear your damn ears steaming from here."

"He has no right," Snod huffed, downing his drink in one giant gulp.

"Are you and Frankie, uh, dating?" Lorenzo asked, smiling shyly.

"No," Snod replied flatly.

"Okay. Right. But you two are sleeping together?" Lorenzo clarified.

"Yes, I have carnal knowledge of his body."

"Got it," Lorenzo said with a few slow blinks. "Okay, so, Obe, let me ask you… Is it okay if I call you 'Obe'?"

"No," Snod growled.

"Fine!" Lorenzo groaned exasperatedly. "What do I call you?"

"My name is Obadiah Penuel Snod."

"The fuck kind of name is that," Lorenzo wondered out loud.

"It's my name!" Snod growled.

"Did your parents hate you?"

"Call me Snod and don't you dare speak ill of my parents—"

"Fine! Okay! Chill out, Sally Psycho!" Lorenzo waved his hands in surrender. "Listen, *Snod*. What do you want from Frankie?"

"What do you mean?" Snod demanded, instantly

suspicious.

Lorenzo presented Snod with a fresh drink, something fruity and tart, explaining, "I don't know what's really going on with you guys, but here's the deal. If you wanna be with Frankie, then fucking be with him. If you're just screwing him because you're some kind of hot for coffins vampire groupie, then you need to back off because Frankie deserves to be happy. He deserves something real, you feel me?"

Snod slowly gulped down his drink, but said nothing. His thoughts were swimming anxiously, teetering between considering his own happiness and the certain damnation that came with it. A life with Frankie, something real, was not possible.

"He could have had that with Mark!" Lorenzo ranted on. "And even though you're kind of scary, and I'm very sure you could probably kick my ass, I swear I will find a way to fuck you up if you break his heart. Frankie kind of gave me the impression that you weren't gonna be sticking around long… So, if you're just passing through, you need to fucking chill with all of this über jelly grouchy bullshit because it's not fair to Frankie to act like you give a flying bucket of crap."

"What?" Snod stared, the slang zooming right over his head.

Lorenzo groaned again, trying simply, "If you're not going to be Frankie's boyfriend, then don't act like a jealous boyfriend."

When Mark's hand reached up to touch Frankie's face and playfully adjust his glasses, Snod couldn't stand it any longer. Boyfriend or not, the rage he felt boiling up inside of him was too much.

Snod began stalking toward them despite Lorenzo yelling after him, "Oh, don't do it, bitch!"

He whirled around to glare at Lorenzo, snarling at the challenge. He stood up to his full height, biting back, "Or what?"

Lorenzo was clearly shaken, but still stubbornly replied,

"Death by robot in your future, dude. Death by fuckin' robot!"

Snod ignored him, getting back on target and moving quickly toward Mark and Frankie. He was stumbling a little bit, and he had no idea what he was going to do. He did not possess a wide array of social skills and any tact he may have had was lost from all the alcohol he'd been guzzling down.

He boldly approached them without any care about interrupting their conversation. He showed his teeth in what could have passed for a smile and said loudly, "Hi."

Mark did not look pleased with the sudden intrusion. He scoffed, scanning over Snod with a very forced smile. He wrinkled his nose as if he smelled something unpleasant, asking politely, "So, Frankie. Who's your… friend?"

"This is Obadiah," Frankie said, gently placing a comforting hand on Snod's arm. "He's new in town, and he's staying with me for a little while."

"Staying with you?" Mark scowled, his eyes wandering back to Snod with a new and intense scrutiny as if he had missed something important. The forced smile returned, and he asked stiffly, "Where are you from, Obadiah?"

"Around," Snod replied shortly.

"He's from the Lancaster area in Pennsylvania," Frankie explained quickly. "He was part of the Amish community there, out on Rumspringa. He's not planning to go back, so I'm helping him get a fresh start."

Snod made a face at the lie, though Frankie told it well.

"Little old for that, aren't you?" Mark asked Snod with a faint smirk. "Thought the Amish did that when they were teenagers."

"Late bloomer," Snod replied with a venomous sneer.

"Well, isn't that sweet," Mark oozed. "You know, that's one of the things I love about you, Frankie. You have such a kind heart. You're always taking pity on the less fortunate."

Snod knew it was meant to be an insult, but he grinned anyway, boldly sliding his arm around Frankie's waist as replied, "Oh, but I've been very fortunate. He's been showing me a whole new world, and it's been… intense."

Frankie laughed weakly, and his thoughts were volatile.

I'm going to kill you.

Snod only smiled more brightly, very pleased with himself when he saw how Mark was beginning to put the pieces together.

"He just means that I've been helping him adjust to life outside of the Amish community," Frankie interjected quickly. "Watching movies, shopping…"

"Sex," Snod proudly added. He clicked his tongue, whispering loudly, "Lots of it."

Mark looked furious, and Snod couldn't have been any happier until he saw Frankie's enraged snarl. Maybe this wasn't such a good idea.

Frankie turned to Mark quickly, meeting his eye and staring at him intently, his voice echoing softly as he commanded, "Forget what Snod just said to you." He snapped his gaze to Snod, growling in that same peculiar tone, "And you! Not another word until I tell you that you can speak!"

Snod felt dizzy, and he tried to bark back, but he found he couldn't get his vocal cords to cooperate. No matter how hard he tried, he couldn't say a damn thing. He grabbed at his neck, cursing that his scapular was back in his pants pocket at Frankie's home.

"It's been really good seeing you, Mark," Frankie said hastily, giving him a quick hug. "We've gotta run, please take care of yourself."

Mark let the embrace linger and rubbed the small of Frankie's back. "Good to see you, too. Whenever you're done doing whatever this is that you're doing? Charity work? Yeah, maybe give me a call?"

Frankie looked surprised, pushing him away with a blink. "Wow!" he exclaimed with a bitter laugh. "It's funny. You told me I was wasting your time because I missed a few of our dates and didn't want to go out anymore. But now that you see me with someone else, you're suddenly interested again?"

"Forgive me," Mark sighed, trying to pull Frankie back into his arms. "I didn't think—"

"No, you didn't think at all, did you?" Frankie's aching heart was very palpable through the bond, and he shook his head as he said, "Goodnight, Mark."

Snod couldn't speak, but he gave Mark the biggest smile he could and wiggled his fingers into a little farewell wave.

"And you!" Frankie snapped, grabbing Snod's wrist. "Outside! Now!"

Snod stumbled along as Frankie dragged him outside the club. The moment they were out of sight from any onlookers, Frankie held him close and blinked them into a secluded alley. For a dumb moment, Snod was hopeful that Frankie wanted privacy to give him that blowjob he had promised him.

But when he saw Frankie's hands planted firmly on his hips and his beautiful face set in a furious scowl, he figured now would not be a good time to bring it up.

"On your fuckin' knees," Frankie snarled, pointing a long finger in Snod's face.

Snod dropped immediately, unsure if his immediate compliance was voluntary or a result of Frankie's power. Regardless, the fire he saw in Frankie's eyes instantly transported him back to that first morning when Frankie had pinned him so aggressively on the sofa.

"You are such an immature, selfish, insecure fucking brat!" Frankie seethed, his fangs fully bared and hissing savagely. "I step away for a few precious moments, a few fucking seconds, and you just had to come barging over like a total jackass!"

Snod still hadn't been given permission to speak, so he had no choice but to listen to Frankie's rage. There was something strangely enticing about seeing him so angry and while Snod couldn't explain it, he could feel himself getting undeniably hard.

"You had no right to say that to Mark!" Frankie continued to shout. "For fuck's sake! We're not together, Obe! I am not yours! I care about you, I do. I am willing to give you a chance when the blood wears off if you really want to be with me. But who's to say you're not just gonna wake up one morning and suddenly decide you don't wanna date an unholy creature, huh? And then what?"

Snod frowned, his cock continuing to stiffen uncomfortably in his pants.

"You're such an asshole, and you know what, so is Mark. You're both fucking assholes!" Frankie raked his hands through his hair, groaning loudly. "God, what is wrong with me, am I just attracted to fucking jerks? God, ugh!"

Snod thought Frankie's lips looked particularly pretty as he panted and huffed, even more turned on as he watched him get more and more worked up. Frankie was unfairly sexy when he was angry, and Snod was doing his best to listen, but it was getting difficult to focus.

"If we're not gonna work out, I don't need you burning my bridges over some petty, bullshit jealousy," Frankie went on. "I'm crazy about Mark, but you… I could be crazy about you, too. But I have to know that you really want this. That you want me."

Snod wished he could speak, although it was probably better that he didn't. All he could think was that he did want Frankie. He wanted him far too much. He reached out for him, gently resting his hands on his thighs and smothering his cheek against his hip.

Frankie gasped softly, his hands moving over Snod's neck, his nails digging in hard. The moment they touched, the desire between them became inescapable. Frankie was pressing closer, growling softly when Snod slid a hand back over his ass. "Stand up," he ordered sharply. "Right now."

Snod was up on his feet and wrapping himself around Frankie in a second. He mouthed along his throat, backing Frankie up against the brick. He would fuck him right here if he could. All he could think about was coming, grinding their hips together as he sought out friction.

"No," Frankie snarled suddenly, grabbing Snod by his neck and switching their positions. He pressed him face first against the wall, hissing angrily in his ear, "Tell me truthfully; do you think you deserve pleasure after the way you've behaved?"

Snod groaned, grateful that he could speak again as he croaked softly, "No… no, I don't. I want you… I want you to punish me. I've crossed you and I need to be punished." He closed his eyes, vividly recalling the way Frankie had spanked him before. He burned deep inside to feel that again, pleading, "Please."

Frankie made a soft sound, something strangled and urgent, his free hand sliding down to cup Snod's ass through his pants. "Do you want me to spank you, Obe?"

"Yes," Snod whined, shamelessly arching into Frankie's touch.

"Fuck," Frankie hissed, squeezing Snod's ass greedily. "Drop your pants. Right fucking now."

Snod wouldn't have needed to be under Frankie's spell to obey. He was so desperate, jerking his pants and underwear down around his knees without any thought to who might be able to see them. He plastered himself across the wall, groaning as his cock rubbed against the cool and rough brick. "Fuck…"

"You embarrassed me!" Frankie growled, barely giving Snod any time to brace himself before his hand came down on his ass with a violent smack. "You made a total fool out of me in front of Mark!" Another slap. "You were beyond disrespectful!"

"Yes," Snod gasped, each brutal spanking rocking his hips against the wall. The burn was making his dick ache, grinding against the brick even though it hurt. He felt so very small with Frankie crowded behind him, holding him so firmly in place as the burn in his cheeks made his eyes water. "I was bad… I'm sorry… I'm so fucking sorry…"

Frankie was relentless, purring in Snod's ear, "I know

you are, Obe. That's okay. I'm going to help you learn. I'm going to teach you how to be good for me…" He spanked Snod's ass again, hard enough to make him cry out. "There, my good boy. You're taking it so well…"

"Fuck, Frankie!" Snod whimpered, clawing at the wall and humping the brick as he sought out friction. The pain was making every other part of his body especially sensitive and he knew he was going to come soon, just from the smack of Frankie's hand and grinding against the wall like a dog. He whined anxiously, his face flushing with shame as he cried, "I'm gonna come… I'm—"

"No," Frankie said, his cool fingers sliding around to cruelly squeeze Snod's cock.

"Urghh!" Snod grunted, the wave of pleasure that was about to wash over him knocked back into a frustrated puddle. He was sweating and on edge, trying to thrust into Frankie's hand. "Please…?"

"This is a punishment, remember?" Frankie gave Snod's cock another firm squeeze before letting go. He nipped at his shoulder, pressing his own hard cock into Snod's hip as he scoffed, "You don't deserve to come, Obe. Not until I'm sure you've learned your lesson, not until I'm satisfied…"

"Then let me satisfy you," Snod pleaded, reaching back to grab Frankie's side to keep him close. "Allow me to earn your forgiveness, Frankie. I can take you right here, right now, however you want me. I'll do whatever you ask of me."

"Mmm, Obe…" Frankie's fangs grazed over Snod's throat as he considered the juicy offer before pulling away suddenly. "No. This is a problem. We can't just fuck the problem away. Especially when the fucking is part of the damn problem!"

"But I want you!" Snod groaned impatiently, pounding his fist into the brick. "I want you more than anything."

"You want to have sex with me," Frankie steadily corrected him, pulling his pants back up with a long sigh and affectionately patting his shoulder.

"Yes, but I want more. I want to watch Disney movies

with you," Snod tried, earnest and vulnerable. The alcohol was an extremely liberating potion, and soon he couldn't believe the things he was saying. "I want to fall asleep next to you, and wake up with you. I want to cook for you, even though you can't eat it. Oh, but you could still watch me. I want to drink more with you. Shirts. I want to fold shirts. Match socks. Dance."

Frankie was honestly touched, warmth flowing over the bond and seeping right into Snod's chest. He cradled his face lovingly, allowing him to draw back in for a tender embrace. His eyes were bright, gazing warmly at Snod as he said, "One month… if you still want that in one month, then yes. You can have it all."

Snod had to kiss him, their mouths passionately crashing against one another's. He didn't care about learning that stupid name or returning to the Order in that moment. His heart was pushing him right into this beautiful vampire's arms, and he never wanted to leave.

The temperature of their kiss turned to boiling within moments, Frankie again being the one with some semblance of willpower and pulling away before things went too far.

"We need to get back and check on Lorenzo," Frankie said, adjusting his glasses that had been knocked askew during their heated make-out. "No telling what kind of trouble he's gotten into."

Reaching down to shift his uncomfortably erect cock, Snod scowled but nodded obediently. His cheeks were still blazing hot from Frankie's strong hand and he was eager for release. He glanced at Frankie, grinning shyly. He didn't have the heart to ask out loud, but he could definitely think it.

Blowjob…?

"You lost all your blowjob privileges when you decided to tell Mark about all the sex we're no longer having!" Frankie huffed, aiming for angry but he was smiling wide. "Come on!"

Frankie brought Snod back to the club to check on his

friend, walking with him arm in arm as they approached the dance floor. At first, Snod thought Lorenzo was having some kind of seizure. His long braids were whipping about violently and his body was shaking as his arms flailed around him.

Most of the other patrons had given him plenty of space, letting him convulse at a safe distance.

"Yup, it's time to go," Frankie sighed, weaving out onto the dance floor to retrieve him.

"Wait," Snod said, gently reaching for Frankie's hand. "I meant it, about… the dancing."

"Huh?" Frankie laughed in surprise. "You mean… you want to right now?"

"Yes," Snod said eagerly, desperately wanting to be close to Frankie again.

"One song," Frankie said, holding up his index finger to emphasize his determination. "Just one, and then we have to get Lorenzo and go home."

Snod grinned victoriously, eagerly wrapping his arms around Frankie. He stayed close, struggling to keep on rhythm. He wasn't very good, but dancing gave him the chance to touch Frankie all over and he loved it. He blushed when Frankie's hands grabbed his hips, helping him find the beat.

Dancing was a lot like sex, Snod began to learn. He wanted to thrust and slam, but Frankie was showing him how to roll his hips against his, seductively moving with the music. It was getting easier, and he smiled brightly when Frankie's arms curled up around his neck.

The tempo of the music had dropped down, now a slow and throaty bass line that begged their bodies to grind together. Snod held Frankie's hips, their foreheads pressed together as they danced, unable to tear himself away from those beautiful eyes for a second.

He knew Frankie wasn't his boyfriend, but what if he could be? What if he forgot all about the Order, what if they could have a life together? With all the alcohol diluting his guilt, such a dream felt within reach.

His head was swimming beautifully. He could feel the bass reverberating in his bones, and the only sensation he could detect through the bond was pure joy. It was Frankie's mixing in with his own, and Snod had never been so happy.

He wished the song could last forever, but the beat changed all too soon and Frankie was untangling their bodies.

"Let's go," Frankie said, taking Snod's hand and leading him over to get a hold of Lorenzo.

Lorenzo's erratic dancing had lost much of its momentum, and he positively melted against Snod and Frankie as they threw their arms around him. "Hey! You guys!" he exclaimed drunkenly. "Where have you been?"

"Sorry, Lorenzo," Frankie said, guiding him out toward the front of the club. "Had to have a little chat with Obe! How are you feeling, buddy?"

"I'm fine," Lorenzo replied in a very slurred voice that indicated he was anything but. He glared, squinting one eye to focus on Snod as he demanded, "What did you do? I swear, robots!"

"I didn't do anything!" Snod growled, nearly dropping Lorenzo on the sidewalk out of spite. It wouldn't have mattered if he had since Frankie could have easily held his friend's weight by himself, but Snod still considered it all the same.

"Robots!" Lorenzo snarled. "Little tiny nano bots that will crawl in through your nose and eat… wait! Wait! Frankie!" He was suddenly excited, almost screaming, "I know how to cure you! I know how to make you not a vampire!"

"Lorenzo!" Frankie hissed, shaking his friend. "Shhhh!"

"Okay! I'm sorry! I'm drunk, but I'm a drunk genius!" Lorenzo cackled. "The special secret thing we can't talk about because it's a secret? It's an endospore, and you can't get through the walls. But we don't have to get through. We can Trojan horse that shit! With robots!"

Frankie stared in bewilderment at his intoxicated friend. "What do you mean? How?"

"The phagocytosis! We couldn't figure out how to penetrate the cell wall, but it weakens when it's nom nom time!" Lorenzo went on excitedly. "I can make a tiny robot, a tiny cargo van robot, to deliver a load into the bacterial cell and boom! Okay. Not literally boom, because that would be bad, but it might work!"

Snod didn't understand a word.

"Mother of God," Frankie murmured, his eyes wide in amazement. "Lorenzo… you really are a genius."

"I know," Lorenzo said, holding his head proudly. He made a sour face suddenly, visibly shuddering as he mumbled, "Aaaand I'm gonna puke."

"I'll hold your hair." Frankie smiled affectionately, guiding Lorenzo around the side of the club to revisit the colorful collection of drinks he had been chugging down all night.

Snod followed at a respectable distance, cringing in sympathy. He could relate.

When Lorenzo had finally finished, Frankie carried him back out to the street to find the car. The whole ride home, Lorenzo was rolling around the backseat and babbling about iron and hemoglobin capsules. Snod thought it sounded like total nonsense.

Frankie seemed to understand most of it, and Snod began to tune them both out. He was still pretty tipsy, but definitely not as bad off as Lorenzo was. He was proud that his second night of drinking had ended with much less disastrous results than his first. He enjoyed the cool feeling of Frankie's skin, smiling when he felt their hands intertwine.

Back at the apartment, Frankie tried to steer Lorenzo toward the couch to crash. Guided by some Pavlovian response, he resisted and stumbled into the guest room where Snod was supposed to be staying.

"I can totally carry him and put him out on the couch,"

Frankie said apologetically, Lorenzo's loud snoring already audible through the door.

"It's okay," Snod said, shaking his head. The apartment was spinning a little, and he desperately wanted to lie down. He stumbled toward the couch, kicking off his shoes as he went, saying, "I'm gonna watch *Aladdin* again."

Frankie seemed surprised, but smiled as he said, "All right."

Snod stretched out, glancing up when Frankie had blinked beside him to offer him a blanket and a pillow. He reached for Frankie's wrist, tugging him down to steal a kiss. The thrill of his theft was lost knowing Frankie could have easily stopped him, but it was sweet all the same.

Frankie petted Snod's cheek, saying, "If you need anything, my door is open."

"And the chances…?"

"Of us having sex are absolutely zero," Frankie cooed, patting the top of Snod's head like a puppy. "Goodnight, Obe."

"Goodnight, Frankie," Snod replied with a sleepy pout. He beamed when Frankie kissed his forehead and put the movie on for him in a flash.

He was asleep before 'Arabian Nights' had even finished, jolting awake at four o'clock in the morning right on the dot. It felt like there was fire in his throat, he couldn't breathe, and his heart was punching violently against his ribs. He didn't know what he had been dreaming about at first, but it hadn't been good.

He could still see bits and pieces, fading images of pain and blood, staring up at the wizened face of Sanguis, and he remembered intense fear.

Screaming.

More pain.

He knew what it was now, sober and gasping for breath as the memory washed back over him like a splash of icy water.

His first lesson.

"Obe?" Frankie's voice was in his ear, his cold arms around him, asking worriedly, "Are you okay? What's wrong?"

"Frankie?" Snod clung to him, trying to shove the memories back down. "It was nothing. It was just a dream." He stared at Frankie's face, hauntingly lit by the light of the flickering DVD menu.

"Obe," Frankie pressed, "I could feel you. You were terrified. I saw something, a little boy and an old man. The old man—"

"You saw my dream?"

"It's possible to share images in the bond, yes. But the old man, he was beating the little boy… was that you?"

"Yes," Snod replied quietly, looking down at the floor. His eyes felt hot, the last few stings of the dream pricking deeply. It was part of the Order's ways. There were many lessons to learn.

The first he had learned when he was seven.

Frankie frowned softly, sliding his arms under Snod and picking him right off the couch. "Come on," he sighed. "Let's go to bed."

"Are you sure?" Snod blinked back his tears, distracted by the obvious temptation. "But you said no sex."

"We can sleep together and not have sex," Frankie assured him with a short laugh. "I don't feel right leaving you out there when you're upset."

"I'm not upset," Snod pouted, flopping into Frankie's bed.

"Uh huh," Frankie said, letting his obvious lie go unchecked. He stretched out beside him under the blankets, pulling him close.

Snod didn't think he'd be able to fall asleep again, but Frankie was holding him so tenderly, his cool hands stroking over his back. They didn't say anything else, only held each other, and Snod couldn't escape the warmth filling him up.

He had never known such happiness, and the Order

wasn't here to take it away. He wanted this dream to be real, a desperate voice deep inside of him telling him that he could have this. He could keep it, he could keep Frankie, and there was nothing wrong with wanting it.

A life together, to actually be his boyfriend, to fall in love, to have something real.

Snod pressed his head against Frankie's chest, and for a precious few moments he thought he could hear the soft thumping of a heartbeat as he dozed off.

CHAPTER EIGHT

Snod woke up snuggled against Frankie's side, his head a little foggy and his mouth dry. He didn't feel too spectacular, but he hadn't had any more bad dreams at least. He grumbled lightly as he peered over to see Frankie smiling at him. He put his head back down, sighing, "Don't you ever sleep?"

"Good morning! I do sleep sometimes," Frankie replied, horribly cheerful and disgustingly wide awake. "I need very little now. Same with blood. I only need to feed once a week. Might be able to even make it a month before I started getting really hungry."

Snod grumbled again and considered going back to sleep, but his curiosity wouldn't allow it. He lifted up his head, asking, "Really? I thought that you had to feed constantly?"

"Young vampires do," Frankie said, propping himself up on his elbow. "Old ones? They can go decades without feeding. Maybe even centuries."

Snod was surprised once again by how little the Order understood what they had sworn to hunt. He was tempted to ask about Frankie's Maker, the mission he'd been given from Sanguis floating there in the back of his mind.

But then he remembered Frankie dancing in his arms last night and he willfully ignored it, asking instead, "Where do you get the blood from?"

"Butcher down the block," Frankie replied. "Pig or cow. He saves it for me; I filter it here, and drink when I need to. You're actually the first human I've fed from in a very long time."

Snod felt his heart flutter at that, smirking. "Mmm, so, you don't get mad cravings for blood and want to attack innocent people?"

"No," Frankie snorted. "I do crave it, but it's not this insane bloodlust. It's no different than wanting chocolate when you're on a diet."

"Isn't that interesting," Snod chuckled, stretching out his arms and grunting as his shoulders popped. "So, I'm… a tasty temptation?"

Frankie's eyes flickered over Snod's body, replying longingly, "In many ways."

"I know all about temptation," Snod chuckled with a smirk, sighing. "I was taught how to meditate, pray, fast. A dozen different ways to resist it to stay pure."

"Does it help?"

"Not when I look at you," Snod replied honestly.

Frankie smiled again, pressing a kiss to Snod's forehead. His gorgeous face twisted up in regret, saying, "I'm sorry about last night. I shouldn't have whammied you, and I know I was… I was upset with you, and I said a lot of not nice things."

"…Whammied?"

"Used my powers on you."

"Ah. I was weak, and I succumbed to my envy," Snod said with a quick nod. "It was overwhelming. I also said some things that weren't 'nice.'"

"It's not your fault. If it's anyone's, it's mine. I wasn't expecting to see Mark there," Frankie said with a frown. "I should have reacted better. You're not weak… you're just, well…"

"What?"

"Sheltered?" Frankie tried. "Maybe that's not quite the right word, but all of this?" He gestured between them. "It's so very new to you. Being intimate with someone is already intense, especially your first, and I know the blood magnifies that times a hundred. I know it does."

Snod felt a ripple of something; pain, regret.

"I'm also afraid that I'm being too rough with you," Frankie went on. "The spankings, telling you what to do and all that? You were beaten so terribly in the Order and I worry that I'm taking advantage of you—"

"I like it," Snod insisted passionately, the very thought of Frankie's hands on him making his body heat up. "I like when you tell me what to do, I like it when you…" he swallowed awkwardly, blushing as the next words came out as a whisper, "spank me."

"You literally just had a nightmare about this last night!" Frankie countered irritably.

"That's different," Snod argued, shaking his head. He desperately wanted to make Frankie understand, struggling to explain himself as he said, "When I was in the Order, the punishments were part of making me into the person they wanted to be. When you do it, it's helping me become the person that… the person that I want to be."

The person that I wish I could be more than anything in the whole world… someone who is free, someone who is happy and loved…

Frankie blinked in surprise, his expression softening as the unspoken words settled over him. He touched Snod's cheek, conceding, "All right, Obe. We don't have to stop, but I still should have been more thoughtful. I could have handled the situation last night better and I didn't. This is all so new for you and you only came out with us because I asked you to. I'm supposed to be helping you find your feet, not putting you down. Can you forgive me?"

Snod's eyes widened, and he tried to speak, but his teeth clicked together in silent failure. Forgiveness was an important part of his everyday life when he lived with the

Order, but it was always because of the need to ask for it. Seek it out, bleed for it, suffer for it.

He'd never had anyone ask him for it, and he wasn't even sure how to respond for a few seconds. At last, his head began to move, nodding as he said, "Of course I do."

"Yeah?" Frankie smiled brightly, and Snod's stomach curled happily in on itself.

"Yes," Snod said softly, overcome by the warmth that bubbled through him. Forgiving someone, allowing Frankie to be relieved of his worries, was an amazing feeling.

He caught himself lingering on Frankie's lips, the warmth in his body moving south as he thought of something else that felt especially amazing. He smirked, saying casually, "Although, I did only go out because you promised me something and didn't deliver."

Frankie's eyes widened, gasping, "What?"

"You left me in an extremely uncomfortable physical state with no satisfaction," Snod scoffed. "It was very rude considering what you had sworn you would do."

"Oh, come on!"

"A broken vow is a very serious offense," Snod said, aiming for stern, but he couldn't stop himself from grinning. "I can forgive your inconsiderate behavior, but not the absence of your integrity."

Frankie bared his teeth, his eyes moving down Snod's lips toward his groin. "Well, I can't have you questioning my integrity, now can I?"

Snod's cock eagerly twitched beneath the blankets, his smile growing wider. "You did make me a promise; I'm only asking that you fulfill it."

Frankie chuckled, kissing Snod as his hand began to wander down his stomach. "Mmm… I suppose that would be fair."

"Very fair," Snod panted, his desire making him start to tremble already. As they kissed, he was fighting to get his pants off, and to his surprise Frankie was just as eager to get his mouth on him.

Frankie pressed him down against the mattress by his hips the moment his pants were out of the way, moaning triumphantly as he sucked every inch of Snod down, his eyes fluttering closed.

I've missed the taste of you…

"God," Snod whimpered, his head flopping back against the pillows, "I've missed this… I've missed you." He couldn't stop the lewd grunts that were spilling out of him, lost in the heaven that was having Frankie's cold mouth wrapped around him.

He could feel Frankie's tongue probing along the ridge of his head and rubbing against the tender tissue. Frankie was usually so slow, so patient, but right now he was absolutely ravenous. He was massaging Snod's thighs, fondling his balls, and Snod was falling to pieces.

Snod wanted more, whining as his hips began to rise up, wanting the friction to increase, begging, "Can I…?"

Yes, God. Yes!

Snod groaned at being given permission, snatching Frankie's hair and roughly thrusting upward. He couldn't believe how effortlessly Frankie took it, letting Snod fuck his tight throat as hard as he wanted to, hissing and sputtering when he felt one of his fangs graze his sensitive skin.

Frankie readjusted himself so his teeth wouldn't make contact again, but Snod started begging, "Please… bite me."

Obe… we shouldn't…

Snod slammed his hips up earnestly, trying to hold Frankie's head down, trying to get his teeth to press into him as he pleaded, "Please!"

Frankie's lust exploded at the urgent request and he growled, his brow scrunching up as his teeth sank in deep, swallowing back a big mouthful of blood.

Snod cried out joyously, loving how the suction from Frankie feeding added more pressure around his cock. It was absolutely divine. His legs were suddenly up on Frankie's shoulders and he moaned when he felt a hard smack on his thigh.

You did want me to spank you…

"Yes! God, please!" Snod whimpered, smothering a sob into the crook of his arm when Frankie slapped his ass. The sting resonated all throughout Snod's body and he knew he couldn't take much more. He needed Frankie to discipline him, but this didn't feel like a punishment. It felt like dying and going to heaven, relishing the stinging sensation of his abused cheeks.

Another hard smack and he came immediately, his cock pulsing hard as Frankie gulped down his load and his blood, swallowing audibly.

Licking and sucking until Snod was whining from severe overstimulation, Frankie finally released him with a low groan. He crawled up his body to kiss him. "Mmm… that was lovely."

Snod was dizzy, panting as their lips connected, tasting the iron of his blood and the salt of his cum. It had no right to be so delicious.

Frankie was pressing against Snod seeking out his own release, his eyes bright as he purred, "Obe, touch me."

Snod's insides twisted immediately, the sweet afterglow tainted by the thought of putting his hand down there, down on Frankie. His hesitation was enough of an answer, Frankie shaking his head quickly.

"It's all right," he soothed. "You don't have to. You don't have to do anything you don't want to. Just… kiss me?"

Snod nodded. That he could do. He kissed Frankie passionately, trying to put everything he had into it to make up for what his hands couldn't do. He could feel Frankie wiggling out of his pants and the rhythmic pounding of his knuckles as they brushed against him as he drove himself to climax.

Snod stroked his hair, slid his tongue into his mouth, and even grinded against him. He did everything he could to wring pleasure from this, hating his inadequacy. He couldn't bring himself to touch Frankie like that. The sin was too much.

Frankie finished quickly against the sheets, gasping and jerking, Snod kissing all along his neck as he worked himself through it. He pressed his hand against Frankie's chest, feeling the beautiful pulse of his heart beating beneath his fingers.

"I'm sorry," Snod managed, their noses brushing together when Frankie was done and his heart had stilled once more.

"It's fine," Frankie insisted, their bond warm and sated. "If you want to, we'll get there one day. If not, that's okay, too."

"What if I never want to?" Snod demanded urgently.

"Obe," Frankie soothed, tracing his nails across his jaw. "I'm not going to pressure you. There's no point in doing anything if you're not going to enjoy it, too."

Like the spanking…

Snod blushed immediately, whispering, "Yes."

"It can all feel so good," Frankie promised, "but we'll take it slow. So very slow."

"You won't… you wouldn't make me do it?" Snod asked, hating how small his voice sounded. "You wouldn't… whammy me?"

"Christ, no!" Frankie gasped, his eyes wide in shock. "Obe, I would never use my powers to do something like that. I promise you. Why would you even think that?"

Snod frowned, silent.

"Let me guess," Frankie sighed, reaching for his hand. "The Order? Vampires voodooing people and draining them dry once they've had their way with them?"

"More or less," Snod mumbled. "We were warned about it. My scapular is meant to protect us from it, but you're the first vampire I met who can actually do that."

"Well, it's a very rare gift," Frankie explained. "I inherited it from my Maker, him from his, and so on."

"When we were trapped," Snod said slowly, realization

dawning on him, "you could have tried to use your powers on me, but you didn't."

"Yes," Frankie replied, "but unless I thought I was truly in danger, I wouldn't have."

Snod sensed a bubble of something vile leaking through the bond, and he saw a flash of blond hair and a charming fanged smile. He frowned, trying to make sense of the vision. "Who is that?"

"My Maker," Frankie said quietly. "It's how he turned me. He forced me. He made me promise him forever, and then he made me a vampire."

"He did it against your will?" Snod felt stupid for asking, but he had always been taught that people outside of the Order were weak-minded and couldn't resist defiling their bodies with the unholy curse if they had the chance.

"What did you think I meant when I said he didn't give me a choice? I told you before. Not everyone wants to be immortal, Obe," Frankie said with a bitter smile, shaking his head. "What my Maker did to me was… horrible."

"You never say his name," Snod pointed out curiously. His interest was certainly influenced by his mission, but he did also wonder why Frankie never said it.

"And I never will," Frankie said simply.

Snod's heart dropped. As much as he had been enjoying this beautiful dream, he was sober now, and he had to wake up. His beloved brother was still back in the Order, and he had to return to him. He had been so damnably selfish, a fresh wave of guilt seizing in his chest.

He couldn't do this.

He had to learn that name.

"Why not?" Snod asked as casually as he could, hoping his true intentions couldn't be sensed.

"It's a long story," Frankie said, his brow quirking curiously. "Why do you want to know?"

"Just… wondering," Snod said, the guilt turning into a stone and dropping down heavily into the pit of his stomach.

Frankie frowned, but before he could question him any further, they heard a very loud retching sound from the bedroom next door.

"Oh, no," Frankie sighed, cringing. "That doesn't sound like he made it to the bathroom."

Snod grimaced.

Frankie sat up, pulling his clothes back on in a blink, saying, "I'll be right back. Let me get him cleaned up, and I'll cook breakfast."

Snod watched Frankie practically vanish through the door to go to Lorenzo's aid, sitting up and getting dressed for the day. He rubbed his hands over his face, trying to get a hold of himself.

The satisfaction he felt from finally receiving the promised fellatio from Frankie was being overrun by a much deeper conflict. The promise of being with Frankie was something he wanted, but he loved his brother.

Snod had taken him under his wing when he first came to the Order, a terrified and confused young boy who had to endure so many lessons because he didn't understand his new home. Snod did everything he could to watch over him and keep him safe, thrilled to have a little brother take care of, no matter how difficult he could be.

Athaliah was stubborn and headstrong, Snod often taking the blame for his various missteps so he wouldn't have to suffer. It took many years, but he was finally getting better. He was learning his place in the Order, and Snod thought he was happy.

But without Snod there to help keep him on a righteous path, he was suddenly terrified that Athaliah would wander off again. He didn't want his brother to follow in his footsteps and be exiled from their home.

Snod headed into the kitchen, busying himself as he began to prep to cook breakfast. He got the coffeemaker going and started pulling ingredients out of the fridge. He was quite an accomplished cook, and he enjoyed it. It was relaxing.

He was already mixing up eggs and milk to make omelets when Frankie came out to see what he was doing, grinning as he asked, "You cook?"

"This is normally women's work," Snod replied with a smirk, stirring at the bowl. "Like laundry, tending to the children. My mother died when I was young, so it was just me and my father for a long time. He was very sick, and I had to take care of our household. So I learned."

"Really," Frankie said, his brow scrunching up. "Chores in the Order are, uhm, assigned by gender?"

Snod was confused, saying, "Well, of course they are."

"Right," Frankie chirped. "So the men do all the hunting and bossing around, and the women do all the housework?"

"Only the men who are fit for the sacred task actually hunt and no, there have been a few female hunters," Snod protested. "Though they're not allowed to hunt when their blood is in. They get sequestered like all the women do."

"Wait. You lock up women when they're on their period?"

"No," Snod snorted, adding spinach and cheese to the bowl. "They're not 'locked up.' They're isolated in a special place until the blood of the first sin leaves their bodies. Then they can come back."

Frankie scrubbed a hand across his forehead, saying, "Oh, Obe. We need to have a long talk about gender roles. And periods. And why all of that is very wrong. But I have to finish cleaning up Lorenzo and wash your bedding."

"Anything I can do to help?"

"You're cooking, that's amazing. Thank you."

"I like it," Snod admitted, blushing softly.

Frankie smiled, blinking forward to kiss Snod's cheek before disappearing back into the other bedroom. A few moments later, a very exhausted Lorenzo came stumbling out, his hair a disaster, and groaning miserably.

"Ohhh, never drinking again," Lorenzo whined as he lumbered into the living room, flopping down defeatedly onto the couch. "Never. Never ever again."

"You always say that," Frankie chuckled, blinking around to bring him a cup of coffee.

Snod smiled when he saw there was a cup for him resting on the counter.

"I left it black," Frankie explained. "Don't know how you take it. If you take it at all."

"This is perfect," Snod said gratefully, sipping slowly. "I've taken more than a few lashings for coffee over the years."

"Lashings?" Lorenzo's head perked up, frowning over the edge of his cup.

"Strict diet plan," Frankie interjected, moving on without missing a beat as he asked, "Do you remember what you were saying last night? About the robots?"

"Killing Snod with robots?" Lorenzo frowned.

"No! The nano bots. The cure."

Lorenzo stared blearily at Frankie before his memory kicked back in, gasping, "Yes! Okay, okay. I got this. I think this could work. It could really fix you!"

Snod poured the mixture into the pan, asking quietly, "How do you fix a curse?"

"It's not a curse, it's a disease," Lorenzo firmly corrected him. "Look, you know Frankie is a vampire, right? Do you know about Bacteria V?"

"No," Snod said flatly.

"V is what we named it. 'V' for vampire, real creative, right?" Lorenzo snorted a small laugh, taking a long drink of coffee before continuing, "It's a very unique facultative anaerobic bacteria, similar in function to bdelloids that it requires fresh DNA to continuously replenish itself and repair damaged cells. Doesn't need water or any other food except the iron from hemoglobin and DNA from inside other cells."

"What?" Snod looked over at Frankie for a translation.

"It's a bacteria that cannot survive in the presence of oxygen," Frankie said patiently. "That's why humans aren't automatically turned into vampires when they drink vampire blood. The bacteria can't survive in a normal human body because there's too much oxygen-rich blood."

"Which is why a potential baby vampire has to be drained almost dry," Lorenzo added. "Once all the oxygen-happy blood is gone, the V will freakin' flourish and take over when the parent vampire gives them their vampified blood. It took us forever to figure that out."

"And what was the thing about a buh-loid?" Snod asked slowly.

"Bdelloid," Frankie answered with a smile. "They're a very special microorganism that are, well, biologically immortal. They can repair their cells indefinitely as long as they have access to fresh genetic material. Namely other bdelloids or other microorganisms, but the function of V is the same. It's how we are able to live forever. As long as we are getting blood, our bodies never age."

"All the V needs is tasty blood to keep on regenerating," Lorenzo chirped excitedly. "It's an incredible, incredible bacteria. It actually repairs not only itself, but the cells of the host body. We've also been trying to study the connection between the bacteria and like, Frankie's powers, but it's been slow going. But! Oh! We do know why he can day walk!"

Snod turned over the first omelet, doing his best to keep up. He had to wonder if the Order would be interested in any of this information, and he was trying to pay attention.

"V is super sensitive to sunlight. Fries it on the spot when it's exposed. But! Some bacteria react to high levels of stress in super magical ways," Lorenzo went on, his eyes bright and excited. "They can revert to a super tough dormant form that we call an endospore. Like suuuuper tough, like boiling for ten hours will not kill these babies. Tuberculosis is like that! Like, oh, where they've found living endospores of TB that are like, thousands of years old.

"V is already sort of like an endospore because it already has this really nasty and rigid cell wall. But here's the fun part. When we compared Frankie's blood to other vampires who can't day walk, his cells are even thicker than theirs! We think when Frankie took his little stroll into the sun, his cells didn't just lie down like a wussy and fry. Oh, no! They went like freakin' super-Saiyan and turned into this badass super resistant endospore type cell, and now sunlight doesn't touch him."

"But why did that happen for you and other vampires die?" Snod asked, frowning as he plated the first omelet and poured a second. "We were always taught that sunlight would purify the unholy flesh."

"I don't know," Frankie answered honestly. "I can only assume it has to do with my Maker. There is so much we inherit from them. The V seems to maintain its own unique genetic material when it's passed down. It would explain how children can share the same abilities as their Makers and be a fraction of their age."

"Like your speed," Snod said, beginning to understand, "and the whammy voice. And the need to feed less..." He poked at the pan thoughtfully, asking, "What other powers do you have?"

"Isn't that enough?" Frankie laughed, not directly answering the question.

"You need to figure out that mist thing," Lorenzo snorted, gulping down his coffee.

"Mist?" Snod echoed curiously, plating the second omelet.

"His vampire dad can totally turn into a freakin' pool of mist," Lorenzo exclaimed. "He told me all about it! When they first met, he—"

"Lorenzo," Frankie interrupted gently, grabbing one of the omelets and bringing it to him in a flash, offering him a fork. "You need to eat, and now maybe you can tell me about your plan? To cure me?"

"Right!" Lorenzo nodded, eagerly chowing down, moaning happily, "Holy crap, this is freakin' fantastic. Like, my God. It's a party in my mouth... okay, right! So! V is a super awesome and crazy tough bacteria. All normal attempts to treat it don't work."

"Like medicine?" Snod said, thoughtfully poking at his food. He was much more interested in hearing Lorenzo's idea, trying to imagine a world without vampires and the peace the Order could find if such a thing were possible.

"Yup," Lorenzo mumbled through a mouthful. "Can't penetrate the cell wall. Nothing gets through. However, all bacteria gotta eat, and V does this through a process that we call phagocytosis. It's where the cell literally wraps itself around the nom and like, absorbs it. It's rare for bacteria with such a thick wall to do this, but V's cell wall actually flexes and softens. It's the only time V might be vulnerable.

"So! This is my idea. If I can create a nano bot with some kind of outer shell made of iron to mimic a blood cell, the V may go in for a nibble. Once inside, the nano bot could drop some kind of super strong antibiotic load like vancomycin or something. It might be enough to finally cure you! Trojan horse that shit with freakin' robots!"

"It might just work," Frankie said, his eyes bright and eager behind his glasses, slapping Lorenzo's arm excitedly. "How soon can you have a prototype ready?"

"Give me like two days," Lorenzo replied, finishing off the plate and licking it clean. "Holy crap, like seriously, Snod. This was amazing."

"In two days, you might be able to cure yourself?" Snod pushed, ignoring the compliment about his cooking.

"We'd have to run tests," Frankie said. "It's not easy to experiment with my blood because of the machines we have to use… I don't know. It may take a few weeks, but this is a great start!"

"When do you work again?" Snod asked, finally eating his food and enjoying Frankie's happiness bubbling through the bond.

"Tomorrow," Frankie replied. "It's my turn to drive, so I gotta pick up Lorenzo and Amy, and, I just… Wow." He actually took off his glasses, beaming more brightly than Snod had ever seen him. "This really might be possible."

Lorenzo hugged his friend tightly, grunting, "We're

gonna do it! We're gonna freakin' unvampify you! No more funky blood drinks, no more worrying about weirdo nut-jobs hunting you! It's gonna be great!"

"Weirdo what now?" Snod snapped, his fingers clenching tightly around his fork.

"These freaks that hunt vampires," Lorenzo replied, not realizing the danger he was walking right into. "Frankie told me about them."

"Lorenzo," Frankie warned kindly, glancing nervously at Snod.

"What? It's only what you told me!" Lorenzo protested. "There are these super religious nut-bags that are like all inbred—"

"Inbred?" Snod growled furiously, slamming his fork down.

"Uh, yeah?" Lorenzo said, blinking, still not understanding why Snod was getting so angry. "Like super inbred freaks that think God wants them to kill vampires or something."

There was a loud knock at the door.

"You told him about the Order!" Snod accused, glaring at Frankie.

"Yes, but—!" Frankie protested, groaning as the knocking continued. "Hold on!"

"Definitely gotta kill him now," Snod sighed.

"Wait, kill me?" Lorenzo squeaked, a mental lightbulb coming on and staring Snod down with a surprising burst of rage. "You're part of the Order? What the hell, were you hunting Frankie?"

"Yes," Snod replied shortly.

"Oh, my dude," Lorenzo chuckled, standing up to his feet and cracking his knuckles. "You're toast. I don't care how good your omelet is, I'm not going to let you touch my best freakin' friend—"

"It's fine now!" Frankie insisted, hurrying to the door to answer it, finding a delivery man with a giant bouquet of red roses. "Oh, what in sweet hell is this?"

"How could you spread such vicious lies about us?" Snod demanded, coming around the counter and staring at the flowers. "And who are those from?"

"It doesn't matter who they're from, and I'm sorry I said those things!" Frankie groaned, quickly signing for the delivery. "You have to understand… oh, shit! Obe, look out!"

Snod looked up just in time to see Lorenzo come barreling toward him, fork in hand, tackling him to the floor. He felt immense pain in his hand and came to a very important decision.

He was definitely going to kill Lorenzo.

CHAPTER NINE

"Dead! You're dead!" Snod roared, the pain in his hand throbbing where the fork was sticking out from his palm. "May God have mercy on your soul for I will have none!"

"Oh, come on! I fuckin' tripped!" Lorenzo protested, his eyes bugging out in horror as he tried to stumble up to his feet. "I didn't mean to stab you!"

"No killing anyone!" Frankie shouted, slamming the front door and throwing the flowers down. He blinked over to grab Lorenzo, safely dragging him out of Snod's reach. "He said he tripped! It was an accident, Obe!"

"Yeah! If I had actually meant to stab you, I think I could have aimed for something more vital than your hand!" Lorenzo wailed, scrambling to hide behind Frankie to use him as a shield.

Snod was on his feet, lunging forward as he snarled furiously, "Liar!"

"I'm not lying, dude!" Lorenzo argued passionately, ducking down behind Frankie. "I was just gonna, you know, wave the fork at you in a very threatening manner! I wasn't actually gonna do anything, you fuckin' whacko!"

Frankie grabbed Snod around his middle, holding him firmly in place and not allowing him to move. "Obe," he soothed firmly, "we can fix this. It's not a big deal! It was just an accident!"

"Yeah! How about we talk about the fact that you admitted to trying to kill Frankie?" Lorenzo piped up, a bit overconfident now that Frankie had a hold of Snod. "Something that you definitely did on purpose!"

"I was following orders!" Snod snarled, trying to reach Lorenzo over Frankie's shoulder. "Obviously, I failed!"

"Both of you calm down!" Frankie pleaded.

"And you! Vile betrayer!" Snod spat, still struggling to get out of Frankie's tight grip. He might as well have been trying to get a concrete wall to budge and he caught himself starting to pant. "How could you say those things about the Order?"

"You mean the crazy group of people who are dedicated to killing my kind?" Frankie scoffed bitterly. "Forgive me if I didn't paint you in a very flattering light!"

"Says the unholy bloodsucking fiend!" Snod fumed, kicking his feet like a child, completely helpless in Frankie's grasp. He hated feeling so weak and Frankie's powerful hold was soon having other unexpected consequences.

"Oh, you see that right there?" Frankie snorted dryly. "The name calling? Real helpful! Very mature!"

Snod wanted to bite back with another insult, but he couldn't think while his cock was pressing so insistently into Frankie's chest. He swallowed back a groan, his hands awkwardly dropping to Frankie's broad shoulders, groping the firm muscle he found there. He was angry, hard, and there was something utterly thrilling to be helpless in the embrace of an immortal.

Frankie was feeling it, too. It was obvious by the hungry way he gazed up at Snod, his hold never faltering, and Snod could sense his raw, hot desire through the bond. He didn't know which one of them thought about it first, but all he could picture now was Frankie's firm hand cracking over his backside.

"Frankie, care to explain to me why you have a vampire

hunter staying with you?" Lorenzo asked, worrying his hands together and retreating several steps away. "Seems like that might be a bad idea and all, seeing as how you're a vampire, and he tried to kill you! You know, just a thought!"

"I'm helping rehabilitate him," Frankie explained urgently, blinking rapidly as the heated moment faded into the background. "He's not a hunter anymore."

"How do you know that?" Lorenzo hissed. "What if this is like a super secret double agent deal? Did you ever think about that? Maybe he's just pretending not to be a hunter, and he's secretly reporting all of your vampire secrets back to headquarters and waiting to kill you! This reeks of bad vibes, man!"

Snod's stomach lurched and his lust rapidly departed. Lorenzo was frighteningly close to the truth.

"He's not," Frankie insisted, finally releasing Snod and inspecting his hand. The tines of the fork hadn't quite made it all the way through, and he tried to soothe his friend's concerns as he said, "He was kicked out. They abandoned him, and I'm going to help him get a fresh start. He's not going to hunt anymore. Isn't that right, Obe?"

"Not vampires anyway," Snod grumbled, his eyes narrowing at Lorenzo. He winced when Frankie pulled the fork out, swearing up a storm as blood dribbled out from the punctures.

"Sorry," Frankie sighed gently, blinking away quickly to grab a bandage to gently wrap up Snod's injured hand.

Snod detected a faint rumble of hunger from Frankie seeing the blood, but it was gone just as quickly as it arrived.

"Seriously, Frankie," Lorenzo said, warily glancing over at Frankie as he tended to Snod's wound. "My head vibes are screamin' that something is wrong here."

Snod flinched slightly as Frankie dressed his hand, but he let his anger reduce to a simmer. Frankie's cool touch was comforting, and he looked up into his bright green eyes. He didn't know what to think, what to say.

He couldn't stop thoughts of Athaliah popping up into

his mind. His brother was why he had to do this. Even stronger than his loyalty to the Order was his love for his brother. The familiar nibble of guilt began to gnaw at his insides.

"Yeah?" Frankie asked his friend with a raised brow as he adjusted Snod's bandage. "And where were these vibes at when you met Obe the first time? It seems a little unfair you're only having suspicions about him after you found out he was in the Order."

Snod's teeth clicked together, anything nasty he had to say stolen away listening to Frankie defend him so passionately. He was surprised, and immediately humbled. Once again, he had misjudged Frankie, and his guilt continued to chew up his guts.

"Maaaybe I had them and just didn't tell you," Lorenzo said stubbornly. "Besides, you're the one that told me all that whacked-out stuff about them! They're not good people… he already tried to kill you once. I'm not letting that go."

"I know," Frankie sighed in frustration. "I know I said a lot of terrible things, and yes, I was very biased because of what they stand for. But Obe's shortcomings are not his fault. It's how they raised him, and I can help him move past all of that."

"Is that before or after he tries to stake you in the middle of the night?" Lorenzo snapped, crossing his arms.

"Lorenzo," Frankie warned. "I think Obe and I met for a reason. There is good in him, I know it. I really believe I'm meant to help him—"

"How did you meet again?" Lorenzo demanded. "Oh! Right! He was hunting you!" He groaned, waving his hands frantically. "Do you not see how this sounds completely nuts? And the two of you are banging now? Come on, Frankie. I'm trying super hard to be supportive, but this… this is not good."

"It's fine," Frankie said with a warm smile. "I appreciate your concern, but I'm in no danger from Obe. I would know if I was."

"The bond thing?" Lorenzo questioned, still regarding Snod with intense suspicion.

"Yes," Frankie sighed, flickering over to give his friend a big hug. "I'm okay."

Lorenzo's rage deflated, hugging his friend back with a big sigh. "I worry so much about you already, Frankie. Now you're like, sleeping with the enemy and shit," he mumbled. "Are you sure it's cool?"

"I'm sure," Frankie confirmed, smiling brightly. "I'm going to get Obe set up with a new identity, get him a job somewhere. It's going to be great. I'll prove to you that your little vibes are wrong."

"Fine," Lorenzo relented, frowning still as he looked over at Snod. "I really hope I'm wrong, too."

Snod bared his teeth in response. He knew if he went after Lorenzo that Frankie would only stop him again. The best thing he could do right now was to be silent and keep his volatile feelings to himself.

Running his fingers through his long braids, Lorenzo took a deep breath. "Okay, Snod? I'm sorry about the fork thing. I really didn't mean to stab you. Unless that actually intimidates you and then I totally meant to do it. No? Right. And about what I said. I'm sorry for that, too. I still don't freakin' trust you… but if Frankie is gonna vouch for you, fine."

Snod said nothing, thinking about grabbing the fork and stabbing Lorenzo in the eye with it. That would be fair, wouldn't it?

The image must have been particularly vivid because Frankie started guiding Snod into the kitchen, exclaiming, "Okay! Everyone's fine! Super fine! Let's go over here now, all right?"

"I'm going to make a drink," Snod growled, reaching for the vodka.

"Fine! Why don't you make a drink, and Lorenzo? I think it's time for you to go home!"

"Yeah, okay," Lorenzo grumbled. "I'll work on the nano bot design tonight. See if I can get something together. I'll see you tomorrow?"

"Yes," Frankie assured him. "I'll pick you and Amy up right on time, I promise."

Lorenzo gathered his things and made to leave, nervously teetering by the door. "You need anything, you call me," he said, giving Snod a nasty look as he added, "And you… if anything happens to Frankie? I don't care if a comet falls down from the sky and hits him, I'm blaming you. And I will make you pay for it. Dearly."

Snod growled, Lorenzo quickly slamming the door upon his departure. He sighed, struggling to get the bottle open with his injury. He briefly considered smashing the top off, desperate for something to soothe both his temper and his pain.

Frankie offered out his hand expectantly and Snod gave him the bottle. He watched Frankie pour him a glass and accepted it gratefully.

"I can heal you," Frankie offered. "Make sure your hand recovers fully, but it would mean more of my blood."

Snod hesitated, trying to make a fist and growling from the pain. He was worried about Frankie sensing his deceit if the bond became stronger, but his hand was useless like this.

"It would just be a little bit," Frankie said, smiling gently.

"Please," Snod said quietly, holding out his throbbing hand toward him, using the other to knock back the drink.

Frankie smiled, gently taking Snod's hand in his own and carefully removing the bandages. He then pricked one of his fingers on his fang, squeezing a few drops of blood directly onto the wounds.

"Thank you," Snod said quietly, enjoying the contact.

"It's the least I can do," Frankie said with a warm smile. "I'm sorry about Lorenzo and all of that… he worries about me."

"I deserve his distrust," Snod said with a faint frown. "We didn't meet under the kindest of circumstances."

"I told you, I've already forgiven you," Frankie reminded him with a teasing smirk. "Lorenzo will come around. He just needs time."

Snod fidgeted uncomfortably, thinking to himself that Lorenzo had a month to realize he was right.

"What is it?"

"Where did the flowers come from?" Snod asked, eyeing the discarded bouquet on the floor as a distraction.

Frankie shook his head as he concentrated on his work, sighing, "It doesn't matter."

"They're from Mark, aren't they?" Snod made a face, flexing his hand as the pain began to fade.

"Yes, they were from Mark," Frankie groaned lightly. "Wanna read the card, too?"

"Yes," Snod replied immediately, though he wasn't entirely sure what the purpose of the card was or why Frankie would ask him that.

"I wasn't being serious," Frankie said dryly. "It wasn't anything provocative if you're really that worried about it. Just another stale apology for his behavior and how much he had taken my company for granted."

"Extravagant gifts like that… are common during courting?" Snod asked, genuinely curious.

"Is that what you call it? Courting?"

"Yes," Snod replied, fidgeting. "It's how things are done in the Order."

"Well, we call it 'dating,' and flowers are hardly extravagant," Frankie said, squeezing out a few more drops of blood from his finger. "They're actually a pretty common gift. What do you do in the Order?"

"If you have an interest in a young lady, you must first ask the council," Snod said, balling up his hand. "They have to approve of the union. If they do, then you have permission to approach the lady's father. If he's accepting, then you can begin and ask the lady if you may court her."

"Wait, so the girl you're after is the last person you ask?" Frankie balked.

"Yes," Snod replied impatiently. "If she agrees, then you may court her. You can have supervised visits, she can invite you over for dinner with her family, things like that until the offer of marriage is accepted. There aren't usually… gifts. But I have heard of women receiving kitchen goods before. Dishes, pots. Things like that."

"What happens if you fall in love with someone outside of the Order?"

"You can't marry someone who isn't a member," Snod said with a shake of his head. "Outsiders can be baptized by the council and join us, but that… that doesn't happen often. Athaliah's mother was such a person. After my father laid with her, he tried to get her to join us properly."

"Let me guess," Frankie said, frowning. "She wasn't a big fan?"

"No," Snod said quietly, poking at his hand where the wounds had all closed up. "She said we were all crazy when my father brought her before the council." He flexed his hand, the injury now completely gone. "She ran away, unknowingly pregnant with my brother."

Frankie scratched the back of his head, asking hesitantly, "And the Order… just let her go?"

"My father was told to retrieve her," Snod replied, pouring himself another drink and moving to sit down on the couch. "He told the council that he killed her because she wouldn't come back with him." He smirked softly, adding, "But then sixteen years later, here comes Athaliah. Quite the surprise."

"He let her escape," Frankie gasped in realization, smiling brightly.

"The council was less than pleased with him," Snod chuckled as he stretched out. "He spent a month in the stocks for it, lashed daily."

"Ouch," Frankie grimaced. He plopped down on the couch beside Snod, pulling his legs over his lap. "What happened to Athaliah's mother?"

"She had died," Snod said with a shrug. "Car accident.

The Order found out everything when social services tracked down my father as Athaliah's next of kin."

"You think about him a lot," Frankie noted.

Feeling a quick flash of guilt, Snod replied simply, "I miss him."

"You know," Frankie began, drumming his fingers over Snod's shins, "you really could go get him. Maybe once you get settled into a place of your own, get a job to support yourself. I would help you."

"I told you how dangerous that would be." Snod hesitated. "You would really do that for me?"

"It would make you happy," Frankie said with a laugh. "Maybe you wouldn't feel so guilty all the time. It's what you do when you care about someone, Obe. You do nice things for them."

"Like… the flowers?"

"Exactly," Frankie chuckled. "Except I'm not much of a flowers or chocolates guy. Just a heads up. Even when I was alive, I enjoyed practical gifts. Books, paper, things like that."

"Practical," Snod echoed, thinking this over for a long moment. "What would be practical for a vampire?"

"Uhmmm… A bunch of blood?" Frankie laughed out loud. "Oh, I don't know. I don't need anything, Obe. Hmm, those flowers are really bothering you, huh?"

"No," Snod said, scowling faintly. He shifted, reconsidering as he added, "Maybe."

"You don't have to court me," Frankie said with a little smile, his fingers playfully drumming on top of Snod's knee. "Although it's very sweet of you."

"But you like that?" Snod pushed. "Someone doing things for you?"

"Yes," Frankie answered hesitantly, his fingers pausing for a moment. "But you don't have to worry about that right now. We still gotta get you set up with a job. I have someone that might be willing to help you out, might not ask a lot of questions."

Snod was watching Frankie's hands, his mind wandering to all the places those hands had been. He was much more interested in feeling Frankie's touch than worrying about a job he wouldn't need in a month's time.

And perhaps, just maybe, he was still a little angry about the flowers.

Mark could send all the flowers he wanted to, Snod thought nastily to himself. That man had no idea what it was like to have those gorgeous cold hands all over him, to hear Frankie moaning his name, to feel his most passionate embrace…

"Hey," Frankie teased, "mind out of the gutter."

Snod smirked, allowing his thoughts to move to even dirtier places. He quickly imagined Frankie's hand smacking against his ass, over and over, leaving his cheeks red and stinging. He grinned when he felt a wave of lust bubbling up in the bond in reply.

"I'm going to go do laundry," Frankie groaned in protest, pushing Snod's legs off of him. "Watch some more Disney movies and try to think clean thoughts."

Snod pouted, his head tilting to follow Frankie's butt as he departed. The very fact that he walked at normal speed made it evident he was inviting Snod's attentions.

"Unholy tempter," he called after him, sighing heavily.

"I just love those sweet pet names!" Frankie called back, laughing.

Snod deflated into the couch, groaning in frustration and downing the remainder of his drink. He rolled onto his side, fumbling for the remote. He decided to watch *Mulan*, cuddling against the cushions.

The movie reminded him even more of his beloved brother, a young person who was also struggling to find his place in the world. He had to get back, he had to help him. In order to do that, he had to learn that name.

Perhaps he could do something nice for Frankie.

After all, if Snod did something nice for him, that would bring them closer together and consequently make it easier to learn the name he so desperately needed. His intentions were entirely focused on his mission.

If it happened to make Frankie happy and possibly smile at him that same sweet way he had at Mark last night, that was merely an unexpected bonus. Nothing more.

But really… what did one do for a vampire?

He mulled it over for a while as the movie played on, starting it again the moment it ended. Frankie kept himself busy around the house, humming along to the songs as he did his chores.

Snod watched more movies, finally moving on to see what *101 Dalmatians* was all about. He hated it immediately. There was something about that horrible woman wanting to skin puppies that made his temper boil over uncontrollably. He got the bottle of vodka, glaring furiously at the television as he drank.

He went back to *Aladdin* after that, almost at the point of napping by the time Frankie returned to the couch.

"Mmm, this one again?" Frankie asked warmly, lifting up Snod's legs and letting him stretch back across his lap.

"I like it," Snod said stubbornly.

"It's a good one," Frankie agreed. A few beats of silence passed. He clicked his tongue lightly, saying, "So, I have to go to work tomorrow, but I'm going to try and get your new identity set up. Can't really look for a job without one, but I know someone who might be willing to look the other way."

"Oh?" Snod quirked his brows.

"He owns the karaoke bar I go to," Frankie explained. "I've known him for years. He's a little rough around the edges, but seriously has a heart of gold. He might give you a job cleaning tables, washing dishes or something, just to hold you over for a little while until we have a social security number and all that."

"Women's work," Snod said distastefully.

"Says the master chef," Frankie shot back with a snicker. "It's a job, okay? And he might pay you under the table to help you out. We could go there tomorrow after I get home from work."

"Fine," Snod grumbled. At least a job would be a distraction from these conflicting feelings he didn't know what to do with. The guilt came back in a wave as he looked over at Frankie thoughtfully. If it wasn't for Athaliah, maybe he could go on pretending he could keep this dream.

That he could keep Frankie and finally be that happy, free person he wanted so much.

But this was the real world, and there were no magical wish-granting genies to be found that could give him a brand new life. All he could do was keep the game going, try to stay a few steps ahead, and do his best to ignore how his heart sang when Frankie smiled at him.

Snod made his way through the rest of the bottle of vodka, allowing Frankie's assistance when he tried to drunkenly cook dinner for himself. He managed to steal a few kisses in between rounds of singing all the songs he'd learned from his Disney marathon.

Frankie would not allow the affection to carry on as far as Snod would have liked, but he enjoyed being close to him all the same.

Frankie holding him steady while he battered chicken was nice. He had never known a mundane task could feel so intimate. It was too easy to imagine doing this every night together, and Snod quickly found one of the bottles of liquor Lorenzo had left behind to drown the unavoidable conflict. He could barely finish his plate of food before he was ready to pass out, Frankie again helping him by guiding him into the bed in the guest room.

Snod hated it.

The bed was too small, the sheets felt scratchy, and it didn't have Frankie in it. He pouted when he felt familiar cold hands tucking him in, longing for more. He reached out, holding onto Frankie's arm, asking, "Won't you stay?"

"Obe…" Frankie sounded torn. "We shouldn't. I told you, one more month and—"

"Do you really see good in me?" Snod demanded

suddenly, trying to turn his head and focus in on Frankie's face.

"Of course I do," Frankie soothed.

"You shouldn't."

"Why?" Frankie asked patiently.

"Because… I'm not good," Snod flubbed.

"Maybe you weren't before," Frankie said carefully, his cool fingers dipping over Snod's scalp, "but you can be now. I wasn't good, but I changed. So can you."

"Are we dating?" Snod asked suddenly.

Frankie paused. "Do you want us to be?"

"I want…" Snod struggled to answer the question honestly. His heart felt heavy, heavy enough to keep him pinned down against the mattress and his chest was so tight that it was hard to breathe. "I want a happy ending."

Frankie gently squeezed his hand, replying, "So do I." He leaned down, softly kissing Snod's forehead. "Goodnight, Obe."

"Goodnight, Frankie."

CHAPTER TEN

Four o'clock in the morning came impossibly soon, Snod grumbling his complaint against his pillow. He reached out to the space next to him, scowling when he found himself alone. The sheets were still itchy, his head was throbbing, and Frankie wasn't here. He tried to roll over and fall back asleep, but his mind was suddenly alive with carnal thoughts.

He was overcome with a wave of desire bubbling back at him through the bond, but he couldn't distinguish if it was his own or Frankie's. His eyes groggily blinked open, and he reached down to palm himself through his pants.

His cock was rigid, uncomfortably hard.

He desperately needed relief, wiggling out of his clothes to take himself in hand. He would handle this situation and then try to pass back out. He had barely begun to stroke when the intense desire began to fade, leaving him hard and frustrated. He didn't understand what was wrong, confused and dragging his hands over his face.

How long had it been since he had cleansed himself? Since he had prayed for forgiveness?

It was four in the morning. This was the time he would always start his day. Wake up, train, pray, shower…

Hunt.

His phone wasn't beeping with a new mission now. It was a dead paperweight in the bedside table with his scapular because he had been kicked out of the Order. He only had a few more weeks before he'd dare attempt turning it back on.

He needed to have a name.

Snod lifted his head, suddenly distracted by someone singing.

It was Frankie.

He rose from the bed as he listened, his erection forgotten for the moment. He didn't recognize the song, but Frankie's voice was luring him out like a siren. He hadn't taken the time to fully appreciate Frankie's singing ability before. There was something about it that was all at once melancholic and riveting, making his heart twist up as he listened.

It was more beautiful than any hymn he'd ever heard, his soul igniting in a fountain of bliss as he hung on every word. He could hear the rattle of dishes in the sink, opening his door slowly as he peered out to see what Frankie was doing.

Frankie was cleaning up Snod's mess from cooking dinner, but instead of speeding through it, he was washing each dish with slow and precise care, continuing to sing to himself. He was only wearing a pair of boxers and a shirt, allowing Snod to gaze over his long legs as he approached.

Snod knew Frankie could hear him coming, but he kept on singing softly, the words soon melting into melodic humming. He stepped up behind Frankie, wrapping his arms around his waist and nuzzling against his shoulder.

"Couldn't sleep?" Frankie asked quietly, glancing over his shoulder up at him.

"No," Snod said softly, his hands fanning over Frankie's hips, seeking the cool flesh underneath his t-shirt. He couldn't say it was impossible to sleep alone now that he knew the comfort of having this body beside him.

Frankie arched his hips back against Snod's as he

continued to scrub a plate, sighing, "Mmm… what is it?"

Snod began kissing up Frankie's neck, using his weight to press him up against the counter. His cock was still hard, wedging itself against Frankie's ass insistently. "Missed you."

"Is that why you're naked?" Frankie chuckled, tilting his head to let Snod kiss all he wanted.

"Yes," Snod replied, his hands slipping up Frankie's sides, dragging over his stomach.

"You need to go back to bed." Frankie's scrubbing was beginning to falter.

"With you?" Snod asked hopefully, pushing his hips forward again.

"You need to sleep in your own bed," Frankie insisted even his ass arched back with a soft gasp.

"Don't want to," Snod said innocently, beginning to grind against Frankie with more purpose.

"Obe," Frankie said firmly, a warning.

"Frankie," Snod sighed, reaching down to hook his thumbs in the waistband of Frankie's boxers and tugging them down.

"Okay," Frankie groaned, the plate dropping from his hands and clattering into the sink. "Last time, this is the last time."

"Last time," Snod agreed, urgently rubbing the head of his cock between Frankie's legs, surprised to find him slick and open. "You're wet."

"May have been playing with myself… while thinking about you," Frankie confessed, offering a cheeky smile.

Snod's brain almost imploded on the spot. To know Frankie had been touching himself like that while thinking of him was the most erotic thing he had ever heard.

"Sweet mother of mercy," Snod gasped, wanting to claim him as his own and fuck him right there at the sink. He remembered the need for protection, fussing, "Do we need to…?"

"No," Frankie answered immediately, certainly reading

his thoughts. "Take me. Now."

Snod groaned as he pushed in without question, enjoying the sensation of cool, tight flesh against his hot cock. It was like dipping himself in silk, intoxicating and wonderful, so grateful to experience this without the pesky layer of latex between them.

Frankie's body was already inviting him in, his hands clenching down on the edge of the counter as Snod settled deep inside. They moved together, rough and fast, Frankie's hips banging against the counter so hard that it might have bruised a mortal man.

Dropping his head down into the sink, Frankie arched his back and let Snod bend him over properly. Snod thought Frankie moaning his name was almost as pretty as his singing, the gorgeous melody punctuated by the smacking of their bodies colliding. Snod knew he couldn't last long, the bare sensation was all too sweet, but he would take Frankie apart while he could.

Frankie was nearly having a fit, groaning and slapping his hand against the counter when Snod hit a particularly ecstasy-inducing angle. He was touching himself, panting out a warning, but in moments he was trembling and his knees buckled as he came.

Snod held Frankie's hips tightly to steady him, grunting as he fell into bliss with him. He could feel his seed pumping deep inside of him, lost in the rhythmic pulsing of his cock. He was gasping, unaware for a few moments that tears were actually running down his cheeks. He slid his cock in and out a few times, amazed at the thick slick of lube and cum enveloping him.

He was at a loss for words, helpless to describe how intense this moment was for him. The Order had always taught him that a man's seed was sacred, and here it was, spilled inside Frankie. Snod didn't think he'd ever share this with anyone, marveling at how quickly the heat of his cum seemed to fade.

Seed was meant for making children and not to be spent

carelessly for physical pleasure. That was part of the sin of lying with a man, that the life-giving fluid was wasted during the unnatural act, but this didn't feel like a waste or unnatural at all.

It was beautiful.

Frankie managed to stand up straight, taking a deep breath and sighing, "Mmmph… Obe… come on." He reached back, grabbing Snod's wrist and blinking them into his bed to enjoy their afterglow together.

"Very, very last time," Frankie said sternly, pulling the sheets up over them with a little grin, "even though that was freakin' amazing."

Snod's insides were a bowl of satisfied mush, and he was thrilled to be back in Frankie's bed. He put his hand on Frankie's chest, happy to feel the last few flutterings of his heart. "I liked it," he said shyly. "Coming in you."

"I did, too," Frankie admitted, his brows furrowing up. "Too much, probably."

"What happened to taking precautions?" Snod chuckled.

"Well, when people are in a committed relationship, it's okay to forego some of those precautions," Frankie replied, shrugging casually.

"Does this mean we're dating?" Snod hated how hopeful he sounded.

"Yes," Frankie said with a warm smile. "If you want that. We're doing things a little backwards, you know. People typically date before sleeping together or living together."

"I'm a fast learner," Snod teased.

"Wait, did you just make a joke?" Frankie laughed. "Did you make an *Aladdin* joke?"

Snod grinned slyly, pleased with himself. He had watched the movie several times already, and he had most of the dialogue committed to memory.

"Go to sleep, Obe," Frankie snorted playfully. "Still have a few more hours before I have to go to work."

"Goodnight, my handsome prince," Snod mumbled, kissing him softly.

"Sleep well, princess," Frankie replied dutifully, still grinning as he got settled down.

"Why am I the princess?" Snod pouted.

"Because you're so very pretty," Frankie chuckled, kissing any further argument from Snod's lips. "Plus, you get a tiger if you're the princess."

"Mmm, you've got yourself a deal," Snod mumbled. It was so much easier to fall back asleep with Frankie's cool body next to his, wrapping his arms around him tight.

When Snod woke up again, he grumpily found that Frankie had returned him to his own bed in the guest room. He flailed around in a huff, staring up at the ceiling and sighing haggardly to himself.

He had the whole day to spend without Frankie, deciding he could spend his time trying to find a gift that would be worthy of a vampire's affection. He got up, made his bed, and dressed for the day. He had a mission to fulfill, a task to accomplish…

And instead he ended up on the couch with more of the liquor Lorenzo had left, getting drunk and watching Disney movies again.

He staggered around to cook himself lunch, doing his best to keep the kitchen clean. He saw Frankie had finished the dishes from this morning, smirking as he looked over the sink fondly.

Oh, this was getting hard.

Frankie had said they were dating if Snod wanted them to be, and God, what a lovely temptation it was. It would be so easy to settle into this domestic bliss and find a happily ever after with this beautiful vampire.

But Athaliah…

Snod heard the front door opening, looking up from where he was sprawled out on the couch. He couldn't believe how quickly the day had gotten away from him, blinking as he sat up to greet Frankie. "Mmm… hey!"

Frankie shut the door and blinked to Snod's side to kiss his forehead in greeting, chirping happily, "Hey! I've got good news." He paused, wrinkling his nose. "And you absolutely reek of strawberry vodka."

"Don't worry," Snod assured him with a stern nod. "I'm not drinking any more of that vile sinner's water."

"You drank it all, didn't you?"

"Yup."

"Okay, you're cutting back on the booze, starting right now," Frankie ordered firmly. "Considering you've never had alcohol before and now you're drinking it every day? For the sake of your liver, I'm not going to let you turn into an alcoholic."

Snod grumbled, pressing a hand over his face. "I'm turning into Dumbo, aren't I," he sighed. "Big, drunk Dumbo."

"Not quite yet," Frankie snorted. "Dry out for a bit, and all the pink elephants should stay away. Alcohol can be fun, like anything, but in moderation. Do you understand?"

"Yes." Snod made a face. "You said you had good news?"

"I've put in the order with my contact for one brand spanking new identity for you! Oh! And Lorenzo is almost done with the first prototype for Project Unvampify," Frankie replied cheerfully. "Today was good! What about you? How was your day?"

Snod waved his hand toward the television where *The Great Mouse Detective* was currently playing. "What you see is what you get."

"You spent the whole day getting drunk and watching cartoons?"

"Idle hands," Snod replied, flopping back down on the couch. "I have no purpose, I have no… mission."

"Well, you're going to," Frankie reassured him, patting his leg. "We're going to go see my friend about that job. Get up, let's get you cleaned up."

"The one that owns the bar?"

"Yes, he owns Cheap Trills," Frankie confirmed, pulling Snod back up into a sitting position. "Come on. You're gonna love Rees, trust me."

Snod fussed, but let Frankie help him up and get him ready to go out. It was still quite amazing how quickly Frankie could move, getting them both dressed in fresh clothes in a matter of seconds. Frankie kissed him fondly, offering him a bottle of water before they left.

Snod drank it on the way over, trying to sober up before he met his potential employer. He knew the karaoke bar well, having stalked Frankie here so many nights before. He had never actually been inside, surprised to find it so worn down and bordering on seedy.

Many of the chairs were broken, and the small stage was in desperate need of repair. All the table tops were scuffed, the neon lights were half lit, and the odor of cigarette smoke permeated every breath.

It was a dump.

It didn't appear to be open yet, but Frankie had no problem walking right up to the bar. Snod was not impressed, sitting down on a barstool and grimacing when he realized the seat was sticky.

Lovely.

There wasn't another soul in sight, but Frankie didn't seem worried. He sat down next to Snod, calling out into the back cheerfully, "Rees! Hey! It's Frankie!"

"For fuck's sake," a sultry and deep voice bemoaned. "You don't have to actually say 'It's Frankie.' I have cameras for a reason, darling!"

Snod stared as a thin man in a sequined dress came out to greet them. The man was wearing heavy makeup and large rhinestone earrings, his tall heels clicking as he approached with a suspicious scowl.

"And who is this?" the man asked, his finely manicured brows furrowing as he looked over Snod. "This the guy?"

"Yup, this is Obadiah Snod," Frankie said proudly, clasping a hand on Snod's shoulder. "Obe, I'd like you to meet Rees Everhart. Rees, this is Obe."

"You're… wearing a dress." Snod was still staring. "You

look like a woman."

"You look like you suck dick," Rees countered smoothly with a sweet bat of his eyes.

Snod grimaced, swallowing back a mouthful of bile. "It's… nice to meet you."

"A pleasure, I'm sure," Rees replied curtly. "You look like trouble, Obadiah. Are you going to give me any trouble?"

"I don't plan to," Snod replied honestly, wishing his head didn't hurt so much. Definitely cutting back on the drinking.

"He really needs a job," Frankie insisted, eyes pleading with Rees. "Anything you need, he'll do it."

"Fine," Rees drawled, looking back at Snod. "What can you do? Know anything about bartending?"

"No," Snod answered slowly.

"What about construction? Uh… how about carpentry?"

"Nope."

"Electrical work?"

"No."

Rees threw his hands up, laughing, "Well, what the fuck, darling! What can you do? Other than hold down a fuckin' chair and look pretty?"

Snod bared his teeth, frustrated with the sudden realization that he was inadequate for even the most menial of jobs. "Well," he growled, "I can snap your neck three different ways. Is that useful?"

Rees laughed right in his face, not the least bit afraid as he cackled, "Ah! Sweet thing has got some balls! All right, tough guy. Bouncer it is. Think you can handle that?"

Snod blinked. "What?"

"It's easy, darling," Rees snorted. "I point at people, you make them go bye-bye."

"He means make them leave the bar," Frankie quickly clarified.

"Be here every day at six, I'll get you up to speed," Rees

went on with a smirk. "I'll pay you fifty bucks a night, plus a small cut of the tips if you do a good job and keep my staff safe and happy. Fair?"

Snod honestly had no idea if that was good or not. He looked to Frankie expectantly, finding an encouraging smile. He nodded, replying, "Yes, I accept your offer."

"Good, you can start right now," Rees chuckled, pointing at one of the broken chairs. "Carry that piece of shit out back to the dumpster."

"How is that bouncing?" Snod scoffed.

"I'm pointing at something and you're making it leave," Rees said slowly. "Come on, sweet thing. I'm an old fuckin' man in stilettos with a bad back. Go move the damn chair."

Snod growled, but got up, hating how his jeans stuck slightly to the unknown mess left on the barstool. He walked over to the chair, dragging it toward the rear exit of the club.

"Wait!" Frankie blinked over to hold the door for him, explaining, "If you let it shut, you'll be locked outside. It's broken. Well, kinda like everything else around here—"

"Why did you, you just—!" Snod stammered, staring at Frankie and glancing back at Rees who had clearly seen him move supernaturally fast. "You just revealed yourself as an unholy creature of Satan to that man!"

"Hey, sweet thing," Rees drawled. "I've known he was unholy since the fucking eighties and I'm not exactly pure myself. Ahem."

Lost for a reply, Snod took the chair over to the closest dumpster and tossed it in. He stomped back toward Frankie, who was still patiently holding the door open for him, demanding sharply, "He knows?"

"Yes, he knows," Frankie soothed. "He's a very old friend, he's not—"

"You're so stupid!" Snod groaned as he walked back inside. "How many people know you're a vampire?"

"Just Rees and Lorenzo," Frankie protested. "And I think Rees' wife. Well, ex-wife now. And you, of course.

And maybe the butcher. I mean, *possibly* the butcher. I think he suspects…"

Staring at Frankie in disbelief, Snod snarled, "How the hell you have not been killed yet is beyond me."

"Because I only tell people that I trust!" Frankie argued defiantly, his irritation boiling up fast in the bond.

"You can't trust anyone," Snod reminded him with a scowl.

"I trust you most of the time!"

"Probably shouldn't," Rees piped up from the bar, leaning across it to watch them argue.

Snod pointed at Rees, scoffing, "See?"

"Obe," Frankie scolded, "it's okay to trust people! It's okay to open up! You trust me, don't you?"

"No," Snod replied bluntly, gritting his teeth, "because I'm not a fool."

"So, wait, you're saying I am?" Frankie scoffed.

"Yes," Snod answered stubbornly.

"Relationships have to be built on trust," Frankie growled, looking so beautifully human when he was pissed off. "And also! Not telling your boyfriend that he's stupid would be good, too!"

Boyfriend.

The word hit Snod right in the stomach, his face flushing brightly. All of his rage was immediately drowned out by something warm and shy, asking breathlessly, "Boyfriend?"

"Yes! Boyfriend!" Frankie said earnestly. "Dating, me and you, remember? Isn't that…" There was a sting of something sharp in the bond, something hesitant. "Isn't that what you wanted?"

"Hey, ahem, lovebirds!" Rees called out. "I've got to open in thirty minutes. Come on. As entertaining as your domestic drama is, it's not good for business."

"Sorry, Rees. Look, Obe, we'll talk about this later," Frankie said flatly, his expression blank though Snod could still feel how hurt he was. He offered his friend a strained smile. "What time should I pick him up?"

"Last call is at two," Rees mused, tapping his long nails on the bar top as he thought it over. "Let's say three."

Frankie flitted over to Snod's side, kissing his cheek. "Rees has my number if you need me. I'll see you tonight."

Snod flinched at the kiss, not used to such open displays of affection. He was afraid that someone would see him, and he would be turned into the council as a sodomite. He was going to burn in hell, and the council would offer him no mercy for such a shameless display of sin.

He had to remind himself that there was no council here and no terrible punishment was awaiting him. He could enjoy this. He could let himself pretend this was real.

Snod offered a small smile, nodding. "Tonight."

"Take care of him, Rees," Frankie warned, smirking at the old man.

"Aw, like he was my own," Rees promised, snickering softly as he gave Frankie a happy wave. "See you tonight, darling."

Frankie smiled sweetly, waving as he left, the door shutting behind him.

"Have a seat, Obadiah," Rees said, gesturing to the bar. He waited for Snod to sit down, asking bluntly, "So, you used to be in the Order and now you're knocking boots with a vampire?"

Snod scowled, furious with Frankie for saying so much to this man, but he held his tongue. He gritted his teeth, replying quietly, "Yes."

"Pretty deep shit, huh? Going from hunting him to rolling in the sheets with him?" Rees pressed, pouring himself a shot of whiskey. "Rather amazing, making that kind of change in your life. Good for you."

Snod tilted his head, watching Rees carefully. "Thanks," he said slowly, "I appreciate that."

"You know," Rees said casually, knocking the rest of the alcohol back with a soft hiss, "just saying, you better be careful with how you proceed. Frankie is very special."

"You gonna threaten to kill me with robots, too?" Snod

asked dryly.

"Nah," Rees chuckled in a friendly tone, grinning wide. "Lorenzo, I'm guessing? Was that him? Sweet kid and all, but meh, lacks imagination."

Snod frowned, his gut lurching uncomfortably. He didn't like how Rees was smiling at him at all.

"I know I don't look like much," Rees went on, gesturing to his slender frame. "Back's worthless and I've arthritis in my knees. But you know what works great? My trigger finger. You may know all kinds of nifty ninja bullshit, but I'm a hell of a good shot. Damn good. Plus, I wouldn't need to aim much to blow your knees out with a shotgun."

Snod was unimpressed at first, saying coolly, "Yes, I get it. If I hurt Frankie, you'll shoot me—"

"Oh, I'm not done yet," Rees spat, his painted eyes narrowed fiercely. "Blowing out your knees is just so I don't get any fuss out of you. Don't worry, I'd tourniquet your legs, make sure you don't bleed out too quick. I may just cut off your legs entirely just to be sure you can't run. Plus, it's less of you to carry. Bad back and all, like I said.

"You see, after I've cut you up a bit, I'm going to make you little concrete shoesies for your nubs. Fix you up with some oxygen and then dump your ass in the river. I don't want you to drown right away. That's what the oxygen is for. I want you to sit down there in the bottom of the river, you and your little nubs, and I want you to have time to think about how badly you fucked up before you die."

Snod shivered at the vivid description, his eyes never leaving Rees' as he replied quietly, "That's very creative."

"Thank you, darling," Rees laughed, still deceivingly chipper. "Way better than death by robot, right? Just making things clear is all. Frankie may not like spilling blood, being the sweet little vamper that he is, but I have no problem. You be good to him, or else it's nubs time."

"I understand," Snod said quickly, trying to frame what he said next very carefully, "My intention is not to hurt Frankie."

"Glad to hear it!" Rees purred, clapping Snod on the shoulder. "Now! We got some more busted furniture that needs bouncing real quick before we open. Let's get to work."

CHAPTER ELEVEN

Snod's first night working for Rees was nothing short of eventful.

After he had bounced out the broken furniture Rees wanted gone, Rees had him carry in crates of beer to put in the cooler behind the bar. A delivery of frozen food arrived next, and Snod had the pleasure of unloading that as well. He wrinkled his nose up at the frozen hamburger patties and fries, complaining, "People actually pay you to eat this?"

"Uh, yeah," Rees snorted as he perched on a stool nearby to supervise. "They get drunk enough, they don't care what they eat. Besides, my cook hasn't been right in the head since he got kicked by this goat a few years back. Dropping stuff in the fryer or popping it in the microwave is about all he can handle."

Snod scoffed in disgust, shaking his head as he finished stocking the last of the so-called food. He snorted, grumbling, "This isn't fit to feed dogs."

"Well, woof woof, sweet thing," Rees drawled. "I really don't think it's that bad." He paused to cough, deep from his chest and noisily clearing his throat. "Pardon me. Hmmph. Employees can eat one meal here a night, so quit complaining, Gordon Ramsay. It's free."

Snod resisted the urge to comment since he wasn't sure who Gordon Ramsay was and certainly had no intention of eating that garbage. "What now?"

"Now, you go work the door. You keep your pretty peepers on the bar and the fine folks on the floor," Rees replied. "We have a strict no asshole policy here. If they turn into an asshole, bounce time. Also, make sure you watch the stage. Anyone gets too drunk and starts hogging the mic, you get them off. Got it?"

"Yes," Snod nodded, suddenly thrilled that he had a purpose. He could absolutely handle this. He'd performed security with the Order before. Manual labor aside, he was surprisingly happy with his new job.

"Now," Rees sighed, leisurely glancing over his nails, "any questions?"

"Why..." Snod hesitated to finish his question, but it was obvious what he wanted to know by how blatantly he was staring at Rees' dress.

"I'm a straight man who enjoys women's clothing," Rees said plainly. "I was married for a while before my wife found me borrowing her things and decided she didn't want to share her wardrobe. I do not want a sex change, I prefer 'he' and 'him' pronouns, and if you have a problem with any of this, you can hit the bricks. We clear?"

"Crystal," Snod said quickly.

"Good," Rees said, holding his head high. "Let's get going."

The bar filled up quickly once the door opened, Snod's presence at the entry garnering several stares from regular customers. He stared right back at them, scowling all evening.

"Amish," Rees would tell the concerned patrons, carrying on Frankie's lie to ease their worried minds as if that somehow explained Snod's grumpy demeanor.

He couldn't believe it actually worked.

Snod learned a lot very fast. The first and foremost was that most people who sang karaoke had no business singing at all. He could only compare the noise to the screaming of cats in heat, wishing desperately for ear plugs. There were a couple of patrons who were moderately talented, but they were few and far in between.

The second thing he learned was that alcohol made people very stupid. It made them believe that they could sing when they couldn't, which Snod particularly hated, and it also made them think they could dance. That at least was amusing. Furthermore, it convinced them that other people were attracted to them when they clearly weren't.

And third, perhaps Snod's very favorite, it granted them the wonderful delusion that they were invincible, and it was a lot of fun to show them that they weren't.

Eyes ever watchful, he had noticed that a short man at the bar was being rather aggressive with the bartender. She forced a smile and continued to serve him, but she was obviously in distress.

Snod was already stalking across the room as the man reached out to grope at the bartender's rear over the counter. "Don't touch her," he snarled. "This is not a proper place for courting, and she has already refused you numerous times. Back off."

"C'mon, buddy," the man laughed, playfully shoving Snod. "Just having a good time here! That's all!"

Growling, Snod snatched the man's wrist and jerked it back with a sickening crunch.

The man screamed, as did a few of the startled patrons quickly scattering from all the commotion. Snod whipped the man's head against the bar, smiling happily as he crumpled to the floor.

Oh, it had been so very long since he'd been able to use any of his training, and he very much enjoyed feeling the familiar rush of adrenaline. He grabbed the man by the back of his coat, cheerfully dragging him out front and letting him spill out onto the sidewalk.

The man whimpered, cradling his broken wrist and cursing loudly.

Snod was grinning from ear to ear. Finally, he'd had a successful mission. Protect the staff, bounce assholes, objective completed.

This job was actually sort of fun.

Snod marched back into the bar with his head held high, surprised when he suddenly felt a hard slap on his arm. He glanced down to see Rees glaring at him, asking flatly, "What?"

"That was Kevin!" Rees spat angrily. "He's a regular!"

"I don't understand," Snod groaned in frustration, massaging his temple as his headache began to return. "Because he's a regular, I allow him to harass the staff?"

"No, you're supposed to carry his bitch ass outside! You don't break his fucking arm!" Rees hissed, smacking at Snod again. "Take it down a notch, Rambo!"

"Rambo?" Snod was lost, but he was certain it wasn't a compliment.

"Listen," Rees said sternly, "no more breaking bones! And don't look at me like I just kicked your fucking puppy."

Snod sulked, crossing his arms as he replied haughtily, "Fine! No more broken bones."

Well, this job *was* fun.

He pouted for most of the evening after that, finding some pleasure in escorting out a couple of drunks who insisted on singing ABBA on repeat and throwing their beers at the audience when they got booed. He promptly deposited them all outside without any permanent injuries as ordered, walking back in to take his post by the door.

He saw the bartender he had helped earlier beckoning him over with a friendly smile. He frowned, glancing around for Rees. He didn't see him, cautiously approaching the bar. He wasn't supposed to leave his post, asking quickly, "What? Is someone else bothering you?"

"I wanted to thank you," she replied, smiling warmly and sliding a shot of something dark toward him. "The way you totally kicked Kevin's ass was like watching art in motion. Thanks."

Snod frowned at the glass, gently pushing it back. "I'm on duty," he said shortly. "I need to be alert."

"Wow! Are you always this serious?" she asked with a soft laugh.

"Yes," he replied. "Especially when I'm on a mission."

"Mission?"

"Working," he tried again.

"Right," she drawled, holding out her hand expectantly. "Well, Mr. Serious, my name is Mandy."

"My name isn't Serious. It's Snod, Obadiah Penuel Snod," he corrected quickly, shaking her hand awkwardly. "You may call me Snod."

"Nice to meet you. So! How do you know Rees?"

"I don't know him. He's a friend of… he's a friend of my boyfriend's." Snod couldn't help the warm little smile that curled his lips. God, to admit that out loud, to say that he had a boyfriend, was absolutely liberating.

"Oh!" Mandy grinned brightly, seeming surprised.

"What is it?" Snod felt a moment of panic at how she had responded.

"I just can't believe Rees has any friends," she replied with a wink.

"I heard that!" Rees' disembodied voice called out from the back, growling in protest. There was a brief fit of coughing before he yelled again, "I have plenty of friends, you nasty little hussy!"

Mandy giggled, shouting back, "You know I love you, Rees!"

"Yeah, yeah," Rees mumbled, strutting out to join them with a dramatic roll of his eyes. "Whatever you say, darling."

Mandy slid the shot she had poured for Snod toward Rees, who drank it back like it was water. It was getting late, and the crowd had begun to thin out. Mandy started to clean up the bar, restocking the little trays of fruit slices and olives.

Glancing at Snod, she said, "Tonight was a good night, Rees. Snod's little rescue really brought in the tips."

"Oh, yeah?" Rees snorted, leaning across the bar with a

grunt. "Maybe Kevin won't press charges."

Snod tensed. He couldn't afford for police to be involved especially without his new identity in place. How could he have been so foolish. He fidgeted, sitting down abruptly at the bar.

Noting the change in Snod's mood immediately, Rees jerked his head at Mandy and asked nonchalantly, "Hey, darling. Last call has hit. How about you go count the potatoes?"

Mandy looked confused, replying slowly, "Rees? We don't have any potatoes. I haven't seen a fresh vegetable in here—"

"Just go find something to fucking count." Rees pointed toward the kitchen, giving her an expectant stare.

"Got it," she said obediently. "Counting the potatoes." She headed into the kitchen to leave them alone at the bar.

"I'll take care of Kevin," Rees said quietly.

Snod perked up expectantly.

"No, I'm not going to kill him, you nut-job," Rees groaned. "I'll make sure it goes away is what I'm saying. You need to learn to control yourself. Isn't some of that shit in the Order all about self-control?"

"It's about resisting the call of sin," Snod argued, his brow furrowing up. "Controlling your impulses through prayer, fasting, and—"

"Damn, your lips are still wet from sucking on that cult's tit, aren't they?" Rees laughed, shaking his head and slapping the bar. He smirked slyly, saying mysteriously, "Allow me to let you in on a little secret… nobody resists sin. We all do it. Maybe a little, maybe a lot, but nobody's clean."

Scowling, Snod dryly retorted, "I know that. That is why we must purge ourselves and pray for forgiveness. We must be the light in the darkness."

"Look, sweet thing," Rees said flatly. "I've been around for a very long time. The whole world is fucking darkness. People are assholes. Like Kevin, he's an asshole. I'm an asshole. It's all nasty with little bits of sunshine to make the horrible shit tolerable if you're lucky enough to find one.

"Frankie? Frankie is like that. Trust me, I've known him for fucking ever. Pure sunshine. The big ol' sun bent right over, spread his cheeks, and shit him right out."

Snod made a face at the description, venturing carefully, "You're saying… he's very special?"

"Goddamn right he is," Rees growled, somehow making the words sound like a threat.

"You already said that when you threatened to make nubs out of my legs," Snod pointed out.

"It's worth repeating," Rees scoffed. "And it's not just because of his, ahem, unique diet. I don't know what you did to make him shine on you, but you better count yourself lucky that he has. Otherwise, I wouldn't give a hang what Kevin does to you."

"What does this have to do with him?"

"Frankie cares about you," Rees explained. "Therefore, I have to care about you. Why else do you think I let him talk me into hiring your crazy ass?"

Snod didn't say anything for a moment, dropping his eyes down to the bar. He knew he didn't deserve this kindness, but couldn't help but be humbled by it. "Thank you," he said quietly. "I appreciate it."

"Don't worry about thanking me," Rees insisted, waving his hand. "I'll make sure Kevin doesn't go crying to the cops. Frankie would be very unhappy with me if I let his sweet thing get arrested. Just keep your ass in line and don't mess anybody else up, okay?"

"Yes," Snod promised. He hesitated as a new idea popped into his head, asking slowly, "What if I wanted to thank Frankie?"

"You can open your mouth and the words 'thank you' can tumble right out."

"No, I mean… I want to court him. Date him. Properly. But I cannot think of an appropriate gift," Snod explained quickly. "You say that you've known him for a long time?"

"Since 1985."

"I was hoping you could help me."

"The fuck do I know about getting him a present?" Rees scoffed, laughing to himself. "What do you get someone like him? Blood?"

"Already thought of that," Snod sighed in frustration. "That's not good enough." He racked his brain, wishing he could think of something. The gift needed to be thoughtful, unique, special…

Just like Frankie.

"He likes old things?" Rees suggested, sincerely trying to be helpful. "You know. Shit that reminds him of when he wasn't on that diet."

"His desk," Snod said suddenly, staring at Rees.

Rees looked confused, but a light seemed to click on as he questioned, "You're talking about the one at the Franklin museum?"

"You know about it?"

"Of course I do," Rees snorted dryly. "He's been bitching about that desk for ten fucking years since he lost it at an auction to some prick who turned right around and donated it to the museum. You aren't really thinking about stealing that desk, are you?"

"Yes."

"Fuck, you are crazy," Rees laughed heartily.

"Would that not be appropriate? Is it not… thoughtful?"

"Oh, it's very thoughtful," Rees cackled. "It also might be a felony."

Snod didn't care about that, curling his lip defiantly. He had finally come up with something that seemed so perfect, and he didn't want to let it go.

"Wait until Friday," Rees said, his slim brows narrowing and suddenly waggling mischievously, "and I'll drive you there myself."

"You will?"

"You know, in all the years I've known Frankie, I've never been able to do anything nice for him. If you really are fucking serious about this, I'll help you."

"Thank you," Snod said, smiling warmly.

"Don't get all mushy on me," Rees warned. "We get caught, I'm telling them it was all your idea and that you took advantage of an old man."

"We won't get caught," Snod said confidently.

"Got a lotta experiences robbing places, Obadiah?"

"I do."

"Mm. Let me guess," Rees purred thoughtfully. "That's why you don't want any trouble with the cops?"

"Yes, but I've never been caught."

"Never say never," Rees said with a wag of his finger. "You jinx us, and Frankie's gonna have to bail both of our asses out of jail."

"How did you meet Frankie?" Snod asked curiously.

"He saved my life," Rees replied with a shrug. Before he could elaborate, he looked up at the door and grinned. "Speak of the devil. Look who's here!"

"Hey!" Frankie had arrived, cheerfully greeting Snod with a kiss on his cheek. "Hi! How did it go?"

"Good," Snod gushed, absolutely drinking in the affection. He was beaming proudly as he announced, "I broke someone's wrist."

Frankie was instantly horrified, sputtering, "What?"

"It was Kevin," Mandy filled in helpfully as she came back to the bar, wiping down the counter. "His usual pervy shit. Tried to grab me, so Snod grabbed him."

"Well, I guess Kevin will finally learn to never do that again." Frankie looked at Snod, scolding, "You need to be careful."

"Already told him," Rees said with a smirk. "I got him, Frankie. It's okay."

Frankie seemed to relax, allowing himself to press up against Snod's side. "Thank you again," he told his friend. "I trust everything else went well?"

"Very well," Snod said, smiling as he looked over Frankie's handsome face. He had missed him, surprised how his heart felt so much lighter just being near him.

"Sweet thing did great," Rees promised. "I think he is gonna be fine here." He nodded at Snod, saying, "See you tomorrow?"

"Tomorrow," Snod agreed, eager to get home and be alone with Frankie.

"See you tomorrow!" Mandy called out cheerfully.

"Bye, guys!" Frankie said with a grin, waving.

Snod nodded his farewell, winding his arm around Frankie's waist and was already hurrying toward the door.

"Hey, sweet thing," Rees called out dryly, leaning on the bar and propping his chin in his hand. "Don't you wanna get paid?"

Snod stopped, quickly turning back to the bar. "Yes."

Rees snorted to himself, moving to the register to count out some cash.

Mandy sorted through the tip jar and pressed a few more bills into Snod's hand, saying, "A little extra. As a thank you for defending my honor."

"Thank you," Snod said, accepting the money and tucking it in his pocket.

"Now," Rees drawled sweetly, "get the fuck outta here!"

Snod grinned, rejoining Frankie and heading outside to the car. Frankie drove them home, excitedly asking him for every detail of his first official day at work along the way.

Snod found himself answering each question happily, realizing he really had enjoyed it. No more breaking bones aside, he was looking forward to returning. The money felt good in his pocket.

It was money he had earned.

As a hunter with the Order, he had been given an allowance and a credit card to handle his traveling expenses. But this money was his, all his, and he didn't even know what to do with it.

Frankie seemed to read his mind like always, opening the front door of the apartment and saying, "Once you get your new identity, we can set you up with a bank account."

"I've never had one," Snod said softly, surprisingly

excited at having something so simple.

"Well, I'm very glad I get to help you with so many firsts. First job…"

"First kiss," Snod reminded, his hands easily finding their way around Frankie's middle and pulling in for a soft kiss.

"Mmm," Frankie hummed as he curled his arms around Snod's neck. "First Disney movie marathon."

"First blowjob," Snod added slyly.

"First drink," Frankie chuckled.

"First time," Snod sighed, tilting his head for another kiss. He loved how easily Frankie melted against him, eagerly sliding his hands down to grope his butt.

"Mmmph!" Frankie squeaked, laughing as he gently pushed Snod away. "Obe…"

"Dating," Snod said breathlessly. "I want it. I do. I want you… to be my boyfriend."

Frankie's eyes were wide and happy, smiling brightly as he said, "Yeah?"

"Yes," Snod confirmed.

"I'm glad," Frankie said eagerly, "and I would very much like to be your boyfriend, too."

Snod surged forward to kiss him once more, all hands and tongue, frowning when Frankie pushed him away again. "What?"

"Still not having sex," Frankie said firmly.

Snod pouted.

"Just a few more weeks," Frankie said soothingly. "Let's wait and make sure it's all out of your system. And then I'll be all yours, okay?"

Snod nodded, taking Frankie's hands in his own, sighing quietly, "Yes."

A few more weeks and Snod knew he would have to leave, his heart aching uncomfortably.

"What's wrong?" Frankie asked gently, seeming to sense his distress, giving Snod's hands a little squeeze.

"I want to enjoy every moment I have with you," Snod

replied honestly.

"There are other ways to spend time together, Obe," Frankie teased, kissing his cheek. "Now, I know this is usually when you're getting up? But I think it's time for you to crash."

Snod laughed, surprised to see that it was getting close to four o'clock in the morning. He accepted defeat, giving Frankie a farewell kiss as he retreated to his bedroom.

"Hey! Obe!"

"What?" Snod glanced over his shoulder.

"I'm really proud of you," Frankie said, his fangs flashing in a big smile.

Snod felt heat creeping up his neck, swallowing hard. "For what?"

"For all of your firsts," Frankie replied warmly, "and all the other ones you're gonna have in the future. Goodnight, Obe!"

"Goodnight, Frankie," Snod replied, offering a little smile as he shut the door. He stripped off his clothes, quickly handling the sinful erection that was plaguing him before getting ready for bed.

After counting out the cash, he carefully stacked it in his bedside table next to his scapular and phone. He seriously thought about smashing the phone. He could stick it in the oven or throw it out the window.

But he couldn't do it. That damn electronic device was a stone around his neck, a terrible obligation weighing his spirit down to the floor. He had to complete his mission. He had to find out the name of Frankie's Maker.

His boyfriend's Maker.

Snod kneeled down beside the bed, clasping his hands together as he closed his eyes. He couldn't keep doing this. All of this sweet joy was a foul sin that he would have to pay for eventually, no matter how much he wanted to keep it.

"O'Lord, my God. I am but your humble servant," he prayed, his voice barely above a whisper. "Please… guide me. I would like nothing more than to one day enjoy the splendor of Your kingdom and sit by Your side, but I… I fear I am lost.

"Everything I feel is… wrong. I know that it is wrong. But I've never been so happy. I've never… I've never felt this way about anyone. We were always taught that vampires were unholy and tainted, but I can find no such fault in Frankie.

"He is one of the most kind and most gentle people I have ever met. He has welcomed me into his home, his bed. I can never repay the generosity that he has shown me, and the things I want now… I want to be with him.

"I don't understand. Please lift me up, grant me strength. These selfish desires are consuming me, they're eating at my soul… I don't know what to do. Please. Help me make the right decision. Tell me what to do."

Snod sadly crawled into bed, hugging his pillows close and wishing they were Frankie. "How can this be wrong," he whispered to himself. "How can… how can something that feels so wonderful, so pure… be a sin?"

CHAPTER TWELVE

The rest of the week did not bring any answers to Snod's prayers. If anything, it only confused him more. When he woke up every day, Frankie would already be gone to work. Snod would tidy up around the apartment and spend his afternoons alone, eating and watching television.

By the time Frankie came home, he would have to whisk Snod away to his job at Cheap Trills. Their time together had diminished greatly, and Snod hated every second that they were apart. He tried to tell himself that it was better this way.

The distance was good.

Except that it wasn't.

It was miserable.

While he certainly mourned the more physical aspect of their relationship, it was so much more than that now. He missed simply being with Frankie, talking and laughing with him.

He wanted to snuggle with Frankie on the couch and hold him close while breathing in the scent of his shampoo. He wanted to watch Disney movies together and show him how many of the songs he now knew by heart. He longed to fall asleep in his arms and feel the touch of his cool skin.

Snod tried several times to rationalize what clearly had to be some kind of insanity. The blood bond should have been wearing off by now, and yet the affection he felt for Frankie was only continuing to grow. It made him ache in a way that made him want to laugh and weep all at once, and he did his best to ignore it and focus on his new mission:

Breaking into the Benjamin Franklin Museum in Philadelphia.

Rees had been letting Snod borrow his laptop to do the necessary research, and it didn't take him very long to formulate a plan. Concentrating on the upcoming heist helped distract him from his conflicted feelings, and he was actually looking forward to it.

The big day finally came, and Snod couldn't hide his bubbling excitement when Frankie strolled through the door. He didn't even say a word before he pulled him into a deep kiss, smiling brightly.

Frankie mumbled in surprise at the intense affection, but held Snod close, kissing him back. It was easy to get lost in Frankie's lips and feel that familiar heat prickling between them.

Frankie pulled away before they got carried away any further, his eyes fluttering as he laughed, "Mmm, wow, someone is in a good mood!" He grinned slyly, teasing, "What are you up to?"

"Nothing," Snod replied innocently. "I am very happy to see you, and I'm looking forward to working at the bar tonight."

"Uh huh," Frankie replied, clearly seeing through the lie, but not questioning it. "Hmmm, just give me a moment, and we'll go."

Snod held on for one more kiss, pressing against Frankie's lips until he earned himself one quick slip of tongue. "I did really miss you," he said softly when their kiss ended. "I do miss you."

"I don't have to work this weekend," Frankie said gently, "and I'm sure Rees will give you some time off. I miss you, too." He looked a little sad. "I promise we'll spend some more time together soon, okay?"

"Soon?" Snod implored, his hands wandering down to Frankie's hips. "More… intimate time?"

"Very soon," Frankie assured him, prying away his fingers and sighing in frustration. "Trust me, you're not the only one who misses the, ahem, intimate time."

Snod kept his hands by his sides and resisted the urge to let them wander. It did give him some comfort to know he wasn't the only one left wanting. He let Frankie leave to get changed, allowing his thoughts to resume their focus on the plan for tonight.

He wondered how surprised Frankie would be to see the desk, a physical piece left over from his actual human life. Maybe he'd actually be willing to discuss the past and finally tell Snod that name he needed so much.

After all, that's why he was doing this, Snod told himself as they drove over to the bar. It was to get closer to Frankie for the sake of the Order, not because his stomach fluttered with the possibility of making Frankie smile.

Kissing Frankie goodbye was bittersweet; the affection felt like a lie on his lips as he headed into Cheap Trills. Mandy directed him into the back to find Rees, and Snod had to blink several times to fully accept what he was seeing.

Rees was wearing black pants, black heels, and a brilliant purple turtleneck sweater dress that was several sizes too large for his slim body. He had on a black beanie, black hoop earrings, and sunglasses despite the early evening hour, scoffing, "What? Isn't this how you're supposed to dress for criminal activities?"

"Your sweater is purple," Snod noted.

"I didn't have anything black that was clean," Rees protested. "This is fine."

"It's *bright* purple."

"Fuck off."

"You look like that little purple creature from the fast food restaurant…"

"You look like somebody whose teeth are about to be on the fucking floor."

"Are we ready?" Snod griped.

"Yes, sweet thing. We are ready. Come on." Rees strolled to the back of the bar and led Snod out through the rear exit. "I got everything we need in the van."

Stopping short, Snod was left gawking at a worn-down ice cream truck. In spite of the rust, the colors were still obnoxiously bright and tacky. There was a large clown head on top, its cracked face leering cheerfully down at them. It was ancient and it didn't look as if it had run in decades.

"No," Snod said immediately. "This is not going to work."

"You said a van, I got a van!"

"I said an inconspicuous van. Do you understand what the word 'inconspicuous' means?" Snod hissed.

"Do you understand what 'kiss my fabulous ass, this was free' means?"

"This is insane."

"It's the only thing I could get on such short notice that the stupid fucking desk would fit in," Rees growled angrily. "Next time, I'll just call 1-800-Inconspicuous-Vans-R-Us and rent something more to your taste, okay?"

"Can't you call them now?" Snod demanded urgently. He paused, searching Rees' flat expression. "Wait. Is this a real rental agency you're referring to or are you—"

"Sarcastic! I'm being fucking sarcastic!"

"You're being an asshole," Snod groaned in frustration, following Rees to the horrid ice cream truck defeatedly. He hopped in the passenger seat, reaching for a seatbelt and finding none.

This just kept getting better and better.

Rees climbed up behind the wheel with a dramatic huff, taking off his sunglasses. He snorted at Snod's disgusted expression and cranked the truck up.

Immediately, a loud and blasting musical jingle began to play over the speakers.

Snod had to cover his ears, gritting his teeth as Rees fumbled around the dashboard to turn the music off.

"Sorry, the guy who hooked us up with this warned me sometimes it does that," Rees chuckled sheepishly.

"Are you actually taking this mission seriously?" Snod demanded sharply. "This is important. Very important. If we fuck up, we are both very likely going to jail."

"I am taking this very fucking seriously, assface," Rees shot back as he began pull the truck out into the street, pointing down to a hot pink duffel bag in between their seats. "Look! I packed a heist bag and everything."

Snod gave Rees an unimpressed glare, reaching down to examine the contents of the bag: rope, duct tape, a bag of trail mix, and two neon pink Hello Kitty walkie-talkies. He held up one of the walkie-talkies, quirking his brow as he drawled, "Really?"

"We have to be able to communicate," Rees argued.

"And the trail mix?"

"My sugar could drop. It's a long drive. I need snacks."

Snod stared out the window helplessly and let his head drop back against the seat. He was definitely going to prison tonight.

"Relax," Rees soothed, guiding the truck out toward the highway. "Everything is going to be fine, sweet thing. Remember, we're doing this for Frankie."

"You never did finish telling me how you met him. You said he saved your life?"

"Yeah," Rees replied with a fond smile. "I first met Frankie when I opened up the bar back in '85. It was all shiny and new then, packed like crazy all the time. And I remember meeting this guy. Came in a few times a week, sang like a damn angel. Called himself Harold. Regular for a few years, then poof. He vanishes.

"About ten years later, he shows up again. Maybe 1997, I think. Same guy, same voice, hasn't changed a bit. I knew it was him. He kept trying to tell me that I was mistaken. Says his name is Lance now, but hmph, I never could forget how that little darling sang.

"Sticks around for a while, disappears again, pops back up after another decade has gone by. And he goes again with this bullshit, trying to tell me we never met before."

"He kept coming back to the same bar," Snod said softly.

"And they say vampires are supposed to be clever, right?" Rees laughed. "I think by the third time he came back it was maybe, eh, 2013. Somewhere in there. It's been almost thirty years now, introduces himself this time as Frankie. I had gotten old and gray, and Frankie hadn't aged a bit.

"He still won't admit that it's been him all of this time, so I play dumb and carry on like it's nothing. My wife had just left me and I guess I wanted a friend. Frankie didn't care that I was wearing dresses and I think he wanted a friend, too. Figured that's why he finally told me his real name. So, we get to talking about all kinds of things. Fashion, history, books. He's at the bar almost every day.

"And then one fuckin' night, some bitch ass punks came in with a gun and itchy fingers."

Snod's jaw tensed. "They were going to rob you."

"They were gonna kill me and then rob me," Rees corrected. "Easier to take what you want from a corpse. I tried to get Frankie to leave, but he wouldn't budge. He jumped right at the gun, and I saw him get shot. Saw him take the full clip. And he was fine. Fucking fine."

"I imagine you had some questions after that."

"You bet your damn ass I did!" Rees exclaimed. "Cops came and arrested the guys. They were all strung out on God knows what. Cops didn't listen to their screaming about some freak being bulletproof, thank God. They finally left, and I had to help Frankie pull all those slugs out of him. I watched the holes close right up. That's when he finally told me."

"How did you react?" Snod asked curiously.

"How the fuck do you think?" Rees cackled. "I freaked

the fuck out. But Frankie was my friend; he'd just saved my life. We got through it."

"How could you rectify being friends with a monster?"

"Easy now, sweet thing," Rees warned. "Frankie is not a monster. Let's get that cleared up right the fuck now. It wasn't what he was that I had beef with. It was him lying about it. Lies are poison."

Snod's stomach clenched.

"Like I told you before, Frankie is special," Rees continued on. "We got through the shit, we got really close. He told me all about the Order, the ancient vampires still running around—"

"Did he tell you how he was turned?" Snod asked quickly, suddenly sensing an opportunity.

Rees quirked his brows at the interruption, but replied, "Yeah. He told me all about it. I know exactly what happened. That bastard Maker of his is one sick motherfucker."

Practically on the edge of his seat, Snod tried to remain casual as he pressed, "Do you know his Maker's name?"

"Yeah," Rees snorted, his brow wrinkling. "Gascard or something. It's French, I think. Uh, let's see…"

Snod waited, tempted to reach over and shake the answer out of him.

"Fuck, I can't remember," Rees groaned, waving his hand flippantly. "Look, if you wanna know about that shit, you need to ask Frankie. It's not my story to tell."

"But you're absolutely sure that you don't remember the man's name?" Snod hated how urgent he sounded.

"Why do you want to know so badly?" Rees snapped back, suspicious.

"Frankie will not tell me," Snod replied defensively. "He will not tell me anything about how he became a vampire."

"If he ever tells you, you'll understand why he's not real keen on sharing it," Rees said quietly. "It's not a nice story. I may not remember the name, but I remember what he did."

Snod sat back in his seat, sullen. To be so close to obtaining that vital piece of information and to be denied because of an elderly memory was frustrating. He did wonder what had happened to Frankie that made him hate his Maker so much. It was easy enough to imagine the man as a monster; he was a vampire, after all.

They drove in silence after that, Snod finding himself hating this particular vampire more than any other. Not only for the crime of being an unholy beast, but knowing that he had hurt Frankie conjured up an intense rage he wasn't sure what to make of.

"Almost there," Rees said, slowly pulling the ice cream truck through the bustling city streets of Philadelphia.

"Remember," Snod said, his focus now on the mission at hand, "pull around back. Keep the engine running. It should take me approximately six minutes to disable the alarm, four more to get the desk out of the—"

"Blah, blah, blah," Rees sighed, thrusting one of the Hello Kitty walkie-talkies into Snod's hand. "Just give me a buzz when you're ready. I'll be waiting to hold open the door and help you load up."

"You can't even lift the chairs at the bar," Snod pointed out. "How are you going to help me load a piece of furniture?"

"Moral support, darling."

Feeling a headache coming on, Snod held back the urge to scream. He watched through the windshield as they crept up toward the back of the museum. They had to be fast. He took a deep breath, running the plan over in his head one more time. He looked at Rees, asking, "Are you ready?"

"Ready," Rees replied, giving a little mock salute.

Snod snorted, tucking the walkie-talkie in his pocket and grabbing his tools. He slipped out of the truck like a ghost, sliding through the shadows to the back door. He had a mask, pulling it over his face well before he was in range of the security cameras' view.

He popped the panel off of the alarm and got to work.

A snip here, a twist there, and after a few minutes he heard a happy beep as the alarm was disabled. He hurried into the museum, tracking his movements in his head by the map he'd found online and memorized.

Snod knew exactly which exhibit room to go to. Thanks to Rees, he also had a vague description of the desk. This was going to be a simple snatch and grab. The alarms for the doors were off, there were no guards, and the only thing keeping him from the desk would be a length of velvet rope.

He strolled right into the exhibit, confident and smug.

Despite the stumbling start, this heist was actually going very well. Once they were back home, Snod would call Frankie to run an errand for him to lure him away from the apartment. Something simple, a quick trip down to the store, just long enough for them to sneak the desk inside while he was gone so it could be a proper surprise. It was going to be great.

Snod stopped short as he walked up to the rope, staring dumbly at the furniture in front of him as all the warm and fuzzy feelings faded immediately.

There were two desks.

Not one, *two*.

Shit.

They were almost identical, both crafted from weathered dark wood. They both had two drawers with brass hardware and even the damn chairs that accompanied them looked practically the same. Neither were overly large pieces of furniture, either would be small enough for Snod to easily carry out on his own. He actually considered dragging both of them out to the truck, but he didn't think it would all fit.

He could only take one, but which one was Frankie's?

Snod quickly grabbed the walkie-talkie and beeped in. "Rees. It's Snod. We have a problem."

"What kind of problem?" Rees' voice crackled back.

"There are two desks."

"What the fuck do you mean there are two?"

"More than one. Less than three. There are two fucking

desks."

"Well, huh, isn't that a kick in the sack."

"What the fuck, Rees?" Snod hissed furiously. "Which one is it? They look the fucking same."

Silence.

"Rees? What the fuck!" Snod kept frantically beeping the walkie-talkie, wanting nothing more than to smash Hello Kitty's cute little face into the floor. The plastic beast seemed to be mocking him. He waited for several more minutes, but there was still no reply.

Snod quickly pulled the rope out of his way, knowing he had to make a decision. Police could be patrolling the area, and they would definitely spot the obscenely suspicious ice cream truck outside.

The chair that matched the smaller desk on the left was upholstered in red cloth. It wasn't as fancy as the other one, simpler and sleeker. He decided to go for that one. Red did seem to be Frankie's color, and his gut told him that this was the one. He heaved the chair up over his shoulder and began preparing to start dragging the desk behind him.

He promptly bumped into some sort of purple shadowy monster, yelping in surprise and dropping the chair. He swung to strike whatever it was in front of him, freezing when he heard Rees' voice shouting, "Slow your fuckin' roll, fuck! It's me!"

"What the hell are you doing!" Snod snarled, wishing he could strangle the infuriating little man.

"Batteries died in the walkie-talkie!" Rees explained.

"You brought equipment out on a mission without checking it first?"

"I did so fuckin' check it!" Rees started coughing. "It went beep beep, I thought it was fine! Quit your bitching!"

Snod could feel a blood vessel distending in his forehead as he growled low, "You're supposed to be waiting for me outside!"

"I had to make sure you were grabbing the right fuckin' desk!" Rees was coughing harder, wheezing, "You're a fucking idiot!"

"I picked the one with the red chair! It's the right one!"

"Well, you're fuckin' wrong," Rees argued, desperately clearing his throat. He took a deep breath, grunting, "It's the other one."

"How do you know?"

"Because," Rees snorted smugly, marching over to examine the desk Snod was going to leave behind, "Frankie told me he had carved his initials in one of the drawers." He opened both drawers with a dramatic flourish, pausing before saying quietly, "Huh."

"What?"

"Fuck, just… Look in those ones!" Rees sighed exasperatedly.

Snod quickly popped open the drawers, smirking triumphantly when he saw a faint FBT scrawled within. He didn't have time to gloat that he had chosen correctly, dragging the chair back over his shoulder and hauling the desk quickly toward the exit.

Rees strolled quickly, managing to move ahead so he could hold open the door for Snod to come through with the furniture.

Even with the adrenaline pumping through him, Snod's back and shoulders were starting to tire. He passed the chair off to Rees, who cursed and complained but managed to get it into the back of the truck with hopefully minimal damage.

When Snod tried to pull the desk through, it wouldn't budge. It was too wide, perhaps only by an inch, to make it through the doorway. "For the love of all that is fucking holy!" Snod hissed, his eyes gazing skyward for any assistance that the divine might be willing to offer him at that moment.

His prayers were answered in the form of shattering glass, whipping his head to the side to see Rees taking his shoe to one of the windows by the door. The windows extended from floor to ceiling and were definitely wide enough to move the desk through unscathed.

Unfortunately, the breaking of the glass set off a loud and irritating alarm, blaring away while Snod cursed furiously.

"I thought you turned off the fucking alarm!" Rees shouted over the noise.

"I turned it off for the doors! Not for the windows! Those are hooked into the display cases, and they're on a separate circuit!"

"Well, why didn't you turn those off? Some big robbery expert, huh!"

"Shut up and move!" Snod quickly picked up the desk and hurried through the broken window, kicking glass out of his way. He loaded the desk into the back of the truck, scrambling to jump into the passenger seat. "Fucking drive!"

Rees crawled into the driver's seat, cranking the truck up. As if their night couldn't be any more horrible, the annoying happy music began to play over the speakers again. Rees kept slapping at buttons on the dashboard, frantic as he shouted, "Fuck, fuck, fuck! I can't turn it off!"

"Just fucking go!" Snod hollered desperately, certain that the police had to be on their way and would be arriving any second. "Why did you turn the damn van off? I told you to keep it running—"

"I didn't want anyone snatching it while we were inside!"

"No one in their right mind would steal this wretched abomination! Now for the love of God, *fucking drive*!"

"Fuck off!" Rees punched the gas and off they went, Snod nearly flying into the floorboards since he had no seatbelt to hold him in place. They scooted through the streets of downtown Philadelphia, that annoying musical tune wrecking any possibility of stealth.

Frantically pounding at every button on the dash, Snod sighed in relief when the music finally stopped. He slumped against the seat, quickly checking their mirrors and all around them. He didn't hear any sirens nor did he see any flashing lights.

Even as they left the city, no one seemed to be in pursuit of them.

Rees broke the tense silence, laughing triumphantly as he cheered, "Holy fuck, that was kind of fun! Anything else you wanna steal, darling?"

"Not with you," Snod replied, but soon he was laughing too. "That was the most unprofessional, disastrous robbery I have ever been a part of."

"Yeah, but it was fucking fun!" Rees exclaimed, grinning wide. "Oof, gimme my trail mix. I can feel my sugar getting low. I need something to eat."

Snod obediently passed the snack over, unable to resist an affectionate smile. Despite the many things that went wrong, he had to count tonight as a success.

They had the desk, they hadn't been arrested, and soon enough they would be back with their prize to give to Frankie.

The rest of the drive was light and happy, Snod surprised by how much he actually enjoyed chatting with Rees. Despite the rough edges, he was kind, and it was obvious how much he cared about Frankie.

When they were only a few blocks away, Snod used Rees' phone to call Frankie and request a bottle of rum from the liquor store. Frankie was a little suspicious, but Snod explained it was a brand Rees had recommended to him that they didn't carry at the bar. Despite his obvious reservations, Frankie agreed.

Once they saw Frankie's car pull away, Snod and Rees jumped into action. Snod carried the desk and chair in the same fashion as he had before at the museum, Rees helping him through the doorways and into the elevator.

"You got a key?" Rees asked when they got to Frankie's apartment door.

"Don't need one," Snod said, easily picking the lock.

"Dirty ol' crook," Rees laughed as he followed Snod inside.

They arranged the desk by Frankie's massive

bookshelves, putting the chair off to the side as if it was back on display. Knowing Frankie would be home at any moment, Snod was beyond excited and he couldn't wait to see his reaction.

"You lovebirds have a good night," Rees said, starting to take his leave. "Seriously, you ever wanna go out on another caper, you let me know. I'll make sure I wear black."

"You're not staying?" Snod was surprised that Rees didn't want to share in the glory of their successful mission.

"This should be just between you two. It's special. Besides, I don't wanna be around when he decides how he's gonna thank you, you know what I'm saying?" Rees waggled his brows suggestively. "Might get sticky up in here."

"You disapprove of homosexuality?" Snod questioned, not understanding Rees' intent and frowning deeply.

"No, dumbass," Rees scolded lightly. "A gift like this is a real panty dropper, all right? I'm leaving you guys alone to be as homosexual as you want."

"So, you do think it's a sin?" Snod pushed.

"Darling, look at me," Rees drawled. "I'm a man in a dress. Passing judgment is not my thing. People should be able to live the way they want as long as they're not being shitheads. Love is love, all that."

Snod was not convinced, glancing down at the floor as his gut flooded with shame. "It's not that simple. The Order taught me that what I want, that wanting Frankie, is wrong."

"Look, darling," Rees said, his tone surprisingly gentle to soothe Snod's obvious distress. "I know you're still kinda fucked up from the Order and all their crazy bullshit. They have a very twisted way of interpreting shit. A lot of people do, picking and choosing what parts they want to follow and ignoring the rest."

"How do you know what to believe in then?" Snod asked in earnest, hating how desperately lost he was. "How do you know what's right?"

"Follow your heart," Rees replied immediately. "Pay attention to the good stuff. There's a whole lot more shit in religion about loving someone than there is about exactly who it is you should love." He cleared his throat, reciting slowly, "Two are better than one because they have a good return for their labor. If either of them falls down, one can help the other up…"

"But pity anyone who falls and has no one to help them up," Snod continued seamlessly. "Also, if two lie down together, they will keep warm."

"But how can one keep warm alone?" Rees concluded with a smirk. "Just think about it, darling. There's nothing in there about whose business is what; it's just about love. You have the chance to have something really beautiful with Frankie. You could keep each other warm."

Snod was surprised to feel his cheeks flushing, saying quietly, "Thank you, Rees."

"Don't worry about it," Rees said with a quick wave of his hand. "Just don't fuck this up because your head isn't right yet. You'll get there."

"Or concrete nubs are in my future?" Snod asked, unable to resist a smug smile.

"Uh huh," Rees replied, clicking his tongue. "Bet your sweet ass there are. Hmmph. You have a good night, darling. I'll see you around."

"Goodnight, Rees. And thank you."

"Don't mention it," Rees chucked. "Seriously, don't. I have a reputation to uphold."

"Wouldn't dare," Snod said, smiling as the door closed. He looked back to the desk, already imagining Frankie sitting there with that brilliant smile lighting up his face. He thought about everything Rees had said, specifically the advice to follow his heart.

Even though the road might lead to certain damnation and hellfire, he already knew where the path of following his heart's desires would take him.

To Frankie Temple, without question.

CHAPTER THIRTEEN

Only a few minutes passed between Rees' departure and Snod hearing Frankie's key turning in the lock. He attempted to act casual, standing very purposely in front of the desk. He grinned with great satisfaction when Frankie was obviously startled to see him home, his whole body flickering visibly for a moment.

Snod couldn't help but feel an inkling of pride. It wasn't easy to surprise a vampire, after all. "Hello," he purred, aiming for sultry but he was far too excited to keep his voice low enough to maintain a seductive tone. "How was your day?"

"Fine," Frankie replied carefully. "What are you doing home? Did something happen at the bar?"

"No, not at the bar," Snod said slowly. "Did you get the rum?"

Frankie held up a brown paper bag.

"Good. I think you might want to bring out your special reserve."

Frankie began to walk toward him, a twinkle in his eye as he teased, "Oh? Are we celebrating something?"

"Yes," Snod said, slowly stepping aside to show the desk behind him.

Frankie froze on the spot.

Snod had almost forgotten how perfectly still vampires could hold themselves, unflinching like stone. He couldn't read Frankie's expression, a tangle of worry knotting up in his stomach.

Had he been wrong about the gift?

Frankie began to approach, every motion slow and measured, graceful and fluid as if he were moving underwater. His delicate fingers reached out to stroke the back of the chair, gasping. He recoiled as if he had been burned, turning to stare at Snod in bewilderment, asking quietly, "How…?"

"I broke into the Benjamin Franklin Museum and stole it," Snod replied honestly with a cheeky little smile.

"You broke into the *what*?" Frankie suddenly bellowed, his rage erupting like a volcano. "What the fuck were you thinking, Obe?"

Even though the bond had weakened between them, it didn't take the exchange of supernatural blood to know Frankie was pissed.

Snod gritted his teeth, hating how the sting of disappointment and shame stabbed at him. This was not the reaction he had been hoping for. He curled his hands into tight fists, tense, replying quickly, "I wanted to get you something. Something special."

"So you risked imprisonment?" Frankie snapped furiously, the volume of his voice rising louder as he ranted on. "Obe, you're trying to start a new life! A new beginning! Your new identity is going to come through any day now! Why the hell would you do this? After everything I've done for you—"

"It's because of everything you've done for me!" Snod found himself yelling back passionately, glaring at Frankie. "You've clothed me, fed me, taken care of me! And I have nothing to give you, nothing that you will take! You've refused me, again and again—"

"I've told you! Because of the blood!" Frankie tried to

cut him off, but Snod wasn't done.

"Fuck the blood!" Snod raged on, raw and hurting. "I wanted to do this for you! Even in spite of the gaping chasm you've created between us, I wanted to do something to show my appreciation!"

"Gaping chasm?" Frankie scoffed, baring his fangs. "Being a little dramatic, don't you think?"

"You won't have me in your bed! You barely stay in my company! All of the things we've shared together and yet we pass each other now like strangers! I wanted to prove myself to you! Prove that my intentions were sincere, and that this has nothing to do with the blood!" His shoulders sagged in defeat, and his anger was blanched by an overwhelming sense of sadness. He didn't know if it was his or Frankie's. "I meant it… when I said that I missed you."

Frankie's expression was impossible to decipher, again reaching out for the desk as if to make sure it was really there. He opened the drawer, tracing the spot where he had carved his initials. He sighed softly, silence spreading between them for several agonizing minutes before he finally said, "And I miss you."

Pressing closer, Snod's tone was strained as he asked, "Then why are you still pushing me away?"

"Because I don't trust you anymore," Frankie replied without hesitation. "I don't trust that everything you're feeling is purely your own. It could still be my influence. You've never even had a boyfriend before, you'd never done… I've been your first for everything."

"And I want you to be," Snod said insistently. "You're the only one I want."

"How can you be so sure?" Frankie demanded, something curling up his lip. Anger, disappointment, an emotion Snod couldn't place.

"I'm following my heart," Snod said, left timid by such a vulnerable answer.

Frankie's eyes cut into him, trying to seek out any evidence of deceit. He seemed torn, but allowed himself to reach out for Snod's hand. "Thank you," he said at last. "For the desk. It's a very thoughtful gift. A very illegal, very compulsive gift."

"It was not compulsive," Snod protested stubbornly. "I had a very concise and detailed plan."

"Oh?" Frankie's face lit up, making a small sound of amusement. "A detailed plan that involved an ancient and absolutely hideous ice cream truck?"

"You saw us?"

"How could I not?" Frankie chuckled. "I am a vampire, remember? Supernatural senses and all of that."

"That was not part of the plan."

"Wait a second," Frankie said, backpedaling a moment as he sharply accused, "What did you mean by 'us'? Who went with you?"

"Rees came with me."

Frankie squeezed Snod's hand almost as if he wanted to break it, sighing haggardly, "You're both freakin' idiots."

"He wanted to help," Snod defended with a small pout.

Frankie looked back at the desk, shaking his head with a short laugh, "Oh! I'm sure he did. He remembers how angry I was when I came so close to getting this back..."

"And lost it at the auction," Snod said quietly. "He told me. He wanted to do something to thank you. For saving his life."

"Mmmm, he told you that tired old story, did he?" Frankie asked fondly.

"Yes," Snod answered with a light smile. "He said you would like the desk, that it would be special because it was from when you were alive."

"It was a gift," Frankie explained slowly. "From Mr. Franklin."

"So you did work for him," Snod confirmed smugly, delighted that Frankie was finally opening up to him.

"I did," Frankie said with a little smirk, lightly tracing his thumb over Snod's knuckles. "I started off as a printer's apprentice, helped run one of his papers for a while, and he was so impressed with me that he took me on as his secretary. I worked for him for many years."

"And you went with him to France when he was an ambassador," Snod said, filling in the gaps now.

"Yes," Frankie said with a nod of his head. "That's when I lost the desk. Mr. Franklin gave it to me while we were still in America, I'll never forget. It was the finest thing I'd ever owned, and I remember weeping over it. He knew how much I loved it, and he insisted on taking it with us overseas."

"But you didn't you bring it back with you?"

"No."

"Why not?"

"Because France is where I met my Maker," Frankie said after a brief pause, his smile now one of grieving. "He was an acquaintance of Baron Friederich von Steuben, an officer that Mr. Franklin was trying to recruit to help General Washington. He… he was charming. Completely wooed me, absolutely swept me off my feet.

"I had no idea what he was until it was too late. Once he had turned me, I had to leave Mr. Franklin's employment. I had to leave everything behind. I never knew what happened to the desk until I saw it at the auction, and… well, here it is now."

Snod was tempted to push about Frankie's Maker. The opportunity was right there to interrogate him, right in front of him, but instead he said, "Yes, and now it's yours again."

"Thank you," Frankie murmured, squeezing Snod's hand and kissing him. "Really. I never thought I would see this again."

"You're welcome," Snod replied, his heart warming right up and all the tension melting away. "So does this mean we're going to celebrate?"

"Yes, this is definitely worth celebrating!" Frankie grinned and blinked away, retrieving the bottle of his special blood and Snod's rum. Another flash and he was in the kitchen, pouring them each a glass. "Also, maybe promise me no more illegally gained gifts?"

"I promise to try," Snod chuckled, raising his glass to Frankie's in a toast.

"Good enough."

One glass turned into two, and three, and Snod quickly lost count after that. They watched more Disney cartoons, drunkenly singing along together cuddled up on the couch. Snod was sure his heart was going to explode from being so full.

This was exactly the evening he'd wanted, and it was perfect.

"I don't have to work tomorrow," Frankie said as the credits of *Aladdin* were rolling, "but I am going over to the lab. Lorenzo has a prototype ready now, and we have a chance to run a few experiments."

Snod shifted his arm around Frankie's shoulders, drawing him in closer, asking, "For the robot cure?"

"Yes," Frankie laughed. He waited, adding carefully, "I wanted to know if you'd come with me."

"What for?"

"To help," Frankie explained. "Even though you're not a vampire, you must carry some form of the disease. Perhaps it's dormant or something. I don't know. We've never been able to work with blood from someone bonded before, only from other vampires. I'd like to just run a few tests if you'd be willing."

"I don't mind," Snod said, his fingers absently trailing along Frankie's bicep. "I want to help."

"Thank you," Frankie said with a warm and happy smile, leaning into Snod's touch.

"You didn't come to karaoke this week," Snod suddenly realized, frowning. "Why?"

"I didn't want to distract you," Frankie teased. "Seriously though, I was busy helping Lorenzo finish up the antibiotic formula for prototype. That's part of what we're going to do tomorrow. Despite your über stalky stalk perception, I really don't always go every Thursday. I'll come next week."

"And distract me?" Snod asked hopefully.

"Probably," Frankie chuckled, leaning in close to Snod and hugging his side. The movie was over, but neither one of them had made any effort to move. "Mmm. We need to go to bed."

"I'm perfectly content right here," Snod argued. This was the most physical contact they'd had all week. He wasn't ready for it to end.

"You actually need to sleep if you're coming with me to the lab," Frankie scolded.

Snod pouted, but he had no choice except to let Frankie go as he pulled away. He missed his touch immediately, but got up to get ready for bed. He waited for Frankie to reach for him first, firmly holding his waist and pulling him in as they kissed.

Frankie wove his fingers over Snod's scalp, humming happily and swaying a little from drinking so much. He was all smiles as he said, "Tonight was amazing. And I really do love the desk. Thank you."

"Anytime."

"Does this mean we're properly courting now?" Frankie chuckled. "We've exchanged gifts!"

"Yes," Snod laughed heartily, "I suppose it does."

"I don't think the council will approve our union!" Frankie continued to snicker.

"Fuck 'em," Snod snapped, the words burning him more than he wanted to admit. He grabbed Frankie tightly and kissed him passionately. He couldn't resist, maddening thoughts of taking Frankie to his bed, any bed, and being inside of him taking over.

He didn't think it was the blood. This was truly his own emotion, his own desire, and all he wanted was Frankie.

Frankie was kissing him back greedily, nails dragging over his neck and shoulders. The little sounds he was making, the deep groans and growls, were going right to Snod's cock.

"Frankie," Snod murmured, trying to regain his senses. He knew Frankie would continue to blame the blood if he didn't stop, swallowing back a frustrated moan and saying, "It's… it's time to say goodnight."

Frankie's lips were pink from kissing, his eyes glazed over with a beautiful hungry luster. It cleared away after a moment, nodding, "Yes, it is." He kissed him again, but chastely now. "Goodnight, Obe. Thank you."

"Goodnight," Snod sighed quietly, remaining still as Frankie disentangled himself from their tender embrace. He watched him vanish off into his bedroom, and he stumbled toward his own bed to flop against the cool sheets.

The smooth fabric reminded him briefly of Frankie's cold touch, rubbing his cheek into the feeling, left wanting when it faded all too quickly. He closed his eyes, and he drifted off into a dreamless sleep.

Snod woke up suddenly, certain that it was his brain telling him it was four o'clock. He would have gone right back to sleep, but he heard an odd whirring noise. It was quiet, but still audible through the wall that separated his bedroom from Frankie's. He didn't move, trying to block it out.

He was very aware that he was aroused, not surprised when he felt a fresh wave of lust hit him. He had been frustrated all week long, again trying to ignore it. It got stronger and heavier, making him pant and instantly hard.

Frankie.

He had to be feeling this from Frankie.

Snod palmed his cock, tempted to touch himself. He slid a hand down the front of his pants, gasping to find his underwear damp. Fuck. He couldn't figure out what the buzzing sound was, listening more keenly, and then he heard Frankie moan.

It was muffled, but definitely a moan.

Snod stared at the wall, licking his lips.

What was Frankie doing?

He realized he was still a little tipsy when he stood up,

and it was suddenly too warm in there. He didn't understand why he felt so hot. He took off his shirt and pants, heading to Frankie's bedroom in nothing but his underwear and socks. He pressed close to the door, listening carefully.

The odd sound was still going, and he heard Frankie moan again. This time sounded almost painful, and Snod wasn't even thinking when he quickly opened the door, demanding, "Frankie, are you okay? What's—"

"Obe!" Frankie cried out in protest, shrill and angry.

All Snod could do was stare.

Light from the hallway spilled onto the bed, revealing Frankie naked on his back, some sort of phallic object wedged up between his legs. There was a cord and a small remote attached, and when Snod's eyes followed the cord back up again, he realized that the object was actually inside of Frankie. His cock was hard, twitching against his stomach and leaking beautifully.

Frankie's pale body was flushed in a way Obe had rarely seen, knowing he had to have fed to achieve such a lovely color. He looked debauched and irresistible, but Snod hesitated to intrude any further than he already had.

He quickly deduced the buzzing noise he'd heard was from the object Frankie was thrusting into himself, blushing down to his bones as he stammered, "I woke up, I'm sorry… I didn't know… what you were doing. I thought… you might be hurt…"

"I'm trying… I'm…" Frankie's head dropped against the pillows, and he growled defeatedly. "Trying to get off."

Snod swallowed thickly, noting the awkward angle at which Frankie had to hold the object to keep it inside of him and control the remote. "I could assist you," he said, trying not to frame the statement as a question, adding more confidently, "If you want me to."

"God, yes."

Snod immediately joined Frankie in bed, stretching out beside him and their mouths meeting in a hungry kiss. Frankie was guiding his hand down to the thing, the toy, inside of him, but Snod didn't know what to do.

"Fuck me with it," Frankie gasped, his eyes bright and practically glowing in the dark. "Just move it, I need… I need it so much. Come on, Obe. Now!"

Snod obeyed, grabbing the base of the toy and pressing it in deep until Frankie was moaning. It felt weird, the vibrations making his fingers numb, but he kept going. He pulled it out, pressed it back in, slowly, again and again. He wished it was his own cock bringing Frankie this pleasure, but he enjoyed the act regardless.

Now that Snod had taken over, Frankie swept his fingers over his cock and jerked himself off frantically while he cranked up the power on the remote.

The whirring sounded nearly as feverish as Frankie did, buzzing away as he twitched and groaned. Snod did his best to keep moving and thrusting the toy inside of him. He couldn't take his gaze off of Frankie, watching his big green eyes flutter shut as he moaned, "Coming, ohhhh, fuck, I'm coming!"

Snod watched Frankie's cock splashing all over his stomach in quick bursts, oozing one last pulse before he was already ordering, "Don't stop! Go, keep going! Go, please!"

Fucking Frankie harder, Snod was amazed as his hips began to tremble again. A second load joined the first, Frankie's lean stomach glistening with an obscene amount of cum, instantly overstimulated when he was finished and moaning desperately, "Okay, okay, stop!"

Snod quickly complied, drawing the toy out with great care. His hand felt numb nearly down to the wrist from holding the pulsing object, flexing his fingers to regain feeling.

Frankie was shuddering and fumbling to turn off the device. He went limp against the mattress, exhausted, but he was smiling with a deep satisfaction.

Snod leaned in to kiss him, pressing his hand against Frankie's chest to feel the pumping of his heart. It was strong, beautiful, and he was certain it matched his own rapid pulse for a few fleeting moments. As it faded away, Snod was still hard and wanting relief, asking breathlessly, "Can I… May I release on you?"

"God, fuck, yes," Frankie nodded quickly, reaching down to touch him. "Here, let me. Let me do it."

Snod grunted as Frankie's fingers wrapped around his cock, hot and strong. The warmth was unexpected, pressing himself against Frankie's side and finding he was hot all over. The pressure inside of him was too much, gritting his teeth and groaning in short, stuttered grunts.

He didn't last but a few seconds before he came under such dedicated ministrations, watching his cum squirt across Frankie's stomach to join the rest. One pulse landed high up on his pale chest, glittering there in the low light like a jewel.

Snod kissed him deeply, his hand cradling the side of his face as their tongues briefly met. He was content, murmuring quietly, "Mmm… that was new."

"I was thinking about you," Frankie confessed. "While I was playing with myself… all I thought about was you."

Snod didn't even have an immediate response to that. Knowing Frankie had been doing that in his honor made him blush. He knew Frankie had done it before, but to bear witness and participate had been almost spiritual.

Snod smiled softly, replying, "I woke up… and I think, I think I could feel you. Wanting me."

Frankie grinned. "Well, I was thinking very, *very* hard… and I fed. Again. Couldn't help it."

"Is that why you're so warm?"

"Mmhm," Frankie hummed. "I pretty much drank everything in the house. Fresh or not, gorging on blood will do it. I don't usually eat this much…"

"Hungry?"

"Frustrated," Frankie admitted with a wry smirk.

"Ah."

"I don't want you to think you're the only one that wants this," Frankie said, kissing Snod's cheek. "I'm just…

concerned. I want this to be real."

"I know." Snod nodded, confessing sincerely, "So do I."

Frankie blinked out of his arms, cleaning them both up before the sticky mess dried any more than it already had. The toy disappeared as well. He slid back into bed, cuddling up against Snod's chest. He seemed to fit so perfectly there, curling up in the crook of his shoulder and draping his arm over his stomach.

"May I sleep in here tonight?" Snod asked hopefully. He didn't want to leave, not yet.

Frankie tugged the blankets up over them in response, burrowing in as close as he could. He closed his eyes, murmuring, "Just for a few hours. Then we're going to the lab. Tomorrow might be the day we find a cure."

"Maybe it will be." Snod smiled, feeling Frankie's body starting to slowly cool down. It was comforting, nuzzling his cheek into Frankie's hair. There was a tiny part of him that hoped they wouldn't ever find a cure. He wanted Frankie as he was now, perfect and powerful and totally beautiful.

He remembered the passage that Rees had quoted to him, about two people in love keeping one another warm. Perhaps being warm was overrated, he mused to himself. Keeping cool was just as good, if not better. He smirked at that funny little thought, sighing happily and slowly dozing back off to sleep.

CHAPTER FOURTEEN

When Snod woke up the next morning, he was alone. He could distantly hear Frankie off in the kitchen, no doubt making breakfast for him. He smiled, rolling over and stretching his legs. He reached for Frankie's pillow, hugging it tight and savoring the scent of him.

He hadn't slept this well all week, his heart aching at the thought of having to go without Frankie being in his arms again.

A distant thought of Athaliah reminded him that his time with Frankie was limited, regardless of whose bed he slept in.

Pulling himself up, Snod stared down at his feet as they met the floor. Maybe he and Frankie could go kidnap Athaliah, he thought crazily to himself. Then he wouldn't have a reason to ever go back to the Order.

He used the bathroom, washed his face, glancing at his reflection in the mirror. He looked at all of his scars, twisting around to glance at the ones on his back. There were dozens upon dozens, dark and twisted, a lifetime of lessons.

Lessons that might have been wrong.

When he looked at his reflection again, he realized how uncertain he was. He didn't even trust the man peering back at him, eyes full of doubt, lips drawn back in a grimace.

There was a time when he knew all vampires had to be cleansed from this earth. He knew that lying with a man was disgusting and wrong. He knew that everyone outside the Order were fools, blind and ignorant heathens.

So much that he used to know had become ash, crumbling away now with a quick puff of scrutinizing breath.

He wondered what else the Order could be wrong about, trembling as the entire foundation of his world was threatening to crack and fall out from beneath him. Wrong or not, his brother was still there. If the Order was wrong, that was all the more reason he couldn't leave him behind.

Snod sighed, pulling himself back together and heading out to the kitchen to find Frankie.

Frankie greeted him with a kiss and a plate of bacon and eggs. He watched Snod eat with a small smile, always surprisingly interested in the food he couldn't share.

"Do you miss it?" Snod asked curiously.

"What? Eating?" Frankie grinned. "Mm. Sometimes. There isn't much variety in blood, I'm afraid."

"No?"

"Some taste richer than others," Frankie confessed. "Some are bitter, almost acidic. The blood of animals is especially sour when compared to humans."

"What do I taste like?"

"Sweet," Frankie replied, tilting his head as if to hide a blush that never came. "Very sweet."

Snod was pleased with that answer, finishing up breakfast and getting ready to leave for the lab. Frankie was dressed in seconds as usual, sliding into Snod's room to help him.

Snod had never seen Frankie use his speed this much since the night they met. Frankie was excited, eager to get going, and his exuberance was positively infectious. Snod was absolutely charmed, holding Frankie's hand as they drove over to his work.

The Hazel Medical Research Facility was a large and modern complex, Frankie breezing right through security with his keycard and a smile. No one seemed to question Snod's presence. Staff was nonexistent once they were inside, hurrying down sterile hallways into a sophisticated laboratory.

Snod had never seen equipment like this, peering curiously at the odd machines and scowling when he saw Lorenzo's beaming face already waiting for them. Frankie embraced him, the two friends chattering away excitedly before Lorenzo finally turned his attention to Snod.

The pleasant expression faltered, recovering quickly as he said jovially, "Hey, Snod! How's the hand?"

"Peachy," Snod replied, flipping Lorenzo off with the hand he had stabbed.

"That's nice," Lorenzo sighed, rolling his eyes. "Very cool."

"Come on, guys," Frankie soothed. "Remember. We only have a few hours to work, let's do everything we can."

Lorenzo nodded, still obviously skeptical of Snod, but more focused on the experiments ahead of them. "Right, okay," he said, sliding on gloves and producing a rack of tubes filled with bright green liquid.

Frankie was practically vibrating with excitement when he saw them.

"Here we go!" Lorenzo said proudly. "Gentlemen and possibly reformed crazy person, may I present to you Devampy Doo-Dad 1.4! A nano bot serum packed full of delicious antibiotic goodness, ready to begin trials."

Whirling around the room like a tornado, Frankie presented Lorenzo with a Petri dish and a syringe of thick blood. Snod saw a small puncture fading away on Frankie's arm that hadn't been there moments before, realizing the blood was his own and he had drawn it that fast.

"Obe? May I have some of your blood to test?" Frankie asking politely, smiling at him.

"Of course." Snod obediently tilted his head to the side.

"N-not like that," Frankie stammered, eyes wide, reaching for his arm instead.

"Oh." Snod tried not to look disappointed, watching Frankie quickly draw a small tube of blood and placing a Band-Aid over the puncture site before he could fully draw a breath.

Snod found a seat out of the way, patiently watching the two scientists get to work.

Lorenzo accepted the tubes from Frankie and took a deep breath. He began by squirting a few drops of Frankie's blood into the dish and piping the serum alongside it. He eagerly slid it underneath a microscope, saying brightly, "Okay. Let's see some freakin' magic!"

Frankie hovered behind him, asking, "Is it working? Is the V responding to the protein antigen coating?"

"Yes! Bacterial receptors are responding, and the V is chowing down!" Lorenzo squealed excitedly. "It's working! It's freakin' working! It's..." His smile vanished in an instant, pulling back from the microscope with a mournful pout.

Frankie's brows furrowed up, taking his place and staring down to see what had upset Lorenzo so much. His joy was stolen away just as quickly, his shoulders slumping in such a vulnerable human way. "Crap."

"We'll try Obe's blood," Lorenzo said, trying to remain hopeful. "See what happens."

Frankie nodded and quickly put on gloves. He made up a new dish and piped a dose of the serum in himself, his eyes narrowed with intense concentration.

Lorenzo positioned the dish under the microscope, peering down and letting Frankie have a turn. They looked at each other, both seemingly confused and at a loss for words.

"Did it not work?" Snod asked, breaking the tense silence.

"It worked too well," Frankie replied quietly, his face completely smooth now.

"Explosively well," Lorenzo chimed in with a grimace.

"How explosive?" Snod quirked his eyebrow.

Lorenzo picked up the syringe of Frankie's blood and squirted its remaining contents into another Petri dish. He grabbed the serum and poured the whole thing in. The dish smoked and the glass cracked loudly as it shattered.

"Shit," Snod hissed.

"Highly explosive," Lorenzo sighed miserably.

"The cell wall ruptured," Frankie said sadly. "Violently. Much more so than we predicted."

"The cure won't work?" Snod questioned, still trying to understand.

"Not for me," Frankie said quietly, his eyes focused on the floor as he got lost in thought. He was completely still, a marble statue of contemplation.

"Okay," Lorenzo said, rubbing his temples as if to soothe away a headache. "Here's the deal. Frankie's blood is like, ninety-nine percent V. He still has some human red blood cells, but like, maybe five. Okay, exaggerating, but still not a lot, all right?

"If we give him the DD 1.4, all those V cells inside his body will rupture and not only will they compromise his entire vascular system, but Frankie won't have enough human blood left over to even, like, get his heart pumping. Not that it would matter, because all of his arteries and veins will be freakin' goo.

"But you, well, there's at least some hope. Your V level is only like, meh, two percent? Maybe? The rupturing would be super minimal, the infection would be cleansed, and you would be cured."

"But I'm not infected," Snod said slowly. "There's nothing to cure."

"The bond," Frankie said quietly. "It would break the bond between us. You still carry my blood inside you, my infection. It's what allows us to be connected."

"The V cells in your blood are dormant," Lorenzo interjected. "When you drink from Frankie, the V can't survive because of all the oxygen, you know, being a person with a pulse. They die, no vampifying, all that.

"However, there are a few very stubborn little buggers that are like in this super sleep mode that stick around. They're still in there, just chilling out. In theory, a few of them will always be with you."

"It's what allows the bond to exist almost indefinitely," Frankie added quietly. "For you, like we've discussed before, its strength would eventually fade with time, and you'd be able to ignore it. As a vampire, I would always be able to feel you to some degree."

"But this cure," Snod pressed. "It would eliminate it?"

"Yes," Lorenzo said, glancing back at the glowing green serum. "The DD 1.4 would. Aaaand maybe, possibly, probably give you a small heart attack."

Snod approached at once, saying, "Do it."

"What?" Lorenzo sputtered.

"Obe?" Frankie blinked in shock.

Snod was already offering out his arm, glancing at Frankie and saying firmly, "You question the purity of my intentions because of the blood we've shared. How better can I prove to you that what I feel is real?"

"Did you hear the part about a heart attack?" Frankie protested.

"I think this is a great plan!" Lorenzo said, entirely too cheerful.

"I need to know this is real," Snod insisted passionately. "Just like you do."

"What happened to being so sure?" Frankie demanded sharply, bordering on offended. "You're the one who has—"

"You said you don't trust me," Snod reminded him firmly. "Let me do this." He took Frankie's hand, pleading quietly, "For us."

Lorenzo made a small gagging sound, but his voice was soft as he asked Frankie, "What do you want to do, buddy?"

"I want..." Frankie peered at Snod, their fingers slowly

entangling. He leaned close, softly kissing Snod's cheek. "I want a fresh start. I want this."

"Then do it," Snod said earnestly.

Frankie nodded at Lorenzo, his eyes bright when he looked back at Snod. He kissed him tenderly, something hopeful and broken in his touch.

Snod didn't understand, but he could sense a deep anguish. As weak as their bond had become, he realized this had to be very strong emotion for him to feel it. Frankie was worried, but what about?

Snod knew this was for the best.

It was the only way to be sure.

For both of their sakes.

Lorenzo already had a syringe drawn up, saying less than confidently, "Okay, based on some rough calculations… uhm. This should be enough? Ish?"

"*Ish?*" Frankie scolded. "You're gambling my boyfriend potentially having a heart attack on 'ish'?"

"I know CPR!" Lorenzo whined as he stepped up to Snod, syringe in hand. "He'll be fine!"

Snod rolled up his shirt sleeve, his lip flinching slightly when Lorenzo stuck the needle in. He was certain that Lorenzo had done it harder than needed to be cruel, but didn't strangle him.

It took a lot of effort, but Frankie's reassuring smile gave him strength.

Snod waited.

He felt a slight burn in his chest, his heart fluttering hard. He was sweating and there was a strange heat washing over him that made him gasp.

Then nothing.

Frankie and Lorenzo were staring at him expectantly, perhaps waiting for a more adverse reaction to occur.

"Anything?" Lorenzo demanded. "Pain in your chest, tingling in your left arm?"

Snod shook his head and looked at Frankie. The thumping in his heart continued, still fluttering sweetly as ever. The burn was gone and he felt no other discomfort. Nothing had changed. "Wait," he said. "I don't think it did anything."

"Why?" Frankie asked, frowning.

"I still feel the same," Snod said quietly. "About you, I mean."

"Really?" Frankie asked, touching his chest. "No bond, no blood, and you really want to keep…" He glanced at Lorenzo, clearing his throat as he shyly said, "Eh, courting?"

"Yes," Snod insisted.

"We should take another blood sample to be sure," Lorenzo said awkwardly. "See if the V is really gone."

Another tube of blood revealed that in fact virtually last drop of V had been eradicated from Snod's system. He had to sit back down, overwhelmed by the implications. What he was feeling for Frankie right now was truly and entirely his own.

He didn't know if that made it better or worse, knowing what he still had to do.

Probably worse.

"This is amazing," Lorenzo gushed. "Like, really? You can't feel anything from him?"

"Like trying to hear a rock," Frankie confirmed with a sad smile.

"Okay, I know you're disappointed," Lorenzo said gently, tucking his hair back behind his ears, "but this is an incredible breakthrough! We know it will work! I mean, sure, right now it would blow you up, but hey! Progress!"

"I know," Frankie sighed. "I just… I wanted it. I feel like we're so close."

"Super duper close," Lorenzo reassured him, "Oh! But one quick thing for your, ahem, courting? No drinky drink for at least four hours. I mean, not that you're going to, since you just, like, broke it. But the nano bots will still be kicking around, and it wouldn't be safe for you."

"That's fine," Frankie said, nodding. He was trying to stay upbeat, but he was clearly bothered by the results of the tests thus far.

Or was it something else, Snod wondered.

"We still have a few hours to kill," Lorenzo chirped, upbeat as always. "How about we try some variations of the antibiotic load, and then we go out to celebrate?"

"Celebrate?" Snod made a face. He knew that probably meant returning to a club. At least there would be alcohol. He liked alcohol.

"Yes!" Lorenzo cheered, playfully nudging Frankie. "Come on. Pleeease?"

"Well," Frankie said slowly, trying to resist a smile. "I did miss karaoke this week…"

"Yes!" Lorenzo pumped his fist triumphantly. "That's a yes!"

"Fine, yes!" Frankie laughed despite his best efforts, a bright smile lighting up his face. "We'll all go out tonight, I promise."

Snod smiled, taking a seat again while Frankie and Lorenzo got back to work. Karaoke wouldn't be so bad, he decided. At least it was somewhere familiar. He watched them with mild interest as the hours went by, dozing off once or twice only to be woken up when something exploded or crackled.

They managed to spend almost the entire day in the lab before they were afraid to push their luck any further. They had made it from DD 1.4 to 2.2 with little to no improvement. Every dose they tried was still quite volatile.

Snod couldn't help but think what an effective weapon the serum would be against vampires, and he quickly tried to dismiss his hunter mentality. This wasn't about hurting vampires. It was meant to cure them, something he knew Frankie longed for desperately.

Frankie's spirits were still rather damp by the time they finally left, and he didn't seem much better when they returned to the apartment and were getting ready to head out. Frankie avoided Snod for a little while, taking longer in the bathroom than he usually did before emerging.

"Frankie," Snod asked carefully, "are you all right?"

"Fine," Frankie replied in a tone that indicated he was anything but. He looked human, broken and hurting.

Snod gently wrapped his arms around Frankie's waist, kissing his cheek and asking more firmly, "What is wrong?"

"I'm… upset," Frankie replied after a moment. "I really thought this was going to be it, that I'd have a cure. I got my hopes up. It was foolish."

"It's never foolish to have hope," Snod said softly.

"You really believe that?" Frankie asked, peering up at him.

"I do."

"Hmmm. What do you hope for, Obadiah Snod?" Frankie asked with a teasing little smile.

"To be happy," Snod answered as honestly as he could. He hoped for many things; never returning home, to not be afraid to fall in love… to finally and truly be happy.

Even without the bond, Frankie seemed to sense something was off in Snod's reply. He looked concerned, but before he could ask anything further, there was a very hyper series of loud knocks at the door.

"Lorenzo?" Snod grumbled.

"Yup!" Frankie laughed, shaking his head. He kissed Snod's cheek and gently pried himself out of his arms as he said, "Time to party!"

It was indeed Lorenzo at the door, bouncing on his toes and ready to go. Frankie seemed to cheer up as Lorenzo got him pumped to adventure out into the world.

Or at least he was faking it very well, Snod thought with a frown. It was hard to be sure, especially now not being to detect a single fraction of Frankie's emotions.

The ride over to Cheap Trills was upbeat, and Snod was begrudgingly looking forward to spending the evening out. He would tolerate Lorenzo as long as there was ample alcohol to help, and it was time with Frankie.

That was worth it.

When they arrived at the bar, Rees was not happy to see

him. He had apparently been expecting Snod to work tonight, and he had lots of choice words for him the second he laid eyes on him.

"Where the fuck have you been? You're fucking late! I oughta rip off your balls and make fuckin' earrings out of them!" Rees was raging, furiously shaking in purple glittered heels. "You stupid motherfucker—"

"It's my fault!" Frankie insisted, sweeping in to save the day. "We made some really great progress on the you-know-what, thanks to Obe, and I wanted to celebrate with him." He gave Rees his most sincere smile, pleading sweetly, "I promise he'll be back at work tomorrow. On time. Early! He'll even be here early!"

"I will?" Snod growled.

"Yes, you will," Frankie scolded him, turning his bright smile back on Rees. "Come on…" He gave his friend a big hug. "And did I mention how much I love the desk? How very thankful I am and what a thoughtful gift that was?"

"Fine!" Rees conceded, rolling his eyes and grumpily giving in. He narrowed his eyes, huffing sharply, "Early! Tomorrow! I fucking mean it!"

"You're the best, Rees," Frankie laughed, taking Snod by the hand and leading him to a table toward the back beside the bar. Snod enjoyed the brief touch, smiling smugly to himself as they got settled.

Lorenzo bought them drinks and Snod tried to relax. The booze was good, and he listened while Frankie and Lorenzo chatted away about their earlier success with the experiments. He was happy to listen, ignoring the horrible wailing from up on stage.

Snod was relieved when the song was finally over, and he was even more pleased when Frankie brought him and Lorenzo another round of drinks.

To his surprise, Frankie leaned down and kissed his lips. Snod did his best not to flinch, blinking slowly. He could feel his heart racing faster, a little uneasy with such a public display of affection, stammering, "What was that for?"

"Because I wanted to," Frankie said with a little smile, "and for making me feel better."

"It's what you do…" *When you love someone*, Snod almost said, quickly stating instead, "When you care about someone."

Frankie smiled, bright and adoring, almost as if he heard what Snod had meant to say. He kissed him again, a bit more chastely than before. "Good. Now stay put. I've picked out a very special song just for you."

"For me?" Snod scowled and shook his head stubbornly. "I'm not singing."

"No! For me to sing!" Frankie laughed, grinning impishly as he headed toward the stage.

"Ohhh, this'll be good," Lorenzo squealed excitedly. "Frankie is a fantastic singer."

"I know," Snod drawled, remembering all too well the night they had danced and sang together, listening to that band who proclaimed things. He was curious what song Frankie could have chosen for him.

Pushing a couple of buttons on the machine, Frankie smiled as a peppy synth song began to play. He took the microphone in hand, confidently grinning out at the crowd, not even bothering to check the screen as the lyrics began to pop up.

He knew this song, Snod realized, tilting his head curiously. It sounded familiar; maybe it was the same song Frankie had been singing in the kitchen prior to their sink escapade.

Even though the beat was energetic, there was something sad and haunting in the sound of the synthesized keyboards, Frankie's eyes closing as he began to passionately sing. It was a song about a man looking back on his life and finding that it was full of sin. In spite of this, he had still decided to live his life as he saw fit so he could be happy.

Snod nearly dropped his drink, his stomach turning to a nauseous pile of goo when he heard that final word, 'sin.'

He was immediately uncomfortable, gulping awkwardly. The words were too much like his own conflicted thoughts, and he felt trapped by Frankie's voice.

"It's a sin," Snod said quietly, whispering the words to himself as Frankie sang them, realizing he was suddenly sweating all over. He anxiously chugged back his drink, his hands trembling as he clutched at an empty glass.

His skin crackled all over with chills as Frankie held several notes longer than any mere mortal could, applause exploding from all around the bar as people cheered him on.

Snod was reading the lyrics as Frankie sang them, just to make sure he was understanding them correctly. It was as if someone had opened up his brain and pulled his deepest and most personal thoughts to create this song. It should have been liberating, knowing that someone else in the world had ached in the same terrible way he did for wanting forbidden things.

He felt sick.

Frankie sang on beautifully, each word cutting right into Snod's soul.

Snod couldn't stand to hear any more. He got up, ignoring Lorenzo's concerned protests and rushing right out the door. He was dizzy, nauseous, not even sure where he was going except that he had to get away. He was in such a hurry that he didn't even watch where he was going and smacked right into a young man.

"Fuck, I'm sorry," he mumbled, his mind still reeling. He sighed, looking down at the man he had slammed into, asking, "Sir, are you all right?"

The young man was gawking at him, his jaw dropping as he squeaked excitedly, "Obie!"

Snod stared in shock, blinking several times for his vision to properly focus, dumbly gasping, "Athaliah?"

CHAPTER FIFTEEN

It was his brother.

Athaliah Zerah Snod.

Here in front of him and smiling and laughing, throwing his arms around his neck triumphantly and kissing his face, squealing loudly, "Obie! I found you! I finally—"

"How did you—"

"Finally fucking found you! I've been—"

"You left? What happened, why did you—"

"I came to look for you!"

Their voices were rushed, crashing over one another and finally falling into a calm silence, holding each other close. He could feel Athaliah's shoulders trembling with sobs, gently cradling a hand into his hair. His little brother had always felt so small in his arms, but especially now.

Snod was holding him so near and so tight that his feet were dangling off the sidewalk, carrying him to the alley beside the bar for some semblance of privacy. Even in the dim light of the street lights, he could see the familiar blemish that had kept Athaliah from hunting.

His brother's right eye was almost white, the pupil exploding out in a white cloud that looked like a starburst. A congenital cataract, the doctors had said. A blemish that made him unworthy, said the Order. It was just part of his brother, thought Snod.

"Father Sanguis told everyone what happened," Athaliah began rambling quickly. "That you'd been excommunicated for carnal sins, and, and, he said I would never see you again! So I said fuck this! I left and came to look for you!"

"You ran away," Snod said flatly, still in shock. "Again."

"Yes!" Athaliah shouted happily. "But it worked this time!"

"Because I wasn't there to stop you," Snod couldn't help but growl with equal parts fondness and annoyance.

Athaliah squealed again, hugging Snod tight as he babbled away, "Your old hunting buddy Ephraim found out the city you were last sent to hunt in and he told me! So I got all my crap together and I took whatever I could, and, and I ran! I've been looking everywhere for you! I never stopped, I just—"

"Took, you took what?" Snod interjected, gaping in horror. "You stole from the Order? What did you take?"

"Uh, duh! Whatever I wanted," Athaliah snarked with a roll of his eyes, giving Snod a little push. "Please don't act like you actually give a crap. Fuck those assholes! They kicked you out for being gay, didn't they?"

The accusation was a slap in the face, the air very choked right out of him as the words of Frankie's song echoed freshly in his mind.

"Obie," Athaliah soothed, his hands reaching up and cradling his face, his eyes calm and comforting. "You don't have to pretend anymore. It's okay to be gay. I'm fuckin' gay, too! Listen to me. They drive all that hellfire bullshit into your head over and over, but it's not true. None of it! It's fuckin' crap."

Snod's eyes were stinging, his chest aching with the need to breathe, but unable to draw a single puff of air. He clung to his brother, overwhelmed by so many different emotions that he couldn't even name them all. There was pain, relief, anguish, and a rush of happiness that made his knees weak.

He had never even thought those forbidden words to himself. He had never put a name to the desires he felt. It was safer if he didn't, easier to deny the sinful things he longed for. He finally sucked in a breath, shaking and desperate, gazing helplessly at his beautiful brother.

"I'm gay," Snod breathed, almost in tears with the admission. He was stunned by how much lighter he felt saying it out loud. Countless decades he'd spent in denial, wrestling with his own nature, condemning himself and punishing his body again and again, praying for a change that would never come.

"I know," Athaliah teased, but not unkindly. "I've known since the day we met." He pulled him into another bone-crushing embrace.

"I can't believe you're really here," Snod whispered, tucking his face against his hair. "You're here."

"And I'm not going anywhere," Athaliah promised fiercely. "We're both free now."

"I don't have to go back," Snod sighed heavily in relief. "I'm done."

"Go back?" Athaliah was untangling himself in an instant, scowling as he demanded, "What are you talking about? Why would you have even thought about going back there?"

"Obe?" Frankie's voice was calling for him, worry evident in its pitch.

Snod turned his head, his pulse thudding in dread. He really hoped that Frankie hadn't heard that, but almost certainly he had. He knew vampires had extraordinary hearing, hoping that he would be given a chance to explain himself properly.

The Order didn't matter now. Fulfilling his mission to Father Sanguis was as pointless as his internal obligation to hate himself because of a lifetime of abusive and perverse lessons. He was finally free to be who he had always wanted to be and love whoever the hell he wanted.

When he saw Frankie coming around the corner with his flawless face wrinkled up in concern for him, he knew exactly who he wanted that special someone to be.

Frankie.

Always sweet and beautiful Frankie.

"I'm fine," Snod said quickly, scowling faintly when he saw Lorenzo tagging along behind him.

"And who is this?" Frankie asked carefully, minding his movements to appear as human as possible.

"This is my brother, Athaliah." Snod smiled brightly, practically gushing as he explained, "He ran away… he's… he's been looking for me." He shook his head, not about to get too personal with Lorenzo standing right there, turning his head to address his brother, saying, "This is Frankie, my boyfriend."

"Oohhh," Athaliah purred, giggling excitedly, "he is freakin' cute! Okay, no wonder you left! Fuck, totally get it now!" He cleared his throat, asking quietly, "And, uh, who is the vampire?"

"Wait, you think…" Snod stared, taking a few seconds to catch up, grimacing miserably. "No! The vampire is Frankie."

"Freakin' cute, huh?" Lorenzo piped up, blushing shyly and tucking his braids back behind his ears.

"I will end you," Snod hissed, possessively pulling Athaliah to his side. He tried to rectify the misunderstanding as he said, "The vampire is my boyfriend, Athaliah. That idiot is Lorenzo."

"Oh! Okay! I mean, the vampire is okay, too," Athaliah said with a little shrug, biting his lip coyly in Lorenzo's direction and waving.

Lorenzo waved back, but didn't dare put himself within Snod's striking range.

Frankie smiled warmly, chuckling to himself as he approached to gently shake Athaliah's hand. "It's nice to finally meet you."

"Ditto," Athaliah said, grinning happily. "Look,

vampire, whatever. I don't care. You got my brother away from those fucking nut-jobs and gave me the chance to follow right behind him. For that, thank you." He surged forward to hug Frankie's neck, sweetly kissing his cheek. "Thank you, from the bottom of my heart."

Frankie would have blushed if he could have, eyes moving to find Snod's in search of answers he couldn't have right now.

"Where are you staying?" Snod asked suddenly, peering intently at his brother.

"A hotel for now," Athaliah replied. "I pawned some of the junk I swiped, been doing okay. What about you? Where are you staying?"

Snod glanced back at Frankie, a silent question that was answered with a nod. He smiled at his brother, replying, "With Frankie. Come with me. Please. We have so much to talk about."

"Got alcohol?" Athaliah chirped, a wicked grin lighting up his face.

"We can totally get some," Lorenzo said immediately, smiling dopily as Athaliah turned that charming grin toward him.

Snod's blood boiled, but he ignored his rage for now. He wasn't going to let Lorenzo drooling over his brother ruin his mood. They were finally together again, and the weight of his terrible burden had been magically lifted away.

"Let's go," Frankie said, reaching to take Snod's hand and offering him a warm smile. "We can keep the celebration going at home."

Athaliah was reaching into his pocket, saying excitedly, "I'm parked right down the block, I'll follow you guys over!"

"How do you even have a car?" Snod marveled, laughing brightly.

"I've been a very busy boy," Athaliah replied with a smug smirk.

"I should ride with you!" Lorenzo said quickly, not even flinching under Snod's furious leer. "You know, just in case you get lost. I know the way back to Frankie's."

"You're so sweet!" Athaliah purred. "That's very thoughtful of you!"

Frankie squeezed Snod's hand to bring him back down out of his rage, soothing, "It'll be just a quick drive home, okay? Nothing's gonna happen."

Snod didn't like the idea of letting Athaliah out of his sight, not when he had just gotten him back. He knew that arguing would be pointless now that he had made up his mind. If nothing else, they had both inherited their father's stubborn streak.

"We'll stop by the liquor store and pick up provisions," Athaliah was going on cheerfully. "God! I still can't believe I found you! This is an amazing fucking day."

"It really is," Snod murmured in awe, shaking his head. The shock still hadn't completely worn off yet. He hugged Athaliah firmly as he warned, "Go to the store and then straight to Frankie's. No shenanigans."

"I will be shenanigans free," Athaliah swore solemnly. "See you soon, dear brother. I love you."

"I love you, too," Snod replied, his very soul warming up to hear those words again.

He hated to watch him leave, but took comfort in knowing that he would be back with him soon. He would be reasonably safe with Lorenzo, he decided. If Lorenzo tried anything, he could break his fingers. That thought was quite comforting, humming contently to himself as he imagined Lorenzo crying and wailing in pain.

"Stop thinking about hurting Lorenzo," Frankie sighed, his observation so spot on that Snod had to laugh.

"Mmm, don't need a bond now to know what I'm thinking?" Snod chuckled, not denying his violent fantasies in the slightest.

"Not when you have that murderous look on your face, and then you start giggling like a crazy person," Frankie scoffed, affectionately nudging Snod's shoulder.

Snod followed Frankie to the car, enjoying a few

moments of silence before admitting passionately, "I still can't believe he's really here. I ran outside, and there he was. Like he was magic."

"It's a miracle," Frankie said with a small smile.

"Yes," Snod agreed, waiting for Frankie to unlock the door so he could slide into the passenger seat.

"My song," Frankie said as he sat down behind the wheel, waiting to crank the engine, "I'm sorry that it upset you. I thought—"

"No, please," Snod said quickly, reaching to rest his hand on Frankie's thigh. "If you hadn't, I may not have run out at the right time. I might not have found him. Thank you." His smile was a little sad, adding hesitantly, "While the song did upset me, it was only because it was so very powerful. It was a beautiful song, and I wasn't prepared for how… how it would make me feel."

"It made me think of you," Frankie said honestly, resting his hand over Snod's, his thumb slowly gliding over his knuckles before finally turning the key.

"I know that it will take more time for me to adjust," Snod said carefully, "but a sin or not, I want you. More than anything. I know who I am now."

"You'll find that being immortal makes one very patient," Frankie teased lightly. "I know this isn't something that will happen overnight. I'm willing to wait because I want this, too."

Snod's chest felt heavy, bowing his head down, the desire to confess and be forgiven suddenly clouding his mind. It wasn't the sins of his sexual desire that were pressing down upon him, but his dishonesty, his treachery, and his guilt.

Old habits were difficult to break, and he needed absolution more than ever. The only person who could forgive him and give him peace was sitting right next to him, swiping his tongue anxiously over his lips as he said slowly, "There's something I need to tell you."

"Oh?" Frankie quirked his brows, keeping the car in

park.

"I have not been honest with you," Snod began, shame making his stomach twist and staring at the dashboard. Now that he had begun, he found he couldn't finish. There was no way that Frankie would still want him after this. His heart was demanding that he be held accountable for the wrongs he had committed, but he was selfish.

He didn't want to lose Frankie, and this confession would certainly cost him everything.

"Obe," Frankie sighed at length, sounding absolutely exhausted, "I already know."

"Know what?" Snod gulped, every muscle in his body tensing with fear. He hated how Frankie was looking at him right now, with such disappointment and yet, a faintly amused smile.

"Don't play dumb. Please, just stop," Frankie said, holding up his hand so Snod would let him speak. "I already know that you were planning to go back to the Order."

"How?" Snod demanded, stunned and immediately defensive. He had been so careful, suddenly exposed and nauseous with the realization that Frankie had been onto him all along.

"Because while your ability to lie is very impressive, I'm a vampire," Frankie replied with a snort. "You think very loudly, and I am much better at reading the bond than you. You spin some pretty tales with your lips, but your mind was like a book."

Snod didn't know what to say. There were palpitations pounding so hard inside of his ribs that it ached and his fingers clawed at the seams of his pants. He gulped, angry at being toyed with, asking sharply, "Why didn't you say anything? Why did you let me… keep going?"

Frankie's hands pressed over his own, halting his frantic picking as he said, "Because that's not all I felt in the bond. I could feel your guilt, your indecision, how conflicted you were. It was tearing you apart… and I could feel your love."

Snod's eyes widened, choking on nothing, terrified at

being put on the spot to admitting the depth of his feelings for Frankie. He wasn't ready, not yet, but Frankie already knew, he knew everything—

"For Athaliah," Frankie clarified, obviously startled by the look of terror on Snod's face, "because of how much you love Athaliah. I know that's why you were going to go back."

"And you never confronted me," Snod accused, blinking in disbelief. "You never said anything… you allowed me to suffer in my own wretched guilt."

"Well," Frankie said with a click of his tongue, "to be fair? You did deserve it." His hands curled around Snod's, tangling their fingers together. "This is what I've been waiting for. For you to finally tell me."

"Why?" Snod croaked, a traitorous sob rising up his throat and tasting of bile.

"So I could forgive you," Frankie said softly, his eyes bright even in the dim lights of the streetlamps filtering into the interior of the car, his smile gentle and adoring.

There were many things that Snod had sworn to himself that he would never do over the course of his life.

He would never know the embrace of a man, especially a vampire, and he would never leave the Order. He would never abandon his faith, and he would certainly never allow a vampire to live.

All of those certainties had already crumbled away into a heap of rubbish as his entire world was torn asunder, but there was one last absolute that Snod had been able to hold out on.

Obadiah Penuel Snod did not cry.

Tears were weak and offensive, especially during his lessons. He could feel some of the scars on his back burning as if freshly struck, reminders of all the times he had dared to let a tear fall and paid a heavier price to remind him not to let it happen again.

In this moment, he was failing.

He had cried with Frankie before in pleasure, but this

new feeling surging through him and snatching sobs from his lips was anything but kind. It was ripping his soul into jagged pieces, wondering what he ever did to deserve the affection of such a pure creature, tears freely running down his cheeks.

Frankie had to reach for him, pull him into his arms and kiss his forehead, murmuring, "I forgive you, Obe… I forgive you."

Snod sobbed openly against Frankie's chest, weak and utterly wrecked, his shattered world starting to pull itself into shape. He had a new world now, a life with Frankie, with Rees, and with Athaliah. All of the pieces were where they needed to be, and he had never been so happy.

Frankie's forgiveness was the glue binding it all together, Snod's tears washing away the guilt that had been haunting him for so long. He finally got to have this, he could fall in love and get his happily ever after.

Joy, he realized, he was crying with pure and unadulterated joy.

Frankie held him, rocking him gently as if he was a child. He was humming softly, a tender melody meant to comfort, pressing little kisses against his brow until Snod finally began to calm down.

Snod looked up, gasping when he realized Frankie's eyes were bleeding, stammering, "Frankie, your… your eyes…"

"Oh!" Frankie didn't seem alarmed, wiping the blood off with his sleeve, absently remarking, "Happens when I run out of tears. Vampires don't make much in the way of natural human fluids. So, sometimes… well, the tank gets low and to provide the function, our bodies will pull from… you don't really want to hear this."

Snod was morbidly fascinated, too curious to not ask, "Does that mean… during coitus…"

"Yes," Frankie chuckled, shaking his head with a snort. "Don't ask me, don't say it out loud, but yes."

Snod groaned and he had to laugh, the sound surprisingly clear, hastily wiping at his face as it ended. He tried to clean away all evidence of his breakdown, but remained curled up in Frankie's arms.

"You still want me," he said, trying his best not to phrase it as a question. "Treacherous and terrible thing that I am."

"Yes," Frankie confirmed, turning Snod's chin so he could kiss him. "Yes, I do."

"And our bond?" Snod asked hopefully.

"May be restored in time," Frankie said, offering a reassuring smile. "I miss it, too. We still have a lot to work on, but I need you to be honest with me from now on. It's the only way this will work."

"I will," Snod said earnestly, surprised how easy it was to make that promise. "I swear it."

Frankie tilted his head, debating something internally before finally asking, "There is one thing I need to understand. You could have fled back to the Order at any time. Why stay, why bother trying to fake your way into something you clearly wanted so much?"

"Father Sanguis would not let me return unless I gave him something," Snod explained, shame forcing his gaze back to the floor mats.

"What was it?" Frankie pressed, a slight frown creasing his mouth.

"The name of your Maker."

"My Maker?" Frankie blinked in shock.

"I don't understand why," Snod said quickly, "and I am being honest. I have no idea why he wanted to know, but that was the price of my return."

"A vampire's true name can be powerful, or so some used to believe," Frankie said, scoffing lightly. "There is old magic, very old, that supposedly can trap a vampire if you speak their true name with the right incantation."

"Is that true?"

"No!" Frankie scolded, laughing softly. "It doesn't work. There is nothing to be gained by it."

Snod frowned, wondering why Father Sanguis would have wanted to trap a vampire. He trusted that Frankie's information was more accurate than the Order's, and it made his secret mission even more curious.

He could no longer begin to hazard a guess at what Sanguis' true motivations had been, but decided it was no longer relevant. "I will never ask you."

Frankie nodded, finally shifting to put the car in gear and drive them home. He let Snod stay cuddled up against him, the ride relaxed and quiet. There was a beautiful sense of peace between them now, all of the deception exposed. Frankie was still willing to forgive Snod and adore him with open arms.

This had to be love, Snod thought, smiling when they finally arrived home. He held Frankie's hand all the way up to the apartment, content to bask in that warmth before it was snatched away when he saw Lorenzo and Athaliah in the kitchen taking shots.

"Obie!" Athaliah cheered, beckoning him over into a ferocious hug and shoving a freshly filled shot glass his hand.

"Sorry, dude!" Lorenzo chuckled, a bit tipsy and grinning at Frankie. "I sort of let us in? I know where you stash your extra key, and you know, our guest wanted a drink."

"And it's rude to keep a guest waiting," Athaliah purred, batting his eyelashes sweetly as he grinned hungrily at Lorenzo.

Melting instantly, Lorenzo guffawed awkwardly. He'd obviously never had someone as handsome as Athaliah show him such attention.

Snod took the shot of liquor immediately, growling at the awful burn. He was definitely going to need at least twenty more of these to stomach the sight of Lorenzo and Athaliah flirting.

His brother was a free man now, yes, free to make his own decisions and love without restraint just as Snod could. But Snod still saw the sweet sixteen-year-old boy he had sworn to protect, and it was too easy to imagine snapping

Lorenzo's fingers.

Frankie blinked over to Snod's side, slinking his arms around his waist. He seemed to sense his discomfort as always, nuzzling against him to keep him calm. Snod leaned into the gentle touch, kissing Frankie's hair and unable to resist a blissful smile.

"Holy fuck," Athaliah gushed, his mismatched eyes damp and definitely far ahead of Snod in how much he'd had to drink so far. "You look so happy, Obie."

Snod couldn't help but blush, grinning shyly at Frankie, who was gazing lovingly right back at him. Trapped in those brilliant green eyes, he felt a sense of completion he had never understood until now. He tilted his head, replying sincerely, "Because for the first time… I really and truly am."

CHAPTER SIXTEEN

As much as Snod loathed to admit it, Athaliah and Lorenzo had a lot in common. They were about the same age, and Athaliah's only references for pop culture were prior to when he had been brought home to the Order.

Kidnapped, he had corrected sternly.

Snod fussed at that, but let the two of them continue their heated discussion about robot men who turned into cars and who would win in a fight. He had no idea what they were talking about, but he had never seen Athaliah smile this much.

Lorenzo and Athaliah returned to the kitchen to take more shots, Snod politely declining to join them. He was already tipsy, and he was content to leave his blood alcohol level right where it was.

"Today's been quite a day," Frankie said, snuggling against Snod on the couch. "Almost gave you a heart attack, could have blown myself up…"

"Found my brother," Snod added, a soft slur in his voice. "Came out as a disgusting liar…"

"Which I forgave you for," Frankie reminded firmly.

"I also came out to my brother," Snod said, wrapping an arm around Frankie's shoulders.

"Really?" Frankie's eyes twinkled fondly.

"He said he already knew," Snod replied, smirking.

"Coming out is a huge deal," Frankie said, kissing Snod's cheek. "People actually have coming out parties now. It's a beautiful celebration of who you are, surrounded by your family and friends—"

"I don't need that," Snod insisted. "Besides, I don't have any friends and the only family that matters is my brother."

"Oh, come on," Frankie scoffed, protesting lightly. "You do so have friends! You have me! And Lorenzo is your friend even though you hate him. Mandy likes you, she's your friend. And Rees! You guys committed a felony together, that's something only friends do!"

Snod did not seem impressed, saying flatly, "I do not want a party."

"Fine," Frankie drawled dramatically, imitating Obe's deep voice. "Hmph. Just wait until your birthday."

"We don't have birthdays in the Order," Athaliah called out from the kitchen, "but mine is the eighteenth of January!"

"What do you mean, you don't have a birthday?" Frankie blinked.

"We don't celebrate them," Snod replied. "I don't know when mine is. Not exactly."

"But what about your driver's license, your ID?"

"They're all fake," Snod explained. "I'm sure the council knows. They probably have the day I was born in their records. Athaliah only knows his because he wasn't born in the Order."

"Ohhh, we should have a birthday party for you, Obie," Athaliah gasped excitedly. "You've never had one."

"No," Snod said, frowning, "I don't want one."

"Oh, shush," Athaliah argued, ignoring his negative reply. "We could have it here! We can get some presents, decorations, a big cake…"

Frankie grinned, cheering him on. "I think that's a great idea!"

"No," Snod groaned, trying to bury his face against Frankie's chest. "No party. It wouldn't be the right day."

"You can just pick what day you want your birthday to be!" Frankie chuckled, kissing Snod's hair. "Pick the day and we'll throw you a party."

"No."

"Fine, we'll pick the day for you."

"No," Snod continued to argue, tilting up to nip at Frankie's neck. It had been so long since they had been intimate, and he could feel desire heating up inside of him fast. Any possible reservations Frankie could have had about their relationship were all gone now; there was no reason to wait.

Frankie gasped a little when Snod began to suck at his throat, a mockery of feeding that made him twitch and stammer, "Mmm, Obe… uhm. Maybe, maybe we should…"

Snod pretended not to hear him, sliding a hand up into his hair and sucking harder until Frankie moaned.

"Hey! There are children present here!" Lorenzo chided. "Innocent, virgin eyes!"

"Oh, there's definitely nothing virgin in this kitchen," Athaliah purred playfully.

Snod's head snapped up at that, barking, "What?"

"Go back to sucking face with your boyfriend!" Athaliah groaned loudly.

Snod growled, finding Frankie's cool hands cradling his face and pulling him in for a deep kiss. "Not fair," he mumbled. "You're trying to distract me."

"Mmm, is it working?"

"Yes."

"Come on," Frankie urged, nuzzling against his cheek. "I've missed you…"

Snod couldn't resist, whining as the heat simmering away inside his body started to boil, quickly stumbling to his feet. He glared at Lorenzo, pointing at him and warning, "Death. Slow, painful death."

"I'll be fine," Athaliah insisted, hugging Snod tightly, swaying a little as he hung from his neck. "I can take care of myself. Now, go have fun! I'm going to start planning your birthday party."

Snod sighed in frustration, but knew better than to argue with him. Athaliah was as stubborn as Snod was, if not more so. He held him close, his anger washing away as a sudden tenderness seized his heart. He tried to fight off the emotional onslaught of having his brother back, murmuring quietly, "I love you."

"I love you, too," he replied, smiling brightly. "Don't worry. I'm not going anywhere."

Snod smiled softly, finally letting go and narrowing his eyes at Lorenzo, warning again, "Very slow, very painful—"

"Death, lots of death," Lorenzo said, bobbling his head. "Yup. Got it. Threats of homicide read loud and clear."

"Goodnight, guys!" Frankie chuckled, taking Snod's hand and pulling him toward his bedroom.

"You're sleeping on the couch, Lorenzo!" Snod called out over his shoulder, pouting when Lorenzo and Athaliah laughed at him. He didn't like this at all, but Frankie's lips proved to once again be an effective distraction.

Frankie had pushed him up against the door the moment it shut, kissing him passionately and mumbling earnestly, "Don't worry. Lorenzo is a gentleman, nothing will happen."

Snod was not going to volunteer any information on his brother's innocence or apparent lack thereof, his concerns lost to Frankie's sweet kiss. Their hands were all over each other, pulling and tugging at their clothes to seek out bare flesh. Snod's heart was pounding so hard that he swore it was skipping beats, moaning as Frankie's cool tongue slipped inside his mouth and pushed against his own.

Frankie was guiding them to the bed, the rest of their clothing vanishing along the way, panting hard, "I really, really missed you. I thought about you all the time."

"I missed you, too," Snod agreed, dragging his hands through Frankie's hair, surprised that his chest was suddenly aching. "So much."

The ache was beautiful and tender, so strong that it was difficult to breathe, but Snod didn't want it to ever stop. He wanted to savor this feeling forever, grunting when Frankie toppled them down onto the bed together. They were a mass of bare limbs, grappling together and grinding close.

Snod managed to work himself on top of Frankie, using his hips to hold him in place. He started kissing and sucking at the cold skin of his throat, his shoulder, biting his collarbone until Frankie cried out. He had missed the taste of him, the smooth glide of his skin, and the sounds he made, fuck, he had missed those so much.

Snod could feel that they were both hard, pushing his hips down until their cocks pressed together in the most amazing way, the resulting friction making his guts clench with pleasure. They'd had a lot of sex over the past few weeks, but this seemed different somehow.

This would be the first time with no deception between them, the first time they were honestly and truly going to lay together because it was what they both desired with no strings attached. Perhaps it was the alcohol or that Snod still had some lingering guilt, but he wanted this to be special.

He wanted to give himself to Frankie, the idea terrifying and exhilarating all at once. He knew he was in love with Frankie, undoubtedly, and there was no one else in the world he could possibly share this with. He lifted up his head, licking his lips nervously.

The maze of scars etched into his body began to twitch, each one a reminder that what he was doing, what he wanted, was wrong. He did his best to ignore it, but Frankie clearly sensed something was amiss.

"Hey," Frankie asked quietly, his eyes searching Snod's. "Where'd you go? What's wrong?"

"I want you," Snod whispered, gulping softly as he struggled to find the right words. "I want you to be… in me."

"Obe?" Frankie's eyes widened ever so slightly, trying not to allow his shock to show through. "Are you really ready for that?"

"Yes," Snod replied stubbornly. "I want to know what it's like… I want… I want to give myself to you, all that I am."

Frankie's eyes were bright and glistening, his expression positively radiating with love. He pulled Snod in for a warm kiss, agreeing, "Okay. We can stop any time, any time it's uncomfortable or—"

"I'm not going to ask you to stop," Snod insisted, smiling as he traced the tips of his fingers over Frankie's cheek. "I want to show you what you mean to me, what your forgiveness means to me. I don't know quite how to say it, but this… this I can do."

Frankie's lip twitched as if he was going to cry despite his happy grin, urging, "Go on and get on your back. I promise I'll make it so good for you. I'll take care of you, Obe."

Snod nodded, rolling over as instructed and scooting up until his head was resting comfortably in the pillows. He didn't know what to do with his hands, fumbling around until he finally let them drop at his sides. There was a nervous fluttering in his stomach, and he asked quietly, "Will it hurt?"

"Maybe," Frankie said honestly, "but I promise I'll do everything I know to make sure it hurts as little as possible. It's not going to be like when you're with me. I'm a vampire, we're more resilient… uhm…"

"What is it?" Snod asked anxiously.

"I have to get you ready for me." Frankie slowly crawled up Snod's body, careful and delicate, adding, "If we were bonded… it would help."

"God, yes." Snod nodded eagerly. "I've missed feeling you. I need, I need it back. I need you to know—"

"Obe," Frankie soothed, smiling from ear to ear, "I

already know." He pricked his tongue with his fang, blood beginning to flow as he pressed his mouth against Snod's.

Snod groaned hungrily, sucking desperately on Frankie's tongue, swallowing back thick mouthfuls of his blood. He could feel his skin tingling all over from the magical substance, every nerve burning bright until his body felt like a mass of exploding stars. He had to pull away, left dizzy from the sensation, gasping, "Frankie… fuck."

"I know," Frankie sighed adoringly, his cold lips beginning to travel down Snod's chest. He hovered over a nipple, grinning hungrily as his tongue lapped around it in teasing circles. He stroked it to firmness with soft licks before he began to suck.

Snod squirmed, the sensitive skin becoming overstimulated quickly, and he could feel his cock jerking absently between his legs. He gasped when Frankie's fangs sank in, tiny pinpricks of pain that vanished as quickly as they'd arrived. His head fell back into the pillows and he tugged at Frankie's hair as he sucked and swallowed, mewling pitifully.

Frankie didn't take much blood, he never did, but it was enough that Snod realized his own desire had increased tenfold as Frankie's was beginning to meld with his own. The bond was back, bubbling over with a new rush of emotions that made the ache in his chest burn even sweeter.

"Frankie," Snod gasped, struggling to speak, to think, but everything was a jumble of words and thoughts.

I need you, I want you, please, touch, I'm so fucking scared, keep touching me, don't stop, feels so good, I can't be without you, I need…

"I've got you," Frankie promised, continuing his slow descent of Snod's body. His lips were so warm now where they touched his skin, his hands like hot irons when they squeezed his thighs and gently pushed them apart. He mouthed along Snod's cock, not enough to give any satisfaction, only a tease, working his way lower still.

Snod's heart began to take off like a jet plane, complete with loop-de-loops and tight twirls, certain that it was going to burst out of his chest and crash against the wall. His hands came up to cover his face, and he hated how he was starting to tremble all over. His skin was on fire and completely numb at the same time, and he was inhaling in short, ragged gasps.

Breathe for me, Obe… just breathe…

Snod tried to, he really did. He was still shaking, a part of him resisting Frankie doing this to him. It was a sin to perform this disgusting act, letting a man be inside of him, touching him, fucking him. He was both filthy and completely elated, tears stinging his eyes as he felt a new wave of warmth, comforting and passionate, pouring through the bond.

It was from Frankie, he realized, only able to describe the emotion as pure sunshine. It was bright and endless, casting away all the shadowy doubts clouding his mind. He moaned when Frankie's mouth pushed up between his legs, holding onto that sweet feeling to keep himself in control.

Frankie's breath was surprisingly hot, his fangs grazing along the ribbed flesh of Snod's taint, pushing his balls back out of his way. He licked slowly just above his hole before his teeth sank in. A quick gash, just enough to bleed, letting the rich liquid pour down over his asshole as his tongue plunged forward.

Snod gasped, both from the brief flash of pain and the new sensation of that thick muscle trying to press inside of him. It was wet and dirty, Snod left moaning as Frankie pressed in a firm digit to aid his tongue's exploration.

"Christ Almighty," Snod whimpered. The burn took him by surprise, tensing immediately.

It will pass… you have to breathe for me…

Snod obeyed, breathing deeply over and over until the pain faded. There was still pressure, intense and sending strange sparks shooting up his spine. But it was starting to feel really damn good, and Snod groaned wantonly.

Frankie was sucking and licking with such passion, feeding from the dripping blood as he fucked his tongue and finger inside of his hole. He was moving so carefully, as if Snod were made of glass, making sure to track every single reaction to ensure an optimum amount of pleasure.

When Frankie thought Snod was ready for a second finger, he flickered away to grab the bottle of lubricant. He had moved so quickly that the transition of one finger to two was completely seamless, as if he had never moved at all.

Snod moaned in delight at the new stretch, amazed that his body was adjusting much more easily now. He could sense Frankie's concern for his comfort, assuring him breathlessly, "I'm fine, I'm fine… keep going."

Frankie's mouth sucked the tender skin around Snod's balls, his fingers fucking in and out of him with such precision that Snod had to shout out loud, gritting his teeth at the beautiful and weird intrusion that was making his toes curl up. He didn't know how to move, what to do, blindly following the will of his body. He wanted more, rocking his hips down to fuck himself on Frankie's hand.

"God, yes, yes, yes," Snod cried out, his hands digging into the sheets, chasing down that sweet moment of perfect pleasure when Frankie's fingers were pressed all the way inside him and he felt completely full. "Ohhhh, Frankie… fuck…"

Wave after wave of lust crashed between them, Frankie struggling to remain patient. He wanted to be inside of Snod, ravage him, fuck him, a flurry of fantastically erotic images filling the bond. Snod saw every one of them, and he wanted them all.

Every possible way, every conceivable position, he wanted every single one.

Snod cried out when Frankie's fingers pressed against something inside of him, something new and sensitive. It was weird but pleasurable, making his cock throb intensely. "Frankie," he whined, "Frankie, fuck… that feels…"

That, keep doing that, feels good, I wanna come, right now, fuck, fuck, please…

Frankie's fingertips began to massage that spot relentlessly, his lips rising to suck Snod's cock into his mouth in one swift gulp.

"Fuck!" Snod yelped, unable to stop himself from jerking upward, trapped between Frankie's wickedly hot mouth and his torturous fingers. He was shaking harder, pressing his hands over his face as he wept, moaning, "Please, God, please, please…"

Frankie didn't stop, sucking every inch effortlessly down, his hand moving in tandem with his mouth, pushing in hard as he sucked. He was merciless, deep-throating Snod's cock while pounding that tender place, over and over, his eyes flicking open to gaze up at him.

Come for me, Obe… I'll keep you coming all night long…

Snod made a needy sound, a moan that lost its strength as he whimpered softly. The pleasure became too much all at once and his cock was suddenly erupting without warning. The tension inside of him created by Frankie's fingers popping off made him see stars, certain he'd never known any other sensation that was half as incredible. He bit down on his hand, trying to muffle his scream of ecstasy, bucking wildly into Frankie's mouth.

Frankie firmly took hold of Snod's hips, bobbing his head to carry him through his orgasm and slurp down every last drop of his cum. He didn't offer a reprieve until Snod was crying pitifully, finally pulling off with a lingering swipe of his tongue and a sly grin.

"Fuck…" Snod sighed, limp and sweating, panting openly. His cock was still hard, the very air hitting it feeling unbearable, and his hole was oddly pulsing in the wake of his climax.

Frankie snaked his way up to wrap Snod's lips up in a heated kiss, his mind alive with warm and lovely thoughts.

I can't wait to make love to you…

Snod became almost frantic hearing those words, sucking at Frankie's lips and tongue, wrapping his legs around his waist and clawing at his shoulders.

Yes, yes, yes, now, right now, fuck me, fuck me up, what the fuck am I saying, just do it, I need it…

Humming as he spread the lube between them with attentive strokes, Frankie kissed away Snod's tears and sweat, murmuring softly, "Are you ready?"

"Yes," Snod croaked, staring intently into Frankie's bright eyes, every fiber of his being consumed with a raw need. "Yes… please…"

"Here, like this," Frankie urged, rolling Snod onto his side and stretching out behind him. Frankie remained propped up on an elbow, kissing Snod's shoulder.

Snod was arching his hips back, suddenly aware of how empty he felt without Frankie's fingers and the insatiable need to be filled was overpowering. He nodded, grabbing onto the pillow beneath his head, whispering roughly, "I'm ready."

Frankie eased Snod's legs apart, guiding him to bend one knee. The head of his cock was pushing against Snod's hole, rubbing there softly, but not yet trying to penetrate.

Snod closed his eyes, clenching his jaw. Frankie's cock felt so slick; he was surprised how sensitive the tissue was down there to detect such a thing. He held his breath, waiting for Frankie to move.

"Relax," Frankie urged, kissing Snod's neck. "If you don't, it's going to really hurt." He lightly trailed his fangs along Snod's pulse, his hunger hot and palpable. "I'm going to feed from you… it'll help."

Snod leaned his head back, his mouth parting in a loud gasp as Frankie's teeth pressed into his throat. He allowed every muscle in his body to turn to sweet goo, Frankie's arm sliding around his chest to hold him steady as he surrendered himself completely.

It was only then that he could feel Frankie's cock starting to slip inside of him. There was no immediate discomfort, but it seemed awkward and out of place. Frankie was still drinking from him in small sips, keeping Snod distracted while he pushed in deeper.

The first wave of pain took his breath away, Snod protesting softly, "Frankie…"

I've got you…

Frankie hesitated only but a moment, pulling his cock back out almost completely before pushing in again.

Snod instinctively wanted to clench down, to pull away from the foreign intrusion, but Frankie's hot mouth kept him firmly in place. He whimpered, clutching at the pillows and sheets, the pain still burning white hot.

Frankie was holding him close all throughout every intense second, his hand at his chest resting right over his heart, caressing his breast adoringly. He stroked his other hand over Snod's thigh, his hip, squeezing down as he finally pushed the final few inches of his cock inside.

Snod cried out in pain and startled confusion. The sting was unbearable but it felt so good to be this full. He was trembling, tears clinging to his lashes and grateful for Frankie's strong embrace to keep him from melting into the sheets.

You're doing so well, so very well, Obe… my good boy…

Frankie was fully seated within his tight heat now, not moving, only holding him as he finally pulled off of his throat. He sighed happily, praising, "You feel absolutely perfect, you're doing so great… are you okay? Does it hurt?"

"Yes… but I want it to," Snod sighed sharply, wishing he knew how to explain it, trying to share what he was feeling through the bond.

He had experienced nothing in his life that he could compare this intimate act to. It was similar to the pain of his lessons, but where his body would always become numb as the lashings went on, the sensations of Frankie being inside of him only seemed to grow.

Pain to pleasure, pleasure back to pain, it was an endless cycle that pulsed and throbbed and fueled the beautiful ache pounding away within the trappings of his ribs.

There was once a time when he had found such

immense comfort in his lessons. The agony would come and lead him to finding peace within himself and grant him absolution. It would never last, however, and he would always find himself seeking it out once more.

Nothing he had experienced from the Order could hold a candle to what he felt knowing Frankie's forgiveness and love. The adoration he had for this vampire was greater than the blind faith that he had bestowed in a nameless god who never once answered a single prayer.

He wished he would take back all the pain he had suffered and give it all to Frankie. Every drop of blood, every tear, every ounce of anguish, rightfully belonged to him.

"I want it to hurt," Snod confessed frantically. "Please, more."

I need to feel it, I deserve it, I haven't been punished, I shouldn't need this, but I do, it shouldn't feel this good…

"Obe," Frankie mumbled, his hips slowly beginning to rock, troubled by Snod's desire for pain. "I am not going to willingly harm you. This is only supposed to feel good…"

"Please," Snod pleaded, trying to push himself down on Frankie's cock, trying to chase that scalding friction. "Faster, please… I want it…"

"No." Frankie refused to thrust any faster, raising his hand and spanking Snod's ass firmly.

"Fuck!" Snod gasped, his hips jerking back from the blow. His skin was immediately left tingling and his cock was absolutely throbbing. He whined desperately, frustrated when Frankie continued the gentle rhythm. He tried to rock back, and was treated to another smart spanking that made him ache. The sting was lovely and somehow made every other sensation a thousand times more intense. He gasped when Frankie spanked him a third time, his eyes rolling back with a low groan.

Frankie slid his hand back up Snod's chest, pressing against his throat as his cock continued to dip inside of him at a maddeningly slow pace. "Be a good boy for me, Obe," he said huskily. "Be a good boy and I'll give you exactly what you want. Can you do that for me, Obe?"

"Yes… Yes!" Snod was moaning, wanting more, but eagerly taking all that Frankie would give. He couldn't think straight, his brain only allowing enough attention to focus on the thrusts of Frankie's cock inside of his tight hole and his own labored breathing. Every time he tried to increase the pace, Frankie's hand smartly reminded him who was in charge with a crack across his ass.

Even Frankie's immortal patience could only hold out so long, Snod's desperate flailing finally pushing him over the edge. A blink and Snod was on his face, Frankie spreading his legs wide as he slipped his cock back inside of him.

Snod gasped at the new angle, trying to reach back to grab Frankie's hip, but his hands were quickly pinned against the mattress. He turned his head and stared up at Frankie in awe, the green of his eyes positively luminous in the dim light, reaching right down into the darkest recesses of his heart. The ache inside of him pulsed again, longing and screaming for release, his heartbeat throbbing in time with Frankie's through the bond.

Each thump left him trembling, hearing and feeling how their pulses were now thudding together in perfect harmony, the words leaving Snod's lips before he could stop himself:

"I love you."

It was but a whisper, though it may have well been a scream. Silence followed, only broken by the pounding of Snod's pulse in his ears. He kept looking into those bright green eyes, fear beginning to trickle in when Frankie didn't respond. Here he was, splayed out like a sacrificial offering and speared on the hot flesh of Frankie's member, his to take, his to claim, to love…

And still, silence.

Frankie was smiling, shining like the sun peeking through the trees of a desolate wilderness. His voice finally shattered the quiet, hoarse with emotion as he said, "Obe… I love you, too."

Snod sobbed, his soul stretched too thin and breaking, giving his tears over as Frankie kissed him. He was lost to those lips and the immediate thrust of his hips that followed, squeezing Frankie's hands as he slammed their bodies together.

There were brief flashes of pain, but all Snod could focus on the absolute pleasure of Frankie filling him over and over again. His body was positively aflame, overwhelmed by the throbbing in his loins and his ass was so raw from being spanked. His spine was arching all on its own, desperate to increase the depth of penetration, his legs sprawling wide to aid his efforts.

He couldn't stop the torrent of filth leaving his lips, pleading, "Please, just like that, harder, I need… Frankie, I love you, fuck, how I love you… more, please, I need it…"

Frankie began to let go of his rigid self-control, his supernatural strength nearly crushing Snod's knuckles against the sheets and his thrusts finally feeling like a punishment. Snod cried out, the tender flesh of his hole blazing with awesome sensation. He took it all, weeping as Frankie fucked him senseless, every slam bringing him closer to the atonement he desperately sought.

In these heated moments of bliss was when Snod had an epiphany. All of his prayers for forgiveness, for peace and happiness; they had been answered.

Frankie.

Beautiful and kind and smart and funny Frankie was the answer he had been seeking out for over thirty years, and every second of suffering he had ever endured was a small price to pay to revel in this bliss.

"Harder," Snod growled, wailing when Frankie gave it to him with a mean slap across his stinging ass. The torment was heavenly, the pressure within heading to levels of bursting. Between breaths all he could do was cry, dragged across fields of physical pleasure he never knew existed. He was the most vulnerable he had ever been, and yet, he had never felt so mighty.

He was in love, and to be loved in return was an invincible armor that no mortal force could ever tear asunder.

Snod didn't even realize he was coming until he was screaming Frankie's name, his hips violently slamming back against his cock as his orgasm stole away any last remaining cognitive thought. They dipped and rolled together, their bodies slick with the sheen of Snod's sweat, sliding against each other in perfect harmony.

Frankie's climax was quieter, but Snod felt the strangely cool rush of his cum unloading inside of him. He was ready to hyperventilate at the thought of his body being stuffed with another man's seed, but the terror evaporated with Frankie's gentle voice in his ear.

"I love you, Obe," Frankie said, kissing his cheek. "I will always love you."

"I love you," Snod replied passionately, his body exhausted and thrumming with joy. "Forever."

They both knew what a commitment that was; love was meant to be an eternal spark, and that was especially true when one of the two people involved was a vampire.

Forever really meant forever, and Snod has already made up his mind.

He wanted his forever to be with Frankie.

CHAPTER SEVENTEEN

"Terrell Guiscard."

"What?" Snod lifted his head curiously, not understanding what Frankie had said. He was still high on the euphoria of making love and had been contemplating going again before Frankie spoke up.

"My Maker," Frankie sighed, snuggling closer. He repositioned himself against Snod's side, tracing his fingers lazily along his chest as he clarified, "His name is Terrell Guiscard."

"Why are you telling me this?" Snod whispered, confused as his stomach flipped with dread. "I don't need to know."

"Because I trust you," Frankie said simply. "Because I love you, and there shouldn't be any secrets left between us."

Snod frowned, reaching for Frankie's hand.

"He took me, he used the bond to manipulate me, and he turned me against my will," Frankie went on, his voice neutral as if he was describing a piece of furniture. "He made me kill, forced me to feed from humans... he wanted to make me into a monster like him.

"I finally stopped and I started feeding from animals to

sustain myself, but he wouldn't leave me be. He couldn't use his powers to control me like when I was human, so he found other ways to torture me.

"The morning I left him, I was determined to die. I couldn't stand living like that…"

There was a pause, Frankie's voice still calm and his expression flat, but Snod could feel a ripple of agony in the bond. He squeezed Frankie's hand hard.

"But I didn't die," Frankie continued. "I lived, and I couldn't believe it. So I spent every second running from him, trying to suppress the bond between us. I told him I would never be his again. I'd rather die.

"Since going into the sun didn't work, I decided to starve myself. Weeks I went without feeding, wandering in the woods, delirious and slowly dying. I remember collapsing by a tree, and I was so happy because it was going to be over soon.

"But a woodsman found me. He tried to help me. He thought I was sick. His young daughter was with him…" Another coil of pain. "I killed them both. I drained them of every drop because the hunger took away any control I had. I had never known a bloodlust like that, and I was terrified.

"I tried calling Terrell. I didn't understand what had happened, I needed his help… he asked me if I was ready to be his again. I said no, that I only wanted answers. That's when he told me to never summon him unless I was ready to be his once more. He would never come, even if I was dying, unless I vowed to be his lover."

"That's why he'll never come," Snod realized, the last piece of the puzzle clicking into place. "No matter how many times you summon him…"

"Because I would rather die than ever be taken in his bed again," Frankie said, unable to soften the bitterness in his tone.

"He hurt you," Snod said quietly, his words framed more as a statement than a question. The answer was obvious.

"It was all a very long time ago," Frankie replied, smiling

as he tilted his head to kiss Snod's cheek.

Snod turned to catch Frankie's mouth, pulling him up onto his chest, hands fanning over his back as they kissed.

"Mmmm," Frankie hummed, "trying to distract me?"

"Depends," Snod chuckled. "Is it working?"

"Hey," Frankie chided, laughing because he had used those same words on Snod earlier. "Well, maybe a little… you are very distracting, after all."

Snod kissed him deeply, his lips sealing a thousand unspoken promises that fluttered through his thoughts.

I will never hurt you, I'll take care of you, I'll protect you, I'll always love you…

"I love you, too," Frankie murmured, the press of his body against Snod's starting to create a wonderfully amorous friction as they kissed.

Snod dragged the tips of his fingers over Frankie's sides, slipping his tongue deep in his mouth. He knew it was the blood allowing for him to get hard again so quickly, gasping when Frankie shifted back between his legs and began to press against his hole.

Snod was wet and sticky, but spread his thighs invitingly, eager for more. He wanted Frankie to take him again. He grinned, purring slyly, "Just can't get enough of me?"

"Never," Frankie promised, gently bumping their noses together. "Mmmm, again?"

"Definitely again," Snod agreed, moaning when Frankie began to make love to him once more. He cried out shamelessly when his legs went above Frankie's shoulders for a while and he sobbed hard when Frankie rolled him over on his stomach, biting down on his neck to feed.

It was beautiful, Snod left with quivering with pleasure as Frankie brought him over the edge of pleasure again and again in all sorts of different positions. They drank from each other, the bond stronger than ever before, Snod comforted by the warm ebb of flow of Frankie's love washing through whenever their eyes met.

Snod finally fell asleep in Frankie's arms, thoroughly

exhausted after the fourth time. When he woke up, he felt absolutely refreshed. There was no lingering pain and he was perfectly sated. He had never been this happy, letting the joy linger when he realized this was real.

He could keep this, always.

Frankie was still holding him, stirring as he did, smiling brightly as he greeted, "Good morning."

"Morning," Snod mumbled, blinking at Frankie's sleepy expression. "Mmm. Did you actually sleep?"

"I did," Frankie chuckled. "I needed to rest. Someone was quite insatiable last night."

Snod blushed, shyly ducking his head as he said quietly, "I enjoyed it."

"So did I," Frankie assured, smiling warmly. "Very much." He touched Snod's cheek as he reminded him, "Don't forget that you promised to go in early today to work with Rees."

"You promised," Snod grumbled, pulling the sheets tighter around himself. "I did not."

"Come on," Frankie scolded, trying to tug the sheets back off of him.

Snod growled softly and held on tighter. Frankie could have easily gotten them all away from him in one quick pull, but he let Snod continue to struggle as he dragged them off inch by inch.

Frankie was chuckling, watching Snod fight like hell to pull the sheets from his hand.

"Fine," Snod grunted, accepting defeat because they both could knew Frankie would eventually win. "I will get up."

With a triumphant grin, Frankie carried Snod into a hot shower. They kissed and touched, enjoying the newly reformed bond bubbling between them. Snod had missed it dearly. Frankie ended up with his face against the tile and Snod pressed inside behind him.

He had missed that, too.

Dried and dressed, they headed out into the kitchen to

make breakfast for everyone. Snod was pleased to see Lorenzo passed out on the couch, snoring loudly. He went to wake Athaliah, finding him curled up in a little ball in the corner of his bed.

His little brother looked peaceful, his hair spread out around his face like a halo and a soft smile on his lips.

Despite his angelic appearance, Snod knew better than to approach without exercising caution. He gently touched his shoulder, preparing himself to be swung at.

Athaliah jerked awake, hands flying to push Snod away, gasping as he looked around, eyes wide in terror.

"You're safe," Snod soothed, catching his hands and gently squeezing them. "We're both safe."

Athaliah nodded breathlessly, smiling as he replied, "And we're free."

Snod sat down beside him and hugged him close. His little brother had been plagued by bad dreams for as long as he could remember. Snod had caught his fair share of elbows and fists over the years trying to comfort him.

"Yes," Snod agreed, smiling happily. "We're finally free."

"Mmm, I may look for an apartment today," Athaliah sighed, taking a deep breath. "Tired of crashing at hotels."

"You can stay here," Snod insisted, scowling.

"Ugh, and listen to you and your boyfriend have freaky vampire sex all night?" Athaliah teased, his eyes sparkling slyly. "Nope! I'm good!"

Snod's face darkened, embarrassed down to his bones, saying flatly, "You heard that."

"Obie," Athaliah sighed, shaking his head and affectionately patting Snod's cheek, "the whole building heard you."

Snod grimaced.

"It's not a big deal," he giggled. "I'm really happy for you, seriously. And yeah, I might crash here for a few days, but I need my own place. You and Frankie got your thing going on, and fuck, I just… I need something that's mine, you know?"

Snod wanted to protest, a gaggle of familiar arguments coming to mind, but none of them applied now. He couldn't tell Athaliah to stay for the good of the Order because they were no longer members. He couldn't tell him that his place was here because he deserved to be happy on his own.

He could only nod, grumbling, "You'll need a job. Whatever you stole from the Order won't last forever."

"Well, where do you work?"

"The bar where we found each other," Snod replied. "I work there as a bouncer."

"I could come work with you!" Athaliah exclaimed, bouncing off the mattress and up on his feet. "I could be a waiter or something!"

"We'll see," Snod said, wondering how far Rees' kindness could be pushed, following his brother out to the kitchen.

Frankie was blinking around getting breakfast started, smiling when Snod stood behind him and wrapped his arms around his waist.

Happiness, pure and warm.

Snod watched Frankie cook, adding a pinch of salt here and there, smirking as they remained tangled together even while scrambling the eggs.

Lorenzo began to wake up, drawn by the smell of food and mumbling, "Anybody get the number of that bus that hit me? Holy crap."

"Told you to drink water!" Athaliah chirped happily, bringing Lorenzo a cup of coffee and kissing his cheek.

Snod narrowed his eyes, but Frankie kept him focused on breakfast.

Lorenzo blushed, sipping gratefully as he mumbled, "Mmmm. I'll try to remember next time."

Snod violently plated the eggs, imaging jabbing Lorenzo in the eye with the spatula while Frankie giggled softly. No doubt he was seeing Snod's thoughts. He scowled, growling softly, "It's not funny."

"It's a little funny," Frankie teased, passing the plates around with a big smile.

Athaliah took his to the couch to sit beside Lorenzo, munching contently as he said, "Mmm, so good. I definitely missed your cooking."

"Yeah, in another life you should have been a freakin' chef," Lorenzo agreed, inching a little closer to Athaliah and the two of them sharing a shy smile.

Snod would not allow the flattery to deter his disapproval, dryly remarking, "Don't you have somewhere else to be? A hole to crawl back into?"

"Nope," Lorenzo replied cheerfully. "I don't have any plans at all." He looked hopefully at Athaliah, offering, "I was kind of thinking maybe I could show you around the city, take you out to that diner I told you about. Not like on a date, I mean, unless you want it to be a date and your brother doesn't murder me—"

"Awww, you're so sweet," Athaliah purred, petting Lorenzo's hair, "but I can't. Obie's gonna help me find a job today!"

"I am?" Snod blinked before nodding quickly, affirming, "Yes, I am. And we need to leave. Now."

"Really?" Lorenzo pouted.

"Sorry," Snod drawled. "I did promise Rees that I'd be in early."

Frankie rolled his eyes, knowing full well Snod was doing all of this to keep the two of them apart.

Snod smirked, kissing Frankie sweetly as he said, "Mmm. Gotta get ready. Don't wanna be late."

Frankie cleaned up the kitchen while Snod and Athaliah got dressed. Lorenzo stretched back out on the couch, still attempting to recover from the toll of last evening's alcohol consumption.

Before they left, Snod swept Frankie off his feet and into a passionate kiss, purring, "I love you."

Frankie laughed at the display, grinning wide as he replied, "I love you, too."

They didn't need any other words, able to feel the warmth and adoration pulsing between each other, the pull of the blood so strong now. It was easy to get drawn in, Snod pouting when Frankie gently pushed him away.

"Go," Frankie teased, "before you start something you can't finish." He glanced at Athaliah, who was fussing over Lorenzo, chuckling as he asked, "Gonna take your brother to see Rees?"

"Yes. Maybe he will be willing to take another stray. He'll need a new identity as well."

"I'll see what I can do," Frankie agreed. "Yours should be ready any day now. And you know, you don't have to keep working for Rees. With a new social security number and a new name, you could do anything you wanted."

Snod frowned a little, saying, "We'll see."

"Small steps," Frankie soothed. "If you're happy working for Rees, then stay there. I just want you to know there's a whole big world out there for you."

"I like this little part of the world right here," Snod admitted, reaching for Frankie's hand. "I don't need anything else."

"Okay," Frankie conceded with a warm smile. "Now go before you really are late and piss off Rees again. I'll see you tonight."

They shared one last farewell kiss before Snod followed Athaliah down to find his car. He shook his head at the gaudy gold sports car, sighing, "How much did you steal from the Order?"

"Lots!" was his quick reply, giggling as he hopped in. "You won't believe how easy it is to buy things when you pay in cash."

"Athaliah…" Snod shook his head, flinching a little when he struggled to get the car into gear. "You do know how to drive, yes?"

"Yes!" Athaliah snapped, slamming down on the gas just to make Snod tumble a little in his seat. "Sit back and enjoy the ride, big brother. I've got this." He quickly got the hang of it once they hit the open city streets, teasing, "Just like riding a bike!"

"I don't know how to ride a bike," Snod griped, making sure his seatbelt was fastened securely.

"I didn't even have my permit before the Order took me!" Athaliah said gleefully. "But don't worry! I've been practicing all week! We will arrive safely!"

They managed to make it over to Cheap Trills in one piece, although Snod felt ready to revisit his breakfast by the time they parked. He groaned lightly as he got out of the car, thankful to be on solid ground again.

"See? Not bad!" Athaliah chirped happily, bouncing behind Snod toward the door.

The bar was empty this time of day, Snod calling out, "Rees! You here?"

"Who's the twink?" Rees grumbled in response, sauntering out to skeptically stare down Athaliah.

"My brother," Snod explained, "Athaliah."

"Let me guess, doll. You need a job, too?" Rees snorted, leaning against the bar and crossing his arms.

"Depends," Athaliah replied sweetly, quirking his brows. "You got a job to give me?"

"Maybe," Rees mused, pursing his lips together. "What can you do?"

"I was a waiter for two weeks before I was kidnapped almost twenty years ago?" Athaliah offered with a quick shrug.

"Congratulations, you're officially more qualified to work here than your fuckin' brother," Rees cackled, shaking his head. "Lemme guess. The Order?"

"You know about the Order?" Athaliah glanced at Snod for confirmation, and he nodded.

"I know lots of things, doll," Rees replied with a smirk. "I'm not just a pretty face, you know."

"Beauty and brains," Athaliah purred, easily charming him with a sweet smile.

"You sure you're related to that boring ol' asshat?" Rees

laughed, jerking his head at Snod. "You, I like. Your brother? Ha! Personality of a cardboard box soaked in piss."

"He takes a little while to warm up," Athaliah said, winking playfully, "but trust me, he's amazing."

Snod made a face at being the subject of conversation, grumbling, "I'm right here."

"Yeah, yeah," Rees said, waving his hand dismissively. He looked over Athaliah again, finally agreeing, "Fine, you wanna be a waiter, you got it. But keep all that vampire crazy turned real low. Nobody else here knows except me, got it?"

Athaliah saluted, promising, "Got it."

"Athaliah? Stock the bar. Just fill up the shit that's empty with more of the same shit," Rees ordered, grunting at Snod. "You. Come with me. I got some trash that needs to be bounced."

Snod got to work, letting Rees order him around for a few hours as they cleaned out the kitchen and stockroom. Rees was showing Athaliah where everything was, and Snod wanted take a break and get a drink of water. He came out to the bar to grab a glass, tensing when he heard the front door open.

"We're closed," Snod called out, filling his glass with ice and scowling when he saw who it was.

"Frankie told me you were working here," Mark said, his eyes moving around with a faint hint of revulsion as he stepped inside slowly. "It suits you."

"What do you want?" Snod snapped, getting right to the point. He hadn't seen Mark since that night at the club, and he had hoped that would have been the last time.

"I want you to leave," Mark replied calmly. "I don't care what it takes, but I'm not giving up on Frankie. That won't happen as long as you're around, so I want to make that problem go away. I want to make *you* go away."

Snod scoffed, shaking his head as he drawled, "Not happening."

"I will write you a check right now," Mark replied, moving closer to the bar but refusing to touch it as if it might be sticky. It probably was. "Name your price. Leave Frankie to someone who can properly care for him. You don't really believe that you'll be able to keep him forever, do you?"

"Yes," Snod growled, gritting his teeth together and resisting the urge to smash his glass in Mark's face, "because I know what forever means with Frankie, more than you ever will."

"I have no idea what you're talking about," Mark sighed, clearly annoyed and reaching into his coat pocket. "You just tell me a number, okay? And I will write it on this check."

"You'd put a price on Frankie's happiness?" Snod demanded in disgust.

"Everything has a price," Mark coldly retorted.

"And what's your price, handsome?" Athaliah piped up, appearing from behind the bar like a siren, fluttering his eyes at Mark.

Mark flinched, replying stiffly, "More than you can afford."

Athaliah stalked toward him, his hands running all over the front of his coat as he pouted, "Awww, really? Huh. 'Cause you look pretty damn cheap to me."

Mark flinched again. "Please, this is a very personal matter."

"Oh, it's very personal to me, too," Athaliah insisted. "See, it's very important for my brother to be happy. And he and Frankie are happy. Like, my God, fucking all night making sweet love kind of happy. And then again this morning, whew, can that Frankie scream! Boy has got some impressive pipes!"

Mark grimaced, his face noticeably darkening at Athaliah's colorful description.

"The last thing they need is some pretty boy fuck like you screwing things up," Athaliah went on, flashing a wicked smile. "The best thing for you to do is turn around and go back to Losersville where you came from. Population one. That's you. You're the one."

"I'm not going anywhere," Mark said angrily. "Now, I've tried being nice—"

"Nice?" Rees' voice shouted from the back, stomping out with a snarl. His face was bright red and he was having a bad coughing fit, wheezing angrily, "Waltzing in here trying to buy off Frankie's boyfriend is your idea of 'nice'?"

"You must be Rees," Mark said, forcing a strained smile. "Frankie's mentioned you, it's a pleasure to meet you finally."

"Ha! Why don't you come over here and get a big ol' mouthful of this dick because a hot splash in the face is the only pleasure I'm ever gonna give you, you yuppie fuckin' punk," Rees spat fiercely, covering his mouth with a handkerchief as he continued to hack into his hand. "Who the fuck do you think you are? Throwing your money around like that, thinking you're hot shit? Please, you're not half the fuckin' man Snod is."

Snod finally understood the real meaning of friendship in that moment, his heart overflowing with affection. He put his hand on Rees' shoulder to steady him, but the old man wasn't done yet.

"Fuck your money, fuck you, and get the fuck out of my bar," Rees seethed. "Don't go thinking for a second that Frankie isn't gonna hear all about this. Your chances of making a deposit in the Frankie booty bank are now officially fuckin' closed."

Snod sputtered at that, his teeth slamming together with a loud click. He ran a hand over his face, mumbling, "God help me."

Athaliah was cackling, grinning at Mark's equally disgusted expression, teasing, "Awww. Poor baby! Can't always get what you want, huh?"

"You're all revolting, subhuman trash," Mark growled, starting to back away.

"So's your mom!" Athaliah jeered, sticking out his tongue defiantly.

Mark threw one last nasty glare at Snod, snapping, "You

won't be able to keep him forever. Eventually, he'll get tired of slumming with you and when he finally does, I'll be waiting."

Snod said nothing, sneering bitterly.

Mark huffed, turning sharply on his heel and stomping out the door.

"That was very nice work, doll," Rees said approvingly, giving Athaliah a little nudge. He cleared his throat, giving one last deep cough. "Mmmph. Very nice."

"Thanks." Athaliah beamed proudly.

"Did you have to touch him so much?" Snod asked sourly. "It looked… sexual."

"Ew, no," Athaliah drawled, rolling his eyes. "I was stealing his wallet. Like, duh." He held it up triumphantly, plucking out all the cash and stuffing it in his pocket. "Rich guys are dumb."

Snod couldn't resist a happy smile, coming around the bar to embrace his brother. Holding him close brought him comfort, but some of the things Mark had said were bothering him.

Forever did mean something different with Frankie. Forever meant an eternity because Frankie was immortal.

But Snod was not.

He was human and the terrifying reality of their relationship was settling over him. He was going to grow old and wither away right before Frankie's eyes; Frankie, who would never age, never change, and never die. He knew Frankie was searching desperately for a cure, but how long would that take?

Would Snod be in his fifties by the time Frankie found one? His seventies? What about his nineties?

Fuck, would he even live that long?

The idea of Frankie watching him grow old and die while he remained perfectly frozen in time made Snod sick to his stomach. That wasn't fair at all. He loved Frankie with every fiber of his being, and he wanted to be with him always.

The solution was obvious.

Snod made up his mind there on the spot; he would ask Frankie to turn him.

He would ask Frankie to make him a vampire.

CHAPTER EIGHTEEN

As the day wore on into evening, Snod couldn't shake off the incredible decision he had come to. The only way for him and Frankie to be together forever would be for Snod to become a vampire. Frankie would eventually cure them, but this way they could stay together without having to fret over Snod's looming mortality in the meantime.

Frankie was very close to figuring it out, and he would be able to cleanse them both of the curse eventually.

No, the *disease*, Snod mentally corrected. It was a disease, and Frankie would be able to cure it. Then they could actually grow old together as humans, and Snod wanted that happy ending for them both.

But would Frankie actually do it?

Of course, Snod convinced himself. Frankie loved him, and he would do anything to keep them together. He didn't like the idea of drinking blood, but he had faith that he wouldn't have to do it for very long.

It was perfect.

All he had to do was wait to ask Frankie when he finished work tonight. It was a slow evening, ignoring the usual drunken caterwauling from the stage as best as he could. He kept an eye on his brother, unable to stop himself from smiling.

He looked so happy.

Watching Athaliah interacting with his customers was a true delight. It was so easy for him to blend in, to laugh and smile, and Snod was curiously envious.

Athaliah's childhood had been normal, and he knew all about the outside world and how to talk to people. He was honestly overjoyed to meet each and every customer and his tips were piling up fast.

Snod's attention was drawn to the bar where Mandy was frantically waving at him. He darted from the door toward him, asking quickly, "What's wrong?"

"Rees has to take Dwayne to the hospital," Mandy replied quickly. "Some sort of seizure from his goat-related head injury?"

"Dwayne the cook? Is he okay?"

"I have no idea," Mandy sighed miserably. "I know Rees is gonna make sure they take good of him. But now we don't have anyone to cook! You any good in the kitchen?"

Snod pursed his lips, replying slowly, "I've some talent, yes." He hesitated. "Where is the nearest grocery store?"

"Huh? Why? All the food is—"

"I'm not cooking that garbage," Snod replied with a disgusted sneer. "Nearest grocery store, if you please?"

"Two blocks down on East Autumn," Mandy told him. "It's small, but—"

Snod was already gone, racing down to the store as fast as he could. He felt the thrill of having a new mission, eagerly ticking off menu ideas in his head. He knew he wouldn't have to buy much as slow as the bar was tonight, filling a shopping basket with fresh bread, hamburger, and an assortment of bright vegetables. He figured the kitchen probably wouldn't have any spices or sauces so he grabbed those, too.

He was a little alarmed at the price at checkout, having to fork over almost all of the money he had earned so far. It would be worth it. Plus, he would keep the receipt and make sure Rees paid him back.

Arms full of bags, he ran back to the bar and practically dove headfirst into the kitchen. Half of the dishes he needed to use had to be washed first, and there was a big pile of tickets that had already been waiting for over thirty minutes.

Once he got everything cleaned, he was ready to begin.

Snod sliced potatoes to make fresh fries, dropping them down into the fryer while he seasoned the meat. Onto the grill the patties went, sizzling loudly. He moved quickly, noting that most patrons had ordered cheeseburgers.

A few had requested chicken tenders, and while he hated to serve the frozen abominations, he had no other choice. He seasoned them with sweet peppers and made a spicy mayonnaise dipping sauce to make them more palatable, starting to quickly plate.

The orders were coming faster now, and Snod was worried that he might run out of ingredients. He didn't understand why there were so many orders now. It finally began to slow down after a few hours, and he was very grateful when the evening was over.

"Last ticket!" Mandy called out, bringing the order to him. "I told everyone the kitchen is closing—"

"Thank you," Snod sighed in relief, quickly making up one final plate of chicken tenders for the ticket.

"Hey!" Mandy grinned wide. "I don't know if you've heard yet. Everyone is going nuts for your food. They can't stop talking about it. They fuckin' love it, Snod. You Amish guys can really cook, huh?"

"They're all asking if this is gonna be the new menu!" Athaliah squealed excitedly as he came bouncing into the kitchen to join them. "See! I told you that you're a great cook!"

Snod allowed himself a little flush of pride, shrugging as he replied, "Thank you. It was nothing, really. I have some talent, yes, but—"

"But nothing!" Mandy laughed. "That sauce you made for the chicken? I saw people licking their plates. Come on.

It's amazing." She smirked at Athaliah, glancing back at Snod as she said, "I think we gotta tell Rees we got ourselves a new cook."

"And why is that?" Rees' grumpy voice rumbled, strutting back to find where all of his staff was hiding. "What the fuck happened in here? What's that smell?"

"I cooked," Snod replied, turning around to tend to the last few burgers he had going on the grill.

"How's Dwayne?" Mandy asked immediately.

"He's okay," Rees sighed, pausing to cough into his handkerchief. "They're keeping him overnight to monitor him. I'll pick him tomorrow whenever he gets released." He eyed the food Snod was preparing, asking, "Those aren't our burgers. Where'd you get that stuff?"

"I bought it because I refuse to serve frozen sewage to living people," Snod huffed, sprinkling a pinch of salt over the fries and placing the burger on the bun. He made up three more plates, serving one to each of them with a little smile.

Athaliah and Mandy immediately dug in, making very happy noises of enjoyment. Athaliah giggled through a big mouthful, grabbing the last plate of chicken tenders to run out to the bar.

Rees didn't look convinced, eyeing the burger skeptically as he demanded, "What kind of cheese is that?"

"Swiss," Snod answered with a quirk of his brows.

"Why is the burger such a weird damn color?"

"Because it's actually made from a cow."

"Huh," Rees scoffed, finally taking a small bite.

Athaliah hurried back from delivering the last order, he and Mandy watching Rees eat expectantly, eagerly awaiting his reaction.

Rees chewed slowly, considering for a long moment before he laughed, "Well, fuck me, that's good as hell!"

Athaliah and Mandy cheered, Mandy saying brightly, "All the customers loved it. And I bet we could get some more butts in seats with a killer fresh menu."

"Dwayne couldn't do this," Rees snorted.

"No, but Obie can," Athaliah said with a wink.

"Then what the fuck do I do with Dwayne?" Rees demanded.

"Let him work the door," Mandy insisted. "He's scary enough with that giant goat scar and all that. Things get too tough, Snod can always come out and help him. You've gotta let him cook, Rees. Come on!"

Rees didn't answer for a moment, thoughtfully nibbling on his burger. He furrowed his slim brows together, staring Snod down as he gruffly asked, "You can make me a whole menu like this?"

"Most likely," Snod replied carefully.

"Fine," Rees sighed, groaning when Athaliah and Mandy started cheering loudly again. "I expect you'll be wanting a raise as well. Fuck."

"And payment for the groceries I purchased tonight," Snod added with a smug smirk.

"Jesus fucking Christ on a cracker," Rees moaned, scrubbing a hand across his face. "Fine! Yes! Yay! Now, everybody's happy. Get your punk asses back to fucking work!"

Athaliah giggled, ruffling up Snod's hair before following Mandy back out front.

"Write me up some kind of menu," Rees said with a roll of his eyes. "I'll do fresh on what I can, but that shit's expensive. We'll make it work."

"Rees?"

"What?"

"Thank you," Snod said earnestly, smiling warmly.

"Yeah, yeah," Rees snorted, waving his hands around. "Forget about it. Thank you for saving my ass tonight." He held out his hand toward Snod. "You're all right, Obadiah Snod."

Snod shook it firmly, nodding his head, replying, "So are you, Rees Everhart."

"Don't get all mushy on me now," Rees chuckled. "Clear

down for the night. We'll talk some more before Frankie gets here."

"Yes," Snod confirmed, cleaning up the kitchen with a content smile. He had enjoyed the rush of the tickets and tending to all the different dishes and preps. For the first time, he felt that he had found a purpose. This was a job he could do and find happiness in.

He knew it might be harder if he was a vampire, what with not being to taste anything. He knew Frankie was still able to cook quite well, wondering if he would be able to function in a kitchen with only his sense of smell. He felt confident that Frankie would help him figure it out, still smiling when he put the very last pan away.

The hour had grown late, and Snod was in a fantastic mood. He had almost forgotten about Mark's rude visit, enjoying chatting about the new menu with Rees at the bar while Athaliah and Mandy tidied up. He felt Frankie before he saw him, his heart flooding with a familiar warmth.

Frankie was there at the door when he looked up, smiling happily and sliding into his arms for a big hug, laughing, "Wow! Someone had a nice night!"

"It was very pleasant," Snod said, kissing him chastely as his joy rushed through their bond.

"Except that creep Mark showing up," Athaliah piped up, making Snod grimace. "He tried to buy off my brother!"

"What?" Frankie blinked.

"He wants me to leave you," Snod explained. "He tried to bribe me. I declined."

"I robbed him," Athaliah said cheerfully.

Frankie's face became like stone, but Snod could feel a glimmer of anger. "Please, give me back whatever you stole. I'll return it to him and make it clear that I won't tolerate this behavior."

Snod growled softly. He had his own ideas for making Mark go away, but he knew Frankie wouldn't allow any of them.

Athaliah pouted, handing over the pilfered wallet,

groaning, "Ugh, whatever. You're no fun."

"Well, what else happened?" Frankie asked, trying to brighten the mood back up.

"Obe's our new cook," Mandy announced proudly, quickly launching into an exciting recap of Snod's culinary adventures that evening, including how successful it was.

Athaliah also emphasized how great the food had been, and even Rees grumbled a few compliments.

"Hell of a night," Frankie laughed, leaning close to Snod. He reached for Snod's hand, asking cheerfully, "So, ready to head home, master chef?"

"Yes," Snod replied, looking to Athaliah. "Are you ready?"

"Actually," Athaliah began, glancing back at Mandy and grinning. "Mandy and I have been talking. She invited me to stay with her until I can get my own place."

"Athaliah," Snod said sternly.

"Obie," Athaliah mocked, imitating his firm tone. "It's just gonna be for a little while, I'll be fine."

"I promise I'll take good care of him," Mandy assured him.

Snod grimaced, but knew this was a losing battle. He pulled Athaliah into a crushing hug, mumbling, "I just got you back."

"It's okay," Athaliah soothed gently. "I'm not going anywhere! I'm here. You've gotta let me be free, Obie."

Despite his heavy heart, Snod couldn't deny his brother's request. They were both free, and he had to respect his wishes. He nodded stiffly, saying, "You'd better be at work on time tomorrow. I love you."

"Love you, too! I will be!" Athaliah promised, giving Snod a big hug and waving at Frankie. "You boys don't stay up too late now. And try not to wake up your neighbors!"

"I'll make no such promises," Frankie teased, playfully nudging Snod's side.

"Ah, to be young again," Rees snickered. "Don't do nothin' I wouldn't do!"

Snod blushed furiously and refused to address any of their comments. He waved farewell to them all as Frankie led him outside to drive them home. He talked excitedly during the entire trip about the menu and all the ideas he had, which ones Rees liked, which ones he didn't. He was getting nervous the closer they got to the apartment.

Snod couldn't wait. He had to ask Frankie to turn him as soon as possible.

Frankie knew something was up like always, turning to face Snod the second the door closed behind him and asking bluntly, "Now, do you wanna tell me what's really on your mind? I know it's not freaking out about whether or not Rees hates truffle oil."

Snod took Frankie's hands in his, smiling shyly as he replied, "No, it's not."

Frankie pressed close, asking again, "What is it, Obe?"

"I love you," Snod said slowly. "I know that I want to spend the rest of my life with you. You have taught me so much, and I never thought I would be able to have this. To be happy, to be free… I don't want to lose it."

"Obe," Frankie murmured passionately, "you're not going to lose me. I told you forever, and I meant it."

Snod's hopes skyrocketed, saying eagerly, "Then you'll do it."

"Do what?"

"Turn me," Snod breathed.

Frankie's eyes widened and his side of the bond closed off immediately. He pulled his hands away, saying, "Obe, I can't do that."

"Yes, you can," Snod insisted. "I'm asking you to. It's the only way we can be together forever."

"I'm so close to finding a cure," Frankie retorted. "It would be pointless to turn you."

Snod frowned, surprisingly angry at Frankie's refusal, scoffing, "How close? How many years have you been searching for one?"

Frankie narrowed his eyes, his voice cold as he replied,

"Obe. You don't know what you're asking of me. I won't do it."

"How many more years is it going to take, Frankie?" Snod demanded passionately. "Five? Ten? How old will I be by the time you finally become human? Will I even be alive?"

"What is this about, Obe?" Frankie snapped. "Is this because of Mark?"

"No," Snod snarled, "it's not!"

"Obe, you don't have anything to worry about," Frankie insisted. "I'm with you. You're the only one that I want. I love you."

"Then why won't you turn me!" Snod shouted, his hands curling into fists. "You'd rather watch me grow old right before your eyes, withering away?"

"Obe!" Frankie snapped back. "It's because I love you that I can't do this to you! I wouldn't wish this existence on anyone, especially someone I care about! I am going to find a cure! I want us to grow old together—"

"Unless I die first," Snod said bitterly, the rejection hurting so badly it made his bones ache.

"That's not going to happen," Frankie said firmly, allowing his side of the bond to open up once more, flooding with warmth and determination.

It was so strong that it nearly knocked Snod to his knees, shaking by the time Frankie reached for him. He was angry and confused, letting himself get drawn into the pull of the bond. Frankie was kissing him, his thoughts bubbling over like a waterfall.

I love you, you're everything to me, we will have forever, I promise, I swear to you, please don't be angry with me…

Snod grabbed Frankie roughly, dominating the kiss and fueling it with all of his frustration. Their tongues met and clashed, teeth clicking together. He could feel the passion reaching a boiling point almost immediately, panting loudly, "Please…"

"I can't," Frankie snarled, a surge of agony ripping

through his soul. "Obe, you can't ask me to do this."

"I'm sorry," Snod gasped as the pain overwhelmed his senses. "I just want you, I want you forever, I don't want to hurt you..." He couldn't help himself, afraid that if he spoke that he would sob, pressing his lips back against Frankie's in a desperate kiss.

I don't want to live without you...

Frankie inhaled sharply, taking a breath he didn't need to fend off a low groan. He was deeply conflicted, and the indecision to do what he felt was right was breaking his heart.

"I'm sorry," Snod whispered, the pain resonating in his chest as if it were his own. "I'm so fucking sorry..."

Frankie shook his head, baring his fangs as he whisked them into the bedroom in a flash, his lovely thoughts continuing to flow.

This is the happiest I've ever been, waking up with you, loving you, please, I will always love you, I will fix this, we will have forever, but please don't ask me... don't ask me again...

"I won't," Snod sighed as their clothes fell away, lube hastily slicked between them in a passionate rush, kissing him hard and saying breathlessly. "I'm sorry, I won't, I promise..."

"I'm so sorry," Frankie said urgently, all of their emotions swirling together in a thick blur. "Please forgive me. Forgive me..."

Something about those words made something deep inside Snod snap and a new flood of feelings drowned out any other coherent thought. He took Frankie against the wall, shoving him hard and lifting him into his arms. Frankie's long legs curled around his waist, gasping as Snod pushed inside of him roughly.

Snod set a fast pace, trying to find somewhere for all of his frustrations to go. He hated being denied, but wounding Frankie so deeply had crushed him. Here he was, drowning in rejection and guilt for being so selfish, and yet Frankie was the one pleading for his forgiveness.

Frankie moaned sweetly, tearing open his neck for Snod to drink from him. He clung to his shoulders, his beautiful lips twisting up in pleasure, whimpering, "Oh, my God, Obe… God, yes!"

Snod growled and crushed his mouth against Frankie's neck, catching the blood with his tongue. He fucked him harder, slamming Frankie's body and bouncing him on his cock relentlessly. He was still angry, the rejection fresh and stinging, swallowing down a thick gulp of blood.

I forgive you, I hate it… I hate it so much, but I forgive you… I love you…

Frankie's head snapped back so hard it hit the wall, overcome with the ecstasy of Snod feeding from him while fucking him so hard. "God," he groaned. "Obe, I love you, too… I love you so fucking much. Fuck! Harder, Obe!"

Snod gasped when Frankie's hand violently spanked his ass. It was a slam that was certain to leave a bruise, making all of his previous spankings seem like a kitten's swipe in comparison. He grunted, roughly biting down on Frankie's neck as he focused all of his anger into his hips, fucking Frankie with everything he had.

He didn't stop until they had both reached their ends, violently trembling together against the wall. He held Frankie close, managing to carry him over to the bed before collapsing. The sex had been quick, rough, leaving him out of breath and his body aching.

Frankie reached up to lick the smeared blood off of Snod's face, gently petting his cheek as he murmured, "Do you really forgive me?"

"Yes," Snod sighed miserably. "I don't… I don't understand, but I never wanted to upset you."

"I know you're angry, and I never meant to hurt you. You must think me selfish, not willing to share immortality with you. But this disease, having to be this way… it would break my heart to make you like me, Obe."

"But why?" Snod pushed gently. "Wouldn't losing me be worse?"

"That's just it," Frankie said with a sad smile. "If I turned you, you wouldn't be human anymore. As a vampire, you might become something else. All of the things I love about you might fade away. You'd truly be lost to me."

"Being a vampire is that different?" Snod asked quietly.

Frankie closed his eyes, nodding as he replied, "Yes. It's too easy to forget who you are… I almost did."

"With Terrell?"

"Yes." Frankie rested up on Snod's chest, the tips of his fingers lightly tracing along his collarbone. "All the terrible things the Order believes about vampires are because of monsters like him."

Snod frowned, watching Frankie blink away to get a towel to clean them both up. Frankie lovingly wiped away the mess of fluids and blood, tucking them both in beneath the covers.

"I will find a cure," Frankie whispered, tangling their bodies together and holding Snod close. "We will have our happy ending, I promise you."

Snod wanted to believe him with all of his heart and soul. He knew Frankie was certain he could cure the disease because he could feel his determination. Doubt continued to linger in his mind, wondering how long would it take.

Years from now, would he lay dying in Frankie's arms, still listening to his empty promises?

Frankie kissed him softly, reading his thoughts and murmuring, "That won't happen."

Snod kissed him earnestly, the kiss turning more passionate by the second and losing himself in Frankie's intimate embrace once more. They made love all night, Snod trying to smother all of his doubts in Frankie's beautiful flesh.

He fell asleep, exhausted and his thoughts still troubled, restless and stirring often. He woke up at four o'clock and stared up at the ceiling. Frankie wasn't in bed; he was able to sense him moving about in the living room.

He sat up, frowning as Frankie suddenly came through

the door carrying a brown envelope, exclaiming, "Hey! I felt you wake up. I wasn't going to bother you until morning, but look! Look!"

Snod stared at the envelope Frankie was pushing into his hands, blinking slowly as he asked, "What is it?"

"Look inside," Frankie insisted, bouncing on the bed beside him.

Snod frowned, pulling out a driver's license, a passport, and other various identification documents. He quirked a brow as he read out loud, "Richard Oberon?"

"It's you," Frankie explained excitedly. "Your new identity. And see, we can still call you 'Obe,' people will just think it's a nickname because of your new last name!"

"Thank you," Snod said, glancing over the papers with a smile. He had seen many forged documents before, and these were flawless. This had not been cheap.

"You can finally start over," Frankie said. "Here is your new life! Your new identity. You are officially a new man. I know you're still disappointed that I won't turn you—"

"I am not."

"You can't lie to me, Obe," Frankie snorted. "I know you're upset with me. But I want this to be a fresh start for both of us, okay?"

Snod couldn't resist Frankie's pleading gaze, trying to shove down his muddled emotions as he agreed, "Yes. I will try."

•••••••

Over the next few weeks, Snod did everything he could to forget his resentment. He busied himself at the bar with his new role as head cook, thoroughly enjoying the menu he had created and its immense success amongst their customers.

Athaliah got his new identity thanks to Frankie and then his very own apartment. He was spending more time with Lorenzo than Snod would have liked, and tried to visit often. If nothing else, he knew how uncomfortable he made Lorenzo and that always made him smile.

Every night he came home to Frankie, falling asleep in his arms and waking up in their bed. He was happy, happier than he had any right to be, but still the doubts crept in.

He couldn't help but focus on a tiny splash of gray in his hair that he hadn't noticed before or how the lines around his eyes seemed more pronounced. He was going to keep getting older while Frankie would remain eternal.

He hated it.

Snod tried to ignore his bitterness as he had promised he would, but it was difficult to let go. He hoped that Frankie would change his mind, futile as it might be.

Especially since Athaliah had now chosen a date for his birthday, he could feel the pressure of his own mortality pressing down upon him more than ever before. He didn't have the heart to tell his brother that he didn't want a celebration because he was so excited, but Snod was dreading it.

What was so great about getting another year older, he thought. It was only bringing him closer to his inevitable death.

He was so wrapped up in his own misery that he hadn't even noticed that the date Athaliah had picked would mark one month since he had left the Order. The morning of his birthday came like any other, sighing deeply when he felt something moving down between his legs.

Well, that was new.

Snod gasped when he felt the prick of Frankie's teeth in his thigh, his cool fingers stroking his hardening cock.

Happy birthday, Obe…

Snod groaned softly as Frankie sucked him so sweetly, starting to rock up against his palm. Frankie's mouth moved to suddenly envelop every inch of him, taking him all down his throat and bobbing his head until Snod was crying out loud.

Huh. Maybe birthdays weren't so bad after all.

CHAPTER NINETEEN

"Happy birthday to me," Snod mumbled dreamily, gasping as his cock thrusted up into Frankie's cool, tight mouth. His thigh was throbbing from where Frankie had fed, and he groaned at the pressure starting to rapidly build between his legs. It was always so perfect with Frankie, and he let him have complete control.

Frankie sucked him hungrily, burying his nose against his skin and sinking his teeth in for a quick taste of blood. His nimble fingers were playing over his balls, his thumb pushing against his perineum as he drank.

Snod cursed, panting haggardly at the intense suction. He was starting to get close, unable to resist Frankie's talented mouth. The warmer he got, the better it felt, his fingers clawing at the sheets and trying to keep his hips from bucking up too hard.

Close…?

"Yes," Snod whined.

How do you want to come? Like this?

Snod shook his head, gritting his teeth as he pleaded, "In you, please… I wanna come in you…"

Frankie pulled off at the last possible moment, slowly running his tongue over the shaft of Snod's cock. He pricked his finger, dabbing his own blood over the wounds he'd left behind and then licking it all away with soft little moans that made Snod's balls ache.

Snod ran his hand affectionately through Frankie's hair, and he smiled ravenously as he purred, "Come on, my love… please."

Frankie had the lube applied in a blink, slinking up Snod's body with a wicked gleam in his eye. "Happy birthday to you," he sang softly, rubbing the head of Snod's cock against his slick hole. "Happy birthday to you…" He began to ease himself down, only a fraction at a time, gasping, "Mmm, happy birthday, dear Obe…"

Snod groaned with him in pleasure, his hands finding Frankie's hips and trying to guide his descent.

Grinning slyly, Frankie wouldn't let Snod move him a bit, dragging out the last few inches for as long as he could. He finally sat all the way down, moaning happily, "Fuck, yes, happy birthday to you!"

Snod loved when Frankie was on top like this, eagerly watching the way his leaking cock bounced as he rode him, tilting his hips to catch just the right angle to make him really sing. He was approaching the precipice of climax sooner than he wanted to, lost to Frankie's ferocious slams.

He couldn't stop staring at Frankie's cock, licking his lips nervously. He could see the little bubbles of pre-cum oozing from the tip, and he wanted to touch it.

It's a sin…

Frankie began to slow down, his teeth pressing against his lip as he said, "You can touch me… but only if you really want to…"

Snod anxiously looked up at him, grateful for the surge of warmth he felt rushing over him to give him strength. His hand was shaking, but he reached, the tips of his fingers touching the slick pre-cum dripping from Frankie's cock.

Frankie's eyes closed, sighing contently, "Yes, Obe… just like that…"

Snod wasn't sure what he was expecting, but it didn't

seem that strange at all. The fluid was sticky like his own, and right now Frankie felt so warm having just fed. He squeezed the head, watching Frankie gasp and another dribble of liquid leak out.

Wrapping his fingers around Frankie's shaft, Snod gave a tentative stroke. He held his hand as he had always touched himself, wishing he wasn't shaking so much. He began to move, glancing up at Frankie often to gauge how he was doing.

Frankie's eyes fluttered back open, and he gazed down at Snod with pure adoration. He leaned back until his hands were resting on Snod's thighs, rolling his hips in time with his trembling fingers. He could feel every slide of his cock as it slipped in and out of Frankie's body, gasping when he realized he could feel a faint pulse beneath his palm.

"You're close," Snod whispered, stroking him faster. "I can… I can feel it…"

"Yes," Frankie whimpered, speeding up to match the rhythm of Snod's hand, "so fucking close…"

Snod could feel Frankie's pleasure, white hot and blazing, bleeding into the bond. He began to pant, jerking his hand even faster, determined to make Frankie come before he did. It was a delicious race of will power, and God, Snod was happy to lose.

He couldn't stand another second of Frankie's tight ass bouncing on his cock, groaning as he stuttered and bucked, unloading deep inside of him. He kept his hand moving, riding out his orgasm and feeling Frankie's body clamping down on him as he came.

Snod was entranced by every pearly stream shooting onto his stomach, the last few splashes coming out as thick drips that ran over his fingers. He kept stroking until Frankie was mewling pitifully, a plea for mercy, and Snod was left staring dumbly at the mess on his hand.

He hesitantly brought it to his mouth, his tongue darting out to steal a taste. Salty, rich, and bitter like minerals and blood. He made a small face of displeasure, prompting

Frankie to laugh.

"Oh, Obe," he giggled, "you're so sweet."

Snod pouted, choosing to wipe his hand off on the sheets instead of tasting any more of it, huffing, "That is vile."

"It's not so vile when I taste you, is it?" Frankie challenged, leaning down to kiss him.

Snod sighed, letting the kiss linger, swiping his tongue just inside Frankie's lips as he mumbled, "No, I like that. Very much."

"Well, I liked you touching me, very much," Frankie said, smiling brightly. "You don't have to do all the things I do, you know… but I'm glad you feel comfortable enough to finally touch me, too."

Snod's cheeks heated up with a faint blush, shyly turning his head as he said, "I liked that, too. I liked how you felt, knowing I gave you pleasure."

"Oh, you always give me pleasure," Frankie promised, snagging one last kiss before leaving the bed to get them both cleaned up in a blink.

Snod stretched out with a contented grunt, his body still thrumming with passionate energy. He watched Frankie zipping around to get ready for work, drawling, "We could always give each other more pleasure before you have to leave."

"No," Frankie chuckled. "I'm driving for the carpool today, I can't be late!"

Rolling over onto his stomach, Snod asked innocently, "Even if I wanted you to be in me?"

"That's just… that's…" Frankie whined, his lust blossoming immediately. "That's not fair."

Snod spread his legs, arching his ass up invitingly as he sighed, "It's been so long since you've filled me, my love…"

"Obe," Frankie warned, his resistance dwindling quickly.

"It is my birthday," Snod said firmly, glancing over his shoulder at Frankie frozen in the doorway. "Is it not customary to receive presents on one's birthday?"

"You'll get plenty of presents later," Frankie insisted sternly.

"Frankie... please?" Snod propped himself up on his elbows and knees, trying to arch his back as high as he could.

"Oh, fuck," Frankie panted, his foot taking a step back inside the bedroom. He palmed his crotch, unable to deny himself Snod's spectacular display any longer. "Okay! But we're going to be quick."

Snod chuckled triumphantly, his laughter stilted as Frankie's slick fingers were suddenly pressing deep inside of him. He moaned, his head dropping against the sheets, rocking back against Frankie's hand, gasping, "Yes... Sweet mother of mercy, yes!"

Frankie was stretching him out patiently, leaning down to kiss his hip, sighing happily, "As if I could refuse you on your birthday."

Snod started to laugh again, but was cut short again when Frankie twisted his hand, forcing him to pant as his body opened up. He closed his eyes, groaning loudly as the burn faded, pleading, "I'm ready... please."

Frankie wouldn't allow it, his fingers continuing to thrust and play until Snod's toes were curling and he was sobbing.

"Please," Snod begged, "Frankie..."

Frankie finally pulled his hand away, his wet cock replacing his fingers and pushing slowly inside of him.

Snod's head snapped back up, gritting his teeth at the beautiful stretch, and he tried to push himself back to take it all.

"Beautiful," Frankie praised, gasping as Snod starting fucking himself back on his cock, his hands spreading his cheeks wide. "You are so beautiful, Obe..."

Snod's face was hot, gasping and panting through clenched teeth, pushing himself back harder, trembling when Frankie's cock completely filled him. He didn't withdraw very far, desperate to keep that feeling, grinding his hips desperately to stay full.

Frankie let him control the pace, let him tease and rock,

chuckling breathlessly, "Mmm, I suppose since you never had a birthday before, you've never had birthday spankings, huh?"

Snod's ears burned, glancing up over his shoulder. "Birthday… spankings?"

Frankie smoothed his hands over Snod's ass, nodding with a smirk. "One for every year, Obe… and one to grow on. Would you like that? My beautiful birthday boy? Would you like me to spank you?"

"Yes," Snod whimpered, his hips slamming back more urgently. Just the mere thought of Frankie spanking him was getting him hot.

"Mmm, but I wonder how many?" Frankie gave Snod's round ass a hard squeeze. "We don't actually know how old you are… but you are making me very late to work. It should be a fair number, don't you think?"

"Thirty-five," Snod blurted out.

"Is that how old you are?" Frankie blinked at the quick reply.

"It's the most… it was the most lashings I've ever taken at once," Snod said quietly, his face burning red hot. "It's not a good memory and now I want you… I want to…"

I want you to make a better one, I want to remember this, being with you, you touching me, owning me…

"Oh, Obadiah," Frankie purred, his tone husky and dripping with lust. "That I can do."

The first pop of Frankie's hand was gentle, Snod able to breathe right through it without any trouble. The ones that followed were also playful smacks and Snod began to wonder why Frankie was holding back. The next one was a hard crack that made him cry out in surprise and pain. He groaned low as the stinging sensation seemed to echo inside his very core.

"Mmm, do you like that?" Frankie teased, rocking his cock forward as he spanked Snod's ass again, mean and hard.

"Fu-uck! Yes!" Snod whimpered, not even recognizing

his own voice. When Frankie spanked him, he realized it was forcing his body to clench down on Frankie's cock and it made him ache. Frankie's cock felt bigger somehow, as Snod whined at another hard smack. "Fuck, yes…"

"We're up to eight now." Frankie rubbed Snod's sore cheek, switching to the other side with a violent smack. "Mmm, and nine… I love watching your ass bounce, how eager you are for it… my beautiful boy…"

Snod felt ashamed and elated all at once hearing the praise, trying to push back on Frankie's cock with an eager whine. He got another rough smack in response, gasping as his eyes teared up. "Shit! Frankie!"

"Shhh, come on," Frankie urged, "you can take it. I know you can, Obe. Relax, breathe… and let me take care of you. We'll get there, I promise you."

"I trust you," Snod whispered, closing his eyes and groaning as Frankie's hand got going again. Rapid spankings in quick succession followed by one or two light slaps to give him a moment to breathe left him reeling in pleasure and the sweetest agony. All he could do was moan and take every wonderful slap, the heat of his abused skin spreading to his hips and his thighs. He felt like his bottom was absolutely on fire and he loved it.

Frankie began to roughly thrust into Snod's tight hole, his hand still occasionally popping his ass when he tried to move again. "Be a good boy, Obe."

"I wanna be good," Snod gasped breathlessly, not even recognizing his own voice for how broken and needy he sounded. "Please, I just wanna be good for you…"

Frankie slid his hand around Snod's hips, squeezing his hard cock with a hungry little growl. "Mmm, you are, Obe. You're so good, so tight… and so very wet." He lightly popped Snod's cock, chuckling when Snod's ass instinctively clamped down in response.

"Oh, fuck."

"Oh, yes," Frankie said, totally delighted. He kept fucking Snod, slowly and deliciously, taunting, "You want me to spank your cock, Obe?"

Those words burned a hole right through Snod, pleading anxiously before he even knew what he was saying, "Fuck, yes, please, do that, spank my cock, please, just do it, just do it!"

Frankie held Snod's cock flush against his own stomach, smacking it hard with his other hand. "Like that, my sweet boy?"

"Yes!" Snod cried out, writhing in Frankie's powerful grip. The burn on his cock was exciting and new, his balls growing tighter and tighter. He could feel his orgasm was only a breath away, but he knew Frankie wasn't done yet. Over and over, Frankie spanked his cock and squeezed his balls while he fucked him, Snod's brain about to overload from sensation.

"Feel good?" Frankie asked, giving Snod's balls a hard twist.

Snod could only moan and shake his head, grinding his teeth together. He had already lost count of how many times Frankie had spanked him, and he then realized that his arms were shaking from the adrenaline flooding his nerves. "Mmm… Frankie…"

"You've been such a good boy for me, so very good," Frankie said with a naughty smile, his hips suddenly snapping forward with unexpected strength as he drove his cock deep inside of Snod. "Mmm, now it's time for your reward!"

Snod groaned, eyes wide at the force behind the thrust, lights of pleasure dancing in his vision. His ass was sore and his cock was positively throbbing, screaming in bliss when Frankie pounded into him again and again.

Frankie forced Snod all the way down flat on his stomach, fucking him hard, holding him at his side and shoulder as he growled, "God, yes, you feel so fucking good…!"

Snod was sobbing, helplessly pinned beneath Frankie and completely blissed out. He could give this to Frankie, he could be vulnerable, he could be happy. All of his old memories were gone from his mind in those heated moments, giving himself over to his lover entirely.

He pressed his cheek against the mattress, his hands clenching into the sheets, his mouth opening but not able to make a sound. Frankie was fucking him so hard, so fast, he was totally lost to it and he'd forgotten how to even breathe.

The pressure was almost painful, the crack of their flesh smacking together echoing throughout the room. He could hear his own heart thumping in his ears, drowning out every other sound, moaning shamelessly as his loins throbbed. He was aching for release, his cock grinding into the bed, clenching his teeth together until they hurt.

Breathe… breathe for me, Obe…

Snod sucked in oxygen, gasping and mewling, listening to Frankie's tender voice. The pressure was so intense that he was wailing, moaning as he realized he was about to come again. The friction of the sheets rubbing against his tender cock and Frankie's relentless pounding was perfect, every muscle locking down tight until he started to quiver.

He came, wave after wave of ecstasy melting his brain into a wonderful pool of nothing, twitching and groaning low when he felt Frankie finishing inside of him. It was warm, slick, and he sighed contently as Frankie lovingly kissed his shoulder.

"Wow…" Frankie lazily pushed his cock in and out, the slide easy with how wet Snod's asshole was. "That was amazing, Obe."

"Mmmmhmmm," Snod agreed.

"Now I'm definitely going to be late," Frankie chuckled affectionately, nuzzling against his cheek. "I trust the birthday boy is satisfied for now?"

"Yes," Snod mumbled, lifting up his head for a kiss. "For now."

Frankie snickered, turning to slap Snod's ass one more time.

"Ow! Fuck! What was that for?" Snod complained.

"One to grow on," Frankie replied with a wink. He grinned, sliding off to clean them up again in a blink, leaving Snod tucked in and a tray of breakfast in his lap. Snod was startled, blinking down at the steaming eggs and bacon, asking, "How…?"

"Magic," Frankie teased.

"Magic?" Snod scoffed.

"Yes!" Frankie said, grinning slyly. "Just wait until tonight after the party that you totally don't know Athaliah is throwing for you. I'll show you how freakin' magical I am."

Snod bit hungrily into a piece of bacon, eyeing Frankie from head to toe as he purred, "Can't wait."

"Love you," Frankie said, kissing him sweetly.

"And I love you," Snod replied, smiling warmly as he watched Frankie hurry off to work. He finished his breakfast and showered carefully, being mindful of his sore cheeks and dick. He lingered in the warm water for a long while, happy and content, finally stepping into the guest room to find a particular shirt he wanted to wear.

They had started moving Snod's things into Frankie's room, bit by bit, but not all of his clothes would fit in Frankie's closet yet. He kept them stored in here, thumbing through the hangers thoughtfully and tightening his towel around his waist.

Athaliah had been as subtle as a sledgehammer about his party, dropping hints like cement blocks for days. He was ridiculously excited for tonight, and Snod knew that he had been working very hard to make it happen.

Snod decided to make the best of it and enjoy the evening to come, picking out one of the nicer dress shirts that Frankie had bought for him.

It was dark blue with silver buttons, soft and sleek. He had a pair of black slacks that would look perfect with it. Maybe a vest, maybe not. He started to put it on as he debated, but he paused when he realized it had French cuffs.

Damn, did Frankie buy him cufflinks?

Snod couldn't remember. He dug around in the closet, moving to peek inside the bedside table to check. He froze, staring down at his old phone sitting next to his scapular in the top drawer.

Setting the shirt down, he sat on the bed and anxiously licked his lips. He should destroy it. Throw it in the trash. Burn it.

The familiar sting of guilt forced his hand and he couldn't help himself. He turned it on and watched it boot up with bated breath.

He clicked through old text messages, finding the picture that Father Sanguis had sent him. It was the painting of Frankie and his Maker, Terrell Guiscard. He frowned when he looked at the date, realizing that it was sent a month ago today.

A month ago, he had pledged to find that name and give it to the Order, desperate to return to their ranks. A month ago, he thought his world was ending.

But now he was in love, deeply and truly. He had new friends and his beloved brother was here. He had a job that he enjoyed and an entirely new purpose for his life.

He had a new world.

When the phone rang, his heart stilled in his chest and his blood ran cold. His new world crumbled away, and he was staring at the ringing device in shock.

It was Father Sanguis.

He drew in a shaking breath and his hands began to tremble. He had to answer it. He had to. He had to report in, he had so many new sins to confess…

No.

He threw the phone at the floor, choking back a broken sob. He held his face in his hands, fear taking away his breath and all of his confidence. He was a scared little boy again and it was his first lesson; the first time he had to learn the pain of punishment and the reward of forgiveness.

The phone kept ringing, and Snod bit down on the heel

of his hand. It was such an innocent melody, a simple pulsing chime of bells, but every time it sounded Snod could feel his soul shattering. He could hear the hymns, the snap of the whip, and he could smell the censers burning their foul incense.

He couldn't stop himself, crawling like a terrified child toward the phone, wishing to God that he was strong enough to resist its pull. He picked it up, answering it with a gasp, his voice trembling as he said, "H-hello?"

"My son," Father Sanguis' voice slithered through the line like a serpent, wrapping itself tightly around Snod's throat. "It has been a month, precious child. Tell me…"

"No," Snod protested immediately. "I have nothing to tell you."

"Oh, my beloved son," Sanguis sighed mournfully. "You've been corrupted, haven't you? Tell me, what has that foul beast done to you?"

"Nothing I didn't want him to," Snod growled.

"You've let the beast blaspheme the sacred temple of your body for carnal pleasure, yes," Sanguis intoned patiently, "but we can wash those sins away, my sweet child. I can take all of that pain away. I know it still festers deep in you. Deep in your soul, you know what you've been letting that creature do to you is wrong…"

It's a sin…

Snod gurgled, tears burning in his eyes as he tried to argue, "No, Father. It's not… it's not wrong. I love him. And he loves me! And love is—"

"Love is meaningless when it's so obviously polluted by sin. When was the last time you prayed? What was the last sin you confessed, my son?"

Sanguis' words were a siren song, calling all of Snod's protests to heel. He was already on his knees, trying not to cry, his teeth slamming together as he croaked bitterly, "I don't… I don't remember, Father."

"Let's pray together, my son," Sanguis soothed, his silky tone demanding obedience. "You must be positively filthy."

Snod bit his tongue to hold back a sob, whimpering, "Yes… I'm… I'm so filthy…"

"Find something to cleanse yourself with," Sanguis purred. "We'll pray together and purify you, my dear child."

Snod started toward his closet, finding a belt and putting the phone on speaker. He sat back on his knees, the once familiar ritual now so foreign to him. The belt wrapping around his hand he knew well, but he didn't feel any comfort for what was to come.

He was angry and afraid.

He didn't want to do this.

"Lord o'God, please forgive Your lost child, Obadiah Penuel Snod, for all of his sins," Sanguis began the prayer. "Forgive him for how he has sinned against You and allowed himself to be a whore for the most unholy of beasts. Forgive him for allowing his heart and mind to be corrupted, for letting him be filled with the vampire's disgusting poison…"

Every word turned Snod's stomach, bile rising up into the back of his mouth. It wasn't true. None of it was true.

"He will repent immediately in blood and with flesh," Sanguis went on. "He seeks to walk in Your light again. Please allow him to be forgiven…"

"How many?" Snod croaked miserably, bowing his head in submission.

"That all depends, my son," Sanguis sighed. "Did you do as I asked? Were you able to learn the name of that fiend's Maker?"

Snod flinched, the leather creaking in his hand. The spell was beginning to fade, saying breathlessly, "How many lashes, Father… how many?"

"The name," Sanguis repeated sharply, all of the kindness vanishing from his voice in an instant. "Tell me! Did you learn it!"

"Yes," Snod panted. "I did… but tell me, Father. I need to be forgiven, don't I? How many lashes will it take?"

"The name, you insolent child!" Sanguis roared

furiously. "Give me the name or I will cast your soul into eternal damnation! You will never see the light of our Father's Holy Kingdom, you ungrateful blaspheming sodomite!"

Snod's upper lip twitched, sneering, "No."

"Pardon?" Sanguis hissed.

"No," Snod said more fiercely. "I will never say it. I won't."

"A hundred lashes," Sanguis spat, "and a hundred more for your insubordination, you disgusting fiend. Flay yourself until I tell you to stop! Begin now!"

A horrible howl tore itself out of Snod's throat, his hand rising up before he could think better of it, striking himself across the back. The buckle struck flesh, and he knew it was bleeding. He hit himself again, whimpering shamefully.

He kept going, crying out with every lash, listening to Sanguis' horrible breathing through the phone while he suffered.

"Now," Sanguis growled, "tell me, you wretched boy. Tell me that name!"

Snod's blood was pumping furiously all throughout his body, and he was able to detect the rich scent of it from his wounds where it was leaking. They hurt, the burn offering not one ounce of absolution. It didn't mean anything. None of this did.

What he had with Frankie…

That meant something. Frankie's affection, his warm passion and his hot punishments; his love was everything to Snod. He reached down deep for that beautiful warmth, clinging to it possessively, wrapping himself up in it tight.

Frankie… I love you…

Obe?

Snod was sobbing angrily, dropping the belt as he snarled furiously, "No! Never! I will never tell you!"

"You dare risk damnation of immortal soul?" Sanguis bellowed. "You refuse your own salvation?"

"I dare anything!" Snod roared back. "You are the one

who is corrupted, taking words of light and tainting them with darkness! There is no salvation to be found in this meaningless torture! I will never tell you, I will never serve you or your false god again! Never!"

Hold on, Obe! Hold on! I'm coming!

It was Frankie, beautiful and sweet Frankie.

"You will regret this, ungrateful child! You were a lamb, and now you've become the wolf!" Sanguis sneered hatefully. "We will hunt you just the same without mercy!"

Snod swallowed hard, picking up the phone to reply directly into the speaker, taking a deep breath as he spat, "Suck my fuckin' dick, Father."

"You disgusting, vile—!"

Hanging up quickly, his fingers trembled as he pulled the battery out of the phone and snapped it in half. He collapsed on the floor, every muscle drowning in adrenaline and causing him to shiver uncontrollably. His back was aching, his soul was on fire, and he was certain he was going to throw up.

He didn't know how long it was before he felt Frankie's strong arms lifting him up, his voice in Snod's ear, comforting and warm, whispering, "Obe, hey, Obe! Tell me. Talk to me. What happened? You were so afraid, what's wrong?"

Snod could only weep at first as Frankie carried him to bed, petting his hair and kissing his tears. He felt something sticky rubbing around on his back, the fading pain identifying the substance as Frankie's own blood.

"Tell me what happened," Frankie urged lovingly. "If you can't tell me… open your mind, show me."

Snod shook his head weakly, not sure how to show Frankie what happened. He tried to think it all back over, tried to recall Sanguis' hateful words and how weak he had been. The memories were too fresh, too painful, as he covered his face with his hands.

Frankie held him close, cradling him in his lap as if he were a child. He kept his side of the bond flooded with love, his voice gentle as he said, "I'm so proud of you, Obe. You stood up for yourself. You were so brave."

Laughing bitterly, Snod scoffed, "Brave?"

"You're finally free," Frankie said lovingly. "You denied him! You had the courage to refuse that creep and totally told him to suck your dick! Do you have any idea how amazing that is?"

Snod blinked, gazing up at him with a crooked smile, replying softly, "You. You made me brave. Your love…"

Frankie gently laid Snod down against the pillows and stretched out beside him, bringing him in for a gentle kiss. He curled their hands together, smiling brightly as he said, "Our love, Obe. It's ours… and I'm so very, very proud of you."

Snod found himself smiling, murmuring, "It did feel pretty good to tell him off… I feel… I feel lighter."

"I bet," Frankie chuckled, kissing his forehead. "Hell of a way to spend your first birthday."

Snod actually laughed out loud at that, his smile brightening as he pleaded, "Can we just skip the rest of my birthday?"

"No," Frankie teased. "Afraid not. Your not-so-surprise party is in a few hours, and I'm pretty sure your brother will murder us both if we miss it."

Snod snorted, taking a deep breath as he tried to collect his thoughts. He looked over Frankie's scrubs, commenting softly, "You left work because of me. The carpool?"

"Nothing to worry about," Frankie assured him. "Lorenzo is on it. I came because you needed me. I could feel your pain. I'll always be here for you, Obe."

"Always?"

"Always," Frankie promised with a kiss.

"Even if I want to bail on my own party?" Snod grumbled.

"Mmm, I dunno," Frankie sighed dramatically. "Your brother can be kind of forceful. We should probably go. At least for a bit. Eat some cake, open some presents…"

Snod groaned lightly in protest.

"If you really don't want to go, we won't," Frankie swore, squeezing Snod's hand.

"No," Snod sighed. "Athaliah worked so hard, it's important. We'll go… but until it's actually time… can we… can we just… could we…?"

"Cuddle?"

"Yes," Snod breathed softly.

"Whatever you want, birthday boy."

CHAPTER TWENTY

Snod drifted in and out of sleep, waking only to pull Frankie closer if he felt like he had strayed too far from his embrace. His body felt as if he had been out hunting for days, exhausted to the marrow and he was grateful for the chance to rest.

There was a giddy and ridiculous voice in his head that couldn't believe what he had done. He had told off Father Sanguis, an archbishop of the Order and a member of the council. He had refused to complete his mission, denied his terrible punishment, and it had been positively liberating.

Decades of training had been cast aside, and the shackles of hatred that had kept him bound for so long had finally been shattered. He was free, completely and totally, of any obligation to the Order.

A trickle of fear still managed to drip into his joyful reverie, stirring and burying his face against Frankie's chest with a soft sigh.

"What's wrong?" Frankie asked, his fingers gently stroking through Snod's hair.

"The Order," Snod replied. "You know they may come after me. Maybe even Athaliah." He sighed again. "They don't care for people outside of their ranks knowing about their operations, especially as intimately as I do having been a hunter."

"I'll protect you," Frankie said without hesitation. "We can always move if you want."

"But your research is here, your friends, my job," Snod said, frowning slightly. "We have a life here. I don't want to throw that away to run from them."

"Do you really think they'll just leave you alone?" Frankie asked, quirking a brow.

"I honestly don't know," Snod replied, uncertain and his brow creasing with worry. "I know they've hunted down others who have left…"

"So you've said," Frankie sighed, his thoughts a little troubled. He cheered up suddenly, suggesting, "Well, why don't we take a vacation? Get out of town for a little while?"

"Vacation?"

"You know," Frankie chuckled, "somewhere with sand and water. Me and you and some bathing suits… a vacation!"

Snod stared blankly, asking slowly, "To what end?"

"To relax. That's the point of a vacation! To relax, to get away."

"But we'd come back?"

"Yes," Frankie said, smirking playfully. "We would come back. We'll take a little break, give time for things to cool down, and then we'll come home. Both you and Athaliah have new identities now, you won't be that easy to find."

"Athaliah found me," Snod pointed out, "and they already know what city we're in."

"We will handle it," Frankie reassured him, his confidence not wavering for a moment. "I promise. Try not to worry so much."

Snod grumbled, turning his head to stare up at the ceiling.

Gently pressing his hand against Snod's cheek, Frankie tilted his face back toward him until their eyes met. He was smiling, soothing, "I love you. We will get through this, just like everything else, together."

"I love you, too," Snod replied earnestly, leaning into Frankie's cool palm. "Don't suppose we could leave on vacation right now?"

"And miss your party?" Frankie gasped in mock horror.

"Yes."

"Nope," Frankie said with a firm shake of his head. "Pissing off your brother scares me more than a crazy cult full of vampire killers."

Snod laughed, Frankie joining in, both of them cackling until they had tears in their eyes. Snod sucked in a deep breath, grateful for the moment of levity, leaning in to kiss Frankie's lips.

"Well," Frankie hummed. "I suppose we need to get ready. Start thinking of some exciting and exotic places you want to visit."

Snod was at a loss, frowning to himself as he tried to think of somewhere, anywhere, that he would want to go. He shrugged, saying at length, "I don't care where we go. As long as we're together."

Frankie kissed his cheek, teasing, "Sweet talker."

"Honest talker," Snod corrected.

"Come on then, my honest boy," Frankie chuckled, dragging Snod out of bed. "Let's get you ready for your big ol' party!"

Frankie moved in a blur, fetching the dark blue shirt that Snod had picked out earlier. He paired it with black slacks, a vest in a complementary shade of blue with a silver tie. Frankie had indeed purchased cufflinks for Snod, helping him snap them into place.

He peeked over Snod's shoulder, beaming at his reflection in the bathroom mirror as he gushed, "You look amazing."

Snod watched his cheeks turn red, shyly turning his head as he said, "Mmm, so do you."

Frankie had chosen a scarlet dress shirt and a plaid bow tie with khakis. The glasses he was wearing were round with thick rims and a pair of suspenders completed his outfit.

Snod thought he looked positively gorgeous.

"Come on, birthday boy," Frankie laughed, kissing him fondly. "Let's get you to your party!"

Snod did his best to look forward to the celebration ahead, although on the drive over his stomach was still clenching with worry. Frankie took his hand, but directly didn't comment on it. He continued to keep his own thoughts positive and warm, and it made Snod feel better.

He was smiling by the time they pulled up to the bar, and the tension in his bones had relaxed.

Perhaps this wouldn't be so bad.

Frankie led him by the hand inside, a giant roar of "Surprise!" greeting them both. The entire bar was decked out with countless balloons and dazzling streamers, and a big banner declaring 'Happy Birthday' was hung up behind the stage.

Athaliah was marching toward him with a brightly decorated cake covered in blazing candles in his arms, his sweet voice leading the crowd in a rousing rendition of the birthday song.

Rees was sitting at the bar, raising a glass as he sang along. Lorenzo was hovering nearby, waving excitedly as he wailed, horribly out of tune but very enthusiastic. Mandy and Dwayne were also joining in, grinning cheerfully at him. Even Kevin, whose arm was still in a cast, was lending his voice to the joyful chant.

Frankie was singing softly, his voice somehow rising above them all despite his quiet tone. He was smiling, squeezing Snod's hand and lovingly kissing his cheek in between each verse.

Snod's heart had never felt so full, surrounded by so many people who cared for him. He was worried that his soul might burst and splatter all over the floor, clinging to Frankie tightly to steady himself.

It was such a simple and benign song, and yet it moved him more than any church chant ever had. It was beautiful, and he could feel tears clogging his vision.

When it ended, everyone applauded and cheered and Athaliah firmly commanded, "Now! You have to make a wish and blow out the candles!"

"Why?" Snod asked flatly, blinking rapidly to dissuade his tears.

"Because duh, that's how you make the wish come true!" Athaliah drawled with a roll of his eyes.

Snod didn't understand, frowning at the little flames, asking again, "Why? What am I wishing for?"

"Whatever you want," Frankie giggled, hugging his waist. "Just remember! You can't tell anyone or it won't come true."

"Why won't it come true?"

"Magic," Frankie replied mysteriously.

Snod accepted that answer, quickly trying to think up a wish. He looked over all the smiling faces beaming at him, his family and his new friends, and he suddenly wished he could he could be this happy for the rest of his life.

That was a pretty good wish, he decided. He quickly blew out all the candles to appease the capricious birthday spirits, smiling as everyone clapped.

"Yay! Now, let's eat this damn thing, and then you can open presents!" Athaliah exclaimed happily.

Smirking bashfully, Snod leaned against Frankie with a shake of his head. Athaliah had truly outdone himself. He let Frankie lead him over to a table to sit down, frowning when he saw a familiar figure out of the corner of his eye.

It couldn't be.

Broad shoulders. Shaved head. Big.

Snod quickly turned around, his pulse beginning to thump dreadfully.

"Obe?" Frankie asked, sensing his fear.

"Ephraim Rosario," he said, teeth tight. "Another hunter from the Order. This place is no longer safe."

"What are you talking about?" Frankie demanded, his panic rising to meet Snod's.

Looking around quickly, Snod jumped up and raced into the kitchen with Frankie right behind him. Athaliah called out after them, but Snod ignored him.

The kitchen, that's where Ephraim would have done it.

Kicking open the door, Snod found himself staring at a large bomb that had been hooked up directly into the gas lines.

"Is that—" Frankie gasped.

"We have to get everyone out of here," Snod hissed. "Right now, we have—"

The bomb ignited, the force of the explosion sending Snod and Frankie flying back through the open doorway and into the bar. Fire erupted over every surface of the kitchen, and an oozing flammable liquid carried the flames all over the floor and right toward them.

People started to scream, panic imploding as they all started rushing toward the front door.

"Are you okay?" Frankie was shouting, pulling Snod up to his feet to get him out of the way of the flaming liquid.

Snod's ears were ringing, and he tried to nod his head. His chest hurt, but he was all right. There wasn't any shrapnel in the explosion. He knew the bomb wasn't meant to tear things apart, it was meant to burn them.

That was always Ephraim's way.

A second explosion by the front door sent everyone running and crying. Fire crawled all over the walls and the stage, incinerating the colorful birthday banner in seconds. Smoke was filling the bar, screams of terror and coughing clogging up the dim.

Snod tried to stay low, covering his mouth and trying to stay focused. The whole building was going to burn down as fast as the flames were spreading. They had to get out of here.

"The back door!" Frankie yelled, grabbing Snod tight and blinking him outside.

Snod grunted as he was dropped on the ground, panting as he tried to clear his lungs and breathe in clean air.

Lorenzo and Athaliah suddenly popped up beside him, quickly followed by Rees. They all scrambled to back away from the burning building, smoke beginning to pour out from the roof.

The other patrons and staff were appearing, all of them being dropped off at lightning speed. Every time the door was about to shut, it suddenly swung open again as someone else was brought outside. Snod cursed, knowing it was a risky use of Frankie's ability, but everyone was disoriented and scared. No one was going to question the nature of their rescue.

Snod rushed over to check on his brother first, hugging him tightly. "It's Ephraim," he hissed in his ear. "I saw him."

"Oh, no," Athaliah gasped, his eyes wide in fear. "Why... why would he do this?"

"I don't know," Snod said, shaking his head. "I think it's because of me. I wouldn't give the Order what they wanted."

Athaliah cried quietly, wrapping his arms around Snod's waist, sniffing defiantly, "I won't let him take you."

Every second miserably dragged on as more people appeared, and Snod kept his eyes on the door as his stomach tightened down. He thought he felt blazing pain and a surge of sudden fear, but he didn't know if it was his own or Frankie's that he was experiencing.

Something was terribly wrong.

"Come on, Frankie," Snod hissed desperately. "Where are you?"

Part of the roof had collapsed, and he could hear sirens wailing off in the distance from an approaching fire engine and police. All of the patrons and staff seemed to be accounted for now, but the door had finally shut.

Still no Frankie.

"Is this everyone?" Lorenzo asked breathlessly, coughing weakly.

"Frankie is still in there!" Snod snarled. He tried to open

the door, kicking it furiously when it wouldn't budge.

"Can't open the door from that side!" Rees woefully reminded him, wheezing from his spot on the ground. "Gotta go around front!"

"Take care of him," Snod snapped at Lorenzo, gently pushing Athaliah into his arms. "I'm going after Frankie."

"Obie!" Athaliah called out in protest. "Be careful!"

Snod took off at a dead run, sprinting down the alley and turning the corner to the front of the building. Frankie was powerful, but fire could still hurt him.

Obe… don't! Don't come for me! Run! Run away! It's a trap!

"No!" Snod roared furiously. The moment his feet touched the sidewalk out front, a burly fist popped him in the face. He saw stars, trying to raise his hands to fight back, but another powerful punch dropped him to his knees.

The world was spinning and his mouth was full of blood. He was dizzy, staring upward and trying to see who had hit him.

"Hi, Snod," Ephraim's gravelly voice greeted him, pushing him down on his stomach. Ephraim crawled on top of him, his knee digging into his back as he sighed, "Been a while."

"Ephraim!" Snod growled, struggling to break free, but Ephraim was too fast. His wrists were zip tied together in a second, and despite his ferocious kicking, Ephraim easily tossed him into the back of a van he had waiting a few yards away.

"Obe!" Frankie cried out, whimpering in pain as Snod collided with him.

"Frankie? Frankie! Are you all right?" Snod demanded, rolling onto his side to look at him.

Silver chains were wrapped around Frankie's neck and wrists, his flesh sizzling softly where the metal was digging in. The wounds were bleeding, each one raw and angry. His glasses were missing, and his shirt was torn.

Frankie was gaunt, weak, smiling sadly as he sighed haggardly, "Of all the damn things to get right… the Order was always right about silver."

"You can't move? At all?" Snod whispered, glancing up to the front seat where Ephraim had climbed in behind the wheel. He would make Ephraim pay for letting Frankie suffer like this.

"No…" Frankie's eyes closed, desperately trying to keep his pain from tainting the bond. "Can't."

He was waiting for me inside… it was a trap.

"Can you… you know?" Snod nodded his head suggestively toward Ephraim.

Whammy him?

"No," Frankie answered miserably.

Tried… he's wearing some… some kind of charm… like your scapular…

Snod looked around quickly. There was no way to open the back doors from the inside and steel mesh separated them from the front. There was no way out. He tried to sit up, grunting at Ephraim took off suddenly, and the momentum sent him flying flat on his back.

"Obe," Frankie yelped, "are you okay?"

"Peachy," Snod grumbled, wiggling back around to stretch out beside Frankie. He turned his head, calling to Ephraim, "How'd you find me?"

"I've been huntin' you for weeks," Ephraim scoffed.

Snod frowned, echoing, "Weeks?"

"Father Sanguis ordered me to keep an eye on you," Ephraim replied. "He had a feeling you wouldn't be able to complete your mission. So I went on and told Athaliah your last location. Let him escape…"

Snod closed his eyes, groaning lightly, "You followed him here. You knew he'd find me."

"Yup. I watched, I waited."

"Waited for what?" Snod demanded sharply.

"Orders to take you."

"Sanguis wants us alive?" Snod demanded, trying to keep Ephraim talking.

"You're breathing, aren't you?"

"What about Athaliah?"

Ephraim paused before growling, "What about him?"

"If any harm befalls him, I swear to God—" Snod began, his rage boiling.

Ephraim reached back and pounded his fist against the steel, shouting, "You ain't got no right swearing to a god that you betrayed!"

"Fuck you! If you hurt my brother, there's no god in the world that'll keep you safe from me!" Snod seethed venomously.

"I don't have orders for him!" Ephraim snapped back. "All right?"

Snod fell silent, glaring furiously.

"I only have orders for the two of you," Ephraim sighed, clearly frustrated. "I'm supposed to bring the two of you alive and brought before the council. Now… shut up."

"It'll be hours before we're back at the compound," Snod sneered. "You really think I won't find a way—"

"We're not going home," Ephraim grunted. "The council is waiting for us close by."

Snod's eyes widened. He had never known any members of the council to leave the sanctuary of their compound before. He didn't understand what was so important about a vampire's name that they would take such a risk.

"We'll be there soon," Ephraim growled. "Don't get any wise ideas, okay?"

Snod felt a wave of pain break through from Frankie, and hearing him gasp in pain made his heart ache. They had to get out of here. He had no idea what was waiting for them, but he had no doubt that the Order would kill Frankie. He swallowed hard, looking at Ephraim and saying urgently, "You don't have to do this."

"Shut up," Ephraim warned.

"Ephraim, listen to me," Snod pleaded. "We've known each other since we were children. We did our very first hunt together. I helped you after your first lesson, do you remember? Just like you helped me."

Ephraim said nothing.

"We were friends! Please, if you ever gave a damn about me, you have to listen to me. The Order is wrong. They're wrong about everything. Vampires, our sins, all of it—"

"Shut up!" Ephraim roared, punching the steel mesh again. "I will not listen to your blasphemy!"

"You know it's wrong!" Snod shouted passionately. "Come on! Deep down inside of you, down in your fuckin' soul, you have to know it's not right! There has to have been some moment, some doubt—"

"Stop trying to confuse me!" Ephraim growled furiously. "I never have doubts, never! I believe in our God, I believe in the word, and I believe in our sacred charge to rid the world of the unholy curse—"

"Disease!" Snod snapped. "It's not a curse, it's a disease! Listen to me! We were wrong!"

"It's a curse born from their unholy pact with Satan, and you fucking know it!" Ephraim argued through gritted teeth.

"Come on," Snod scoffed bitterly, trying another angle now. "Don't you think it's strange that Father Sanguis wants us alive? He's up to something. He wanted me to find a name, a name of an ancient vampire..."

Ephraim growled faintly, but he held his tongue. He cocked his head, listening expectantly.

"There are old spells for summoning vampires if you know their name," Snod said quickly. "Why would the council want to summon a vampire, huh?"

"It is not my place to question their wisdom," Ephraim replied stiffly.

"You don't find it odd that they're very interested in summoning the very thing we are sworn to destroy? I mean, right now, you're allowing an unholy beast to live just a few feet away from you! On their orders!"

Unholy beast?

Frankie rolled his eyes.

Snod grimaced.

Unholy beast that I love and adore?

Hmmph…

"I do not question my orders," Ephraim repeated, but this time he didn't sound certain.

"Father Sanguis wants that name. I don't know why, but I think they want to summon this ancient vampire. But Frankie told me that the spell won't work. They won't be able to summon him or hold him or whatever else it is that they have planned!"

"Frankie?" Ephraim questioned.

"The vampire," Snod replied, sighing.

"That beast has warped your mind," Ephraim said sadly. "He's totally corrupted you. He's forced you to doubt the wisdom of the council and poisoned you."

"No, Frankie loves me," Snod defended, "and I love him. He's shown me how people can truly live happily and free outside of the Order, that the world is so full of beauty that—"

"Stop."

"Not until you fucking listen to me!"

"I will pull this van over right now," Ephraim said with a dangerously low snarl. "I will take my knife, and I will cut into you until you pass out if you don't fuckin' shut up."

Obe…

Frankie was gazing at him with pleading eyes, pain throbbing pitifully through their bond.

He's too far gone… you tried…

Snod grinded his teeth in frustration, turning back toward Frankie. He leaned their foreheads together, taking a deep breath and closing his eyes. He tried to be strong for them both, but he was so afraid.

Frankie was scared, too.

"I love you," Snod murmured softly. "No matter what happens, whatever they do, they can't take that away from me."

Frankie managed a weak smile, his eyes bright and lashes fluttering as he replied, "I love you, too. Being with you… you're the best thing that's ever happened to me. You make me feel… I feel human again when I'm with you."

Snod's face twisted up with anguish, pressing a soft kiss to Frankie's lips, trying to swallow back a sob. "I treasure every moment I've had with you," he said quietly. "Even if these are our last moments together, I regret nothing."

Frankie whined and weakly shook his head. He was losing his strength as the silver chains continued to burn into him and drain away his energy. He couldn't speak, concentrating on the bond instead.

I'm not afraid of death… I'm afraid for you…

"I'm ready," Snod said earnestly. "I can face whatever comes in the next world. My soul is prepared."

Ephraim scoffed loudly, but made no other comment.

Snod snarled, but resisted the urge to start another fight. He tried to focus his thoughts, closing his eyes tight.

We're alive. They want something from us.

Frankie fidgeted slightly.

Terrell… his name. Summoning him, if that's even what they're trying to do… It won't work, Obe… they're crazy.

They don't know that yet. We will find a way to escape, I promise you. Although I am ready to meet death, this will not be the day we die…

I love you, Obe.

I love you, too.

CHAPTER TWENTY-ONE

The van came to a stop approximately thirty-two minutes outside of the city, give or take a few seconds. Snod had been counting anxiously while trying to press himself as close as possible to Frankie. Tears of blood were drying on Frankie's face, and he was no longer able to keep the bond clear of his pain.

It was constant agony.

The silver was burning his flesh and not allowing it to heal, leaving the wounds ragged and aching. Frankie was exhausted, and Snod had never experienced feeling him so frail. That bright light that always blazed so beautifully inside of him was getting dim.

From his training with the Order, he knew silver could not kill Frankie. It would weaken him, but once it was removed, he would be able to heal. Snod had tried pulling at the chains with his teeth, but it was of no use. He couldn't free Frankie.

He had attempted to free himself and also found failure. The zip tie would not break, and he knew his wrists were bleeding from his efforts. He watched Ephraim climb out from the front seat, immediately sitting up and pulling himself into a crouching position.

The moment the doors opened, he would launch himself at Ephraim and head butt him. He would bite his face, kick him in the balls, anything to get the upper hand. He had to escape from him. He had to get Frankie away before they were both killed.

Snod was determined not to go down without a fight.

When the doors swung open, he was ready to spring into action until he saw that Ephraim was not alone.

There were at least a dozen other hunters with Ephraim, all fully armed.

Fuck it.

Snod launched himself anyway, managing to give Ephraim a good crack in the jaw before he was grabbed by the others. He got punched in the face for his efforts and barked out in pain as his lip split wide open. The sensation of the wound seemed far away, so very minuscule compared to Frankie's suffering.

Frankie cried out when they came for him, and not an ounce of kindness was offered as they dragged him out of the van. A few of the hunters kicked him, spat at him, and Snod's fury was uncontrollable.

He tried to jerk away from his captors, snapping his teeth and snarling, "Leave him alone, you fucking cowards!"

This only seemed to spur them on more, and the assault continued. Snod broke away, throwing himself down on top of Frankie to shield him, groaning as the next boot found its way into his ribs.

Obe… it's okay…

"Stop! Fucking leave him alone!" Snod demanded, another kick in his stomach snatching away his breath and making him gasp. He refused to move, trying to keep Frankie as protected as he could.

"Father Sanguis wants them both alive," Ephraim growled sharply. "Remember your orders."

The hunters finally relented and grabbed Snod, roughly yanking him to his feet. Frankie couldn't even stand, and Ephraim knelt down to scoop him up like a rag doll. Snod swallowed back a mouthful of fresh blood, panting softly as he was dragged forward.

At first glance, he thought they were in a parking deck. They were in a vast space surrounded by smooth, plain concrete and fat pillars. They were definitely underground judging by the smell of dampness and mildew. There was a steel door they were brought through that led into a narrow hallway.

At the end of the hall was another door that led into a large room. There were dozens of candles lit, and he could smell incense burning that immediately made him nauseous. There was a long table behind which sat all the members of the council with Father Sanguis sitting right in the middle.

Sanguis was leering at Snod triumphantly as he declared, "Our little wolf has returned."

Snod bared his teeth, grunting as the hunter on his right kicked the back of his knee and forced him to kneel.

There was an elaborate sigil painted on the floor with multiple glyphs marked around its border. Snod had never seen anything like it, glancing desperately over to Frankie.

What is that?

Ephraim had dropped Frankie on the floor, and he immediately curled up into a little ball. His quiet whimpers were miserable to hear, and his eyes fluttered open to look at the sigil.

Summoning circle…

"Now, there is the matter of your mission," Sanguis went on, casting a disgusted grimace toward Frankie. "You said you were able to learn the name of this fiend's Maker. What is it?"

Snod glared at Sanguis, growling defiantly, "Why should I tell you?"

"Because if you do, I'll offer you both a merciful death and send you into damnation as if you were merely falling asleep," Sanguis soothed. "Continue to be difficult, and what I do to you will make hell seem like a welcome reprieve."

"Never," Snod hissed, groaning as he received a swift crack in the side of the head. It sent him off balance, and he couldn't use his hands to catch himself. He toppled onto his face, grunting as he was promptly dragged back into a kneeling position.

"You want his blood… don't you?" Frankie gasped, fighting through the agony to glare up at Sanguis. "You've had it before… I can smell it on you…"

Snod stared at Frankie in bewilderment, and he flinched as Ephraim kicked Frankie right in his mouth.

"Quiet, fiend!" Ephraim roared, keeping his leg reared back to hit him again. "Don't you dare speak so of our holy father! They would never partake of your foul blood, they—"

"It's all right, my son," Sanguis urged, raising his hand for Ephraim to stop. He leaned across the table to regard Frankie with a cool smile, replying to him calmly, "In our war against your kind, we've all sinned. Perhaps we elders most of all. Your blood is very powerful, especially the blood of your unholy heart."

"What…?" Ephraim stuttered, grimacing in horror as he realized the full implications of what Sanguis was saying.

"Calm yourself, my child," Sanguis urged, sparing Ephraim a soft smile.

"Tell me it isn't true," Ephraim demanded hoarsely. He was trembling all over, and his eyes were wild and fierce.

Several of the other hunters were murmuring amongst themselves, and the air was becoming frighteningly tense.

"Has this council not served you all well?" Sanguis challenged with a click of his tongue, his smile vanishing in an instant. "Have we not guided you, provided our vision and our wisdom? Have we not taken care of you? For over two hundred years, we have been able to lead you! We made a pact with a fiend for the good of the Order so that we could go on fighting!"

"You sold your soul to the devil," Ephraim accused, his upper lip curling in revulsion.

"No," Sanguis insisted. "We took on a sin, a burden, so that we could be everlasting—"

"No!" Ephraim roared in disgust. "Every word you've said is tainted by that unholy blood inside of you! All of you are corrupted! Blasphemers! Hypocrites and fiends, every last one of you! None of you are fit to lead us!"

"Stand down," Sanguis spat furiously. "That is an order!"

"No," Ephraim snapped, angrily pointing at the council. "I see you now, all of you. You're all fucking liars! I will never take another order from your foul lips ever again… never."

Snod's heart ached for his friend. He knew the pain of finally seeing the truth behind their faith and being left wanting. Even though he had no affection left for the Order, he was still equally stunned that they had been abusing vampire blood.

It had to be why they wanted Terrell, he realized; they wanted his ancient blood.

"My children," Father Sanguis growled, rising to his feet and leaning heavily on the table. His eyes passed over all the hunters present as he announced, "Your brother conspires against us! He openly defies me. You must remain vigilant! Do not listen to his lies! He's been weakened by his association with Brother Snod! Obviously, he has been bewitched by that foul vampire just as Snod has been!"

"Liar!" Ephraim yelled, taking a step back when he realized his own brethren were ready to turn on him. "Did any of you actually hear anything he said? He's just confessed to the entire council using vampire blood! Polluting their own bodies! For centuries!"

"Take him," Sanguis commanded, slamming his fist into the table. "Bind him! He will suffer a thousand lashes before he dies!"

"Run!" Snod shouted suddenly. "Ephraim, for the love of all that is holy, *fucking run*!"

Ephraim turned and gave Snod a pleading look, his eyes

sad and pained.

In that moment. Snod knew they understood each other. Ephraim knew Snod had been right and regretted not hearing his friend out now. Ephraim bolted, and a few of the other hunters gave chase after him.

Snod heard doors slamming and a flurry of gunshots. He closed his eyes, hoping to God that Ephraim was able to get away.

"Now," Sanguis said, sighing deeply and looking back to Snod with an unfriendly smile. "Where were we? Ah, yes. You were going to give us the name."

"The name of the vampire whose blood you've been guzzling for the last two hundred years?" Snod retorted dryly.

"Yes, I was hunting him," Sanguis chuckled fondly, as if remembering an old friend. "I'd never seen a vampire that could move like him, like a ghost… He offered us the blood of his heart in exchange to never be hunted again. For the good of the Order, we accepted his bargain."

"To extend your own wretched lives," Snod bit out angrily, receiving a fist upside his head in response. He shook it off, scoffing, "And what's wrong now? Huh? Tank's running on empty?"

"We have need of the blood, yes," Sanguis growled softly. "For the future of the Order, for the lives of all our brothers and sisters… now, give me that name."

"You've run out, haven't you?" Snod cackled. "That's why you're so desperate. You're used up all that precious heart blood, and now you're all finally dying."

"The name," Sanguis demanded.

"No," Snod said, plastering a big smile on his face.

Waving at one of the hunters, Sanguis instructed him, "Bring me the whip. Perhaps if we cleanse Brother Snod's body of some of its sin, his mind will follow and cooperate."

Obe, just tell them!

Snod shook his head, grunting as the hunters tore off his tie and vest, cutting his shirt down the back and ripping it open. He looked at Frankie with a sad smile.

Even if I do, they're going to kill us anyway.

There was a loud crack as Sanguis unfurled the whip, rising to his feet.

Snod shuddered at the sound, but even as terror clutched at his heart, he refused to give Sanguis the satisfaction. He stared Sanguis down and held his head up high.

Sanguis stalked toward Snod. "Tell me the name… right now."

"Never," Snod replied firmly.

Sanguis circled around Snod and raised his arm, the whip ready to snap forward as he growled, "Last chance, my child."

"Rot in hell," Snod quipped, spitting at Sanguis' feet.

"May God have mercy on your soul," Sanguis intoned, his hand jerking to strike.

"Terrell!" Frankie gasped from the floor, writhing in pain as he struggled to raise himself up. "Stop… his name… is Terrell…"

"Frankie, don't!" Snod protested.

"Let Obe go," Frankie panted, his eyes shining bright as he glared at Sanguis. "Let him go, and I will tell you the rest."

"Frankie! No! Don't you fucking dare!" Snod roared, fighting to get to his feet and tear away from his captors. They grabbed him and held him firmly in place.

"Fine," Sanguis said curtly. "We have an accord, vile fiend. Tell me the name, and I swear to Almighty God that I will release him."

"Terrell Guiscard," Frankie replied breathlessly. He had managed to sit up, calling on some incredible inner strength to fight through the horrible pain he was in. "His name is Terrell Guiscard… Now, let Obe go."

The elders of the council quickly gathered around the sigil on the floor to write out the name. Sanguis was watching with a nasty smile, and then he suddenly cracked the whip across Snod's back.

Snod yelped in pain and surprise, the kiss of the whip digging in like a hot blade. He gritted his teeth, but couldn't stop another cry when Sanguis struck him again.

"What are you doing!" Frankie screamed as he struggled against the silver chains. "You said you'd let him go! You swore—"

"I swore that I would release him," Sanguis corrected savagely, "and so I shall. I shall release him from this mortal life, and I will pray that God will be merciful."

"You fucking bastard!" Frankie seethed, baring his fangs ferociously and writhing in agony as he fought to free himself.

Snod sobbed when the whip struck next, closing his eyes and trying to place his mind anywhere else. He thought of Frankie; lying in bed with him, cooking with him, all the hours they spent cuddled together on the couch.

Frankie's beautiful smile when he laughed, the arch of his brows when he was excited, the way his lips parted so sweetly when they made love, or that little furrow that would appear on his forehead when he was concentrating. All of these moments were flashing before Snod's eyes like photographs in an album, turning the page every time the whip tore into his flesh.

I love you, please, I love you so fucking much, I love you…

Frankie was weeping loudly, helpless and desperate, screaming furiously.

I love you, Obe! Don't die, please! Please, please don't die!

"The summoning didn't work," one of the elders hissed, momentarily interrupting Sanguis' torture. "The name must be wrong!"

Sanguis grunted in frustration, snapping the whip viciously across Snod's neck as he yelled, "You and your little vampire whore think me a fool? Don't you dare try to lie to me! Tell me the name!"

Laughing weakly, Snod fell forward onto his face. He was too weak to remain upright any longer, grateful for the cool feel of the floor against his cheek. He panted haggardly, his entire back flaming with agony. He couldn't tell where one lash began and the other ended, every bit of flesh stripped raw and throbbing. He continued to laugh, weakly replying, "That is… the name…"

"Then why didn't it work?" Sanguis howled, kicking Snod in the face. "Why!"

"Because you're a fucking idiot?" Snod suggested, groaning as Sanguis struck him with the whip again. He had lost so much blood, and it hurt to breathe. He closed his eyes, tears running down his cheeks.

This was it.

This was going to be how it ended.

I'm sorry, Obe… I can't watch this, I can't watch you die… I love you…

Snod shook his head, his vision blurring as he stuttered, "F-Frankie… what are you doing…"

No.

He wouldn't.

Please forgive me, Obe.

"Frankie! Don't!" Snod managed to shout, wiggling and trying to push himself off the floor. "Don't do it!"

"There's only one way to summon a vampire," Frankie hissed quietly, ignoring Snod's pleas as he glared furiously at Sanguis. "Here… let me show you."

Snod became immediately aware that the temperature was dropping. So quickly did it plunge that within the space of a blink, he realized that he could see his own breath.

Father Sanguis and the others were all looking around, puffing in terror and chattering anxiously. "What is this," he demanded, his voice trembling in fear. "What are you doing?"

A thick mist began to appear, heavy and black, snaking along the floor and filling the room. It never rose higher than a few feet, but it enveloped everything it touched in freezing cold.

Shivering, Snod rolled back on his knees so he could try to see what was going on. His captors had released him for the moment, and he took the opportunity to crawl out over to collapse beside Frankie. He pressed close, pleading urgently, "Please tell me you didn't… please…"

"I couldn't watch you die," Frankie whispered, blinking away bloody tears. "I'm so sorry, Obe. I love you."

"Ahhh, how touching," a smooth voice drawled, echoing off the concrete menacingly. It seemed to come from everywhere, but there was no visible source.

"Unholy creature of the devil!" Sanguis commanded. "Show yourself!"

"Mmm, only because you asked so nicely," the voice chuckled, apparently enjoying this as if it was all a big joke. The mist began to rush together until a solid figure began to form. It was a man, tall and beautiful with thick blond hair and a nasty smile.

Snod recognized him immediately from Frankie's memories and the painting.

This was Terrell Guiscard.

Sanguis was trembling, but still as arrogant as ever. He scoffed, pointing at Terrell and demanding, "It is you! Finally, you have come to us. We want to renegotiate our deal, fiend. In exchange for not hunting you, we—"

"No," Terrell said calmly, "there will be no more deals. Please don't mistake what was only a curious experiment for anything more."

"You, you were at our mercy!" Sanguis protested. "I could have killed you that day!"

"Oh, please," Terrell cackled, grinning down at Frankie and Snod. "Can you believe this blood bag?" He leaned in close to Father Sanguis to taunt, "I only made the deal with you because I was bored… I wanted to see what you would do. I thought perhaps the gift of everlasting life might inspire your puny mortal brains to seek out a new purpose for yourselves. Break the hold of those treacherous religious trappings…

"Maybe become artists? Wander the earth and help little children? Cure disease? Write poetry?" Terrell pursed his lips before sighing in disappointment. "But alas, it only reinforced your madness. Ironic that the blood of a vampire made you into more devoted vampire killers."

"No… this isn't true… that's, that's not how it happened," Sanguis wheezed as he backed away toward the table. "You are a liar, fiend! I will take every drop of blood right from your dead heart!"

"See? This is what I'm talking about!" Terrell laughed, lunging forward faster than Snod could see. There was a wet crunch, Sanguis screaming as Terrell sank his fangs in and tore out his throat.

There was no art in it and Terrell made no effort not to make a mess of himself. He enjoyed the kill, laughing like a madman as he dropped Sanguis to the floor with a slick smack.

Snod's heart seized up in horror, staring at his blank, unseeing eyes.

Sanguis was dead.

The other hunters started firing their useless guns and shouting angrily. Blinded by their fear, all of them started to swarm toward Terrell to attack and avenge their fallen father.

"Look at me!" Frankie snapped suddenly, nudging at Snod's cheek. "Don't look, please, just look at me! Don't watch!"

Snod grunted, blinking rapidly as he forced himself to stare into Frankie's gleaming eyes. He could hear men screaming, gunfire, and the heavy thump of bodies hitting the floor.

He knew them all; the hunters, young and old, the elderly members of the council.

They were once a part of his family, his very identity, and Terrell was slaughtering them all without mercy. He was angry, grieving, and completely helpless to stop it. He knew each of these men would have let him die, but his heart still ached for them as they took their final breaths.

Snod had never known any vampire that could move like

Terrell could, much less kill like him. All the while he could hear Terrell laughing, and it was the most bone-chilling sound he had ever heard. None of the hunters stood a chance. He truly was a monster.

"I love you," Frankie whispered, kissing Snod's forehead, trying to get as close as he could. "It's almost over. You'll be safe now."

"He's going to take you," Snod accused, flinching at a particularly loud cry of terror from one of the dying hunters. "You agreed to… to be with him!"

"To save you," Frankie insisted urgently. "Because I love you so much. Please don't ever forget that. Please forgive me. I couldn't… I couldn't let you die. Even if we're not together, I'll know you're alive."

Snod cried quietly, closing his eyes and tried to tune out the sounds of carnage. The smell of blood was thick and he could hear the hunters screaming as they fought Terrell. After what seemed like an eternity, it finally stopped.

Silence.

Footsteps broke the stillness as Terrell strolled toward them, whistling lightly. He crouched beside Frankie, grunting softly as he pulled off the chains, shaking his hands from the brief burn.

Frankie groaned in relief, rubbing at his wrists and neck. The wounds were slowly starting to close, and Snod could feel Frankie's suffering beginning to ease.

Terrell pulled Frankie up into his arms with an adoring sigh, cooing, "My beloved Francis… it has been far too long."

Snod rolled onto his back, growling when Terrell passionately kissed Frankie on the lips. He was even more furious when he saw Frankie kissing him back despite an overwhelming wave of revulsion bleeding through the bond.

Snod had never felt such fury, narrowing his eyes into venomous slits and snarling, "Don't you fucking touch him!"

Snorting in amusement, Terrell picked Snod up and pinned him against the far wall in a blink. He smiled, looking over him curiously as he said, "Ah, this is the one you wanted me to spare… your little human lover. Feisty."

"Untie me, and I'll fuckin' show you how feisty I am," Snod spat furiously.

"You know," Terrell teased, "the rest of these men tasted so bitter and weak." He leaned close, lewdly smacking his bloody lips together. "I bet you taste fantastic…"

"Leave him alone," Frankie warned, appearing right beside them. "You got what you came for. I'm going with you. Don't you dare harm him."

Snod's hands were still bound behind his back. He tried to jerk away and kicked at Terrell violently. Assaulting a dumpster full of cement would have been an easier opponent.

Terrell didn't budge.

"I'm going to kill you," Snod promised him with a horrible grin. "You will not take him from me. He is mine. I will fucking hunt you down, I swear it!"

"Such spirit!" Terrell praised, lightly smacking Snod's cheek. "I can see why you fancy him so, Francis."

"Let him go," Frankie demanded again, a faint hint of pleading softening his tone now.

Terrell shrugged, dropping Snod promptly as he sighed, "Say your farewells, and let us be on our way."

Snod never hit the floor, Frankie catching him and holding him tightly. The zip tie was snapped away like a piece of straw, and Snod quickly embraced Frankie the moment he was free. He leaned into him, shaking his head and trying not to cry.

Snod wanted to stay angry and seek out the strength in his rage, but all he could think about was this might be the last time he would ever hold his beloved boyfriend.

Frankie bit deeply into his palm and let his blood flow freely over Snod's wounded back. All the cuts were vanishing, and the pain faded away until the only agony left was Snod's heart splitting into fragments.

I'm sorry, I'm so fucking sorry, please, forget about me, get on with your life, find someone else, I love you so much!

Snod growled miserably, kissing Frankie passionately as he panted, "No, no, no. I'm not, I won't! I won't let you go!"

You don't have a choice…

"Yes, I do!" Snod snarled, possessively curling his fingers into Frankie's shoulders. "You taught me that! There's always a choice! I can make my own fucking decisions, and I am not giving up on you!"

Take the cure, break the bond, and forget about me, please. Terrell will kill you if you try to come for me… please, Obe. I love you…

Snod kissed Frankie with every ounce of love and anguish twisting around inside of him, convincing himself that this wouldn't be the last time. This would not be their last kiss.

Frankie was pulling away all too soon, his eyes red with bloody tears as he whispered, "I'm sorry, Obe… I love you."

"Don't go," Snod begged, trying to hold onto him. "Don't fucking go! Don't—"

Frankie was gone along with Terrell, both of them vanishing before Snod could even draw another breath. He fell against the wall, holding his face in his hands as defeat crushed him.

Frankie, please. I love you. You're everything to me, you're my whole fucking world… I will find a way to save you from him. I swear it.

Silence was all he received in response, straining to reach out and sense anything he could from Frankie. He couldn't feel anything, and he tried to get his scattered thoughts together. He was alone, surrounded by corpses, and he was completely lost.

Snod knew that Terrell was immensely powerful, but he refused to give up. There had to be a way to defeat him.

There had to be some fucking way.

In a moment of hopeless depression, he briefly considered what Frankie had told him to do; to take the cure and move on. It would certainly be easier, but how could he…

Wait.

The cure.

Snod was on his feet in seconds, flying toward the exit. A plan began to form, pushing aside his emotions and focusing on the task at hand. He had an ancient vampire to kill and a beautiful boyfriend to rescue. He had to get back to the city as quickly as possible. As much as he hated to admit it, there was only one person who could help him save Frankie.

Lorenzo.

CHAPTER TWENTY-TWO

Snod had never run so fast in his life. He raced back through the hallway and out the door, nearly tripping over more corpses. He paused long enough to identify them, realizing they were the hunters who had gone after Ephraim.

The van was gone.

Ephraim had escaped.

Snod felt a flicker of hope for his old friend as he tried to navigate his way out of the building. He had no idea where the other members of the Order had left their vehicles, groaning as he came to the miserable conclusion that he may end up walking back to the city.

The drive here had been approximately thirty-two minutes, and Ephraim had been driving at an average speed of forty-five miles per hour. That meant the trip was roughly twenty-four miles and walking at about three miles per hour would take Snod…

Way too damn long.

Fuck!

He had to try.

Snod had no idea where Terrell would have taken Frankie or where to even begin looking for them. They could be on the other side of the world by now, but he refused to give up hope. He wouldn't allow his love to be held captive a second longer than he had to be.

Just thinking about what Terrell might be doing to him made him shudder.

He had to get to Lorenzo as quickly as possible and get a sample of the cure. He needed something special to take on an ancient fiend like Terrell, and that explosive green serum might be enough to even the odds.

Snod took off at a brisk pace, heading back toward the city. He had only made it a few blocks before Ephraim's van was zooming up behind him.

"Oh, shit!" Snod cursed, jumping up on the sidewalk to get out of the way. He thought for sure that Ephraim was going to hit him.

The van roared right past him, skidding to a stop and slowly began backing up. Ephraim rolled down his window, staring blankly at Snod and demanding, "What happened?"

"They're all dead," Snod replied honestly, still poised to run.

"Your vampire lover?" Ephraim scoffed in disgust.

"No," Snod said, shaking his head slowly. "The one the council was trying to summon… The old one. He came. He took Frankie… it did not end well."

"But you survived," Ephraim said suspiciously.

"Yes," Snod said slowly, hesitating to elaborate.

Ephraim sighed, glancing out the windshield for a long moment. He was thinking. He looked back at Snod, snapping, "You can explain on the way."

"On the way where?"

"You're going after your vampire, aren't you?" Ephraim quirked his brows. "Which means you're gonna try to kill the other one."

"Yes."

"As long as I get to kill a vampire today, I'll be happy," Ephraim grumbled, jerking his head to the passenger seat. "Let's go."

Snod jumped in and Ephraim took off, following his directions to Athaliah's apartment. He suspected that they would find Lorenzo there. Along the way, Snod did his best to explain what had happened and his plan for going after Terrell.

"So," Ephraim said slowly, taking a few seconds to process everything, "you really think this green goo is gonna take out an ancient vampire who just ripped over a dozen of our best hunters to pieces?"

"I have to try," Snod said earnestly. "I've seen what it can do." He paused, looking out the window before adding, "You don't have to come with me."

"I should have listened to you," Ephraim replied quietly. "You tried to tell me, and I thought you had been blinded by lust. I had no idea how open your eyes truly were."

"For what it's worth, I'm sorry."

"No," Ephraim said sternly. "These sins are not yours to carry. The elders will pay for them when they meet God." He sighed, pressing a hand briefly to his forehead. "Without leadership, the Order will certainly crumble."

Making a sour face, Snod kept his eyes focused on the city passing by as he said, "Maybe it's better this way."

"And all those people left behind?" Ephraim snorted. "Our families at the compound? What about them?"

"Not my family," Snod corrected bitterly. "Not mine."

"You wouldn't come back to help?" Ephraim demanded roughly.

"Not even an hour ago, you and all our brothers were going to stand by and watch Father Sanguis beat me to death and murder the man I love," Snod replied coolly. "Forgive me if I'm feeling a little less than charitable."

"Fine," Ephraim scoffed. "I'll help you slay this vampire and then leave you to your life of sin."

"At least I'm free," Snod drawled, the very words empowering him and smirking smugly. "At least I'm happy."

"Hope that's comforting while you're rotting in hell,"

Ephraim grumbled, shaking his head in dismay.

Snod wanted to snap back and say something foul, but he took a deep breath to stop himself. Calmly, he replied, "Ephraim, I really hope that someday you know what it's like to love someone. Then you'll understand that the only real hell is being without them."

Ephraim had nothing to say to that, returning his attention to the road. They didn't say another word to each other until they arrived at Athaliah's apartment building when Snod briefly instructed him where to park. He quickly led Ephraim upstairs to Athaliah's door, banging loudly.

Athaliah answered immediately, his face raw from crying, gasping when he saw him.

"I'm okay—" Snod began, cut off with a grunt when Athaliah tackled him into an oxygen-depriving embrace.

"I was so fucking scared!" Athaliah wailed, burying his face against his chest. "I just knew that fucker Ephraim had taken you and Frankie! Damn him! I didn't know what to do!"

Snod held him close, glancing over his shoulder and finding Lorenzo and Rees perched anxiously on the sofa.

"I swear, I'll fucking kill him," Athaliah was ranting, pulling away to wipe at his face. "I'll rip off his balls, and…" He froze, howling furiously when he saw Ephraim standing in the hall, "You!"

Snod managed to catch Athaliah as he lunged, hugging his middle tightly and dragging him into the apartment. "He's here to help! It's all right!"

"You son of a bitch! You're fuckin' dead!" Athaliah screeched, kicking and trying to wiggle free.

Rolling his eyes, Ephraim followed them in and shut the door.

Rees was on his feet, his little body shaking with rage as he cursed, "This is the motherfucking piece of turtle feces that burned down my fucking bar?" He took off his earrings and kicked off his shoes. "Oh, bitch! You're a fucking dead man!"

Lorenzo yelped, grabbing Rees' arm and trying to keep him away from Ephraim. "Rees! Don't! Come on! Big scary hunter man, bad idea!"

"Let me at 'em!" Rees snarled, slapping Lorenzo's hands. He started coughing, wheezing angrily, "I'm going to claw his fucking eyes out!"

Ephraim did not look impressed by their threats. He crossed his arms, tapping his foot impatiently.

"Please!" Snod groaned, carrying Athaliah to the sofa and forcing him to sit down. "Terrell took Frankie! I need Ephraim's help!"

"Who the hell is Terrell?" Athaliah snapped, throwing his hands up in frustration.

"Frankie's Maker!"

Rees stopped struggling immediately. He stared at Snod, worry draining away all of his rage as he asked hoarsely, "He took him… why?" He hacked into his hand. "That fuckin' monster has him? What the fuck happened!"

"The Order wanted to summon him to use his blood," Snod explained, trying to talk as quickly as he could. "The council has been secretly abusing vampire blood for centuries. They needed his name for the summoning spell, but it didn't work. They were going to kill me…"

"Obie," Athaliah murmured, gently resting his hand on his arm.

Swallowing back the painful memory, Snod continued hastily, "Frankie called Terrell to save me. He allowed himself to be taken and made Terrell promise to spare me. He killed everyone else there… all the hunters, the elders. They're all dead."

"How did this lovely piece of human garbage survive?" Athaliah asked sweetly, batting his eyes at Ephraim. "Terrell decided that fuckin' morons with fat heads and big stupid ears weren't a tasty idea?"

Ephraim's upper lip twitched.

"Ephraim tried to confront the council about using vampire blood," Snod replied gently, offering his friend a sympathetic smile, "but they turned on him. He ran."

"So, what?" Rees huffed defiantly, taking a handkerchief and pressing it over his mouth as he started coughing again. "Little fucking pyro pants here is now suddenly on our side?"

"For now," Ephraim grumbled.

"If we're going after Terrell, we will need him," Snod said sternly. "Ephraim is a very skilled hunter." He glanced at Lorenzo, adding, "We also need your help."

"Me?" Lorenzo squeaked, blinking rapidly.

"The cure."

"But the cure doesn't actually… ohhhh!" Lorenzo's eyes nearly bugged out of his skull. "Fuck! Yes! That's genius! You wanna make Terrell go boom! Holy crap! The DD would be so freakin' nasty. Uhm, I mean, shit. Right. We've got to get to the lab."

"We need to weaponize it," Ephraim pointed out.

"I guess just trying to stick a needle in Terrell's neck wouldn't be such a hot idea," Lorenzo mused, rubbing his forehead. "Uhhhh…"

"I can get tranquilizer guns," Ephraim suggested. "Slugs can hold up to two milliliters. Used to fill them with holy water and silver, but we could use that green shit."

"How many you got?" Lorenzo asked, raising his brows.

"Lots."

"Oookay. Don't suppose you have any other weapons? Pointy stakes? Whatever else it is you crazy people use to hunt vampires?"

"I've got what we need," Ephraim assured him, allowing himself a very pleased smile.

"Okie dokie!" Lorenzo anxiously looked to Snod. "So, the million dollar question. Do you know where Frankie is?"

"No," Snod replied hesitantly. "I honestly don't know where to begin."

"Uh, hello?" Lorenzo snorted. "You're still bonded, right? Use that."

"I can't. I haven't heard Frankie since he left. He's shut

me out."

"Try harder!" Rees snapped, waving his handkerchief angrily. "We've gotta get Frankie away from that fucking monster! He's spent fucking centuries running from him, and he just went waltzing right back to him to save your stupid ass!"

"I know!" Snod snarled as he whirled around to glare at Rees. "Frankie is everything to me! You don't think I would have rather died than let this happen?"

"Gee, I dunno," Rees drawled sarcastically before roaring, "Maybe I'd fucking believe you if you were really fucking trying, you fucking punk!"

"What the fuck, Rees!" Snod was stunned by the man's attitude, and his own temper rapidly began to boil.

"Fuck you!" Rees growled loudly. "Now, listen here, you limp dick fucking twat. Take all of that shit, all of that anger, and you fucking reach into that stupid brain of yours and find him!"

Grinding his teeth together, Snod closed his eyes and did as Rees instructed. He concentrated all of his fury and anguish, trying to reach out for Frankie. Their bond had been so strong.

There had to be some way to get through.

His heart was thumping with the rush of his rage, focusing on the memory of how it had beaten so sweetly alongside Frankie's in their most intimate moments. In his head, their pulses were like the beating of a drum in an oddly familiar tune.

It was the song by the people that proclaimed things, the one about walking hundreds of miles. He remembered how beautiful Frankie's smile had been that night and how magical it was to see him so happy as they danced together like fools.

Frankie's hands had felt so good in his, strong and gentle, and Snod could still hear how loudly he had smacked them against the most tender parts of his body as they made love. The recollection of Frankie's moans made him shiver even now, every gorgeous sound more lovely than the last, his soul cringing as he realized there was a very good chance he would never hear them again.

Even worse than that, he might not hear Frankie tell him that he loved him.

Frankie, please… I love you…

Obe…?

There.

Frankie was close, somewhere not far from the city. Even through the bond, he sounded so sad. There was so much pain and misery that it took Snod's breath away, and he desperately locked onto it even as it made him ache. He could see a house sitting in a large field with an oak tree in the yard.

"I know where he is," Snod gasped, not even realizing he had been crying until he felt hot tears rolling down his cheeks.

"Let's go," Ephraim urged, already heading back to the door.

"I'm coming, too," Rees barked, straightening out his dress and stomping after him.

"Rees." Snod grimaced. He very clearly remembered what a disaster the desk heist had been.

"You'll just get in the way," Ephraim said with a revolted leer.

"Ha! Me? Get in your way? Please, darling. You're gonna be the one getting all in the way of my giant dick swinging around, you fucking washed-out Schwarzenegger-looking prick," Rees shot back. "I'm fucking coming."

Ephraim actually laughed. He grinned at Snod, saying cheerfully, "I like him."

"Fine," Snod groaned, nodding his head. "You can come. But you're going to do exactly as we say for your own damn safety." He looked at Lorenzo, asking briskly, "Are you ready?"

Lorenzo gulped. "Oh, yeah. Sure. Totally ready to go fight an ancient super crazy vampire with my lame tiny robots. Yup. Ready."

"Come on," Athaliah said as he hurried to the door. "We need to hurry."

"Uh uh," Snod grunted, grabbing his brother's arm. "You're not going."

"What?" Athaliah exclaimed, growling indignantly. "No fuckin' way! I'm not staying here!"

"You're not fit to hunt," Ephraim reminded him grumpily, pointing at Athaliah's eye. "You will endanger us all."

"Suck my dick, fathead! Rees is over there coughing up his fuckin' lungs and you're letting him go!"

"Athaliah," Snod pressed. "You're staying here."

"For once, I totally agree with your brother," Lorenzo said gently. "Mark this day down on your calendars. Holy crap. But seriously. This is super freakin' dangerous. Like, bungee jumping into a Sarlacc pit dangerous."

"Okay, first of all, you say that like I'm supposed to know what that means—" Athaliah snarled, baring his teeth viciously.

"*Star Wars* was already out way before you were kidnapped!" Lorenzo protested passionately.

"—and second of all," he raged on, "if any of you think I'm letting you leave me behind, you're all out of your fuckin' minds! There is no force on God's whole damn planet that is gonna fuckin' stop me!" He crossed his arms firmly with a furious glare, daring any one of them to take on his challenge.

In the end, it took all four of them to drag Athaliah into the bedroom. He bit Lorenzo, kicked Ephraim in the stomach, and scratched Snod's face. Rees managed to remain unscathed, finding a pair of handcuffs and securing his wrists to the headboard.

Snod didn't immediately understand why his brother had handcuffs or why Lorenzo was blushing so hard when he saw them. He'd worry about that later.

"I love you, dear brother," Snod said. "I promise we'll

come back for you."

"I love you, too," he grumbled, narrowing his eyes. "I am so kicking your ass when I get out of these."

"I look forward to it," Snod declared, scowling when Lorenzo leaned down to not so sneakily steal a kiss.

"We'll be back, I promise," Lorenzo assured Athaliah, tenderly touching his cheek.

"Totally kicking your ass, too," Athaliah said sweetly.

"I kinda like it when you hurt me," Lorenzo gushed, waggling his eyebrows playfully. "Although I'm kind of digging the cuffs on you… maybe we can switch up, huh?"

"Wait… the two of you… you've been… With the *handcuffs*? Oh, for the love of all that is holy," Snod sputtered, groaning in disgust. "Let's fucking go!"

Cackling away, Rees wheezed hysterically, "He didn't know! That big idiot didn't know! Hahaha, that's fucking awesome!"

Snod stalked to the door, trying to ignore both Rees' laughter and the rush of horrible mental images that were trying to invade his mind of Lorenzo and his brother. He stopped short, freezing when he heard a quick series of little knocks. He looked back at Lorenzo and Rees, asking flatly, "Expecting someone?"

"Oh, crap!" Lorenzo exclaimed, smacking his forehead. "It's Amy! She used to be an ER doctor!"

"Amy?"

"You know, the lady from our carpool! I forgot we had called her to come by and check on Rees."

Snod groaned heavily. He hadn't met the mysterious carpooling buddy Amy before and tonight was the absolute worst time to make a good impression.

"I'm fuckin' fine," Rees sniffed stubbornly.

"Says the old stubborn bastard who almost passed out twice and refused to go to the hospital!" Athaliah yelled from the bedroom.

"I'll get rid of her," Ephraim growled impatiently, reaching for the door. "We don't have time for this shit."

He hastily turned the knob, revealing a petite brunette woman peering up at him on the other side.

"Oh! Uhm, hi!" the woman said, suddenly blushing at the giant man leering at her. "I'm Amy, Dr. Amy Bean. Are… are you a friend of Lorenzo's?"

Ephraim had the funniest look on his face, wordlessly staring at her in shock.

Smiling sweetly, Amy offered her hand. "Tongue-tied? I don't usually have that effect on people. Well, it's nice to meet you!"

Ephraim gently took her hand, opening his mouth but still nothing came out.

"You can let go of my hand now," Amy whispered loudly, looking for a familiar face and spying Lorenzo. She sidestepped around Ephraim, greeting brightly, "Hey! Uh, wow, full house tonight."

"Look, sorry we called you," Lorenzo said quickly. "Something came up, and we gotta go."

"Go?" Amy frowned, looking suspiciously at Rees. "Are you feeling better now, Mr. Everhart?"

"I'm fuckin' fine, doll," Rees huffed. "Never better."

"Why do I not believe you?" Amy drawled, herding Rees to the couch. She had a small black bag with her, pulling out a blood pressure cuff and a stethoscope. "Let me just get some basic vitals, and I'll leave you alone, okay?"

Rees was fighting, swatting at Amy's efforts to get the cuff on him. He coughed again, clenching his handkerchief. "I'm absolutely fine, never better."

Snod saw that Ephraim was still gawking, stepping up beside him and asking quietly, "You're acting like you've never seen a woman before."

"I've never seen one like her," Ephraim replied honestly, unable to keep the awe out of his voice. He saw Amy struggling with Rees, quickly offering, "I could hold him down for you."

"That's, uhm, sweet of you, but I think I got him," Amy chuckled nervously, wrangling Rees' arm in and checking his blood pressure. Frowning at the result, she removed the cuff with a hiss of air.

"Just dandy, see?" Rees coughed.

Amy ignored him, clipping a small pulse oximeter to his finger and moving the stethoscope against his chest to listen to his lungs.

"Fiiiine," Rees insisted. "See? Perfectly fine."

"Mr. Everhart," Amy said urgently as concern creased her brow. She grimaced at the pulse ox reading, and she clearly didn't like what she was hearing in Rees' chest. She pulled the stethoscope off, blinking at him worriedly. "How long…"

"I've known for a few years," he replied quietly. "Keep your trap shut, doll."

Snod quirked a brow, asking, "What's wrong?"

"Fucking nothing! Now, don't we have something really fucking important to do?" Rees said sharply. "Like, need to leave right now important?"

"You need to go to a hospital," Amy said firmly. "I don't know how you're walking right now, much less breathing."

"I am fueled by spite, Chanel, and Mountain Dew," Rees drawled.

"I am going to call an ambulance," Amy said, reaching for her phone. "I'm sorry, Mr. Everhart. This is for your own good."

"For fuck's sake!" Rees groaned. He turned his head, calling out, "Hey, Athaliah! Got any more handcuffs in there, darling?"

"Sure do!" Athaliah replied.

"Hey, Dumbo," Rees quipped at Ephraim. "Wanna help me cuff the pretty lady to the bed?"

"What?" Amy squeaked.

"Sure!" Ephraim effortlessly lifted Amy over his shoulder and carried her to the bedroom.

She squealed helplessly while Athaliah cheerfully chirped, "Hey, Amy! Nice to meet you! That giant hemorrhoid is Ephraim. Ephraim, this is Amy. No hard feelings or anything, but I hope you get eaten by that vampire!"

"Vampire?" Amy whimpered. She whined as Ephraim cuffed her to the bed, staring stupidly at Athaliah. "Will someone please tell me what's going on?"

"Sorry, Amy," Lorenzo sighed. "We have to go help Frankie. Just stay put, okay?"

"I'll explain everything," Athaliah said, nodding his head. "See, Frankie is a vampire—"

"Athaliah!" Snod snapped.

"A vampire?" Amy scoffed.

"What?" Athaliah blinked innocently. "She deserves to know! Right, so, Frankie is a vampire, and he got kidnapped by his vampire ex-boyfriend who pretty much murdered the entire cult I used to be in with Obie and Ephraim. Now they're gonna go rescue Frankie and slay his nasty ex."

Amy looked very concerned, asking quietly, "Is this some kind of mass psychosis?"

"Love you, Amy," Lorenzo said, patting her leg, "but we gotta roll!"

"It was very nice meeting you," Ephraim mumbled shyly, and Snod swore he saw his old friend blush.

"Uhm," Amy squeaked, "nice meeting you, too?"

Snod and Ephraim led the charge toward the door, Snod snapping, "Let's fucking go, for fuck's sake! If anyone else is on the other side of that door, just punch them."

"Bye, boys!" Athaliah sang out. "Have fun hunting the vampire!"

"Did you just make a Miracle Max joke?" Lorenzo gasped adoringly. "Oh, my God! Athaliah! I love—"

"Bye-bye time!" Rees grunted, shoving Lorenzo through the doorway. "Mushy shit later!"

"But I might freakin' die!" Lorenzo whined in protest.

"See? Now you've got a great reason to live!" Rees barked.

They finally left, Ephraim and Snod following Lorenzo and Rees over to the lab. They waited in their cars while

Lorenzo ran inside to get the serum. He reappeared carrying a giant briefcase, quickly rejoining them. Ephraim led next, driving over to an abandoned gas station on the outskirts of town where he said he had a weapons cache stashed.

It was a small arsenal packed with dozens of silver-tipped stakes and silver-coated knives, several large rifles, and the promised tranquilizer guns. Ephraim grunted wordlessly for Lorenzo to join him, bringing him a case of darts to begin filling with the cure.

Snod left them to their work, taking the moment to speak to Rees, who was having another coughing spell. He frowned deeply when he spotted blood in Rees' handkerchief, asking him carefully, "Are you okay?"

"Fuckin' ducky," Rees replied sharply.

"What's wrong? Are you… sick?"

Rees groaned lightly, shaking his head. "Look, just drop it, all right?"

"Rees…"

"Motherfucking stubborn jackass," Rees growled. "It's fucking cancer, okay? I've been sick for a long time, and I'm dying."

Snod's heart lurched uncomfortably, and he murmured, "I'm sorry."

"Fuck your apology," Rees laughed bitterly. "There's nothing to apologize for. The cancer isn't sorry. It's just doing what it does. Now I've had a good life, and I'm not worried about what comes next. God is already going to have an entire boutique of Dolce and Gabbana waiting for me. What concerns me right now is helping my fucking friend. So quit your worrying about this old crossdresser and focus on tracking down Frankie."

Snod nodded briefly, saying gently, "For what it's worth, I do consider you a friend, Rees. Thank you…" He took a deep breath. "For everything."

"Jesus Christ bouncing on a pogo stick, will you shut the fuck up?" Rees drawled disgustedly despite a big grin. "Save it. You can slobber all over me when this is done."

Snod smiled softly, looking up to where Lorenzo and Ephraim were finishing up. "Are we ready?"

"Yup!" Lorenzo cocked one of the guns, declaring dramatically, "Splash on some Windex and pull on your garlic t-shirts, gentlemen. We have thirty-four darts packed full of undead eating goodness. Let's go kill us a goddamn shit-sucking vampire!"

Snod nodded fiercely. "Let's." He closed his eyes, saying a quick and fervent prayer to whatever God might be listening. He prayed for strength, for his aim to be true, and to hold the man he loved in his arms once more.

Frankie… I'm coming for you.

CHAPTER TWENTY-THREE

As Snod pulled on a black tactical vest and began to strap in stakes, he was reminded of when he and Frankie had first met. He had been wearing a vest almost exactly like this. It seemed like a lifetime ago when he had first been sent to hunt him, and he was amazed at how much had changed between them.

They were lovers now, and Snod could not imagine spending a moment of his life without him. Frankie had shown him a beautiful new world, and he was determined to live in it with him by his side. He would save him.

Or die trying.

Ephraim and Snod were armed to the teeth as they would be for any hunt. Ephraim passed around charms to keep them from being manipulated by any vampiric powers. The majority of the darts were divided between him and Snod for their tranquilizer guns, offering a few over to Rees to whom Snod gave a tranquilizer rifle.

"What the fuck is this thing for? Hunting elephants?" Rees snorted at the large gun.

"Today it's for hunting vampires from a safe distance," Snod said with a smirk.

"Don't suppose you guys have another one of those?"

Lorenzo asked sheepishly.

"No," Ephraim and Snod replied in unison.

"Right," Lorenzo sighed, adjusting the holster at his hip that Ephraim had given him. He was clearly not comfortable with the gun, but he seemed determined to try. "I was hoping the distance was, you know, optional."

"Most hunting is done at very close range," Snod explained.

"Figured with the whole staking them through the heart thing," Lorenzo said, holding out a few unusual-looking syringes. "I also cooked these up. They're epi-pens, but instead of epinephrine? Oh, yeah. They're packed full of DD."

Ephraim and Snod accepted them, Snod sliding them in his pants pocket.

"Your skills would have been greatly appreciated in the Order," Ephraim noted as he tucked his away.

"Sorry, dude," Lorenzo laughed. "Way too into free will and really gay premarital sex."

Snod glared.

"Not with Athaliah!" Lorenzo sputtered quickly. "No! Not with him. Nope. I never want to have sex with your brother. Not like ever. He's just, no, he's sooo not my type. Not attracted to him at all, no—"

"Lorenzo?" Snod massaged his temples gently, sighing wearily. "Shut the fuck up."

"Shutting up now," Lorenzo squeaked.

"We're going to have a very long conversation about my brother," Snod promised him, "but only after we rescue Frankie, all right?"

"Can't wait."

"We ready?" Ephraim grunted, itching to hunt.

Snod nodded, leading them all back out to Ephraim's van. He let Rees ride up front with Ephraim, climbing into the back with Lorenzo. He closed his eyes, concentrating on reaching out to Frankie and giving Ephraim directions.

He still couldn't tell what was happening to Frankie. He

had no idea what Terrell was doing, but he thought he sensed sadness. There was no pain, only a broken emptiness that he tried to fill with his rapidly spiraling thoughts.

Frankie, I love you, I'm coming for you, I'm not giving up on you. I'm going to take you home, we're going to our bed, I'm going to hold you and never let you go again…

Snod only heard a mournful echo ringing through the bond, but no other response. Frankie was pushing him away, but he refused to relinquish his hope.

"We're almost there," Snod said quietly, a rush of adrenaline making the tips of his fingers tingle. This was going to be the most important hunt of his life, and the consequences of failure were immense.

Ephraim began to slow down, the tires of the van crunching on gravel as they turned onto a dirt road. Up ahead was the house as Snod had described it, Ephraim confirming, "That's it?"

"Yes," Snod replied. "Pull over here."

"What? You really think we're gonna just sneak up on the ancient vampire and catch him unawares?" Rees snorted, fidgeting with his seatbelt.

"Terrell is arrogant," Snod said, stretching out his legs with a grunt. "Most vampires are. You'd be surprised how easily that can be used against them."

"Even if they can turn into smoke and blink around like Sonic the Hedgehog on crack?"

"I… I don't know what that means, but yes."

Ephraim was watching the house carefully, saying, "Snod and I will take the front. Rees, stay by the door. Lorenzo, follow behind us."

Lorenzo gulped audibly.

"Time to go," Ephraim grumbled, hopping out of the van and coming around to open the back doors.

Snod's skin was tingling with excitement. The thrill of the hunt was always a rush, and this one was easily the most important mission of his entire life. He and Ephraim had their guns drawn as they began advancing toward the house,

Lorenzo and Rees falling in line behind them.

The house was an old Victorian with a wraparound porch and high turrets piercing the cloudy night sky. It did not look like anyone had lived there for quite some time. The yard was wild and thick, nearly every inch of the house engulfed in creeping plants as if the very earth was trying to reclaim this land and drag the home down into the dirt.

Snod could see faint light glowing through the windows, perhaps the illumination of candles, tightening his hold on his gun as he crouched down low. He saw no movement, heard nothing, and could not sense anything in the bond.

Ephraim looked back at their unlikely team with a small sigh, nodding sternly and began edging toward the front door.

The steps creaked under their weight, and Snod cringed at the sound. Ephraim took a breath and advanced, finding the door unlocked and pushing it wide open.

There was a massive staircase that led up to a large landing with several hallways trailing off into darkness. A shadowy balcony jutted out from the third floor, and an old chandelier was sprawled across the foyer in front of them. The house smelled of must and death, candles flickering in dozens of sconces scattered along the walls.

Obe?

"Frankie," Snod hissed, zeroing in on his location and bolting up the steps.

"Snod!" Ephraim hissed in warning. "Be careful!"

Gun still aimed and at the ready, Snod marched right to the door where he knew Frankie was waiting on the other side. He kicked it open, his heart jumping into his throat when he saw him laid out across a massive canopy bed.

Snod was relieved to see that Frankie appeared unharmed, but his blood boiled to see him in nothing but a red silk robe and long silver chains binding him to the headboard.

"Fuck, it is you!" Frankie sat up, gasping loudly. "Obe! What are you doing here?"

Snod holstered his weapon, hurrying to his side and pressing a desperate kiss to his lips. He could taste blood, but refused to pull away until Frankie pushed him.

"Obe! You can't be here!" Frankie said angrily. "Terrell left to feed, but he's going to come back! He will kill you!"

"Not today," Snod said passionately.

"Obe, please, go! Now!" Frankie ordered firmly, his strong voice cracking as he begged, "Please!"

"I'm not going anywhere," Snod insisted, kissing Frankie's forehead and gazing at him adoringly. "Not without you."

"You beautiful fool," Frankie sighed sadly. "I love you."

"I love you, too," Snod said earnestly, reaching up to remove the chains that were holding Frankie. He suddenly felt an icy breeze, the hair on the back of his neck standing up.

Frankie's eyes widened and his mouth parted to speak, but it was too late.

Snod found himself suddenly flying over the railing of the stairs, crashing down onto the floor. His gun fell out from the holster, clattering several yards away. There were cold fingers curling around his throat, lifting him up and pinning him to the wall.

Terrell.

He was grinning madly, laughing happily. "Oh, yes. Hello, Obadiah. I was so hoping you'd be stupid enough to come for Francis."

"I missed you, too," Snod hissed defiantly. "Couldn't stop thinking about killing you."

"I love that fire in you," Terrell purred nastily. "I can't wait to put it out." He bared his fangs to strike, but suddenly roared in pain.

Snod grunted as he fell to the floor again, looking up as Terrell turned around to face Ephraim.

There were two darts sticking out of his back.

"What the hell is this poison!" Terrell shouted furiously, reaching over his shoulder and clawing at the darts. He ripped them out, knocking Ephraim across the face so hard he spat out blood.

Snod dove for his gun, but Terrell had blinked back beside him and kicked him ferociously in the side. He couldn't reach the weapon, groaning and trying to catch his breath. He was certain a few of his ribs were broken, hissing at the pain when he inhaled.

Ephraim tried to use the moment to attack again, but Terrell was too fast. There was a loud crash as Terrell slammed Ephraim into the railings of the stairs before he could fire another shot, the wood cracking and giving way beneath his weight. Terrell lunged for him, but screamed out in rage when Lorenzo fired at his exposed back.

"Ha! Suck on that, you undead freak!" Lorenzo cheered triumphantly, pumping his fist into the air.

Terrell snorted, an eerily calm smile playing over his lips as he sized up Lorenzo.

Climbing up to his knees, Snod panted, "Lorenzo… time for you to run away now…"

Terrell wasn't using his unnatural speed, stalking toward Lorenzo at a mortal pace. He was enjoying this, watching the boy tremble before him. He had managed to pull out the darts, dropping them on the floor one by one as he strolled along.

"It's not working," Lorenzo gasped stupidly, trying to back away. "Why isn't it… the concentration of V in his blood must be greater than Frankie's, the dose… he needs a bigger dose! I must have fucked up the calculation somehow!"

Terrell snatched Lorenzo by his hair, running his tongue over his throat, drawling, "Ah, are you the clever little one that created this poison? My gratitude… I haven't felt this alive in centuries."

Snod finally managed to grab his gun, shooting everything he had at Terrell's back and reloading.

Terrell growled, Lorenzo reaching up and bravely socking him right in the mouth. Terrell didn't even flinch, grabbing Lorenzo's arm and snapping it back with a horrible crunch.

Lorenzo screamed, collapsing to his knees and cradling his broken arm.

Ephraim was back up on his feet, firing at Terrell while Snod finished reloading. Terrell moved like lightning, cackling as he sent Ephraim crashing into Lorenzo. The two of them tumbled against the far wall, Lorenzo howling when Ephraim landed on his injured arm.

Terrell came for Snod next, holding him by his head and squeezing down hard.

Snod roared in protest, firing the last of his ammo directly into Terrell's stomach. It didn't seem to faze him in the slightest, his grip only tightening even more. Snod dropped the gun, punching desperately at Terrell's arms and chest.

The pressure in his head was becoming unbearable, and Snod stupidly realized that Terrell was slowly crushing his skull. He closed his eyes, his ears ringing frantically. He was getting dizzy, clenching his teeth as he continued to fight.

"Say night-night now, little blood bag," Terrell chuckled. "I'm starting to get a bit bored…"

Snod realized in a terrible panic that Terrell was only toying with them.

Neither he nor Ephraim had ever faced a vampire like this, not one that could have easily killed them all in seconds. He had been such a fool, and his selfishness was going to cost them all their lives.

For the first time, the idea of dying was devastating. When he was a loyal member of the Order, he wasn't afraid to lay down his life for the cause. He understood the promise of life eternal beyond this mortal existence, and while he never hurried to it, he didn't fear it.

Even now, it wasn't death that terrified him. It was knowing he wasn't going to be with Frankie again, that he was leaving Frankie alone with this wretched fiend and was helpless to stop it. He summoned every prayer he knew, pleading desperately to God for a miracle.

Frankie… I love you…

Obe! No! I love you! Hold on!

I love you so much…

Snod stopped struggling, waiting for the inevitable moment for his head to collapse beneath Terrell's palms. Right when he was certain he was about to meet death, the pressure suddenly released.

Terrell growled softly in frustration, spitting, "Well, that was just rude."

Snod blinked as he collapsed on the floor, staring stupidly up at Terrell to see what had happened. There was a dart sticking out right between Terrell's eyes, Rees' voice taunting from above them, "Ha! Have some of my big ol' swingin' dick!"

Rees had climbed his way up to the balcony on the third floor, lying down on his stomach with the rifle. Apparently, it had taken him the entire battle thus far to make the journey up there. He bowed his head down, firing again and a second dart thunked dead center in Terrell's forehead.

Terrell groaned as he pulled out the darts, his skin bubbling and popping around the tiny punctures. He bared his teeth, sighing, "I'm beginning to grow tired of these games… it's been fun and all, but I think we're done now."

Snod struggled to get to his knees, glancing up to see that Ephraim was on his feet again and Lorenzo was limping up the stairs, holding his injured arm. Ephraim had stakes in both of his hands, throwing himself at Terrell with a loud roar.

Terrell vanished into a puff of black smoke, leaving Ephraim to tumble headfirst into Snod. He caught his friend, helping him regain his balance and looking all around.

There was no sign of Terrell.

"Where the fuck did he go?" Ephraim spat, searching every inch of the house with wild eyes.

"Fuck! I don't know!" Snod growled impatiently, pulling

a stake out from his vest. They were all out of ammo now unless Rees had more…

Rees!

Snod quickly looked up, eyes wide as black smoke began to fill the balcony. He started running up the stairs, screaming, "Rees! Watch out!"

Rees scrambled clumsily to get out of the way, but he was too slow. Terrell had materialized behind him, picking him up and sinking his teeth into Rees' throat.

"No!" Snod screamed furiously, his heart seizing violently in his chest, running as fast as he could. He had to get to him, he had to save him!

Rees was cussing, groaning in agony as Terrell tipped them over the edge of the balcony. He crashed both of their bodies right into the broken chandelier, glass flying everywhere, glittering like exploding stars in the candlelight.

Snod quickly turned around, trying to run back down the other way. He made it to the top of the stairs and threw himself over the edge at Terrell.

Terrell was laughing again, easily tossing Snod aside and watching him slide along the floor.

Snod grunted, the air knocked right from his lungs. His ribs screamed in protest, and his head was absolutely throbbing. The world was spinning as he rolled over onto his stomach. He looked up, gasping, "Rees!"

Rees was lying on his back, his head flopping over to stare at Snod. He was still alive, but he was pale and sweating, blood oozing from the gaping holes Terrell had left in his neck.

Ephraim tried to intervene, lunging at Terrell once more. Terrell laughed, effortlessly knocking him across the room. Ephraim was ready for him this time, catching himself on his hands and knees. He was back on his feet quickly, continuing to pursue Terrell and shouting roughly, "Get Rees!"

"Rees! Get the fuck up!" Snod grunted, trying to crawl over toward him. Every part of his body ached as he dragged himself through bits of shattered glass to reach Rees' side.

"Save Frankie... you asshole..." Rees coughed, a strained grin curling his lips. "Take care of him... for me. Tell him I love his stupid ass..."

Snod's eyes were burning, grabbing Rees' hand and squeezing tight. "You'll tell him yourself," he hissed. "Get your ass up!"

"Hey... I told you I was... a good shot," Rees laughed weakly, not seeming to hear him. "Got that bitch right in the dome..."

"Yeah, you did," Snod sighed miserably, watching Rees' eyes begin to dim. "Stay with me, Rees. Fuck! Please... God, my sweet and merciful God! Please give strength to your devoted child, Rees Everhart. Please help him, fucking save him! Christ!"

"I'm hardly... devoted," Rees moaned with a short laugh, reaching over and weakly pawing at Snod. "Shush now, darling... I'm... ready. Been ready."

"Good," Terrell purred, sauntering back toward them, dusting off his hands. "I want to finish my appetizer, and then I'm thinking about skipping right to dessert."

Snod's eyes searched for Ephraim, finding him face down on the floor by the stairs. He couldn't tell if he was alive or dead.

Terrell plucked Rees up from the floor, sinking his teeth back into his throat.

"No!" Snod roared, rising up struggling to pull Rees away, but it was impossible. His friend was dying, and there was nothing he could do. He tried to grab a stake, but Terrell reached out and smacked him across the face.

The force of the blow sent Snod reeling and his vision blurred, the stake clattering to the floor.

"Hey," Rees croaked, "you rotten sack of regurgitated cat shit..." He had something in his hand, one last dart, and he jammed it into Terrell's eye, growling, "Fucking suck on this!"

Terrell howled furiously, throwing Rees to the floor and clawing at his face as he tried to remove the dart. His skin was starting to bubble and hiss all over as he stumbled away, moaning in pain.

Snod watched as Terrell's flesh continued to boil, taking a stake in hand and pouncing to make the kill.

Terrell was still too fast even while wounded, effortlessly catching Snod's hand and twisting it until he cried out and dropped the stake. He snatched Snod by the back of his head and viciously chomped down on his neck.

Snod cried out, trying to grab another stake from his vest, but Terrell pinned his hand to his chest. He tried to reach up with the other hand, but Terrell grabbed hold and kept it down at his side.

Feeding with Frankie had always been pleasant, beautiful; this was utter agony.

Terrell was draining him in long, deep swallows, moaning and grunting hoarsely. Snod could feel his entire body burning, growing weaker by the second.

"Francis was right," Terrell purred softly, pausing and licking his lips. "You taste so very, very sweet..."

Snod could see Terrell's skin was still actively bubbling and slipping off. The DD was working, but it still wasn't enough. He needed more, but they were out of ammo.

What did it matter?

He was dying.

Terrell was taking his time, drinking every last drop of his blood. Snod could feel darkness beginning to close in around him, wishing to God he could see Frankie just one more time.

Obe!

Frankie...?

Your pocket! Lorenzo says to check your fucking pocket!

Snod couldn't move his hand very much with Terrell still holding it down, but he could move his fingers. His pocket, yes, he could reach his pocket, and he felt...

The DD pens that Lorenzo had made!

There was no way he could pull it out to stab Terrell, but a wild idea came to him in his desperation. He felt the tip of the syringe, turned it against his own leg through the thin fabric, and jammed it down.

Frankie… I love you…

Obe! No! What are you doing? I'm almost free, I'm…

It was like a switch had been flipped. The bond was broken again, and Snod reached for the second syringe. He heard Terrell starting to choke and pressed the second needle into his thigh.

"What… is this?" Terrell groaned, releasing his iron grip and starting to gag.

Snod didn't even feel it when he hit the floor. He distantly wondered if he would have a concussion from his head being slammed around so much. He wanted to laugh, knowing potential brain damage was the least of his problems right now.

Terrell had taken too much; he was not ever going to leave this house alive.

Though his vision was blurring, Snod could see Rees' body a few yards away. His eyes were closed, and he looked peaceful. Snod was certain he was dead, trying to turn his head to find Ephraim. He couldn't see him, groaning quietly from the effort.

Snod did have an excellent view of Terrell, watching black liquid pouring down his face as his skin began to burn and melt away. He was screaming, trying to keep his flesh from sloughing off, steam wafting from his body as he fell to his knees.

It was done.

Terrell was dying, and Frankie would be free.

Snod closed his eyes with a delirious smile. The man he loved was going to be okay, and that was comforting. He grunted when wet, slimy fingers clamped down on his neck, blinking as he stared up at the horrible, disfigured visage of Terrell leering down at him.

Most of his flesh had peeled away to the bone beneath

and he choked and gurgled furiously, "You'll… die now…"

Snod wished he had the strength to give one last clever line, but all he could do was grin. It seemed to do the trick regardless and he gasped as Terrell bit down at his throat to finish him off.

Terrell suddenly screamed in utter agony, his eyes blazing brightly and his body arching backwards. His head flopped to the side and black ooze poured from his lips as death took him. Snod didn't understand what had happened until he saw the tip of a stake protruding from Terrell's chest.

Behind him, fangs bared, was Frankie.

Frankie roared and sobbed, driving the stake deeper and deeper until he had practically pushed it all the way through Terrell's back. He didn't spare another thought for his dead Maker, hurling his putrefying corpse out of his way and gathering Snod into his arms.

"Frankie," Snod sighed weakly.

"Obe! No, no, no! You can't leave me!" Frankie pleaded tearfully, biting into his wrist and pressing the wound against Snod's mouth. "Drink. Hurry! Please drink for me, okay?"

Snod managed to swallow some, but God, his entire body felt like it was on fire. He turned his head, vomiting violently and gasping.

"What's wrong? Why isn't it working?" Frankie screamed.

"The DD!" Lorenzo's voice answered. "He took the cure! Every time you give him blood, it's being attacked!"

"Fuck, fuck! No, keep drinking, Obe! I love you, but you have to drink," Frankie whimpered, holding Snod's mouth open and filling his throat with blood.

"What are you doing?" Ephraim's voice, angry, afraid.

"I'm trying to save him!" Frankie yelled furiously, massaging Snod's neck, trying to get him to swallow.

The burn was white hot, every fiber of nerve screaming with terrible pain. Snod threw up again, coughing violently, gazing at Frankie. He wished he had the bond back so he could tell Frankie how much their time together had meant to him, how much he loved him.

His eyes began to close, and it was so cold now. The pain was beginning to fade away, and while it was a relief, Snod knew it meant he was dying. He shivered, gagging again as more blood gushed into his mouth.

"Frankie," Lorenzo whimpered, broken and afraid. "You have to stop. You're losing too much blood…"

"No!" Frankie protested, tearful and determined.

Snod could feel himself floating, and all of their voices were becoming harder to hear. He was sinking down into a cool fog, the agony of his body far away now. He was cold, numb, although he could distantly feel the thick blood Frankie was still desperately trying to get him to drink.

It was too much, too viscous, and he realized he wasn't breathing anymore. He should have been frantic, panicked, but he was surprisingly calm. The darkness was coming for him now, and he wasn't afraid. He managed a small prayer for God to watch over his friends and family, giving himself over to the nothing completely.

His last thoughts were of Frankie; beautiful and sweet Frankie who would finally be free now. The vampire he loved, the kindest being he had ever met, could go on with his life. Snod wasn't sure, but he was pretty confident that he was smiling.

Frankie, I love you…

I love you, too… Obe!

CHAPTER TWENTY-FOUR

Frankie was right.

Being a vampire was… *different.*

When Snod first opened his eyes, he didn't understand what had happened to him. He thought he had died. But there was Frankie, smiling down at him with bloody tears streaking down his face like crimson waterfalls.

The blood was glittering so beautifully, and Snod could smell life in it; something ancient and warm and absolutely breathtaking.

Breath.

He wasn't breathing.

Huh.

All of his injuries had vanished as well. He'd never felt so refreshed and energized. There was a strange sort of electricity surging through every inch of him, buzzing just below the surface, and coiled to release at any given second.

Reaching up to touch Frankie's face, he was alarmed at how very sensitive he was now. He'd always thought Frankie's skin was perfectly smooth, but now he could feel that it had a very distinct texture. It was voluptuous and soft like velvet, and he couldn't stop touching it.

Frankie was kissing him, and his lips were a hundred

times sweeter than they had been before. There was so much love flowing through the bond that it made Snod ache deep inside with a wild passion.

His desire was unfurling at an alarming rate, and he had never felt this ravenous, this hungry.

Hunger.

That's when he noticed the others' blood; the human blood. It didn't have the same life as Frankie's. It was oddly devoid of intensity but still savory, and Snod had never been so damn hungry. He was starving.

Snod pulled away from Frankie, his keen new senses focusing in on Lorenzo, who was standing right beside them.

He smelled delicious.

"Obe," Frankie warned gently, firm hands holding him in place. "I'll feed you, I promise. We have to go home, okay?"

"Why is he looking at me like he wants to eat me?" Lorenzo asked worriedly.

"Because he does," Frankie replied quickly. "He's a newborn vampire, and he's very hungry."

"We need to torch this house," Ephraim was grumbling, "and dispose of the bodies."

"I'll take care of Rees," Frankie said quietly. "I'll clean him up, and I'm going to take him home. He deserves to rest in his own bed."

Snod's eyes moved to their fallen friend, frowning gently. Rees had died helping him save Frankie. He should feel something, anything, but the hunger was all he could focus on.

Lorenzo nodded, saying, "Look, we gotta set Athaliah and Amy free. They're probably going nuts by now. Then I really have to get to a hospital. The whole broken arm thing, you know?"

"I'll drive you," Ephraim grunted immediately, addressing Frankie next. "Go get him fed. I'll meet you back here and help you."

"You don't have to do that—"

"You have much experience setting things on fire?" Ephraim asked dryly.

"Well, no," Frankie admitted.

"I'll help you," Ephraim repeated, moving around the house and gathering the discarded weapons. He spared a quick glance at Snod, his lip twitching. "Just… take care of him."

Snod couldn't quite read Ephraim's troubled expression; anger, disgust, fear. All of the emotions were dripping from every pore, and Snod realized he was smelling them. He could almost taste them.

Beneath all of it, there was relief. It was small and a bit bitter, but Ephraim was relieved that Snod was alive.

"Meet me here at sunrise after you put that one to bed," Ephraim continued, jerking his head at Snod.

"I will," Frankie said firmly.

"I'm really glad you're both okay," Lorenzo gushed, clapping a hand on Frankie's shoulder. "I mean, you are okay? I'm so sorry about Rees… and you did just murder your Maker and turn your boyfriend into a vampire."

"I'm fine," Frankie soothed, gently embracing Lorenzo while being mindful of his injured arm. He smiled sweetly, reassuring him, "Everything is going to be okay."

Lorenzo didn't seem to believe him, but left with Ephraim after making several promises to check in later from the hospital.

Snod watched them leave, absently licking his lips. He had the oddest urge to chase after them, trying to quell the hunger gnawing at his gut.

"Obe?" Frankie asked quietly, holding out his hand and taking Snod's. "Are you all right?"

"I love you," Snod replied, smiling softly at his first spoken words as a vampire.

"I love you, too," Frankie said, squeezing Snod's hand, "but are you okay?"

"I'm with you," Snod sighed, grateful for Frankie's

gentle touch to ground him, ignoring the painful stabs of hunger. "That's all that matters."

"Let's go home," Frankie said, pulling Snod close and holding him tight. "I promise I'll take care of you."

"I know you will," Snod nodded, nuzzling gently against Frankie's cheek. "Forever."

"Forever," Frankie agreed, locking his arms around Snod's waist. "Hold on."

The entire world breezed by in a blur and he watched it all twirl around him like a wild kaleidoscope.

Normally when Frankie moved this fast, Snod couldn't see anything. Now he found that if he focused his eyes, he could see the streets and buildings as they breezed by, and he knew exactly where they were going.

Home.

Frankie brought Snod inside the apartment, blinking away to grab a large bottle of blood. He handed it to him, urging, "Drink. You'll feel better."

Snod eagerly tipped the bottle up, chugging it back. It was bitter, cold, and not nearly enough. He wiped his mouth, licking at his hand as he gasped hopefully, "More?"

"Yes," Frankie promised him with a kiss. "Much more."

"What about you?" Snod questioned. He didn't know how, but he knew Frankie was drained and hungry. "You gave me almost all of your blood… you need to feed, too."

"I'm fine," Frankie chuckled, kissing Snod's cheek. "Trust me. You need it a lot more than me, Obe."

While Frankie exchanged text messages with Lorenzo to check on everyone, Snod ended up drinking every drop of blood in the house. His hunger was sated for the time being, but he didn't feel satisfied. Frankie took him into the shower to get him cleaned up, pulling away his battle-soiled clothes and tugging him under the spray of hot water.

Snod could feel every individual drop as it hit his skin, nearly overwhelmed and clinging close to Frankie.

"I've got you," Frankie whispered, his green eyes brighter than ever. "I promise I'm going to take care of you."

"Does it always feel like this?" Snod asked quietly.

"Like what?"

"Like…"

My body is ready to explode, I can't feel anything, but I feel everything, it's all so loud and bright and it's too much, and I'm still hungry…

"Yes," Frankie assured him. "It does, but it'll get better. I'll make sure you get enough blood. The most important thing right now is making sure that you're fed."

Snod sighed contently as Frankie began to wash him. He could hear the bubbles of the lather popping softly and he leaned into Frankie's adoring touch. It sounded like music.

"I still remember what it was like to be born again," Frankie said with a bittersweet smile. "Everything is suddenly new and the most trivial things become beautiful. It's easy to be absorbed in your new senses and forget who you were before."

"I know who I am," Snod said stubbornly.

"You haven't asked once about your brother," Frankie pointed out with a sad smirk, "and you still haven't said a word about Rees."

Snod was startled, blinking a few times as he realized Frankie was right. Rees was dead, and he had last seen Athaliah handcuffed to his bed. He pressed his hands against his face, a deep pain plunging into his heart and then fading almost as quickly as it appeared.

"Obe," Frankie soothed lovingly, kissing him, "it's okay."

"What's wrong with me?" Snod asked hoarsely.

"You're a vampire," Frankie replied gently. "It's easy to forget. But I won't let you. It took me a long time to remember…"

Because of what Terrell did to me…

"He wanted you to be this way," Snod whispered brokenly. "To be this… empty."

"Yes," Frankie said, tilting Snod into the water to rinse

him off, "but you can fight it. You can wake up from it."

"Athaliah's okay?" Snod asked urgently, forcing himself to focus.

"He's fine," Frankie chuckled. "Lorenzo is getting his arm set at the hospital, Athaliah is trying to un-brainwash Ephraim, and from what I understand? He's, ahem, become very fond of Amy."

"Really?" Snod snorted in disbelief.

"He refused to be seen by the doctors at the hospital, but he apparently let Amy patch him up," Frankie laughed. "Athaliah said he's totally in love."

"I hope so," Snod said, surprised by how much he meant it.

"Everyone is fine," Frankie repeated, hesitating to add, "Well…"

Almost everyone…

"Rees is really gone," Snod said, frowning.

"Yes," Frankie said sadly, "he was my friend, and he… I am going to miss him very much. He was like a father to me in a way, and he was always so kind."

"Me, too," Snod said, a wave of sadness coming over him. He didn't know if it was Frankie's mourning or his own, but he held onto it tightly before it slipped away again.

"It's okay," Frankie murmured, cradling Snod's face and pressing their lips together. "There… it's okay to miss him. It's okay to feel pain."

"He told me to tell you that he loves you," Snod said, the sadness digging in deeper as he thought of his best moments with the old man. "He wanted me to take care of you."

"We'll keep each other warm," Frankie said softly, a playful smile lighting up his face.

"How did you…" Snod stared awkwardly.

"You're my progeny," Frankie explained fondly. "Our bond is even stronger now. Thoughts, memories… they'll pass between us without even trying. You were remembering that night with Rees, and I saw it."

"I do miss him. I know I miss him."

"I know. We'll make sure he has a proper burial decked all out in Chanel or he'll come back and haunt us both."

"Will I be able to go?" Snod asked, suddenly aware that there were extreme limitations with this new life.

"I'll make sure we hold it at night. I know he'd want you to be there."

"No sunlight for me," Snod said with a click of his tongue.

"No," Frankie said with a quick shake of his head. "I don't think you would have inherited my immunity… maybe. It's certainly possible. But I'm not willing to test it right now. We need to be safe."

"I trust you," Snod whispered. "I know you'll help me… you love me."

Despite so many of his memories and emotions seeming so far away right now, what he felt for Frankie hadn't dwindled in the slightest. He was more drawn to him than ever, and their love was a palpable living force.

He could sense it pulsing between them, vivacious and beautiful, whispering, "You love me so much…"

"Yes, I do," Frankie said with a warm smile, finally turning the water off and grabbing towels to dry them with.

Snod closed his eyes, enjoying the warmth of the friction from Frankie's vigorous rubbing. Each little thread of the towel was squishy and soft, invigorating to his sensitive skin.

A new hunger was beginning to grow from Frankie's attentive efforts, Snod reaching for his hips and pulling him close.

Frankie shuddered, murmuring passionately, "Obe…"

Snod began to kiss along his shoulder and his neck, scowling when a strange image flickered before his eyes.

He could see Terrell kissing Frankie, touching him while he was chained to the bed, and he could feel how much Frankie had hated it. It was a memory, fresh and terrible, and it made Snod's temper flare erratically.

"I'm sorry," Frankie said sharply. "I don't… I don't

want you to see that. I'm yours, only yours."

"Only mine," Snod growled, nipping possessively at Frankie's throat. "Everywhere he touched, I will reclaim. Every inch of you will belong only to me. I am going to fuck away every memory of him inside of you until all you know is my name."

"Obe," Frankie gasped, his eyes fluttering as a spike of lust drilled its way through the bond. He had to crash their lips together in a wildly passionate kiss, moaning loudly.

Snod picked Frankie up, carrying him right to their bed and laying him down. He was amazed how light Frankie was in his arms and how effortless it was to move him. He kept kissing him, enjoying all the new shivers and tastes.

"Oh, Obe," Frankie sighed, his body rising up to press against Snod's, already hard and wanting. All the little sounds he made were even more beautiful to his ears, each making Snod shudder with pleasure knowing how happy Frankie was to be with him. "Come on, please… touch me. Right now!"

Snod began to move as ordered, gracing every bit of Frankie's flesh with his mouth and fingers. It felt like their first time, as if Snod really hadn't been able to see Frankie before now. He was even more exquisite than he remembered, a flawless masterpiece for him to devour.

No one else would ever have this, no one.

Snod wanted all of him, his lips tracing along Frankie's stomach and hips, not hesitating to move along his throbbing cock and inner thigh.

He wasn't afraid.

Any inhibitions Snod had before had been lost with his human self, and he eagerly lowered his mouth down between Frankie's legs. He found his hole, tilting up his hips to get a proper look at it. He'd never taken the time to appreciate how pretty Frankie was down here, licking slowly around the tight ring of muscle and up behind his balls.

Frankie parted his legs, groaning quietly, "My God… Obe…" He hugged his knees, bending back to let Snod have full range of his body, rocking down against his mouth. "Come on, just like that... keep going."

Snod eagerly explored, licking and sucking around Frankie's hole, soon finding that he was slick and open enough to slip his tongue within. The taste was lovely, but the way Frankie cried out for him was even more satisfying.

His cock was heavy and hard, pressing against the mattress as he ate Frankie out, hungry for more of his moans. He loved how frantically he squirmed and shook, finding that he could push his tongue even deeper and curl it up with surprising strength.

Frankie was groaning, his dick twitching against his stomach as he snarled hungrily, "Oh, fuck, Obe! Yes, just like that, fuck, yes!"

The strangest sensation began to overwhelm Snod, an odd pulsing that thrummed through his entire body. It reminded him of a heartbeat, but he knew neither his heart nor Frankie's would ever beat again.

Not unless...

Frankie was getting close, his orgasm fast approaching and rumbling like thunder through the bond. He could feel the building intensity as if it was his own, fucking his tongue in and out of Frankie's slippery hole.

He knew exactly what angle to hit, how to touch, how hard to go, because he could feel what Frankie did. He knew what to do to make him utterly fall apart.

When Frankie came, he could feel lightning streaking up and down his spine from the intensity. Frankie was shaking with every pulse of his cock, roughly dragging Snod up for a kiss while he was still twitching.

Snod was already pressing his cock into place, seeking out the wet and clenching hole to slide into. He kept Frankie's legs up, holding him tight as he began to thrust. He was gasping for oxygen he no longer needed, bracing himself for an entirely new onslaught of sensations.

Pushing into Frankie's body was divine, the snug and slick pressure of his ass clenching down all around him making his cock throb. Frankie's fingers were grasping at his shoulders as his tongue dipped into his mouth, moaning happily in their kiss. He could smell the salty aroma of Frankie's seed sticking between them, savoring every second.

More… Obe, please…

Snod growled, snapping his hips with more force, groaning at the way Frankie screamed for him. God, he'd never heard him wail like this, realizing that his new strength was allowing him to properly wreck him in a way he never could before.

He could make Frankie absolutely ache, he could blind him with pleasure, and so he did.

Snod fucked Frankie savagely, pinning his wrists down to the bed. When they'd done this before, it was only because Frankie was allowing it. He knew Frankie was still stronger, but it was wonderful that he was no longer worried about holding back. Feeling him squirming with such abandon beneath him, truly writhing in ecstasy, was spectacular.

Still, Snod wanted more.

"Frankie," he pleaded without shame, breathless and groaning. "Please… spank me."

Frankie's eyes twinkled wickedly and he easily wrenched one of his hands free to pop Snod's ass with a ferocity that would have bruised a mortal man. He slapped him again, even harder, baring his fangs as he snarled, "Want more, my sweet boy?"

"Yes!" Snod could feel the sensation of pain where Frankie had struck him, but it was eerily far away. It still felt good, but those few taps weren't nearly enough. He needed to fill up that strange emptiness inside of him and he closed his eyes as he begged, "More! Please! Fuck!"

Frankie spanked Snod's ass again, hard enough to make him cry out. There, that, that one had felt fantastic and left behind the familiar burning sensation he loved so much. Snod's hips jerked forward in reply, smothering his frantic moans against Frankie's throat as another brutal slap drove him to fuck him harder and faster.

"Fuck, yes!" Frankie groaned low, clinging to Snod's shoulders. "That's my good boy! Just like that!"

Snod gave Frankie everything he had, drowning in bliss and the sweet collision of their bodies. He could feel the thunderous approach of their climaxes, fucking Frankie to the insatiable rhythm. The bedframe was shaking from his awesome thrusting, Frankie groaning and grunting lustfully as he spread his legs wide to take it all.

It was then, Snod realized, how gentle Frankie had been with him before when their positions had been reversed. No mortal could have ever handled a tryst this rough, and it was difficult to hold back. No, it was impossible. His desire to ravage Frankie was overwhelming and he was not yet capable of controlling his passions.

Frankie was more than happy to let Snod fuck him as hard as he wanted, his lips parting in a guttural cry as his lean body began to tense up. "Fuck, Obe," he gasped, his eyes flickering brightly. "Don't stop, don't stop, don't you dare, ohhhh, God!"

"Never," Snod grunted, throwing himself into the beautiful oblivion of their bond, roaring as they came together. Time seemed to slow down, and he felt every single nerve of his body firing off as the pressure inside him promptly exploded. His heart was beating so hard he swore his ribs were vibrating, tears stinging his eyes as he shook all over.

He was sobbing, every single beat thumping in time with Frankie's, the heat between them reaching an impossible apex before finally beginning to ebb. His hips stuttered, his cock sliding in and out for one last intense slam. He grinned, seizing Frankie's lips in a smothering kiss.

Frankie wrapped his arms around Snod's neck, humming softly. The kiss lingered on and on, neither pulling away for breath because they didn't have to. Their hearts stilled at last, one final beat thudding between them and echoing warmly.

"Wow," Frankie murmured, content and deeply satisfied. "That… that was amazing."

"Uh huh," Snod chuckled, smiling wide, kissing the tip of Frankie's nose. "It was incredible… and I'm not even tired."

"Mmm, ready to go again?" Frankie teased.

"Yes," Snod replied without hesitation, growling as he crashed their lips together once more.

Again and again they went, Snod testing all the limits of his new abilities. The supernatural strength was perfect for pushing Frankie up against the wall and finding impossible angles to stretch him into while they made love. He knew exactly what Frankie wanted, just as Frankie knew what Snod did, and the sex reached mind-boggling levels of passion.

Every time they came, they climaxed together, their bodies quaking victoriously until Frankie was absolutely dripping with Snod's cum.

They held each other close in bed once they took another shower, fingers and legs tangled together, Snod gazing adoringly at Frankie. He knew the sun was going to be up soon, his newfound energy betraying him and leaving his body exhausted.

"You have to sleep now," Frankie whispered, sensing how tired he was and smiling happily. "The older you get, you won't have to sleep as much."

"Don't want to," Snod grumbled in protest.

"Sleep," Frankie urged. "I'll be here when you wake up and I'll bring you more food."

"From the butcher?" Snod asked, grunting. "Hmm, if he didn't suspect you were a vampire before…"

Frankie laughed, a lovely and clear sound, grinning brightly. "Well," he teased, "I'm sure I can persuade him to mind his own business if need be."

"Thought you didn't like using your powers?" Snod mused.

"I don't," Frankie confirmed, "but I have a very hungry baby vampire to feed. I have a responsibility to take care of you."

"Forever?"

"Forever," Frankie promised, tilting his head thoughtfully. "At least until I find a cure."

"Still want to be human again?" Snod asked quietly, not sure why anyone would want to give this up. This power, this strength, it was all so amazing.

"Yes," Frankie replied, "and in time, I think you'll understand why."

Snod frowned, but he was too tired to formulate an intelligible response. He didn't have the faintest idea why anyone would want to be mortal after experiencing this. He managed to grunt, closing his eyes and trying to fight off the call of sleep.

Frankie kissed his forehead, blinking away to make sure the windows were all properly covered and sealed up tight. He wouldn't dare risk Snod's safety while he was gone, ensuring that not a drop of sunlight would peek through.

"I'm going to meet up with Ephraim," Frankie said, flitting around as he got dressed. "We'll take care of the house, and I'm going to get Rees home. I'll call for a welfare check so someone can find him."

His neck…? Won't someone see?

"I'll take care of that," Frankie replied. "Rees has been sick for a long time. His doctor should have no trouble signing off on his death certificate, and his death shouldn't arouse any suspicion."

Snod fidgeted, still struggling to stay awake. He could feel how upset Frankie was, his emotions flowing like a river of endless misery. Snod had to try to say something. This was important.

I'm sorry.

It didn't feel like it was enough. There should have been some other words he could share, something deep and profound. He hated that he could do nothing to relieve

Frankie's anguish, realizing all of these abilities were useless to comfort the man he adored.

"It's okay. I know," Frankie said, a sad little smile twisting his lips. "I'm sorry, too."

I love you, Frankie.

"I love you, too," Frankie said, leaning down to kiss Snod's brow. "Now sleep… tomorrow is the first day of the rest of your life as a vampire."

Even moments from passing out, Snod couldn't resist a smug little smirk curling up his lips.

Don't you mean 'night'?

"Whatever."

CHAPTER TWENTY-FIVE

Nearly a hundred nights passed before Snod finally understood why Frankie wanted to be human again.

Rees' funeral was a simple but intimate affair. They made special arrangements to have the burial in the evening for Snod to be able to attend.

Dwayne and Mandy were there from the bar, Lorenzo and Athaliah as well. Amy came to be supportive, and even Ephraim was hovering a few yards away to pay his respects. He waited until the service was over before tossing a silver-tipped stake down on top of the vault.

Ephraim left abruptly, but Amy followed him. No one heard what was said, but she kissed his cheek before he drove away.

After the funeral, Snod spent most of his time at home. His appetite was nearly insatiable, both for blood and for Frankie. It took a few weeks, but he was finally starting to get it under control. The hunger was tolerable, and he finally felt safe to leave the apartment alone.

He visited Athaliah often, and he had only tried to bite Lorenzo once. It wasn't his fault that Lorenzo told him he was moving in with Athaliah right after his stomach happened to grumble.

Truthfully, Snod was happy for his brother. Lorenzo was good to him, and he could sense how in love they were. He also knew how horribly afraid Lorenzo was of him, and that pleased him endlessly.

Ephraim returned home to take care of what was left of the Order. Athaliah gave back the rest of the valuables he had stolen, and Ephraim used the money from selling them to relocate everyone. He returned to see Amy a few times a month when he wasn't helping them get settled.

They were all getting new lives, a fresh start.

Ephraim told him that there were still a few hunters that refused to give up their old lives, but he wouldn't be joining them. He was going to retire, hang up his stakes, and he was proud to announce that he had a date with Amy coming up soon.

Frankie received quite the surprise when Rees' will was finally read. He had left everything to Frankie, including the bar. It wasn't much now since the fire had torched it to the ground, but Frankie was determined to rebuild it.

"It's what Rees would have wanted," he stubbornly insisted, and Snod couldn't have agreed more.

A brand-new bar was constructed, Frankie using the money from the insurance claim as well as some of his own to make it even more grand than before.

The sound system was top of the line, sparing no expense to ensure they had the very best. He took special care to make sure it was still a very casual and comfortable atmosphere, picking out elegant wooden tables and plush chairs, but nothing too snooty.

Rees wouldn't have liked that, Frankie would say, smiling sadly to himself.

Snod was the one who suggested they change the name and picked out the photograph to hang by the front door. It was the man himself, Rees Everhart, and the bar was no longer Cheap Trills.

It was Everhart's.

The grand opening was a fantastic affair, Frankie

working the front and Snod taking his place back in the kitchen. He used the menu that he and Rees had originally designed, surprised how easy it was to cook by smell alone. He realized that he did miss food, missed tasting it, but he still enjoyed preparing it all the same.

He and Frankie shared a bottle of the special reserve blood to properly join in the festive drinking, everyone partying long into the night. As the alcohol flowed, there were many tears as everyone began to share their favorite stories of Rees.

Mandy had several particularly hilarious ones, as did Frankie, and the tears were soon mixed in with joyous laughter. The energy was warm and bittersweet, and that was when Snod finally understood what he was missing.

He knew he missed Rees, and he knew that he should be moved by everyone's sweet reminiscing. He should feel inclined to shed a tear or two, especially when he could feel how much Frankie mourned Rees' loss through the bond.

But he felt nothing.

This group of people, friends, co-workers, and clients were all coming together for a singular purpose. The love they all had for Rees was palpable and infectious, and yet Snod was entirely immune. He could see it, sense it, but he couldn't share in it.

He felt… cold.

Snod isolated himself behind the bar to make another drink, the rich blood making his head spin. He watched the party as if he was a total stranger, wishing he could join them, but he knew any further participation would have been false.

Frankie came up beside him, resting his chin on his shoulder with a warm smile. "It seems so far away," he mused. "Doesn't it?"

"I don't understand," Snod said quietly, tilting his head to press against Frankie's cheek.

"You're not human," Frankie sighed, his arms wrapping around Snod's waist. "Your emotions aren't as easy to access anymore. They fade away until you feel nothing but the hunger."

Snod closed his eyes, finally sensing an emotion he could focus on: anger. "I should be out there with them," he said stubbornly. "Sharing stories, laughing, crying… I know I miss him. I know that I should miss him."

"It's all right," Frankie soothed, always so comforting. "Just try to remember. Think about something with Rees that you liked, something fun." His eyes lit up, and he laughed, "What about when you stole the desk?"

"That was a disaster," Snod grumbled, but went on as Frankie had instructed. "The ice cream truck he had was horrendous. He told me to take the wrong desk. And then he broke that window so we could leave…"

The memories began to tumble over Snod, unable to stop smiling when he recalled the hideous purple sweater dress Rees had worn. He had looked ridiculous and suddenly there was something stirring in Snod's chest.

He was feeling… agony.

Rees was gone. He'd never hear that cackle again or shake his hand.

Rees was dead.

Snod suddenly couldn't breathe, which was insane because he didn't need to, but his throat was too tight. He couldn't speak, choking back a sob. All of the emotions he had been without were rushing back to him, and his eyes began to sting despite how hard he tried to hold back.

He hadn't yet shed a single tear, but when he remembered Rees' casket lowering down in the grave, the pressure inside of him broke. He wasn't just crying for the friend he had lost, but for the part of himself that had died with him.

Frankie held Snod close to hide his tears as they quickly turned bloody, gently pulling him into the back and away from the party. He cradled him tenderly as he sobbed, urging, "It's all right, Obe… I'm here."

"Athaliah," Snod whimpered. "He's going to die, too.

I'm going to watch him grow old, get sick…" He shut his eyes, the bloody tears thick and sticking to his face. "It'll be like this. I won't be able to feel a fucking thing."

"It doesn't have to be that way," Frankie said quickly, grabbing at some napkins to wipe Snod's face. "You can get it back. It'll come in crazy bursts like this for a while, but it gets easier. I promise it does."

"This is why you want to be human again," Snod whispered miserably. "To feel… normal."

"It's why I liked being with you," Frankie said with a warm smile. "You made me so happy. Angry at first, very angry. Pretty frustrated, too, but I felt so much, and it was easy. It's why I fell in love with you. Because you made me feel human without even trying."

"I love you," Snod said passionately. "If nothing else, what I feel for you has not changed. The entire world can fall down, let it all burn to ashes… I know that I will always love you."

"I love you, too," Frankie replied with a sweet smile. "I promise you. We'll get through this. We will do it together."

Stronger than even the hunger that was always chewing away inside of him was his love for Frankie. He had no doubt that Frankie meant every word, and Snod could feel a faint flicker of a pulse in his heart. Every other possible emotion was a thin wafer of experience when compared to the intense and burning passion he felt for this man.

Vampire, Maker, lover, boyfriend, his entire world.

Snod's hands began to wander, nosing along Frankie's throat and letting his fangs softly graze against his flesh. "I do hope you find a cure then," he murmured. "For both of us. We'll grow old together, watch the world go by side by side."

From love to passion and inevitably into lust was where Snod often found himself falling. Those were the easiest feelings for him to acknowledge and definitely the most powerful after the hunger. He squeezed Frankie's hips, his other voracious appetite demanding to be satisfied.

"Uh uh," Frankie protested, lightly smacking at Snod's hands. He was grinning, and Snod knew he was interested, but he still argued, "Later. We have a huge party going on out there."

"We can have a little party in here," Snod countered, pouting. "Just the two of us."

"Your brother is here," Frankie reminded him. "You need to remember him, too. Go talk to him. Threaten to eat Lorenzo if he ever hurts him. That's always entertaining."

Snod whined, bumping his mouth against Frankie's throat insistently.

"Come on, Obe," Frankie scolded. "It sounds like the worst of the crying has passed. Just… try not to forget Rees again, okay?"

Snod could easily recall Rees scowling in that purple sweater dress now and he smiled at the bittersweet memory. He let it sink into him and he allowed himself to miss his friend. "I won't," he promised. "Let's go have a drink to him, hmm?"

"Let's have several," Frankie agreed happily, kissing Snod's cheek and leading him back to the bar.

They finished off the bottle of blood before Frankie sent Snod stumbling over to find Athaliah. He had taken a break from dancing and laughing, currently leaned back in a chair near the stage.

Athaliah's face brightened up at his approach, kicking out a chair for him to join him. "Hey, dear brother," he gushed. "Fancy meeting you here!"

"Not really," Snod drawled. "I work here."

"Ugh," Athaliah groaned, rolling his eyes. He reached for Snod's hand, a little sloppy from all the alcohol, giggling, "Even as a fucking vampire, you have no sense of humor."

Snod pouted at that.

"I love you," he said suddenly, trying to focus on Snod's face. "Even as an undead fiend. You know that, right?"

"Yes," Snod said, raising his brows.

"I'm glad Frankie saved you," Athaliah went on. "I don't

care what you are, as long as you're here. It was too hard to get away from all that shit in that fucking cult, and I wasn't ready to lose you."

"Are you happy?" Snod asked quietly, glancing down at their joined hands.

"Yeah," Athaliah chuckled. "I'm free, I have you, I have a job I don't totally hate, and I got a guy I'm super crazy about."

Snod's lip twitched.

"Lorenzo wants to marry me, you know," Athaliah teased, enjoying Snod's scowl. "He loves me. And I love him." He tilted his head expectantly, saying, "This is the part where you say you're gonna drain him dry and all that shit?"

Snod smirked.

Love was a spectacular emotion; not just to experience himself, but to smell it on his brother made him happy. It rivaled his supernatural urge to feed, and when he focused on it, he could remember how much he adored Athaliah.

Snod had always tried to protect him and take care of him. He had no doubts that Lorenzo would do anything for him because he knew that he really did love him.

"I don't think that will be necessary," Snod said at last. "Although I do enjoy terrifying him, I know that you'll both be very happy together."

"And what about you, brother dearest?" Athaliah asked, his eyes sparkling. "Are you happy?"

"Yes," Snod replied immediately, smiling brightly. He found Frankie chatting with Dwayne and Mandy a few yards away; their eyes met and they exchanged a smile.

I'm going to fuck you so hard when we get home…

Frankie grinned.

Bring it on.

"Very happy," Snod purred.

"And being a vampire?" Athaliah asked curiously. "You happy with that, too?"

"I'm working on it," Snod said honestly, frowning for a moment. "Am I really so different?"

"Yup," Athaliah laughed. "You sort of… I dunno. You go away for a while, like it's not really you. Like right now, yeah, you're my Obie. But later, you won't be."

Snod's frown deepened.

"It's okay," Athaliah reassured him, squeezing his hand tight. "It makes the moments when I know you're awake in there even more special."

"I do love you," Snod said earnestly. "It's… harder now. But I always will."

"Damn right," Athaliah scolded affectionately, glancing up to say farewell to some of the departing patrons. He looked back to Snod, finding him gazing longingly over at Frankie and snorted, "Why don't you two go home?"

"We still have to close up."

"Mandy and I can handle that," Athaliah scoffed. "Besides, isn't it getting close to your bedtime?"

Snod scowled, but he knew the sun would be up in a few hours. He also knew better than to argue with Athaliah once he had made up his mind, nodding as he sighed, "Fine."

Athaliah giggled, standing up to embrace him. He held him close, rubbing his hands over his back, murmuring, "Mmm. Go eat something. You're so cold."

"Will do."

"I love you, brother dear."

"And I love you, little brother."

Frankie came along to collect Snod, saying their final goodbyes and thanking everyone for such a successful evening. The reopening of Everhart's had been a hit, and it was clear that the bar had a bright future ahead of it.

The future was promising for all of them, Snod thought.

Lorenzo and Athaliah were happy as could be, and Snod had spotted Ephraim and Amy cuddled up in a corner booth as they were leaving. Snod was in love with a beautiful vampire who loved him just as passionately, a man who would never give up on finding a cure for them.

Until such a time came, they had eternity to spend together.

It would be hard, especially if Frankie couldn't find it before too many years went by, but Snod wasn't afraid.

He didn't have to do it alone.

Back at home, Snod fed again before falling into bed with Frankie. Tonight had been exciting, having taken weeks of planning and hours of hard work, and he was ready to have his own private celebration with his beloved boyfriend before the sun came up.

He enjoyed the foreplay almost as much as the intimate act of sex itself, no longer held back by any voices telling him that what he wanted was sinful. The only driving force in his passions now was his own insatiable desire to make Frankie fall apart beneath him.

Sucking down every inch of Frankie's cock while his fingers pressed inside of him was a particular favorite, stroking along that one special place that made his lover moan. He could sense Frankie getting close, backing off when he could feel his heart starting to thump.

"Obe," Frankie pleaded, gasping and desperate, "please…"

"Someone once told me that waiting is good," Snod teased, rubbing his tongue along the base of Frankie's cock.

"Obe!" Frankie growled, jerking his hips impatiently.

"Yes?" Snod asked innocently, continuing to thrust his fingers and slowing down to a devastatingly torturous pace.

"Ohhhh, I will not forget this," Frankie warned him, moaning loudly when Snod took him back into his mouth. His hips rose up again, fucking up into Snod's throat. "Fuck, I'm so close!"

Snod loved knowing that he could make Frankie this desperate. It made him feel powerful, and nothing brought him more pleasure than being able to take Frankie to such heights of ecstasy. His heart was pounding so beautifully through the bond, and Snod couldn't deny him any longer.

Come for me…

Frankie cried out, his entire body shuddering as he orgasmed. Snod sucked down every last drop, bobbing his head in time with the frantic pulsing of Frankie's heart. He curled his fingers to intensify the feeling, stopping just short of the sensation becoming painful.

Frankie was groaning contently, stretching out his trembling legs with a happy sigh. "My love, that was incredible."

"Mmm, just you wait. I'll show you incredible." Snod crawled up Frankie's lean body, dragging hot kisses along the way before pressing their lips together. He was already trying to push his cock inside when Frankie suddenly changed their positions. Frankie was now sitting on the edge of the bed with Snod stretched across his lap, ass up.

"What are you doing?" Snod breathlessly demanded even though he already knew what was coming and his cock was twitching at the very thought of it.

"It was very rude of you to tease me," Frankie said, aiming for serious but Snod could see him smiling. He stroked his hand over Snod's cheeks, taunting, "I think someone needs a little reminder of who's in charge here."

"Please," Snod pleaded softly, arching himself up eagerly. "Help me be good, Frankie."

"Always," Frankie promised, holding Snod's hip firmly as his other hand came crashing down with a vicious slap.

Snod groaned, the impact sending wonderful bursts of pleasure all throughout his body. Frankie didn't have to hold back anymore. He could spank Snod as hard as he wanted to without worrying about hurting him and it was unbelievably liberating. He groaned again when Frankie spanked his other cheek, grinding his hard cock against Frankie's thigh.

Each smack forced his body forward, and Snod's head was spinning. He felt so small and safe in Frankie's arms, his ass stinging sweetly as Frankie spanked him repeatedly. He knew that Frankie didn't like to be teased, but he had done it anyway. He loved the power he had now to make his lover fall apart and the punishment that was always sure to follow was entirely worth it.

"Fuck!" Snod actually cried out when Frankie drove one final and ruthless smack against his tender cheeks. The throb of pain faded slowly, and he tried to hang onto every last pulse of burning sensation. He whined when he felt Frankie's cool fingers sliding against his hole, slick with lube and spreading him open slowly.

"I think you need more, don't you?" Frankie asked, his voice husky and deep. "I don't think you've quite learned your lesson yet, my sweet boy."

"Yes," Snod replied weakly, trying to move his hips and catch Frankie's fingers on his hole. He could feel his own heart fluttering softly, the tease of an orgasm that felt like it was only a breath away. "Come on, my love. It's been too long since you've filled me."

"Mmm, since yesterday." Frankie pushed a single finger into Snod's hole and chuckled when he clenched around it. "So hungry for it, aren't you?"

"Yes." Snod whispered the word like a prayer, turning his head to look up at Frankie over his shoulder. "Please…?"

"Only because you asked so nicely," Frankie said, grabbing Snod by the back of his neck and effortlessly flipping him onto the bed.

Snod took a deep breath that he didn't need, always thrilled when Frankie showed off his full strength. He found himself pressed down into the mattress face first, Frankie's cool fingers curling into his hair.

Frankie tilted Snod's hips and pushed himself between his thighs. He began to push his cock inside, hugging Snod's leg against his chest with a wickedly toothy grin.

Snod started to pant as Frankie slid deeper inside of him, the angle a little awkward but unbelievably intense. He moaned when Frankie popped his ass and slammed all the way inside, the pleasure crawling up his spine and back down to his balls. The ache of Frankie's cock and the burn of his hand against his flesh was perfect, his vampiric senses eating all of the sensations up like precious pieces of candy.

He could feel the velvety texture of Frankie's cock thrusting in and out of his hole, and the tender tissue there between his legs was absolutely throbbing from the sweet pressure. Even the smooth skin of Frankie's palm cracking against his skin was especially exciting, and he was almost certain he could feel the ridges of his fingerprints leaving their mark behind. His heart was thudding loudly, and his orgasm was so very close.

Snod knew Frankie could feel it, but he sensed nothing urgent from his side of the bond. Frankie was calm and quiet, rolling his hips in deep thrusts perfectly aimed to drive Snod closer to the edge. And yet, Frankie was ignoring Snod's cock completely.

Snod reached down to carry himself to completion, but Frankie snatched his hand and pressed it into the bed.

"Not yet," Frankie taunted, his smugness radiating through the bond in tangible waves. "Be a good boy, Obe… and maybe I'll let you come, mmm?"

"Please!" Snod begged, desperate to relieve the pressure between his legs and his stuttering pulse. "Just let me come, Frankie!"

"No," Frankie said firmly, pushing Snod flat against the bed and holding him by the back of his neck. He began to slam into him with bruising force, fingers squeezing around Snod's throat.

No matter how much Snod struggled, he would not have been able to break away from Frankie's strong grip. Not that he would have wanted to; being held like this made him feel owned and safe deep inside. He was Frankie's, totally and completely, and he knew his lover would take care of him.

He clawed at the bed, only in an effort to find some way to relieve the beautiful anguish of Frankie fucking him at full strength. Frankie's hold on his throat tightened, and Snod almost forgot he didn't need to breathe. "Oh, Frankie! Fuck!"

"Good boy," Frankie sighed in a sultry purr, bowing his head to drag his fangs over Snod's shoulder. "Are you ready to come, my sweet boy?"

"Fuck! Yes!" Snod sobbed, moaning when Frankie bit down. "Please!"

Come for me, Obe…

Snod slid his hand down and barely touched the head of his cock before he was coming. Frankie's savage thrusts rocked him through every pounding quiver, his skin on fire as his lover continued to feed. He could feel Frankie coming inside of him and he moaned excitedly, "Yes… oh, God… Frankie…"

Frankie released Snod's shoulder with a wet slurp of blood, licking his lips hungrily. He sat up, smacking Snod's ass one last time and chuckling when he jerked beneath him. "Mmm, teach you to mess with me again, huh?"

"Mmm, you may find that your punishments actually encourage me to keep misbehaving," Snod taunted, enjoying the dwindling rush of their hearts beating together.

"Oh? Do they?" Frankie asked coyly, rolling Snod onto his back and playfully pinning him down.

"Yes." Snod's hands greedily slid up Frankie's thighs. His cock was already hard again and pressing insistently up against Frankie's ass.

Frankie leaned down for a kiss, smiling against Snod's lips. "Mmm, well, we have plenty of time to work on your behavior."

"Indeed we do," Snod said, grinning as he began to push inside Frankie, both of them moaning softly together as Snod pushed and pushed until he was all the way inside.

Every single time was heaven. Being with Frankie, being connected like this, was utterly divine. He would never tired of how Frankie's body swallowed him up, his arms embracing him so tenderly, and the roll of his hips on top of him.

Snod took him to the limits of bliss over and over, carrying him over to the wall to fuck him until he screamed. He loved how easy it was to lift Frankie up like this, hissing at the nails digging into his back. He buried his face against

Frankie's neck, pleading, "Yes?"

"Yes," Frankie gasped, tilting his head. "God, yes!"

Snod pressed in his fangs, groaning at the first splash of blood that hit his tongue. He slowed down, thrusting hard every time he swallowed, listening to Frankie sob passionately. He could feel their climaxes approaching together, their heartbeats thumping all over the place before beginning to pulse in sync.

Frankie was clawing at the wall, the edge of the window, panting erratically as Snod continued to slam him down on his cock. "Fuck, yes, right there, there! Ooooo-oh! Fuck!"

The rush of Frankie's blood flowing into his mouth combined with the clenching of his lovely body was the perfect way to tip over the edge. The strength of his orgasm made him dizzy, clinging to Frankie as he released inside of him, fucking them through every delicious shudder.

Snod moaned frantically, smothering his bloody lips against Frankie's in a heated kiss. Frankie blinked them back into bed without sacrificing their connection, on top of Snod now and sliding their tongues together.

They drank from each other and made love until Frankie finally had to pry himself away to get ready for work. Snod wanted to keep going, but his internal clock was demanding that he rest and he couldn't keep Frankie in bed if he couldn't even keep his eyes open.

Frankie tucked Snod into bed, kissing him sweetly. "Mmm, goodnight."

"Good morning," Snod drowsily corrected.

"Sleep," Frankie laughed, blinking away to finish getting ready.

Snod tried to go to sleep, frowning when he couldn't drift off right away. Usually, he couldn't fight it and sleep took him under almost immediately. His stomach grumbled lightly, and he tried to ignore it.

Snod happened to notice that one of the window coverings had been torn during their passionate exercises. There was a tiny streak of sunlight peeking through, lighting up a corner of the bed near his foot. His curiosity got the better of him, and he scooted down toward it.

Frankie hadn't let Snod try this and he had warned him of the anguish and pain that even a small amount of daylight could cause.

Without Frankie here next to him, Snod was already feeling empty again, and he wanted to feel something, anything to distract him from the nagging hunger.

He stretched his foot out toward the light, dipping in a toe and quickly pulling back, blinking rapidly.

Nothing.

Braver now, he pushed his foot into the sunlight and held it there.

Again, nothing.

He wiggled his pale toes, grinning at the little shadows flickering around his foot. It didn't hurt at all. He could feel warmth, the happy glow of the morning sun, but no pain.

Could it be…

Snod sat up, summoning all of his willpower to stay awake and approaching the window. He let the sunlight hit him directly in the face, squinting at the brightness, but otherwise he felt no discomfort.

"Obe? What are you doing?" Frankie's voice called out sharply.

"I think I can…" Snod began, his hand on the window covering and beginning to pull it down. He didn't have a chance to finish his sentence, Frankie moving like a blur and tackling him back into bed.

"Are you crazy!" Frankie yelped. "You'll be burned!"

"Look!" Snod grunted, sticking his foot back out into the sunlight. He waited for Frankie to see it and wiggled his toes like he had before.

Frankie blinked, staring back at Snod in complete disbelief. "You're… you're immune?"

Snod gently pushed Frankie off of him, returning to the window once more. He peeled down the covering under Frankie's watchful eye, knowing he was ready to pounce at the first sign of singed flesh.

Allowing the sunlight to spill over him, Snod grinned smugly. He could feel the warmth and energy of the sun, closing his eyes as he basked in it.

"I can't believe this," Frankie murmured, standing beside him and running his hands over Snod's chest. "You must have inherited my immunity… this is incredible!"

Snod pressed a soft kiss to Frankie's brow, smiling happily. He knew he had to sleep soon, hungry and exhausted, but he wanted to savor this moment. He drew Frankie in close, enjoying the warmth of the rising sun as he noted, "Never realized how much I missed it."

"It's beautiful, isn't it?" Frankie chuckled, glancing out to where the sun was starting to rise above the horizon, lighting up the city below.

"You're beautiful," Snod whispered, his eyes only focused on Frankie's face, delighted when his eyes grew brighter. They looked like emeralds, glittering perfectly in the sunlight, and he was completely lost in them as he said, "You are truly the most beautiful thing I've ever seen."

"Mmmm, sweet talker," Frankie said softly in reply, though he tilted his head as if he was blushing. A playful smirk twitched his lip, and he scolded softly, "You know you need to go to sleep."

"After the sunrise," Snod insisted stubbornly, hugging Frankie close.

"All right," Frankie agreed, leaning into Snod's embrace. They watched the sun crawl its way up into the sky together, holding each other close and watching all the colors change as the day began.

Snod dropped his head down, mumbling defiantly as the need to sleep suddenly began to overpower him. Frankie picked him up, gently placing him back in bed and tucking him in. He pulled down the rest of the coverings on the windows in a flash, returning to kiss Snod goodbye.

"I'll be home when you wake up," Frankie promised, stroking his fingers through his hair. "Maybe we'll see what other fun powers you might have gotten from me, hmm?"

Snod smiled sleepily, sighing, "I love you, Frankie."

"I love you, too," Frankie replied sweetly.

"Always?"

"Forever."

THE END

STORMY NIGHT PUBLICATIONS WOULD LIKE TO THANK YOU FOR YOUR INTEREST IN OUR BOOKS.

If you liked this book (or even if you didn't), we would really appreciate you leaving a review on the site where you purchased it. Reviews provide useful feedback for us and for our authors, and this feedback (both positive comments and constructive criticism) allows us to work even harder to make sure we provide the content our customers want to read.

If you would like to check out more books from Stormy Night Publications, if you want to learn more about our company, or if you would like to join our mailing list, please visit our website at:

www.stormynightpublications.com

Printed in Great Britain
by Amazon

21597195R00210